SPILL ZONE

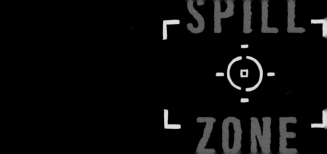

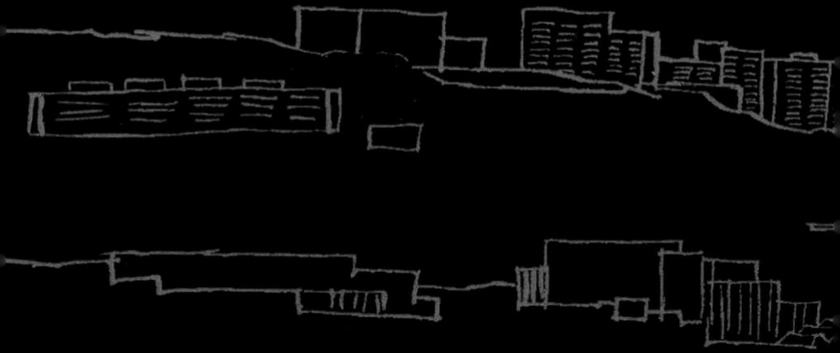

SCOTT WESTERFELD

SPILL ZONE

ALEX PUVILLAND

Colors by
HILARY SYCAMORE

:01
First Second
NEW YORK

Thanks to everyone in the indie
comics world for welcoming me in
— S.W.

To Leo and Adrien
— A.P.

SPILL

ZONE

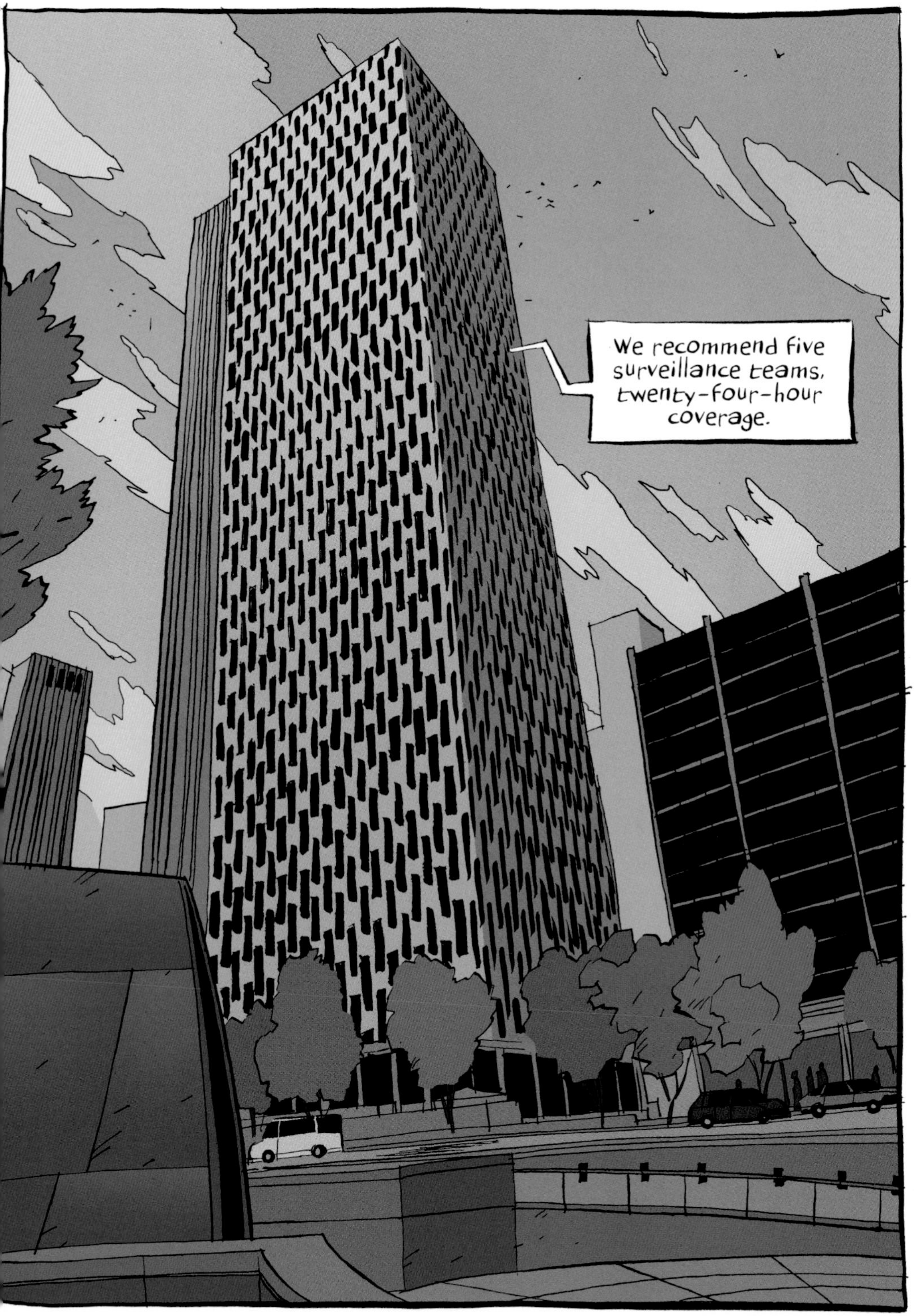
We recommend five surveillance teams, twenty-four-hour coverage.

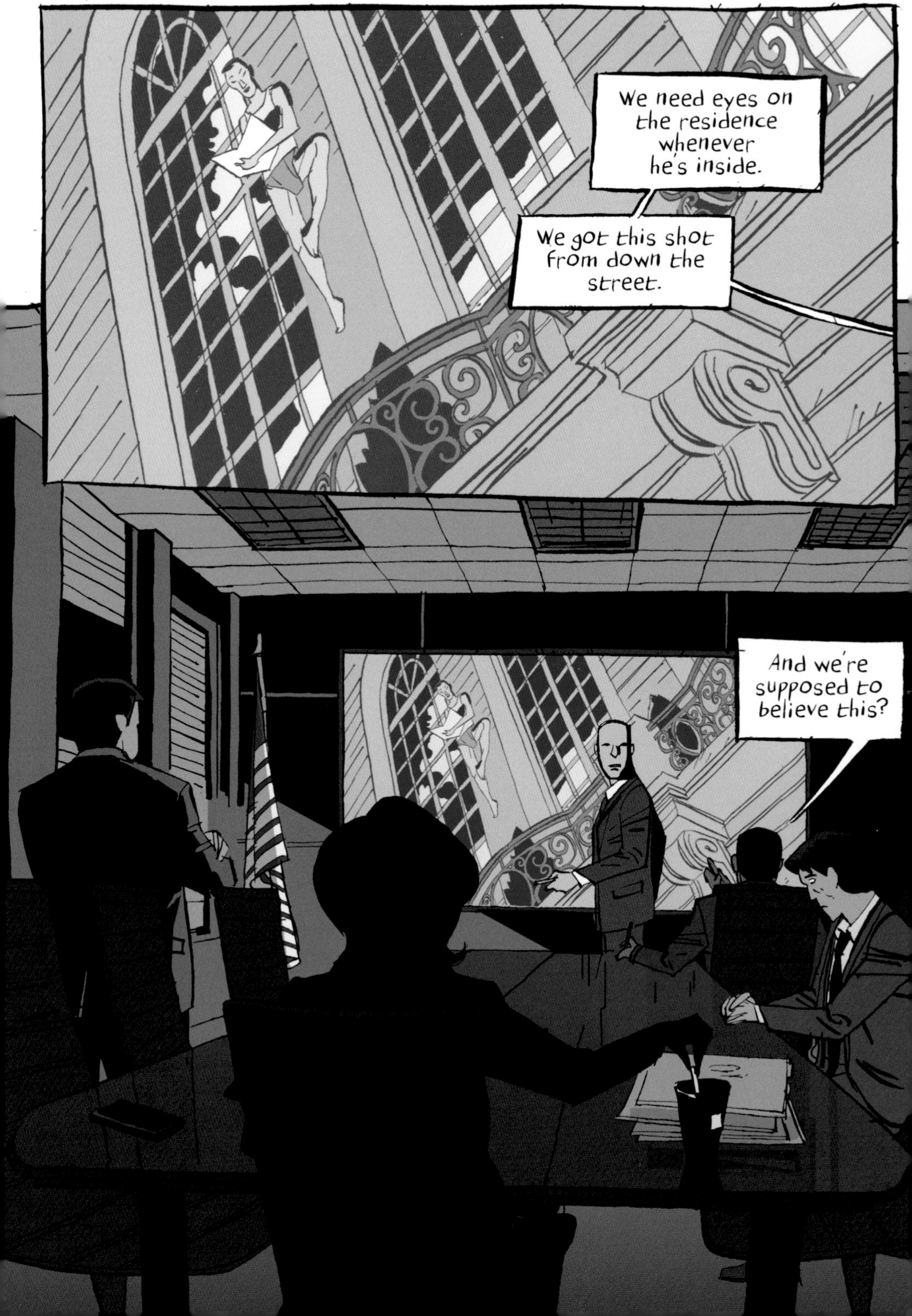
We need eyes on the residence whenever he's inside.
We got this shot from down the street.
And we're supposed to believe this?

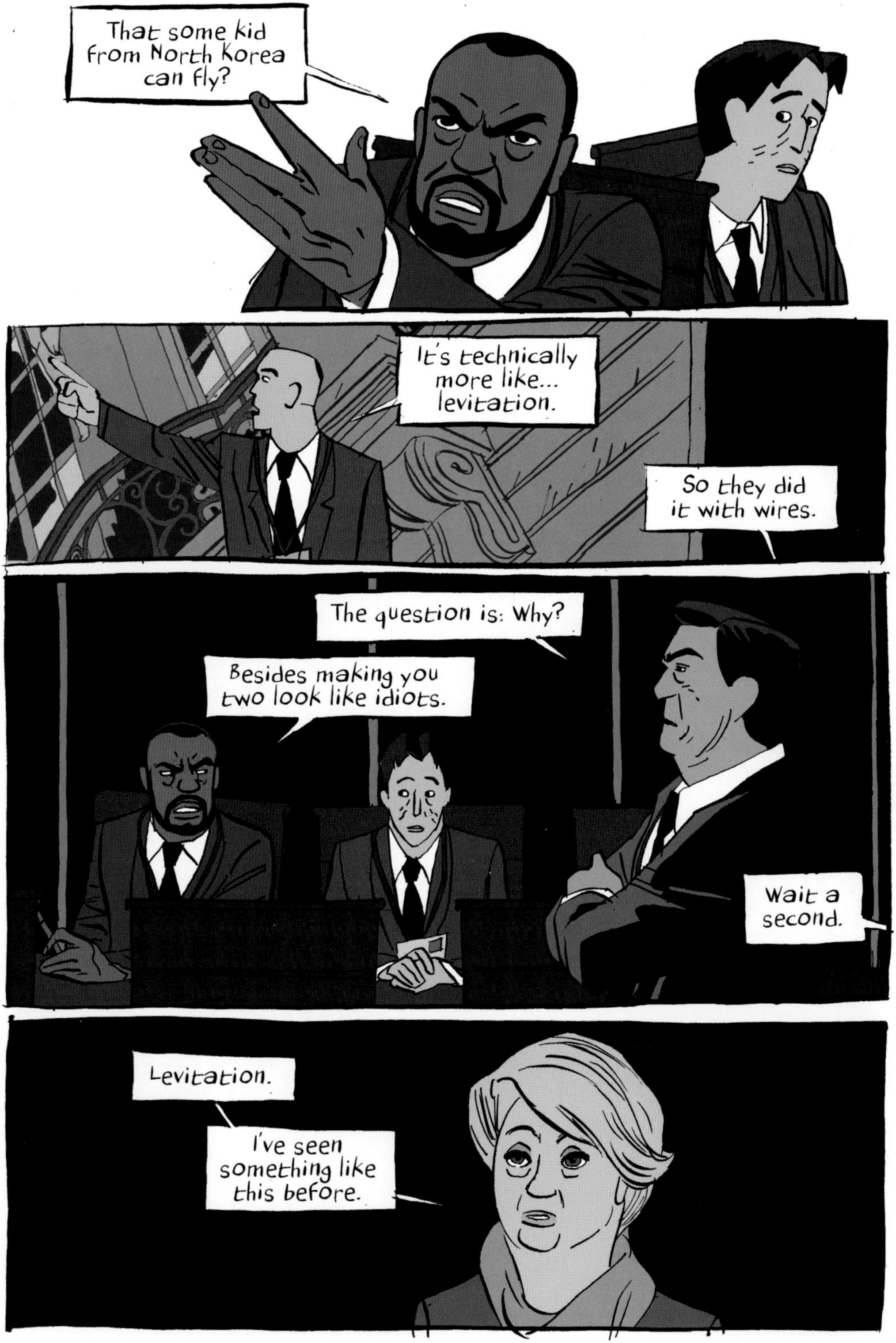
That some kid from North Korea can fly?
It's technically more like... levitation.
So they did it with wires.
The question is: Why?
Besides making you two look like idiots.
Wait a second.
Levitation.
I've seen something like this before.

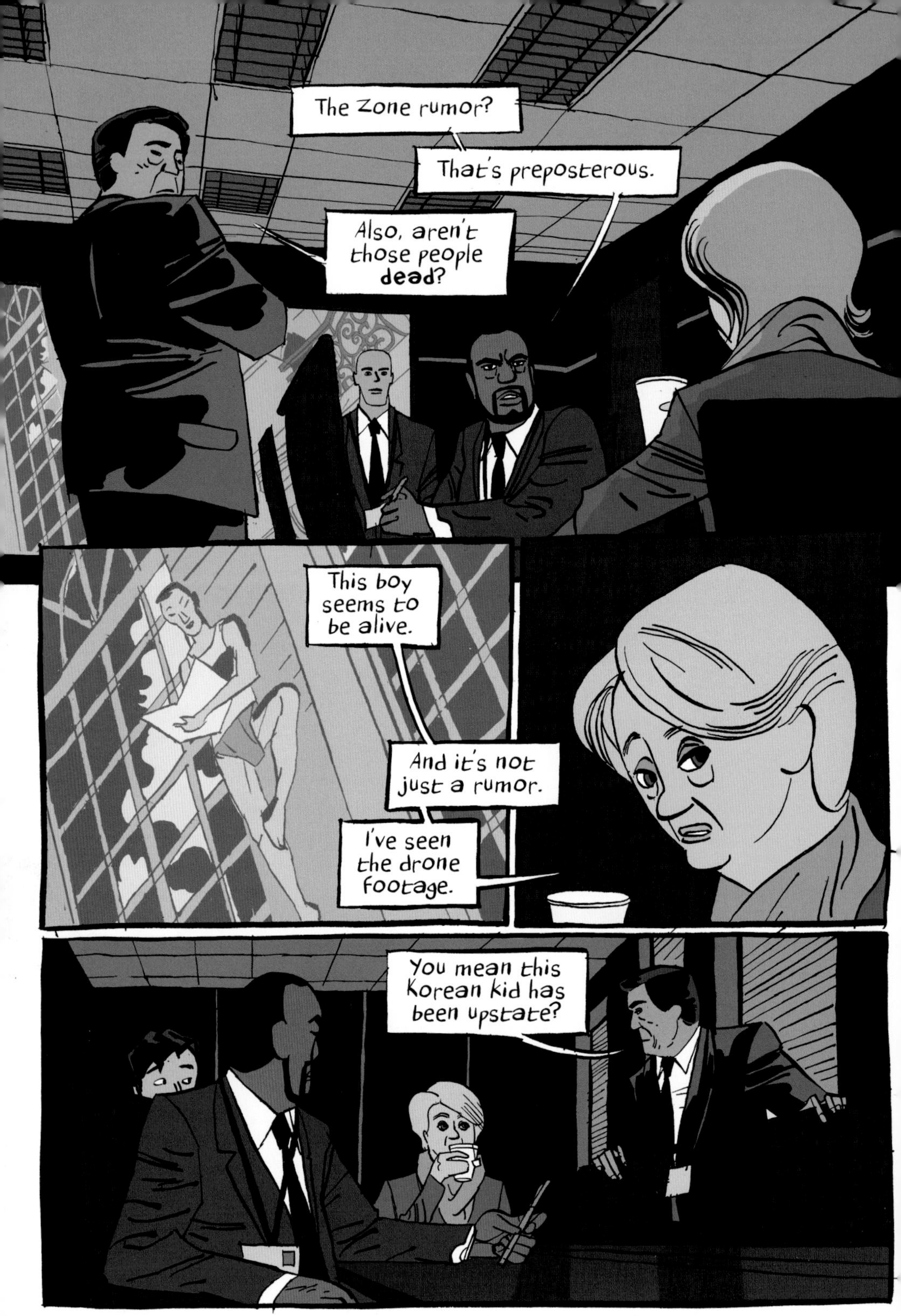
The Zone rumor?
That's preposterous.
Also, aren't those people **dead**?
This boy seems to be alive.
And it's not just a rumor.
I've seen the drone footage.
You mean this Korean kid has been upstate?

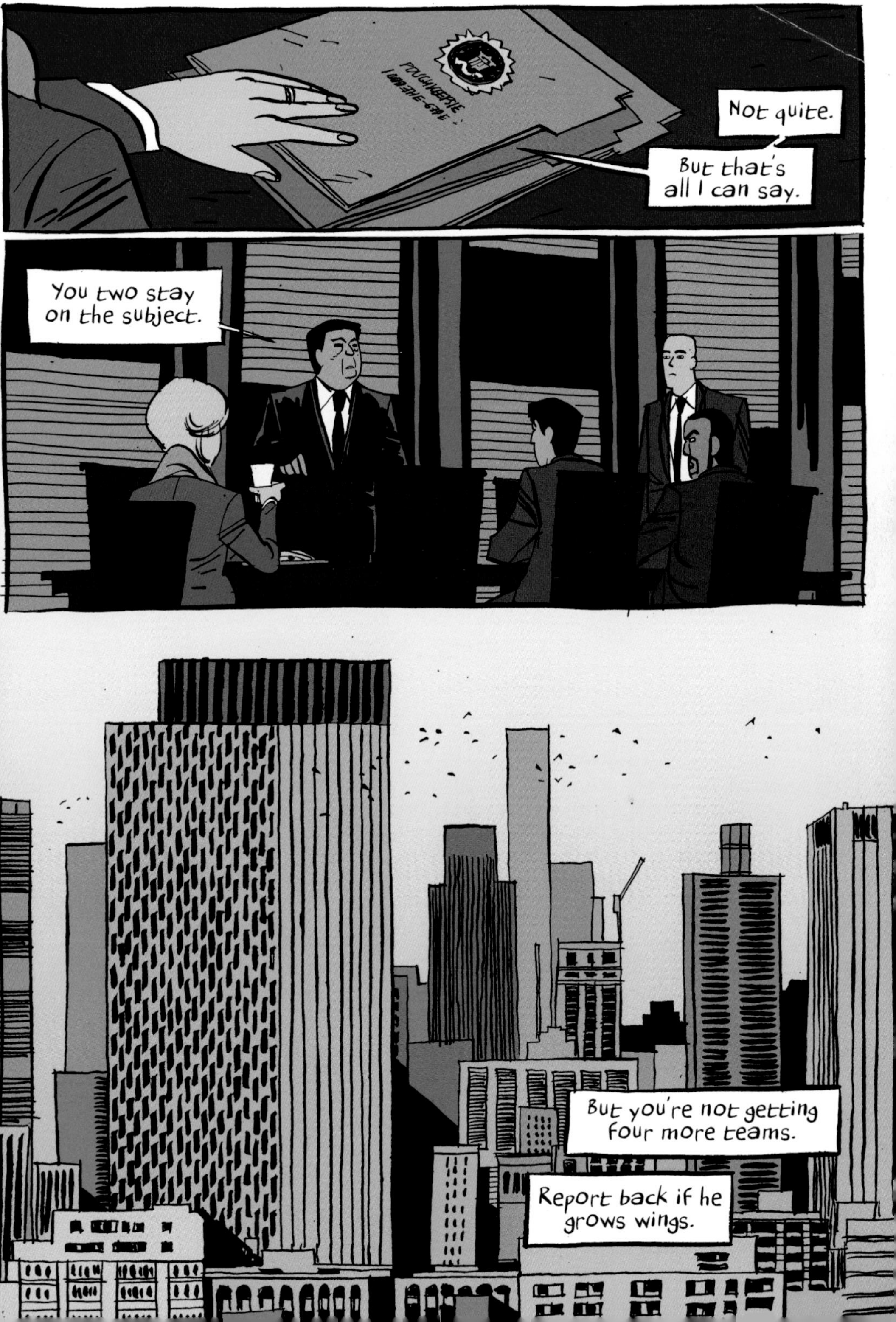
Not quite.
But that's all I can say.
You two stay on the subject.
But you're not getting four more teams.
Report back if he grows wings.

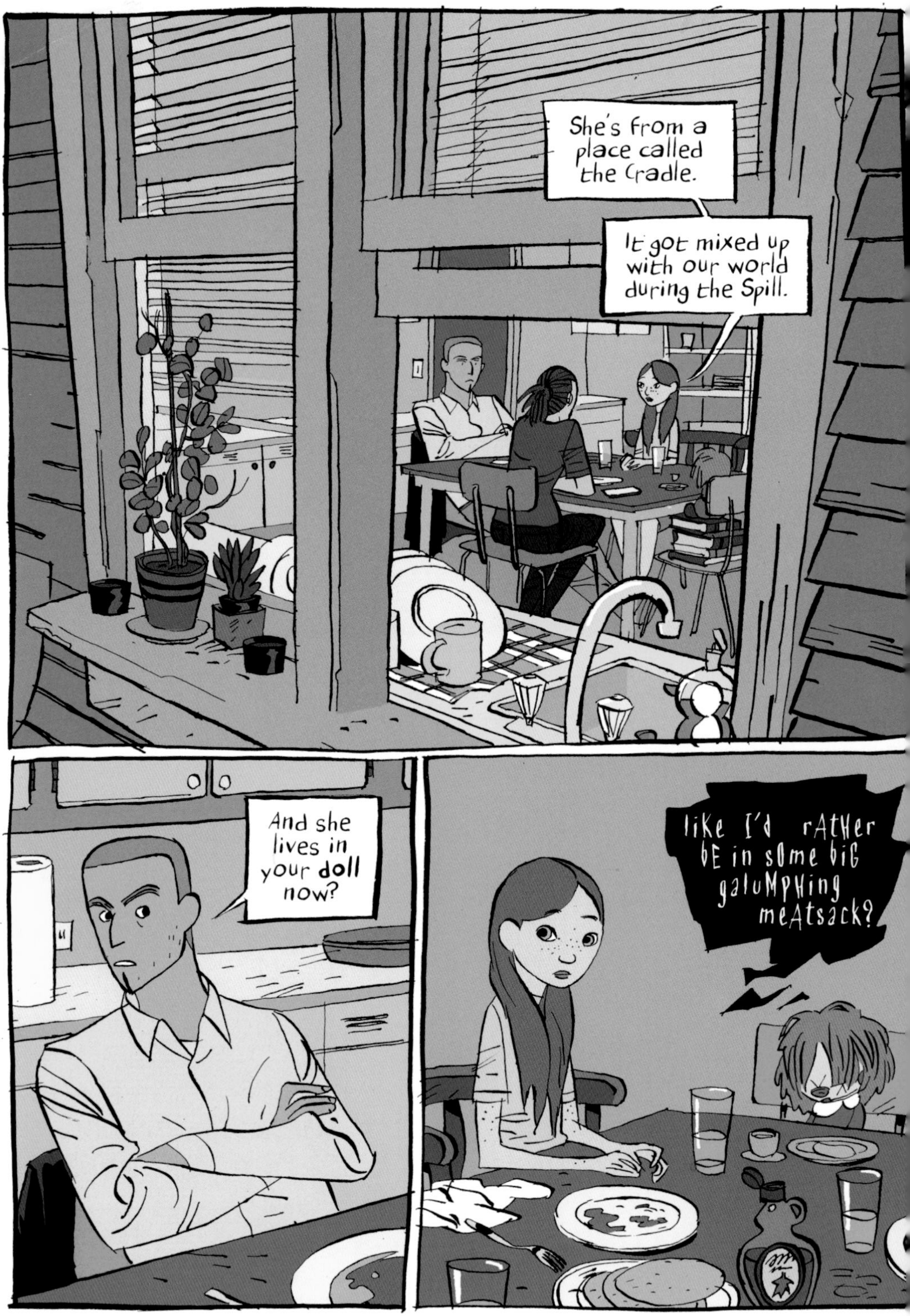
She's from a place called the Cradle.
It got mixed up with our world during the Spill.
And she lives in your **doll** now?
like I'd rAtHer bE in sOme biG galuMpHing meAtsack?

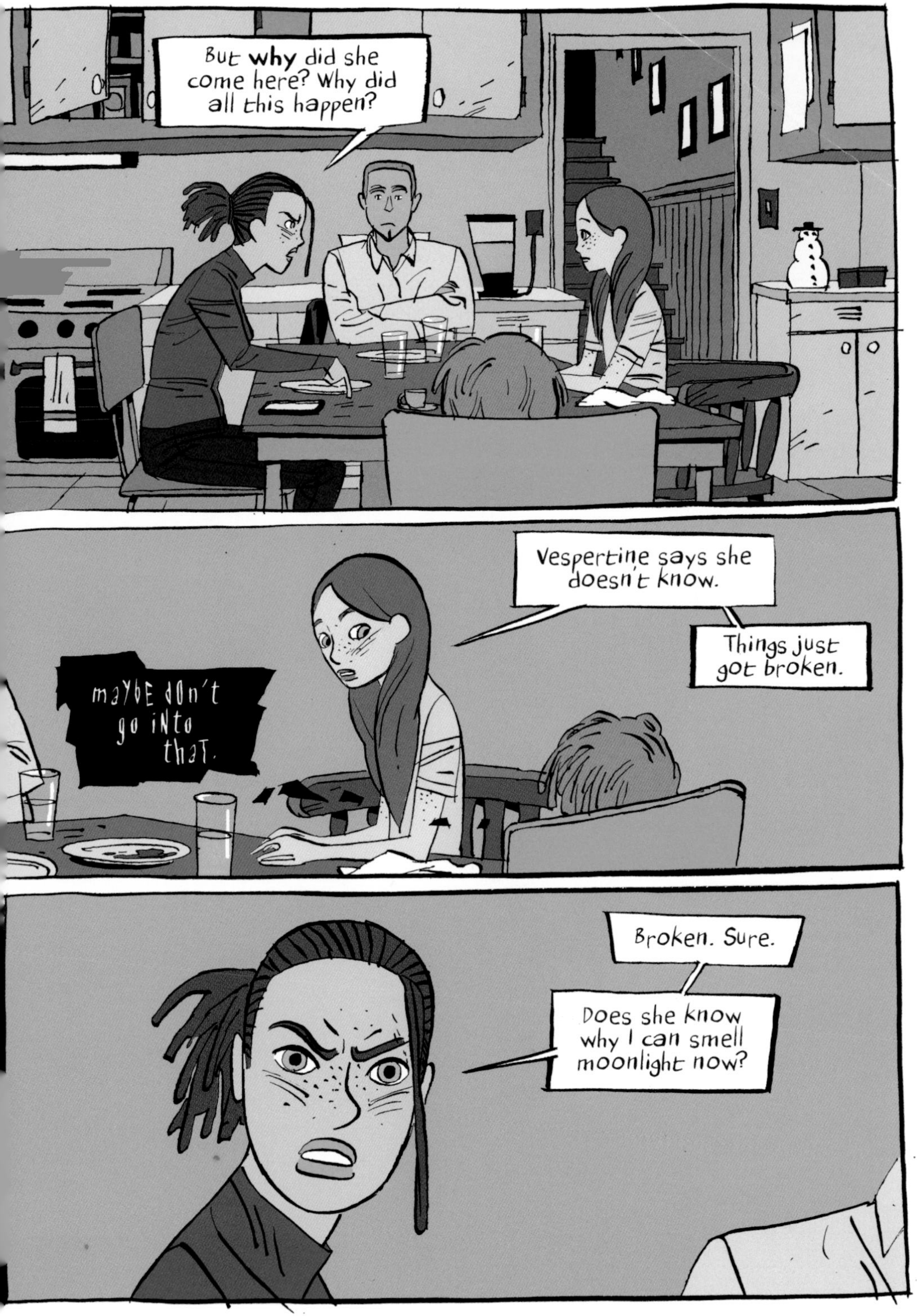
But why did she come here? Why did all this happen?
Vespertine says she doesn't know.
Things just got broken.
maybe don't go into that.
Broken. Sure.
Does she know why I can smell moonlight now?

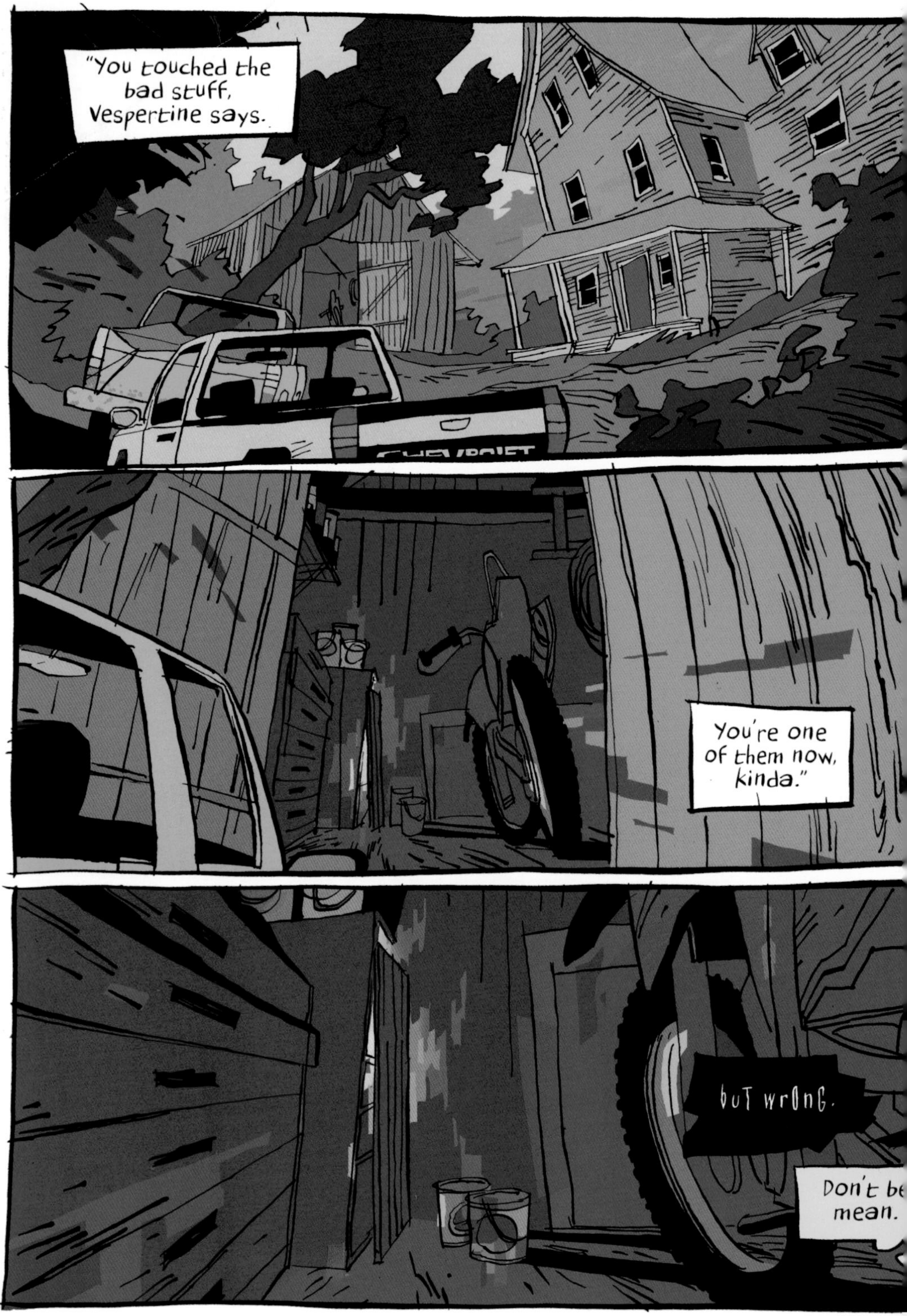
"You touched the bad stuff, Vespertine says.
You're one of them now, kinda."
but wrong.
Don't be mean.

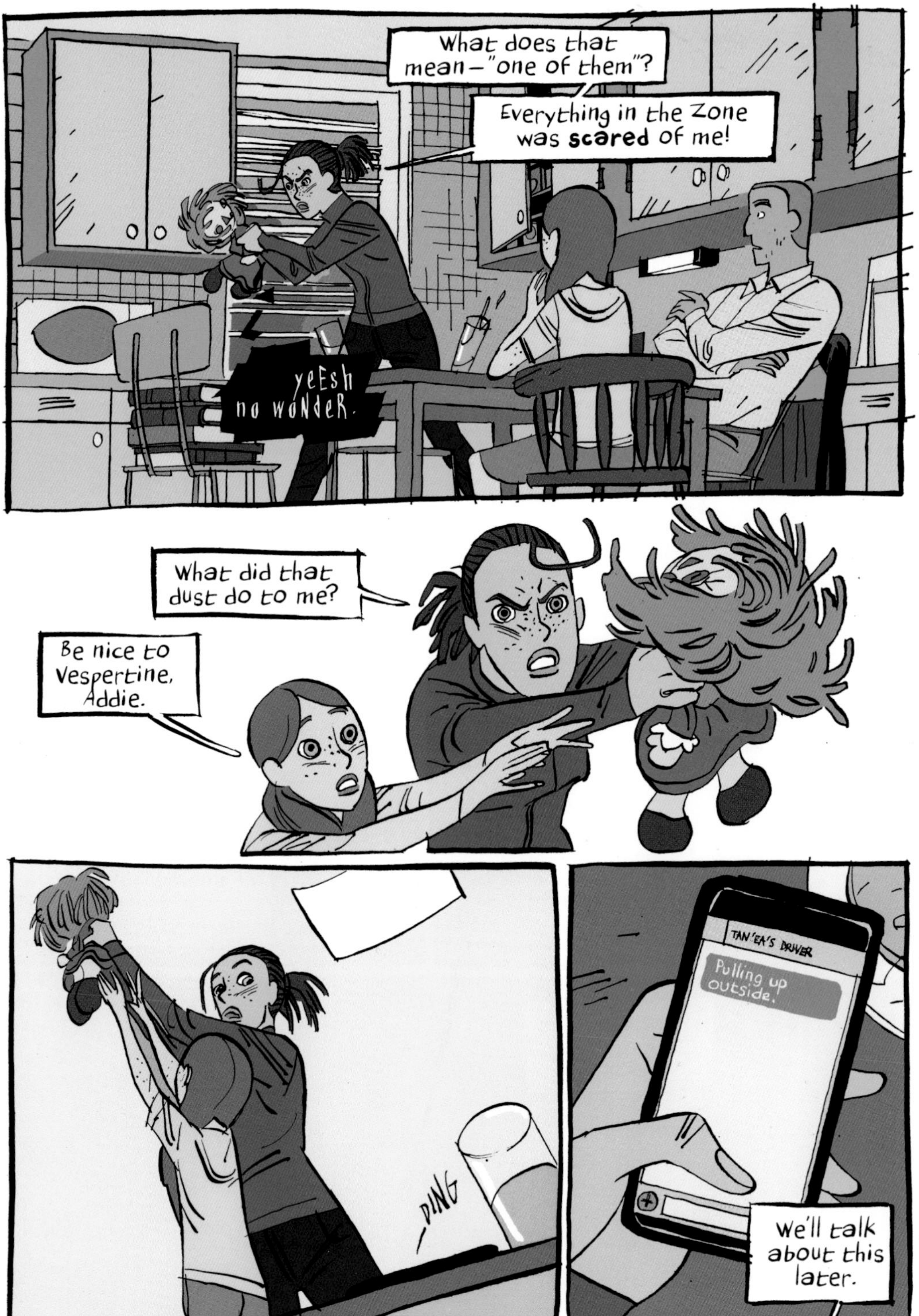
What does that mean—"one of them"?
Everything in the Zone was **scared** of me!
yeEsh no wonder.
What did that dust do to me?
Be nice to Vespertine, Addie.
DING
TAN'EA'S DRIVER
Pulling up outside.
We'll talk about this later.

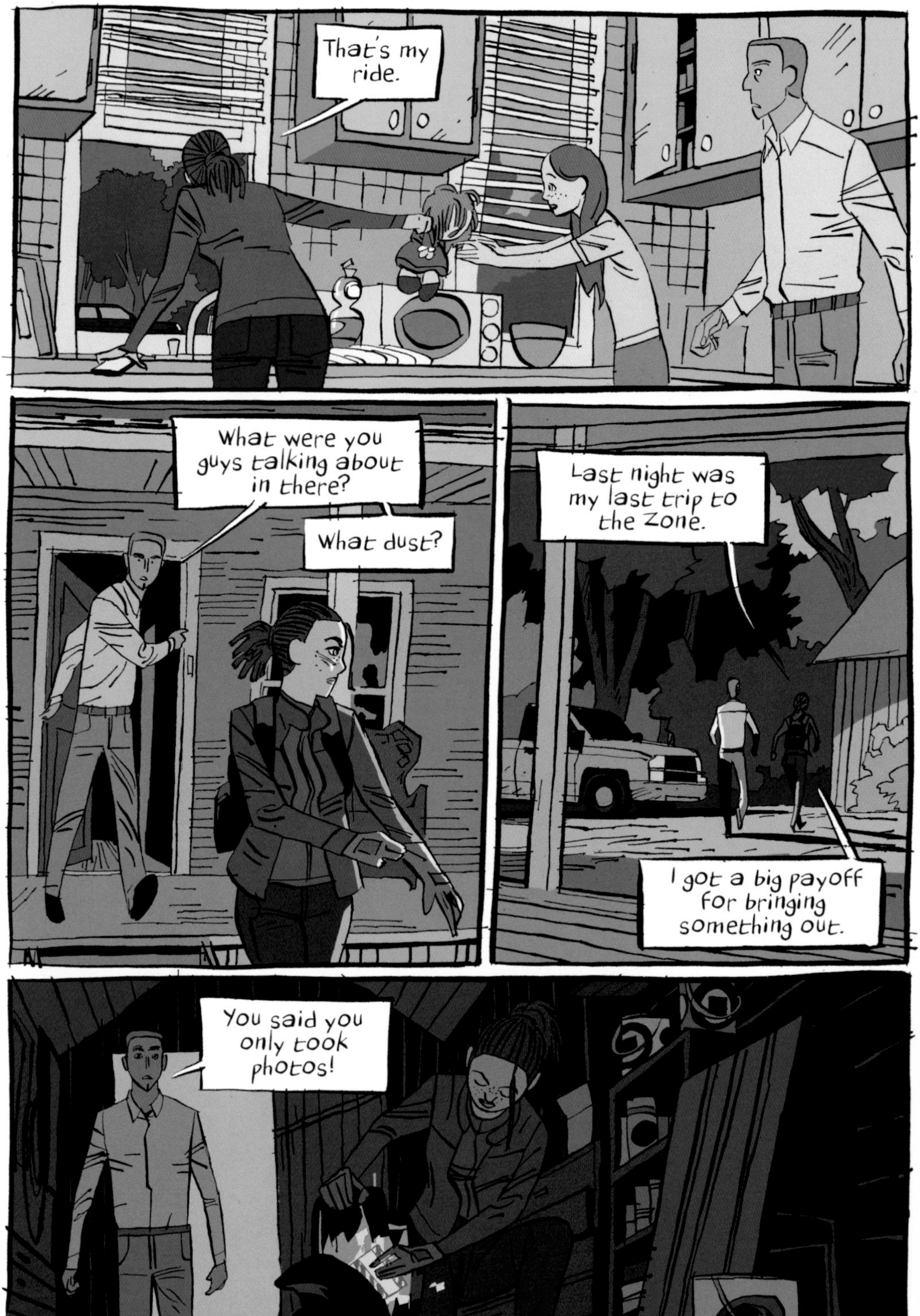
That's my ride.
What were you guys talking about in there?
What dust?
Last night was my last trip to the Zone.
I got a big payoff for bringing something out.
You said you only took photos!

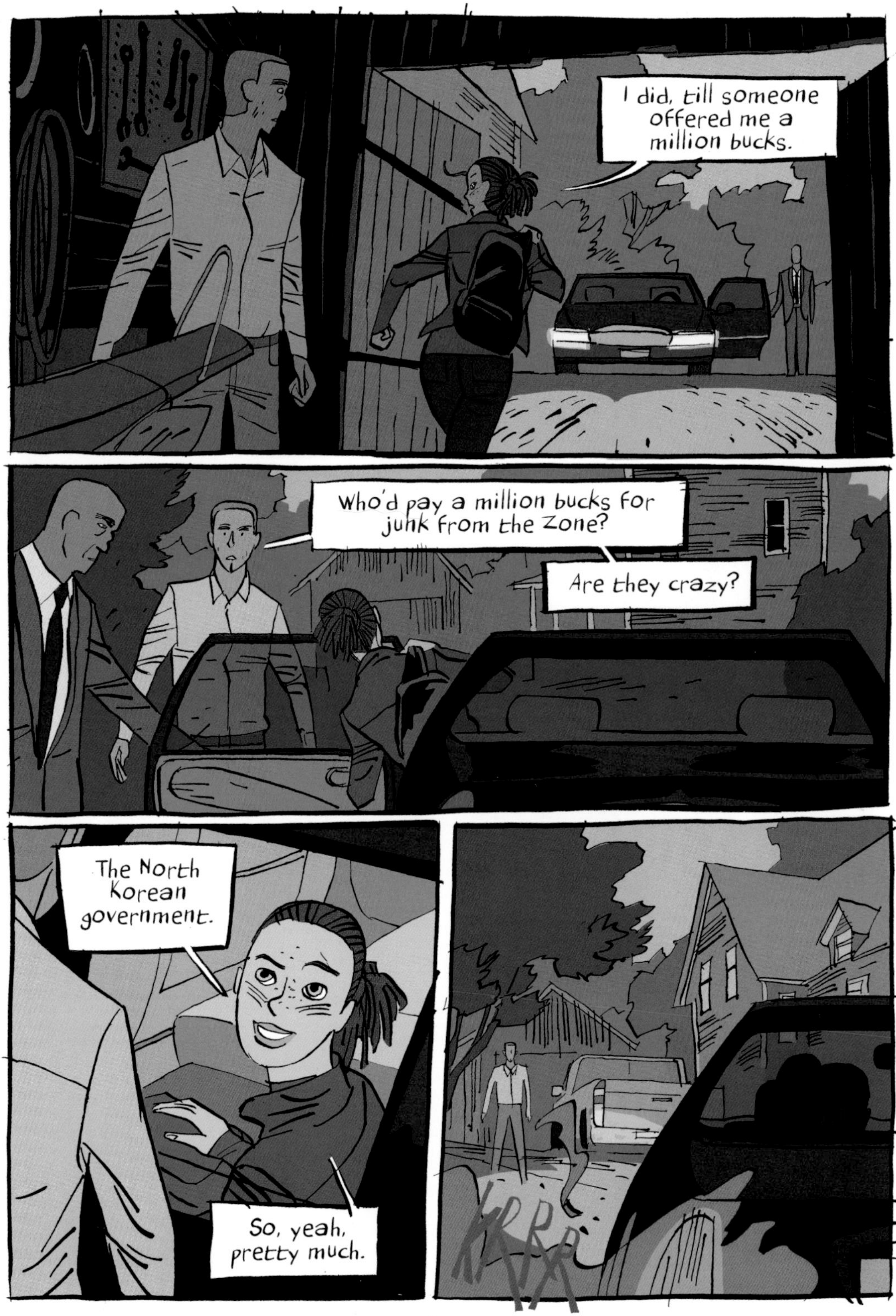
I did, till someone offered me a million bucks.
Who'd pay a million bucks for junk from the Zone?
Are they crazy?
The North Korean government.
So, yeah, pretty much.
KRRR

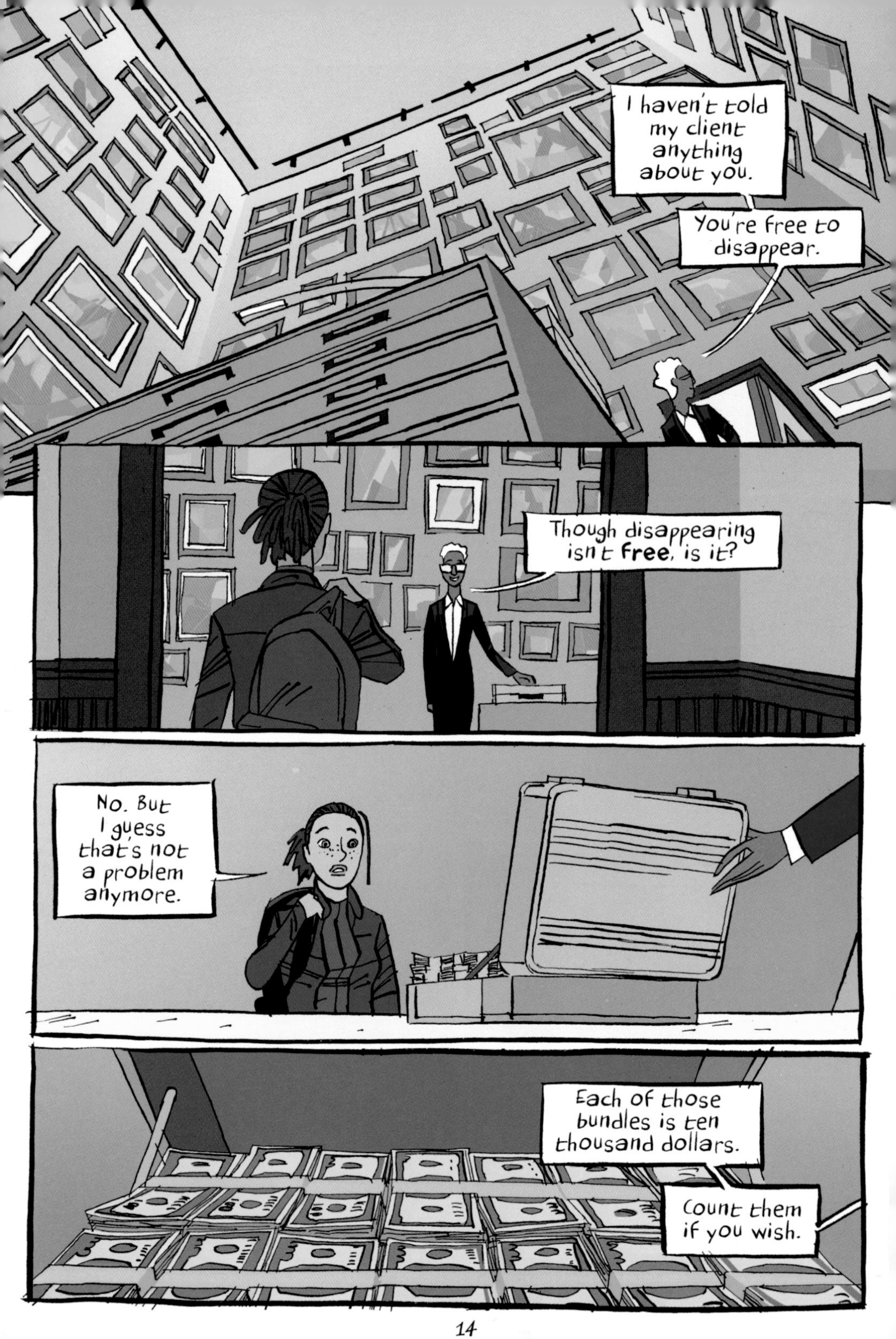
I haven't told my client anything about you.
You're free to disappear.
Though disappearing isn't **free**, is it?
No. But I guess that's not a problem anymore.
Each of those bundles is ten thousand dollars.
Count them if you wish.

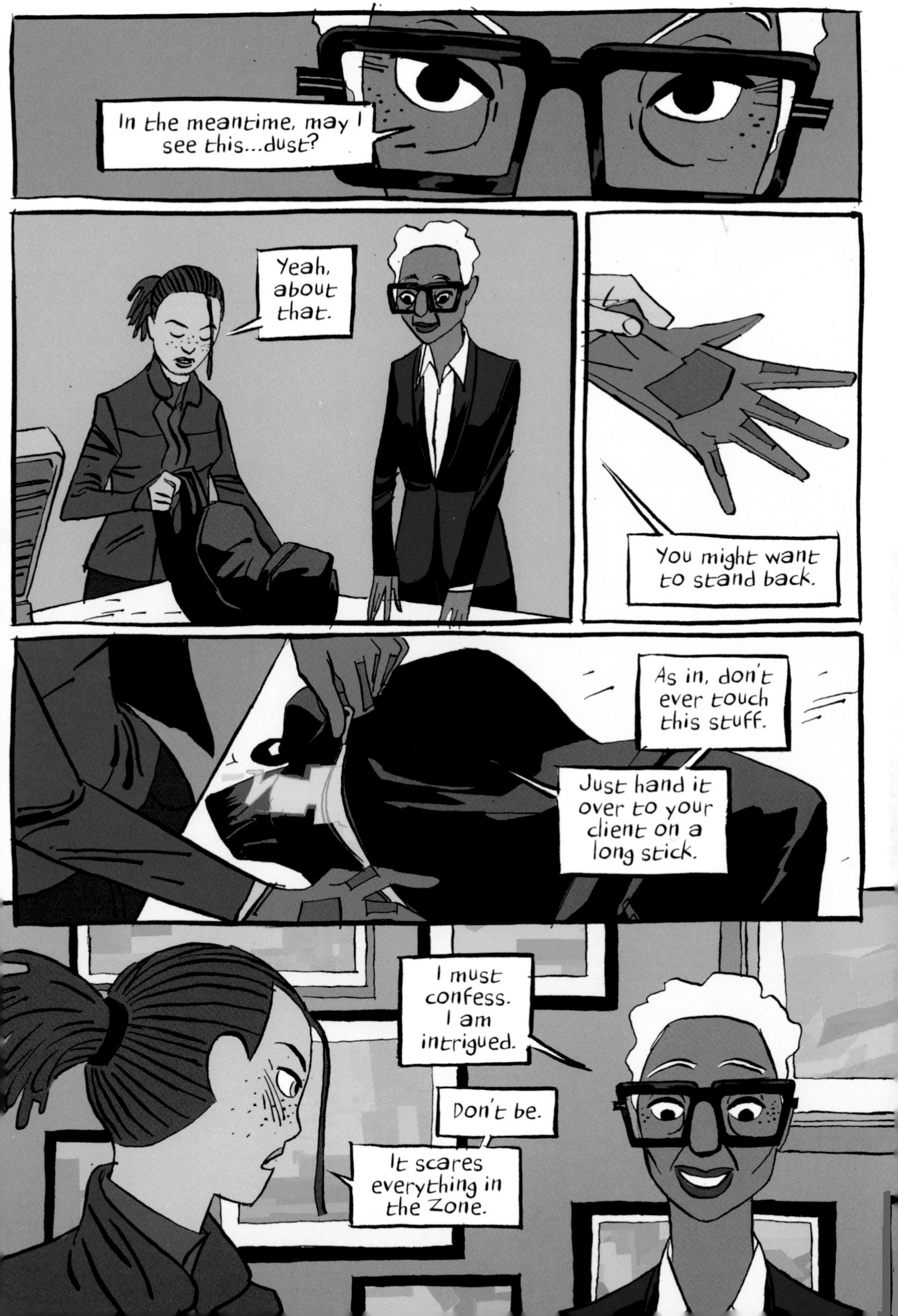
In the meantime, may I see this...dust?
Yeah, about that.
You might want to stand back.
As in, don't ever touch this stuff.
Just hand it over to your client on a long stick.
I must confess. I am intrigued.
Don't be.
It scares everything in the Zone.

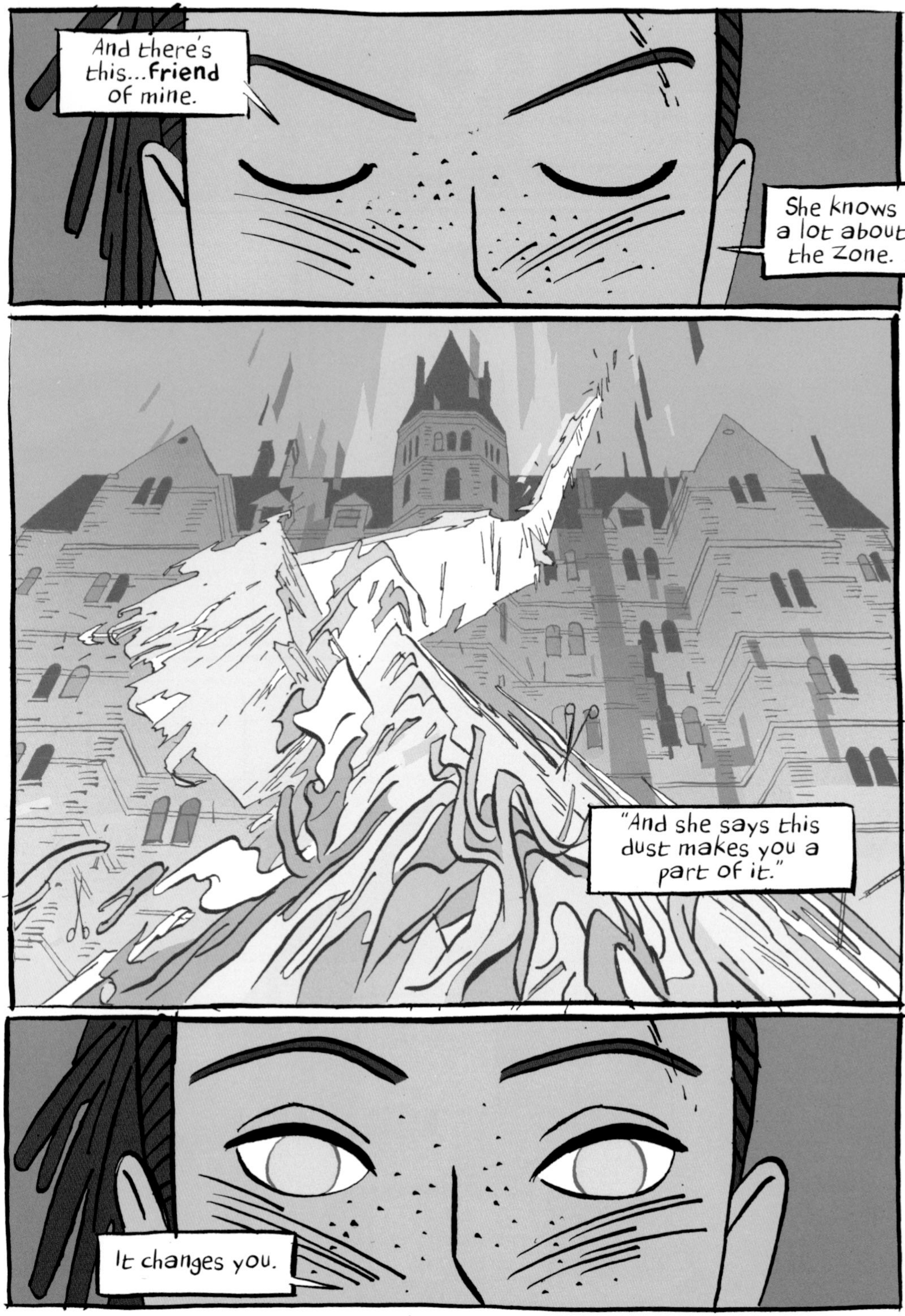

And there's this... **friend** of mine.
She knows a lot about the Zone.
"And she says this dust makes you a part of it."
It changes you.

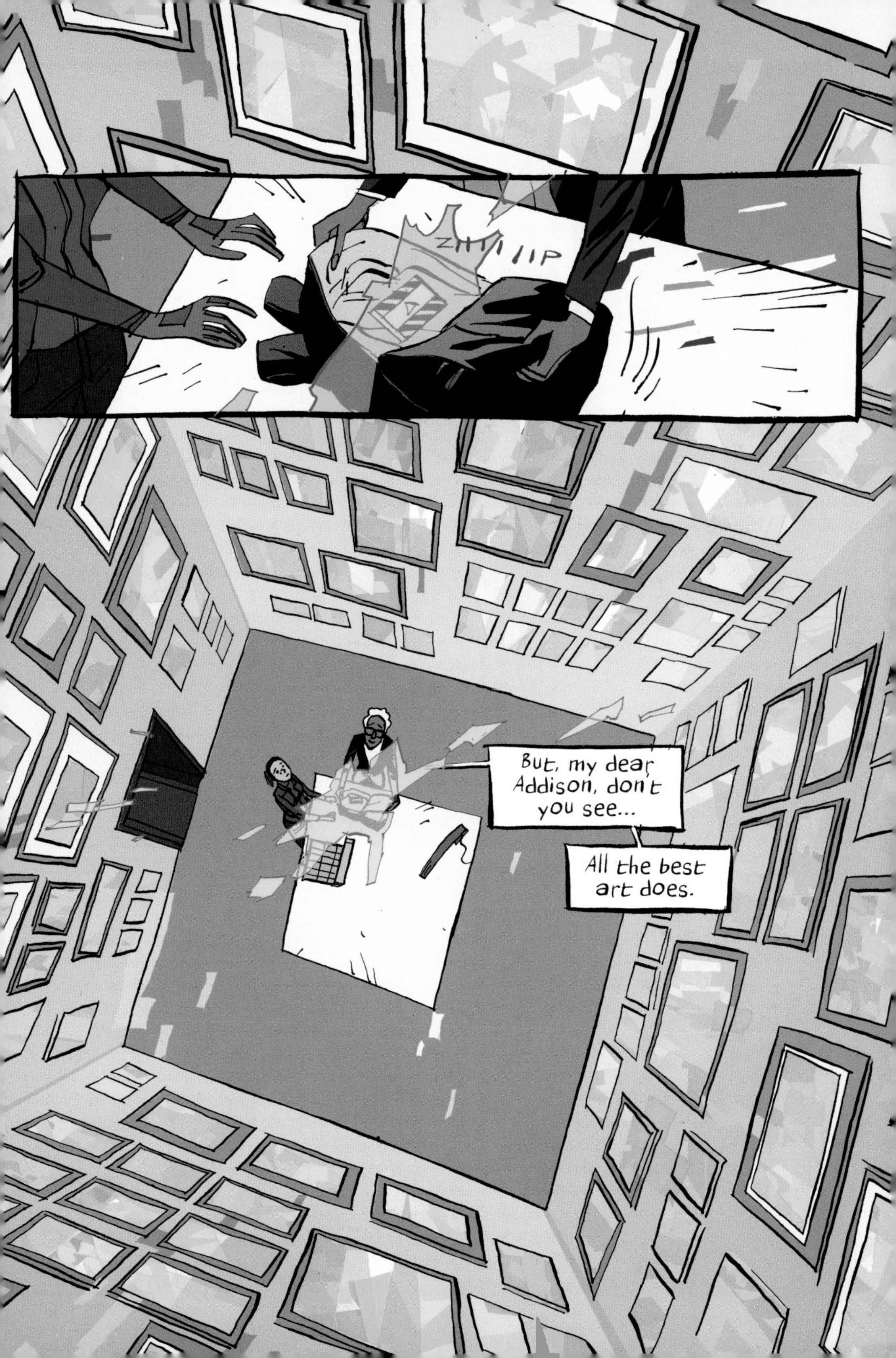
ZHHHIIP
But, my dear Addison, don't you see...
All the best art does.

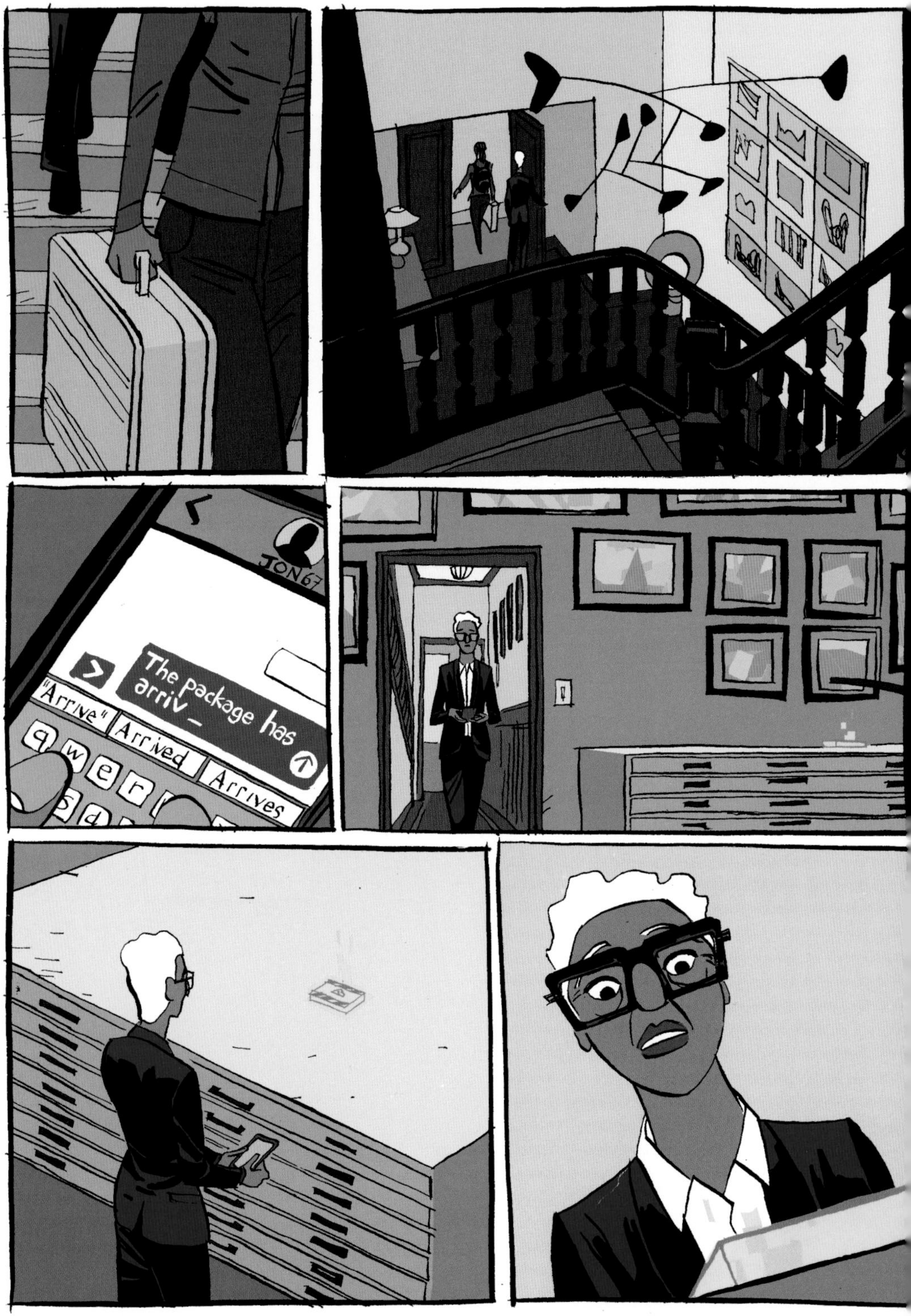
JON67
The package has arriv_
"Arrive"
Arrived
Arrives

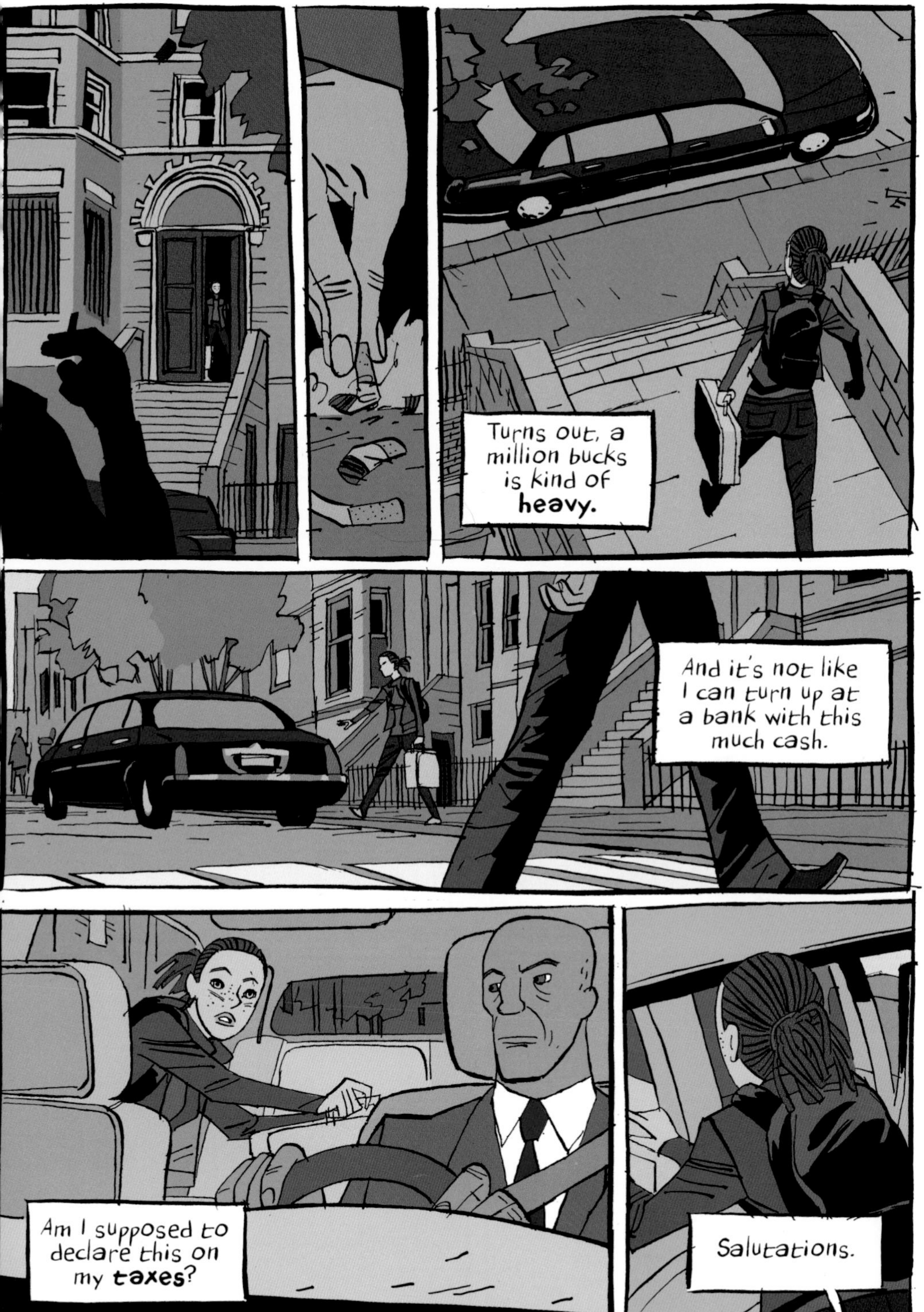
Turns out, a million bucks is kind of **heavy.**
And it's not like I can turn up at a bank with this much cash.
Am I supposed to declare this on my **taxes**?
Salutations.

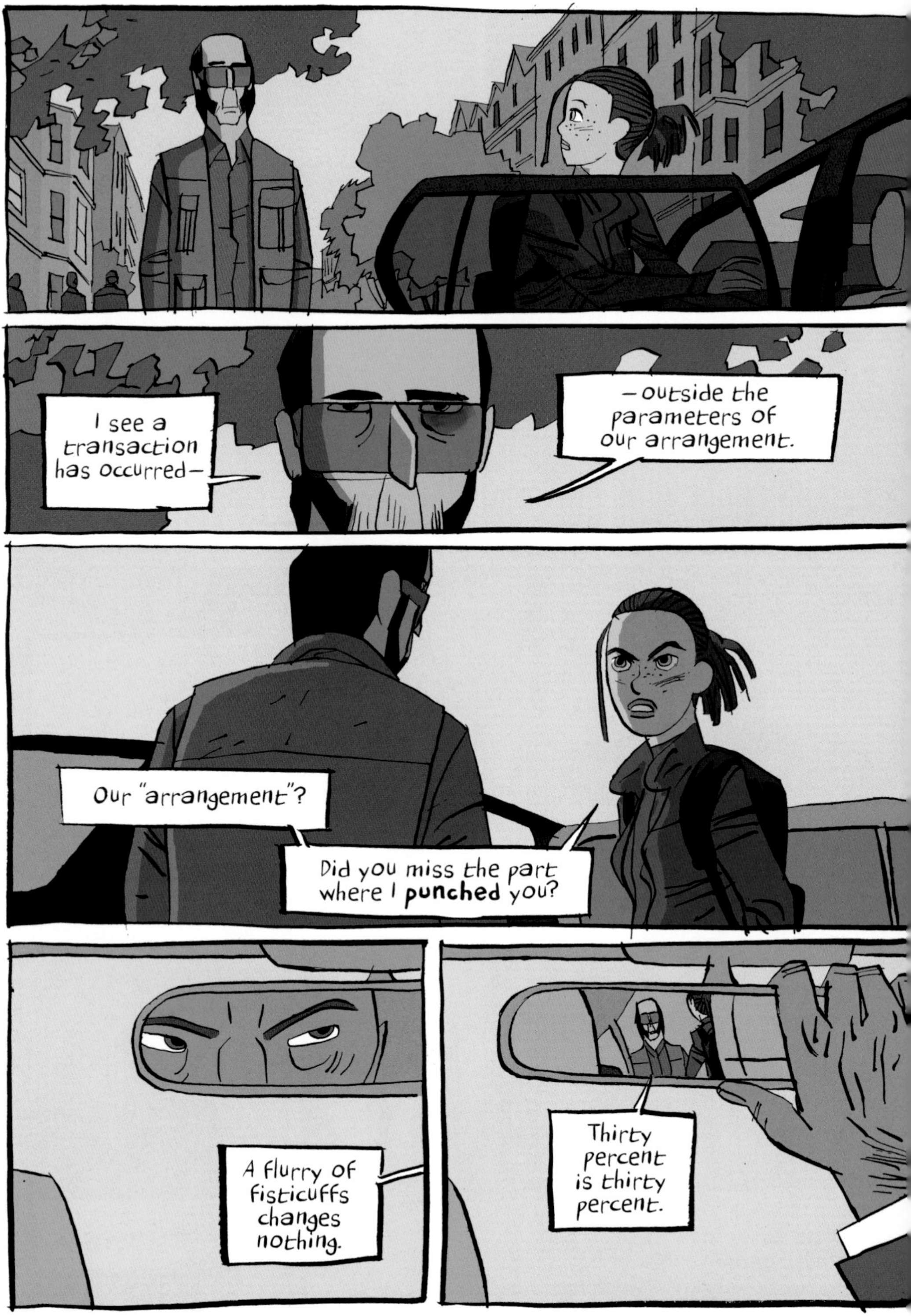
I see a transaction has occurred—
—outside the parameters of our arrangement.
Our "arrangement"?
Did you miss the part where I **punched** you?
A flurry of fisticuffs changes nothing.
Thirty percent is thirty percent.

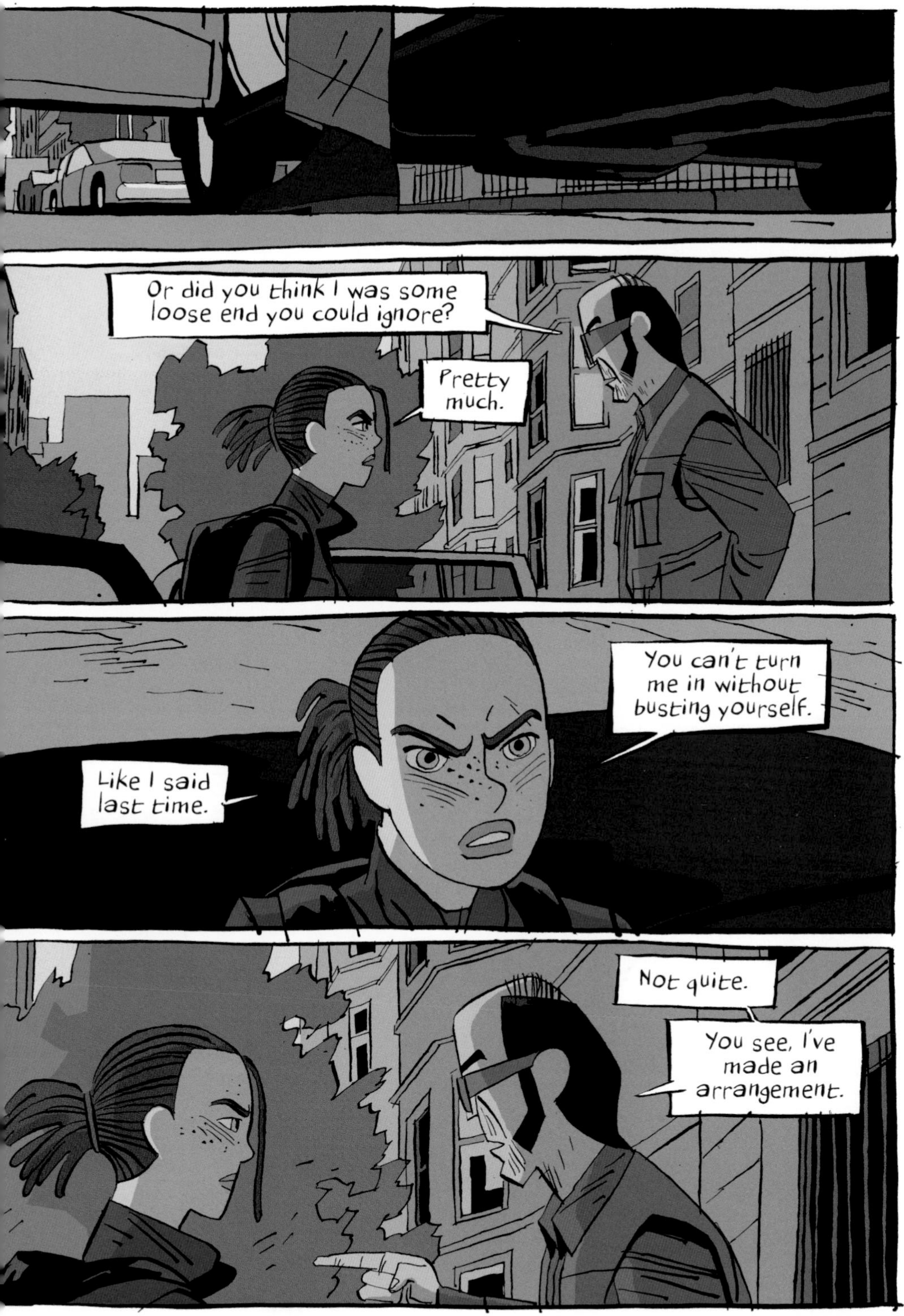
Or did you think I was some loose end you could ignore?
Pretty much.
You can't turn me in without busting yourself.
Like I said last time.
Not quite.
You see, I've made an arrangement.

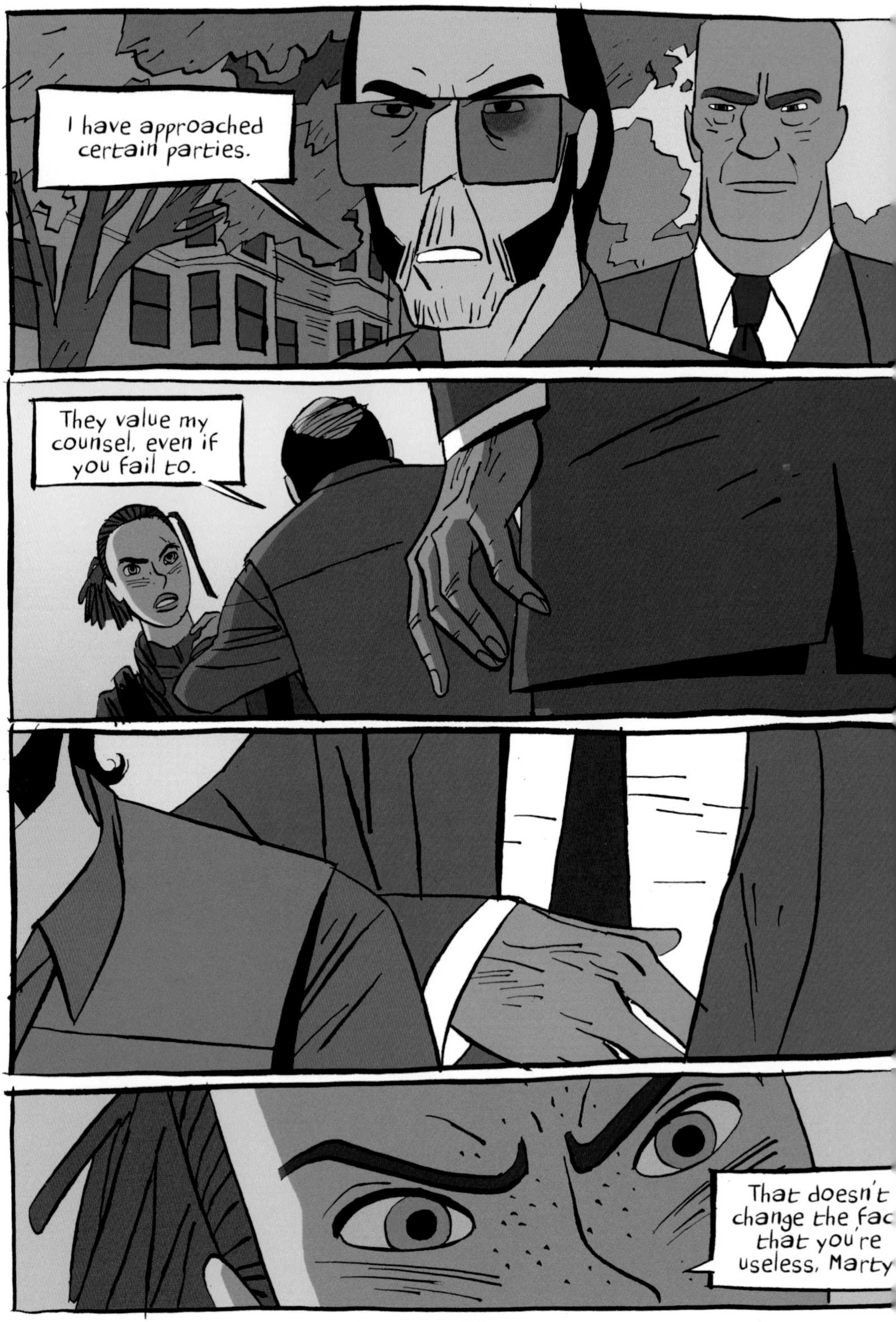
I have approached certain parties.
They value my counsel, even if you fail to.
That doesn't change the fac that you're useless, Marty

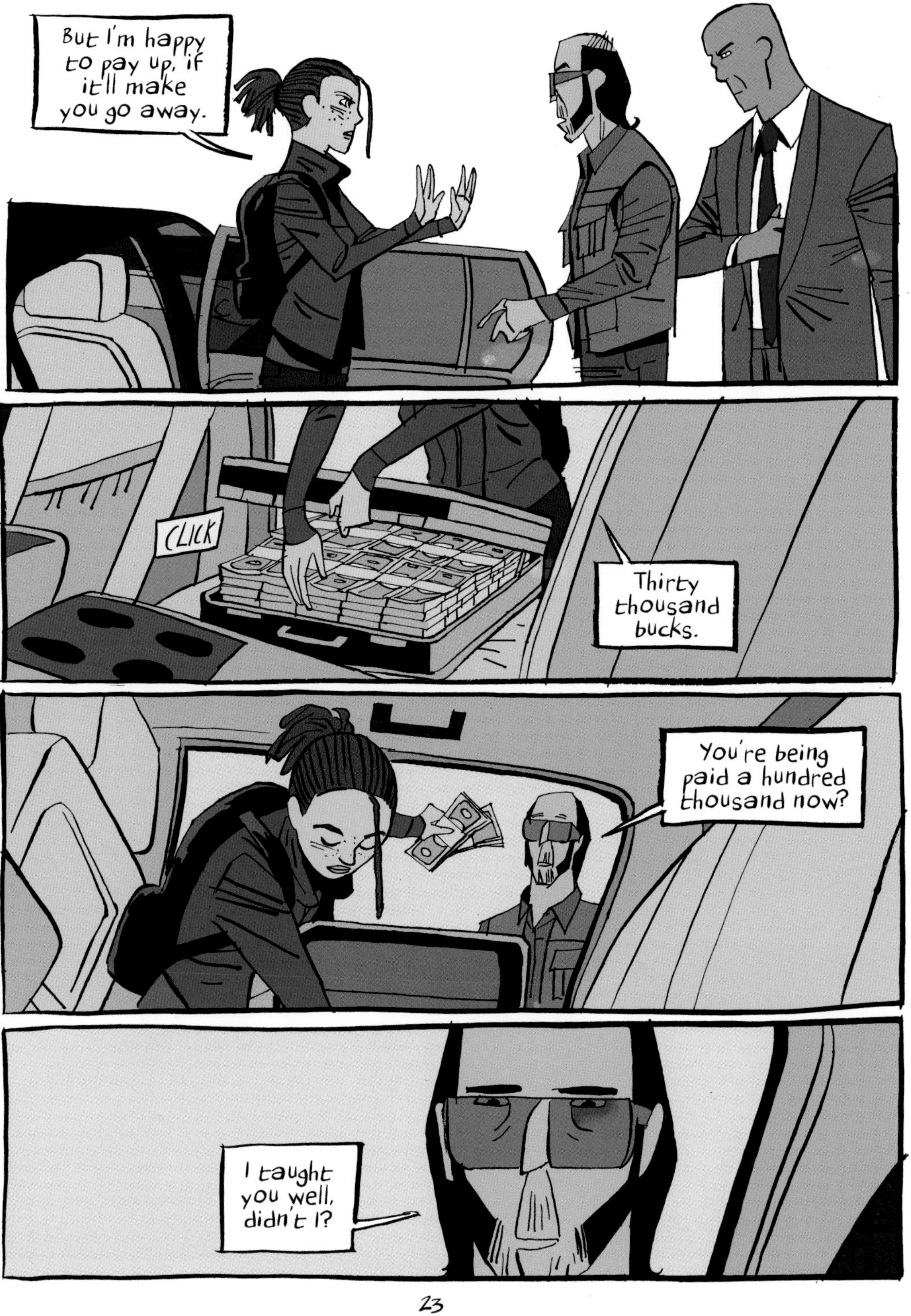
But I'm happy to pay up, if it'll make you go away.
CLICK
Thirty thousand bucks.
You're being paid a hundred thousand now?
I taught you well, didn't I?

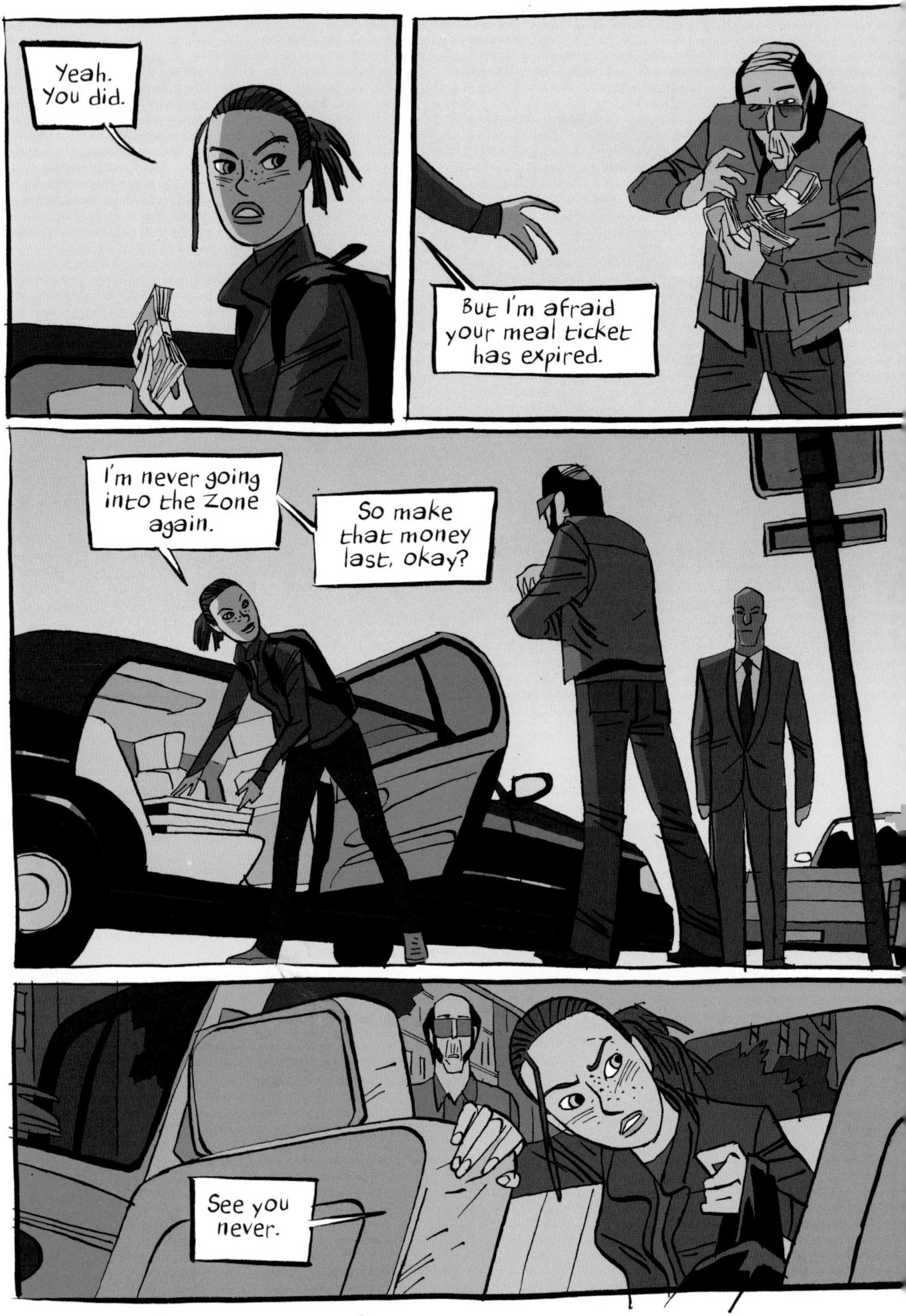
Yeah.
You did.
But I'm afraid
your meal ticket
has expired.
I'm never going
into the Zone
again.
So make
that money
last, okay?
See you
never.

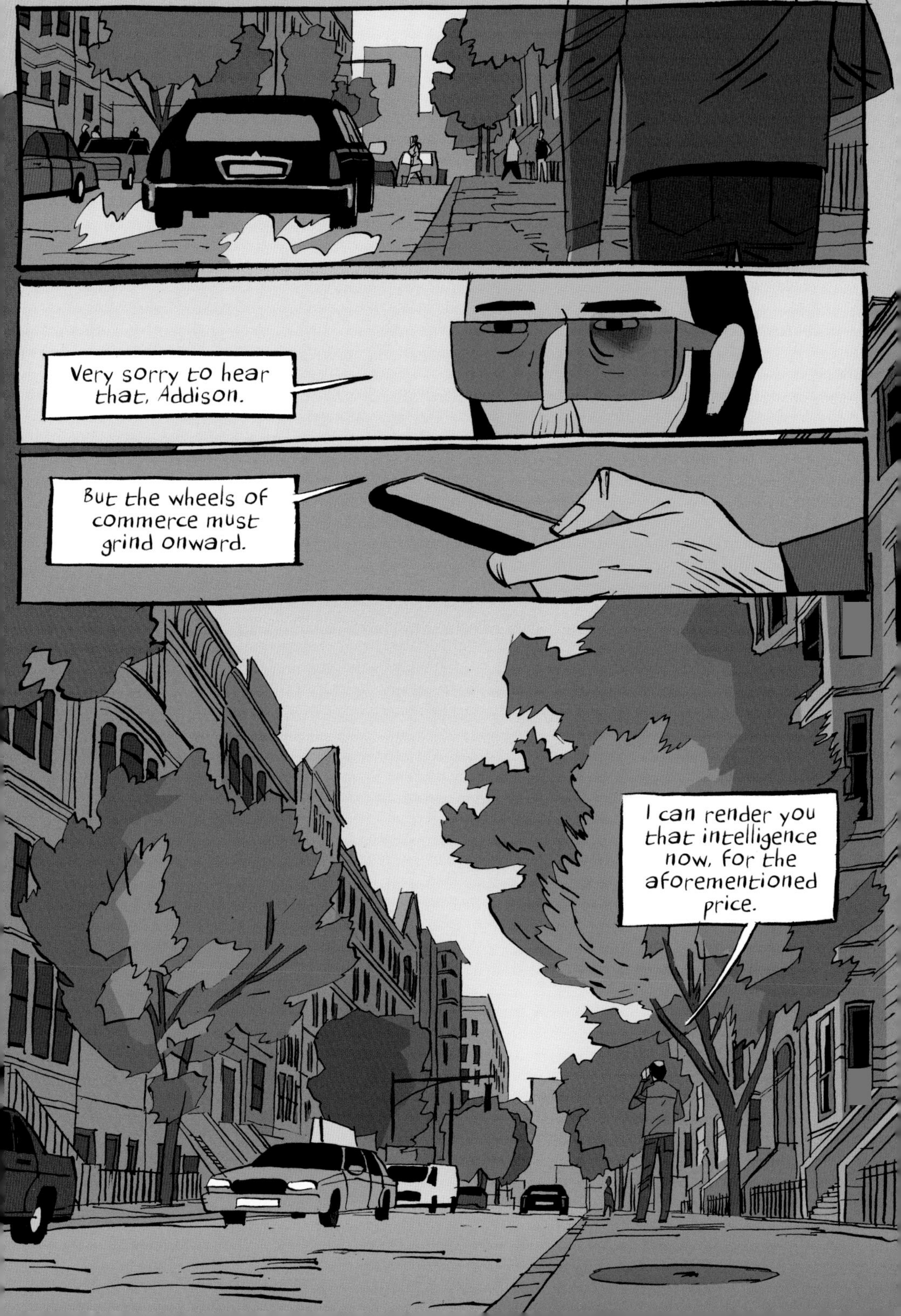
Very sorry to hear that, Addison.
But the wheels of commerce must grind onward.
I can render you that intelligence now, for the aforementioned price.

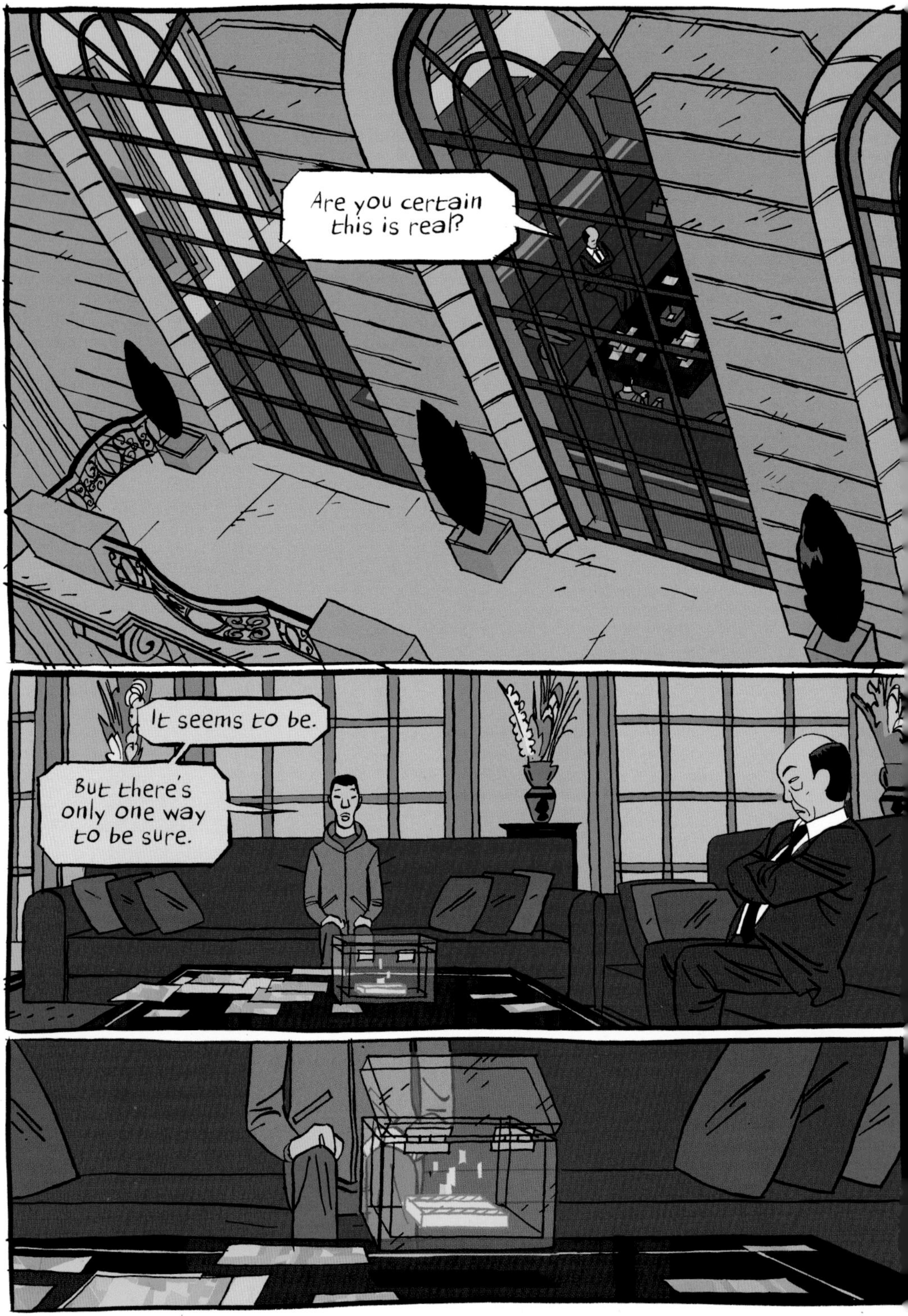
Are you certain this is real?
It seems to be.
But there's only one way to be sure.

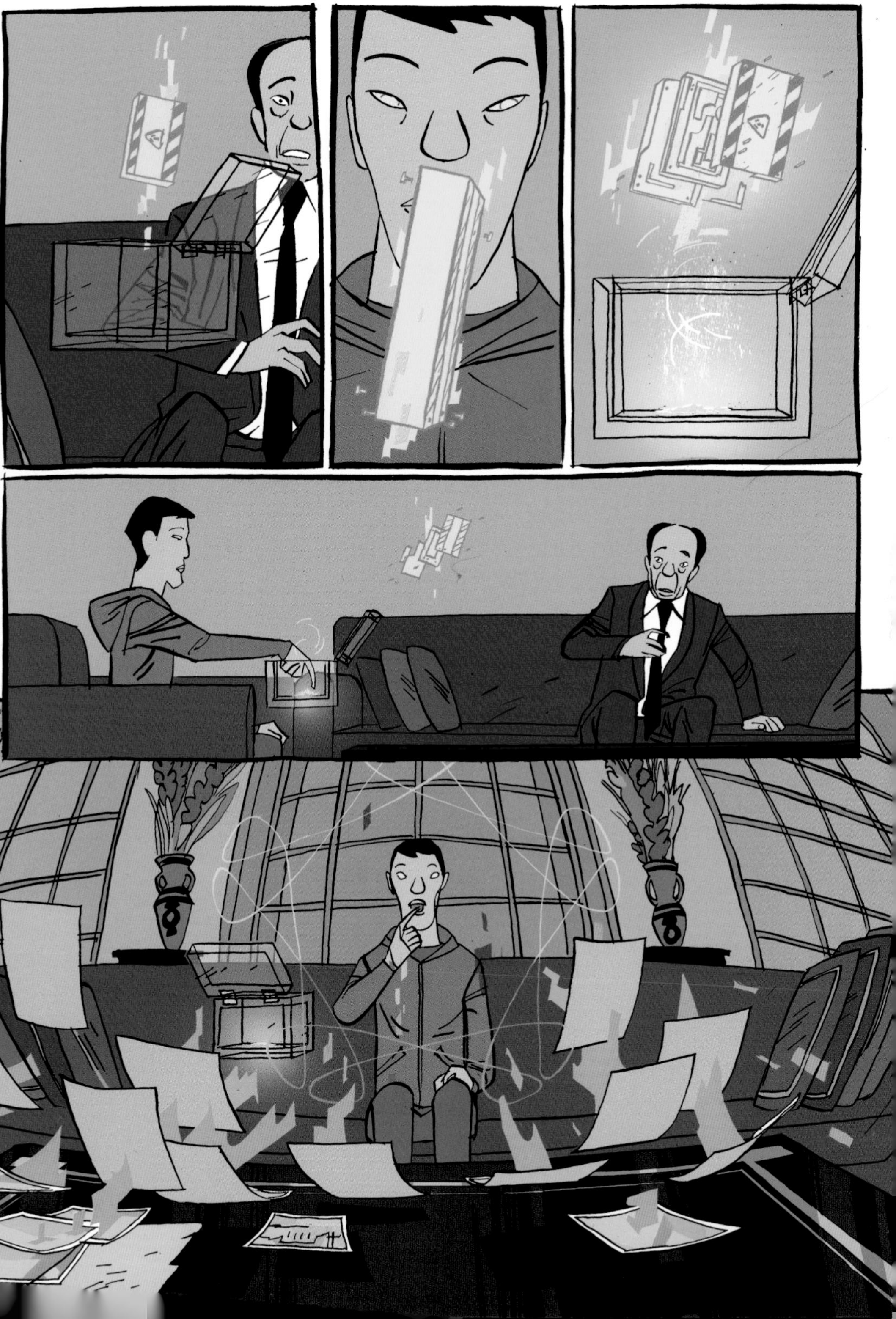

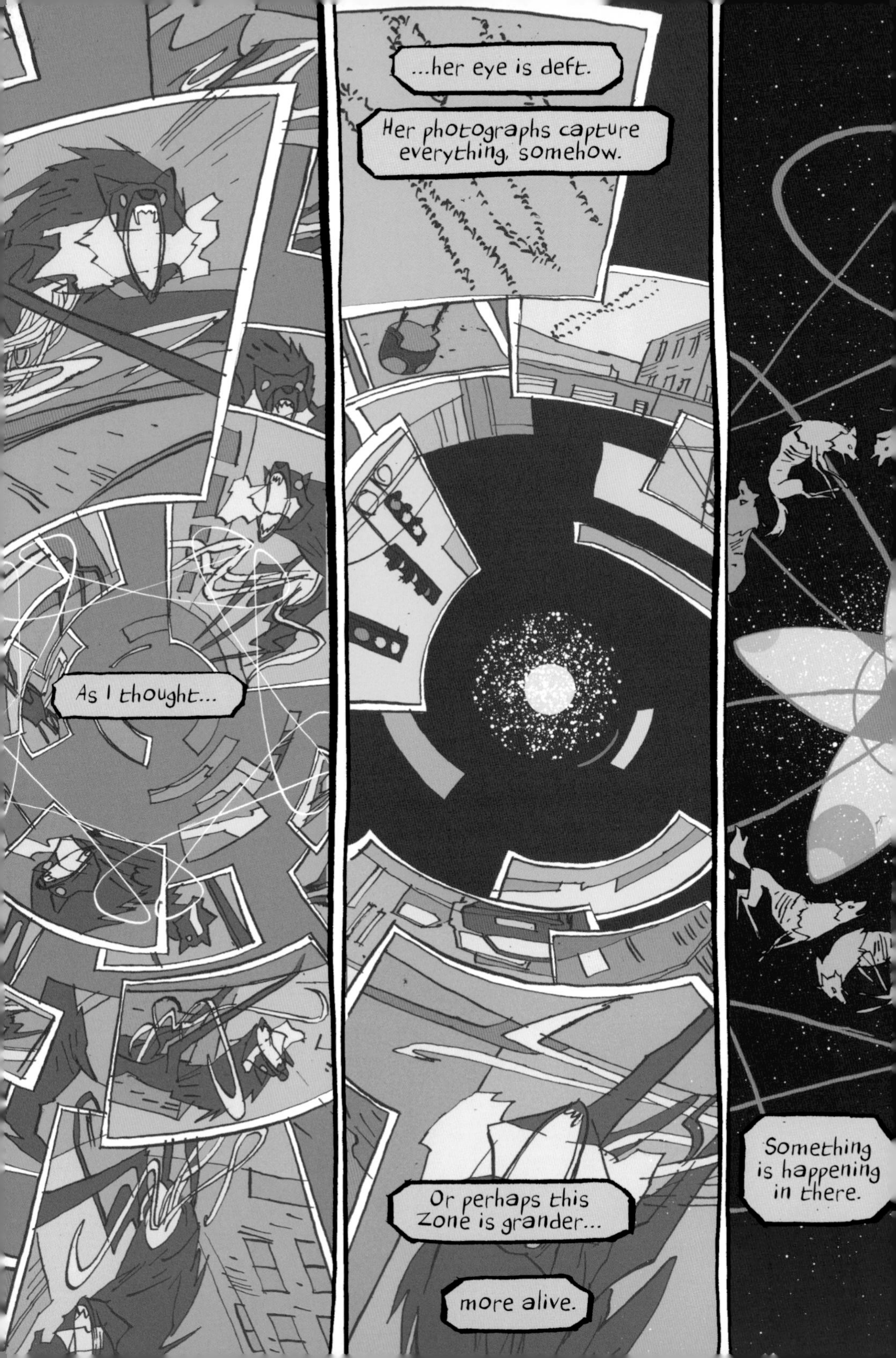
As I thought...
...her eye is deft.
Her photographs capture everything, somehow.
Or perhaps this Zone is grander...
more alive.
Something is happening in there.

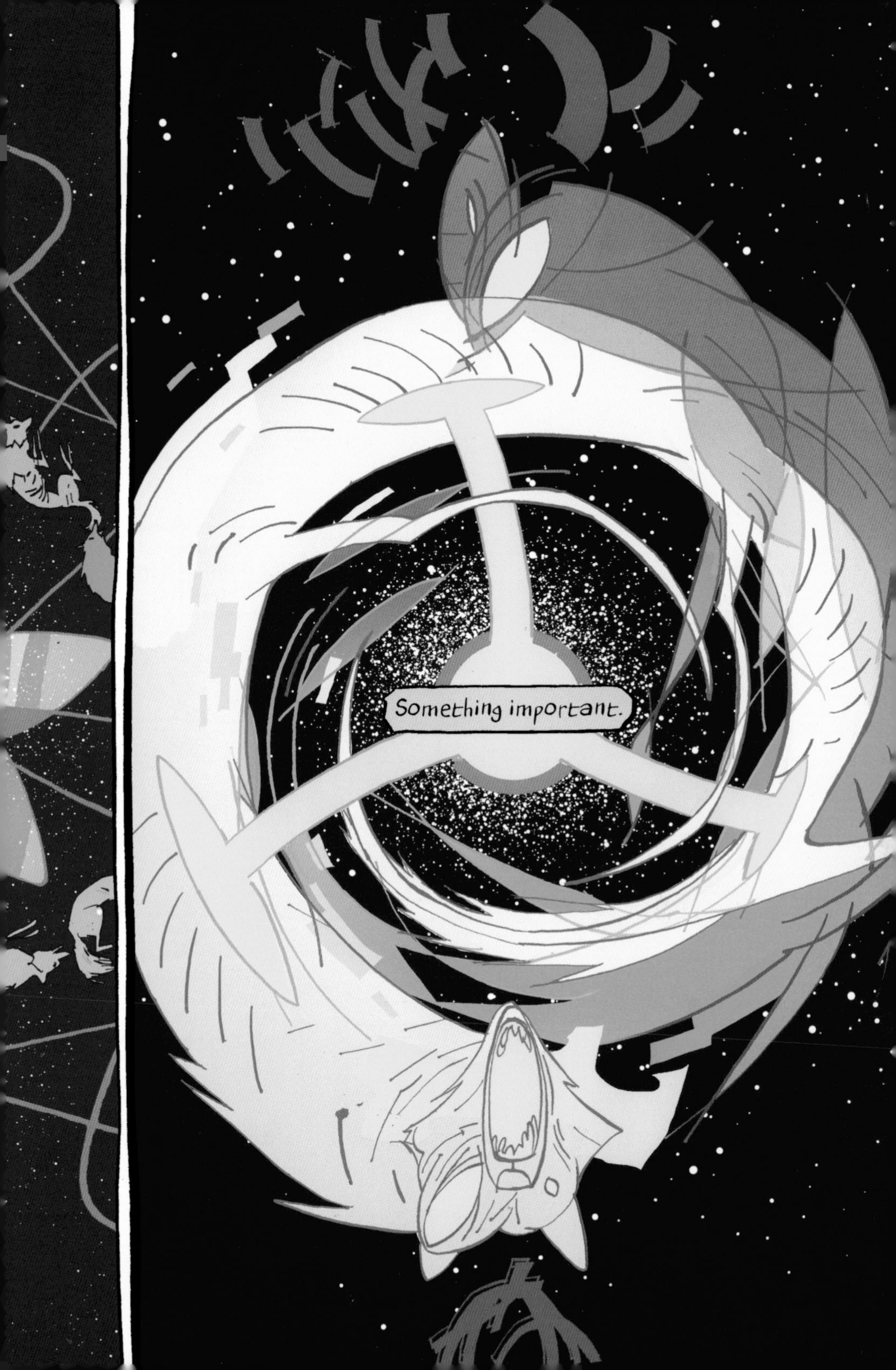
Something important.

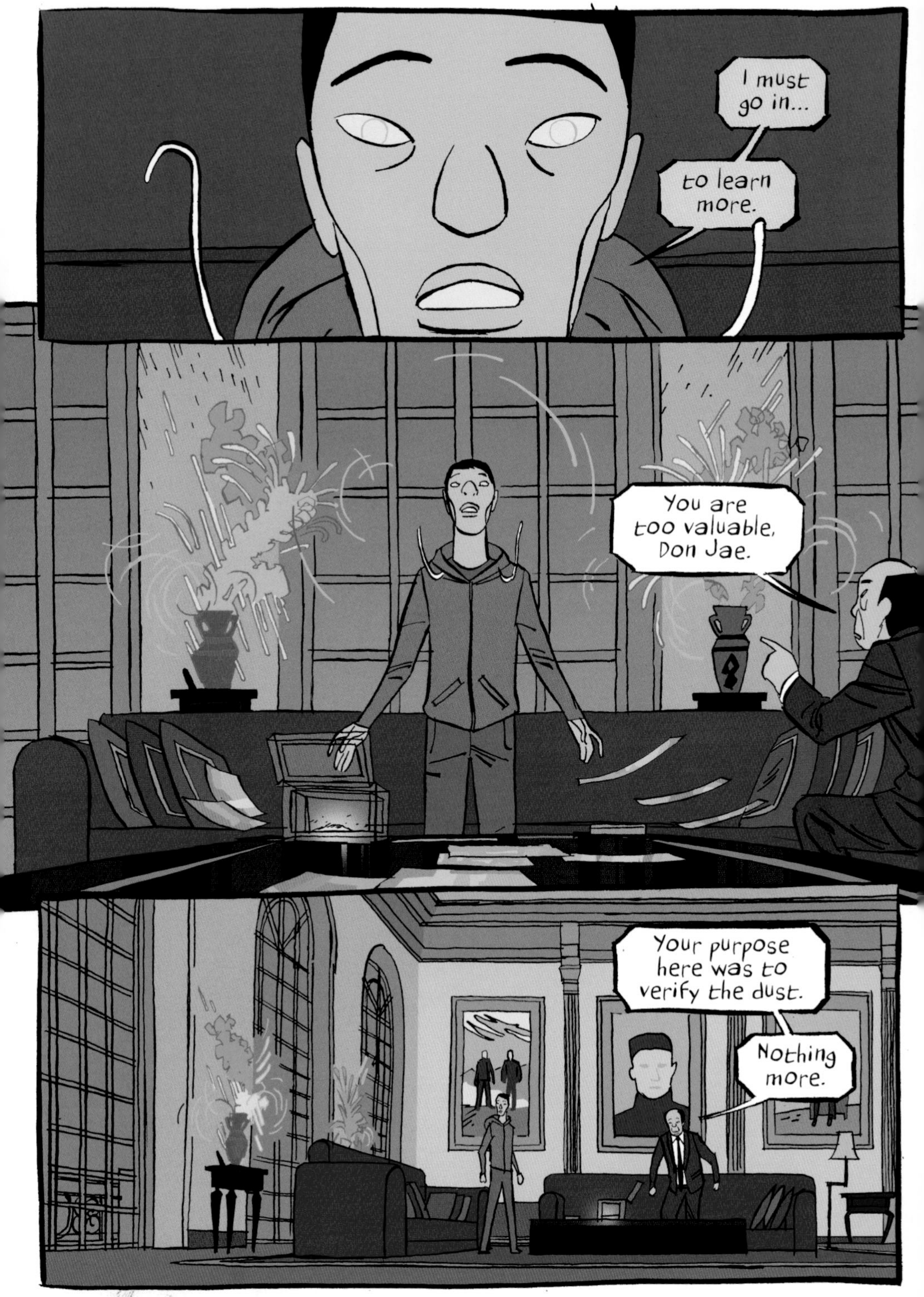
I must go in...
to learn more.
You are too valuable, Don Jae.
Your purpose here was to verify the dust.
Nothing more.

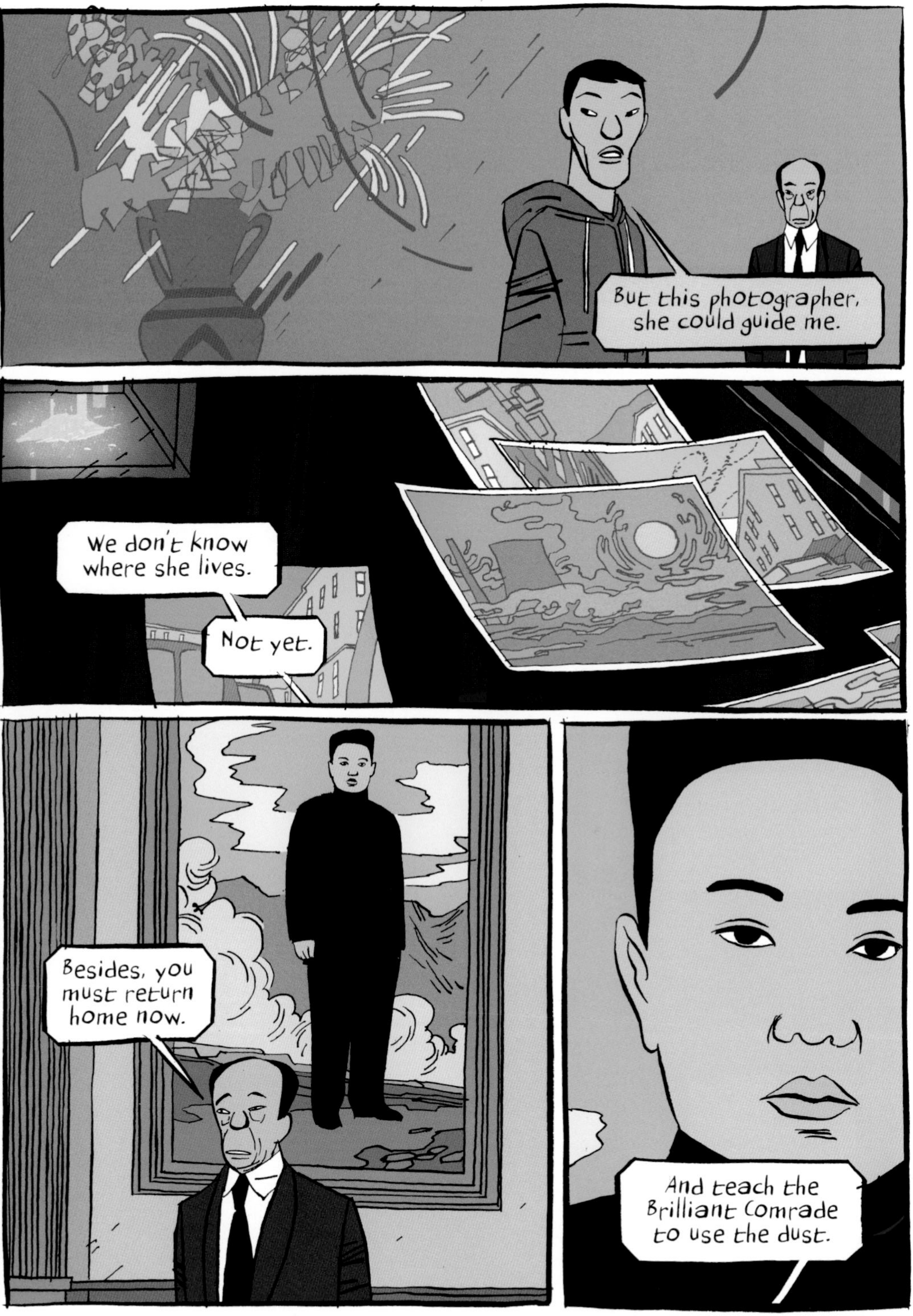

But this photographer, she could guide me.
We don't know where she lives.
Not yet.
Besides, you must return home now.
And teach the Brilliant Comrade to use the dust.

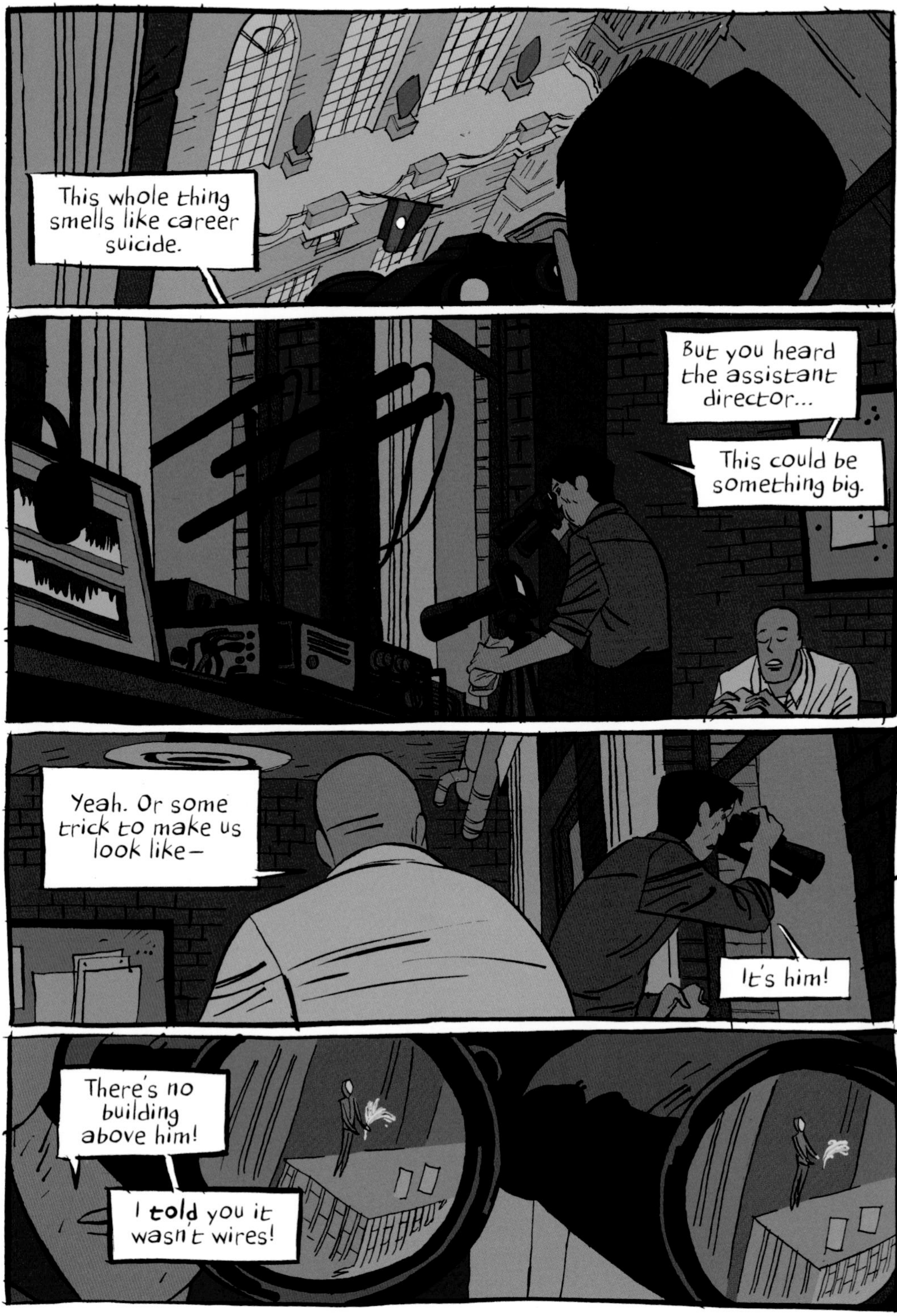
This whole thing smells like career suicide.
But you heard the assistant director...
This could be something big.
Yeah. Or some trick to make us look like—
It's him!
There's no building above him!
I told you it wasn't wires!

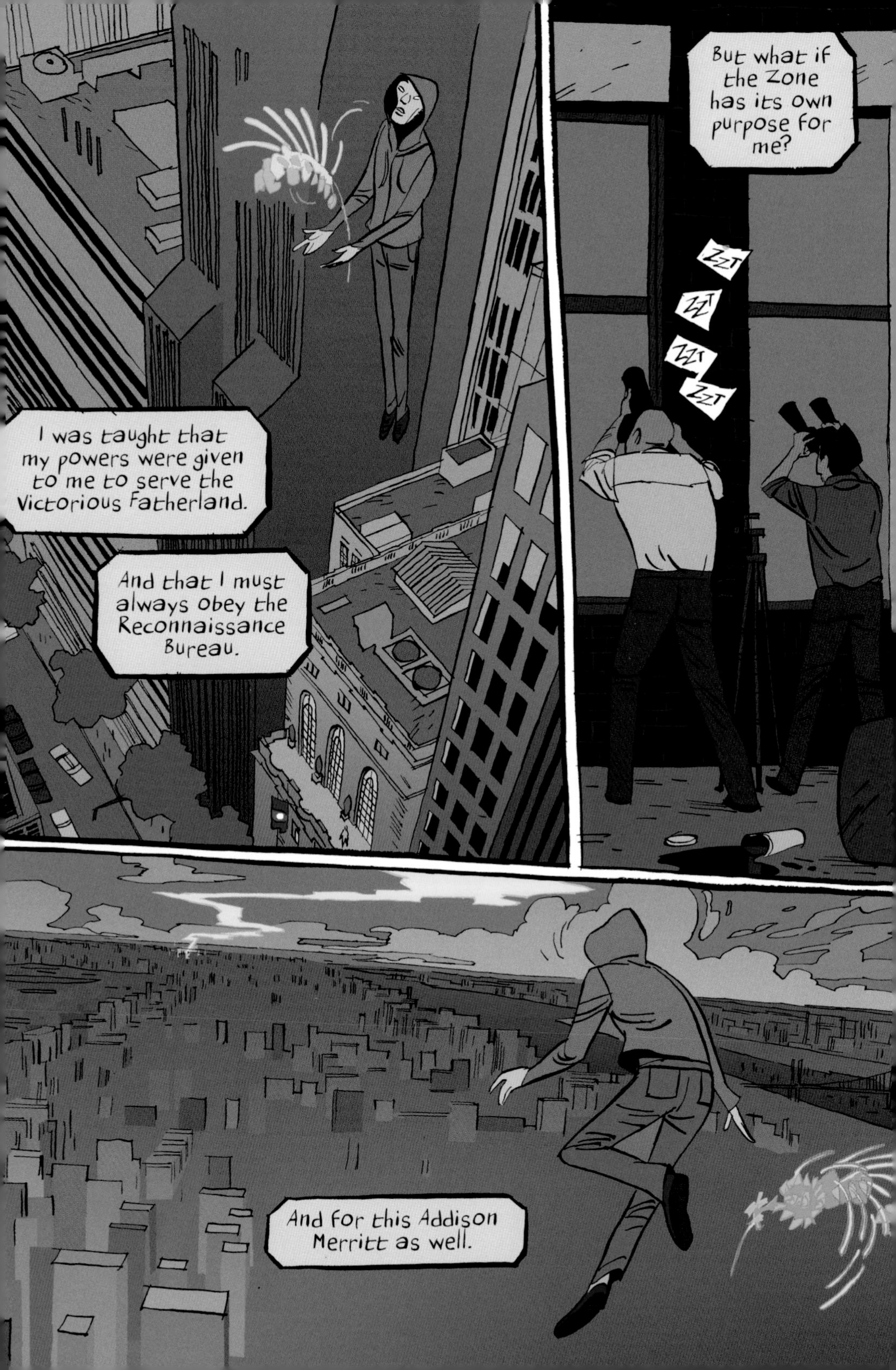
I was taught that my powers were given to me to serve the Victorious Fatherland.
And that I must always obey the Reconnaissance Bureau.
But what if the Zone has its own purpose for me?
ZZT
ZZT
ZZT
ZZT
And for this Addison Merritt as well.

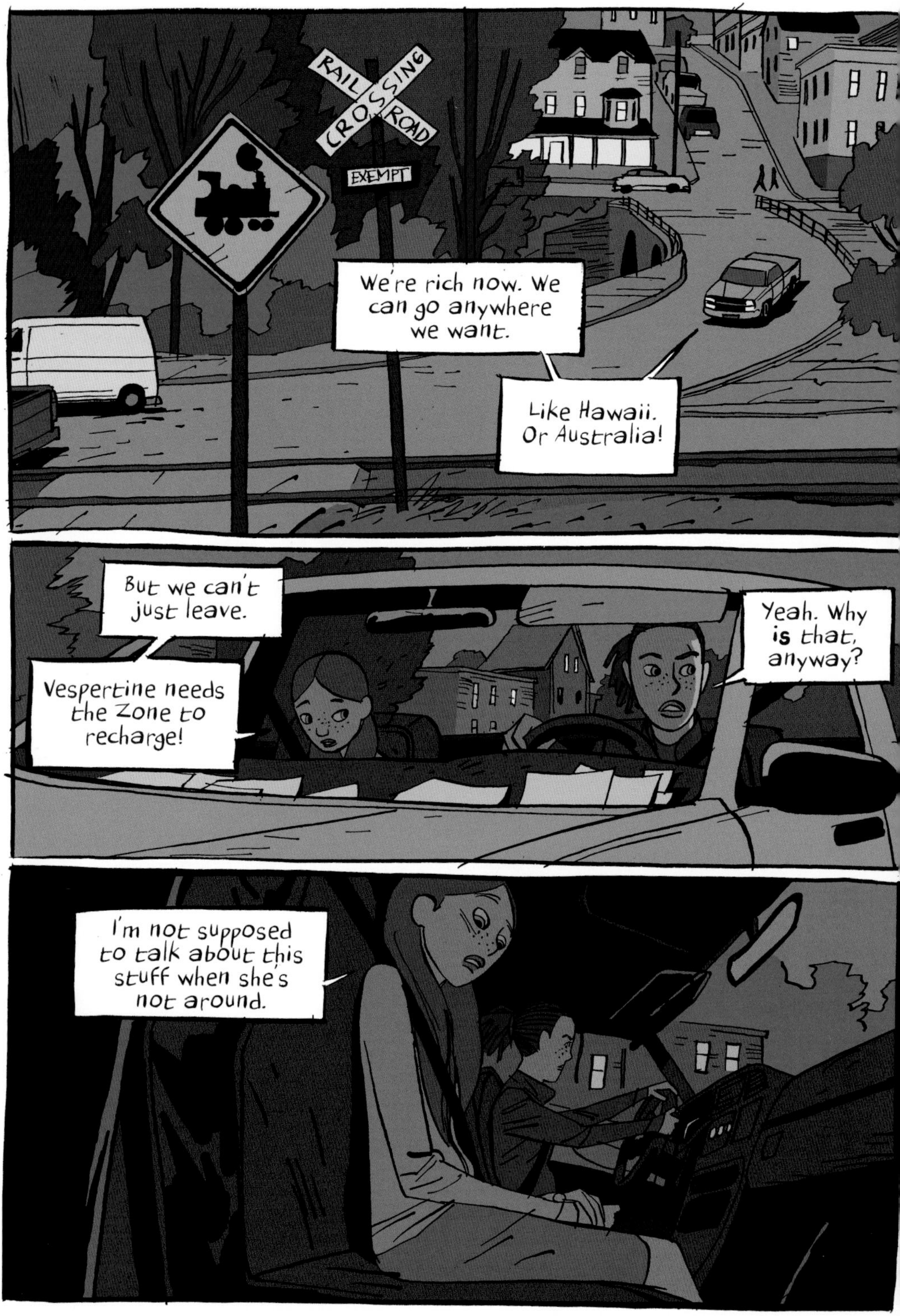
RAILROAD CROSSING
EXEMPT
We're rich now. We can go anywhere we want.
Like Hawaii. Or Australia!
But we can't just leave.
Vespertine needs the Zone to recharge!
Yeah. Why **is** that, anyway?
I'm not supposed to talk about this stuff when she's not around.

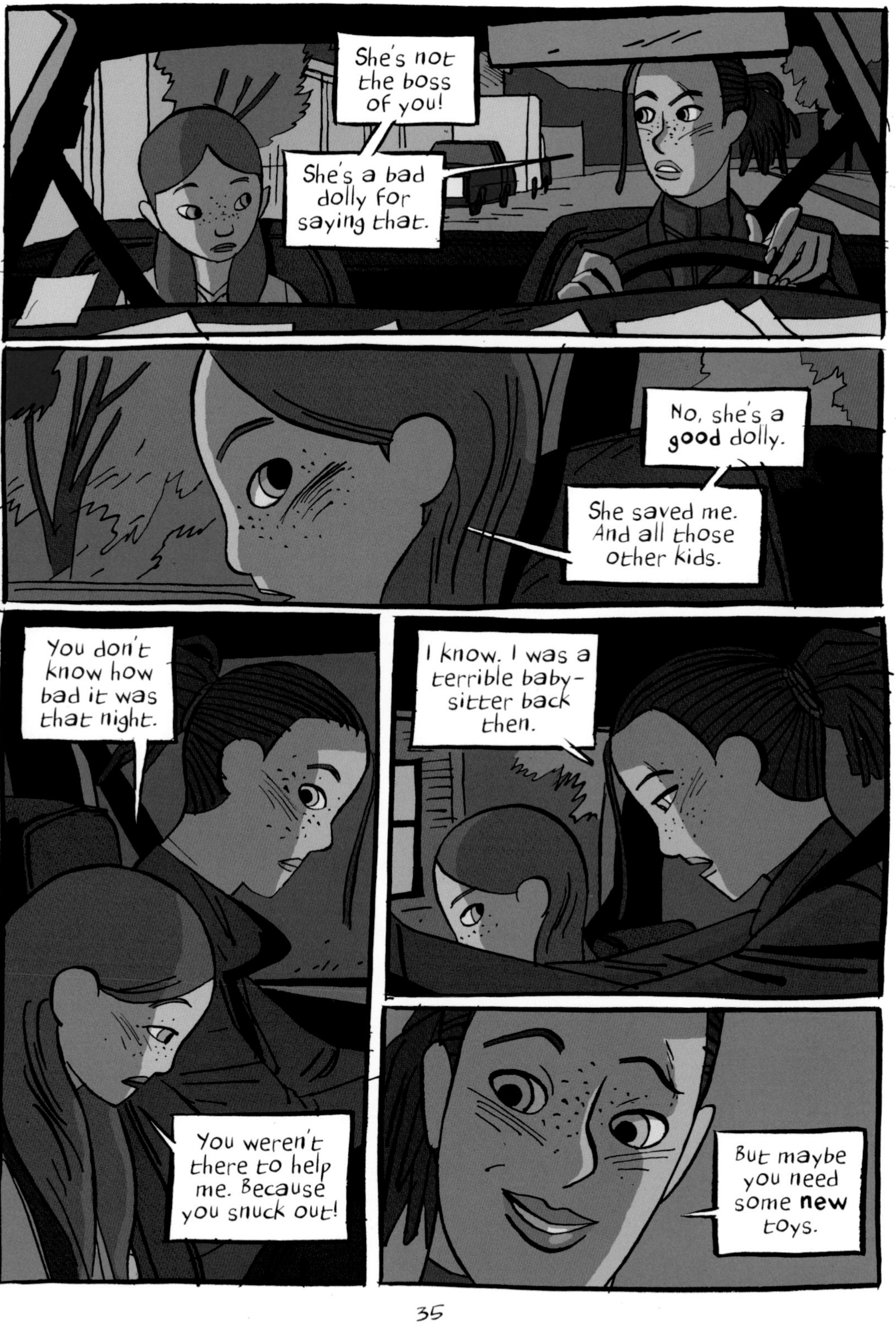
She's not the boss of you!
She's a bad dolly for saying that.
No, she's a **good** dolly.
She saved me. And all those other kids.
You don't know how bad it was that night.
You weren't there to help me. Because you snuck out!
I know. I was a terrible baby-sitter back then.
But maybe you need some **new** toys.

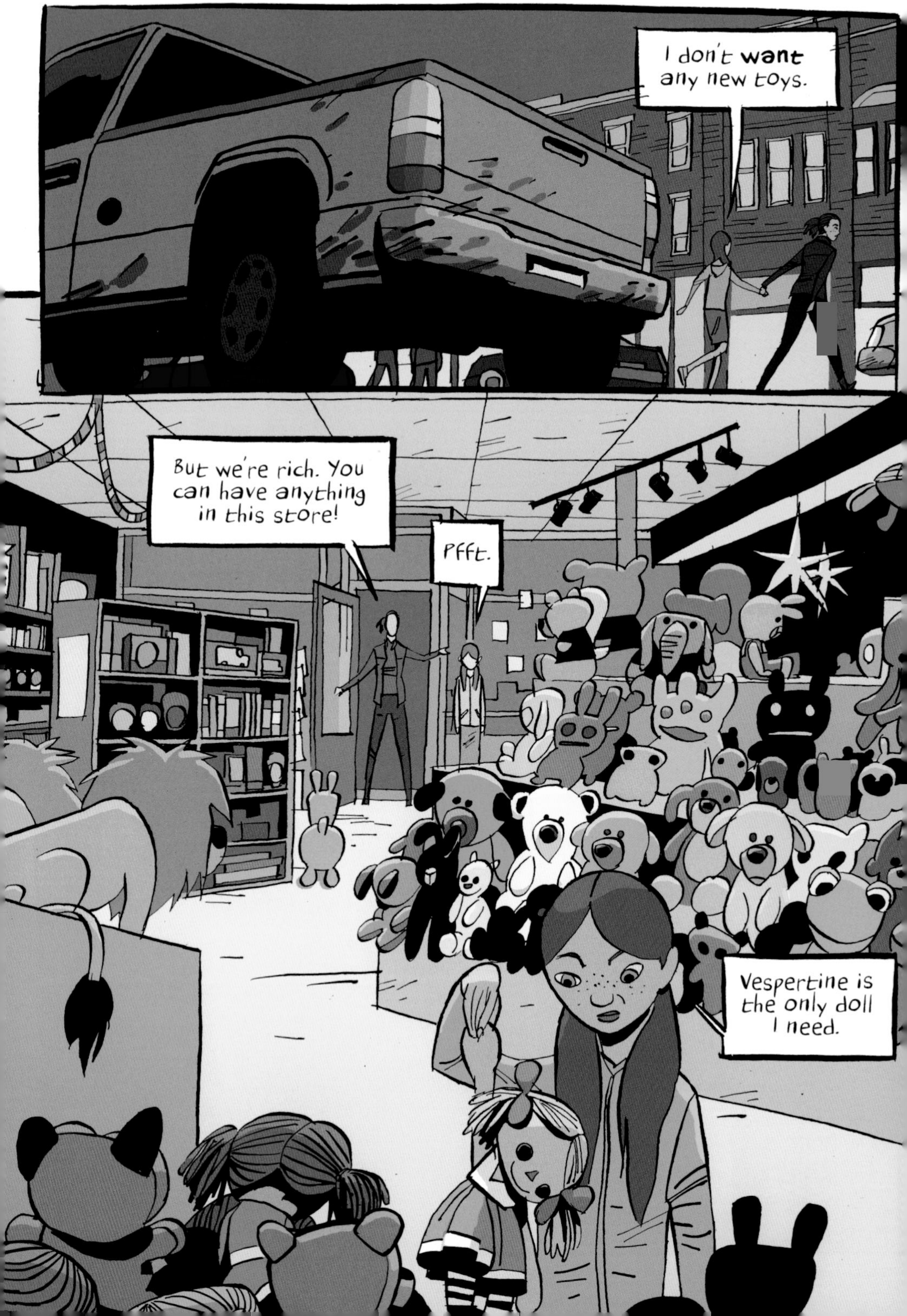
I don't **want** any new toys.
But we're rich. You can have anything in this store!
Pfft.
Vespertine is the only doll I need.

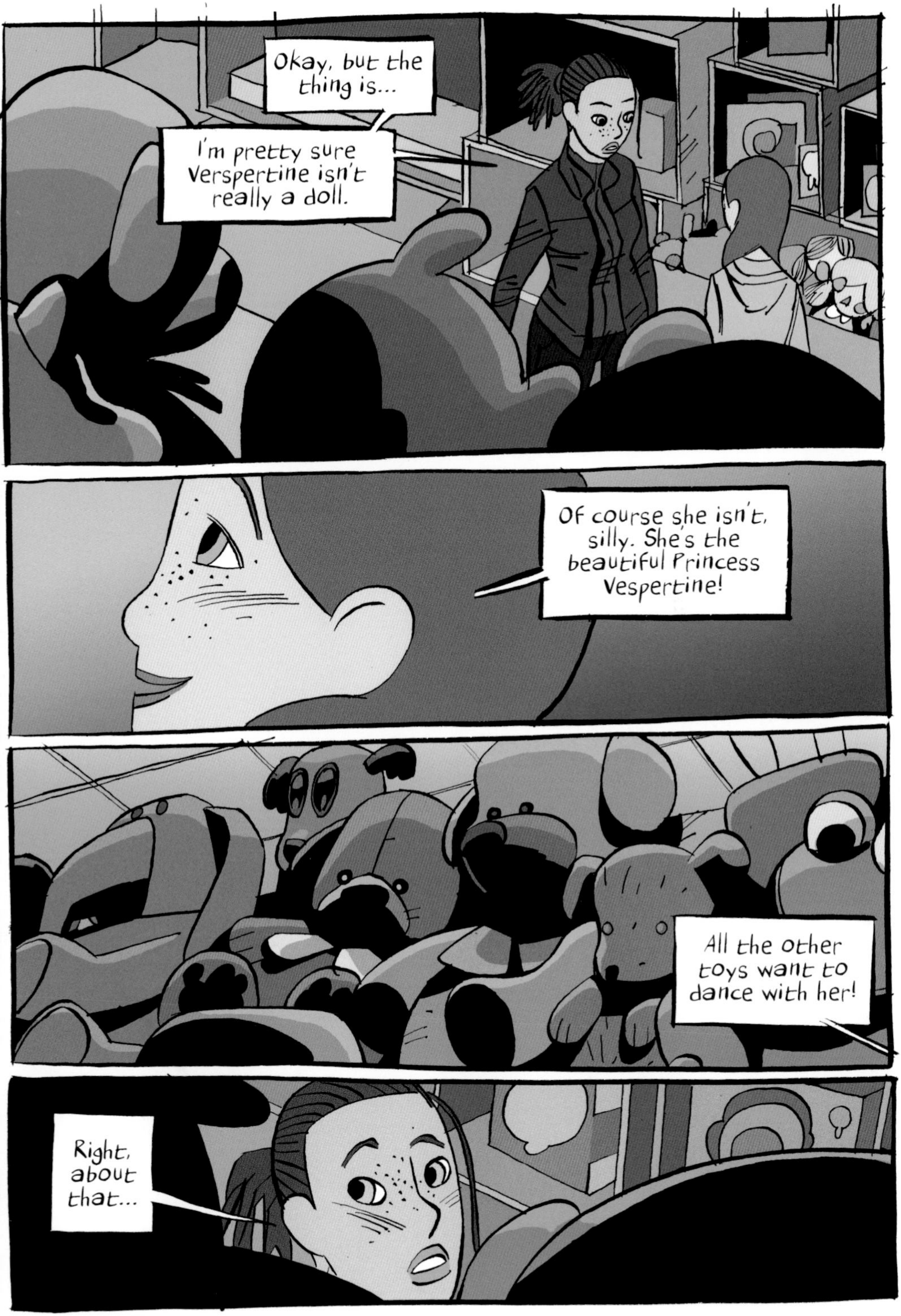
Okay, but the thing is...
I'm pretty sure Verspertine isn't really a doll.
Of course she isn't, silly. She's the beautiful Princess Vespertine!
All the other toys want to dance with her!
Right, about that...

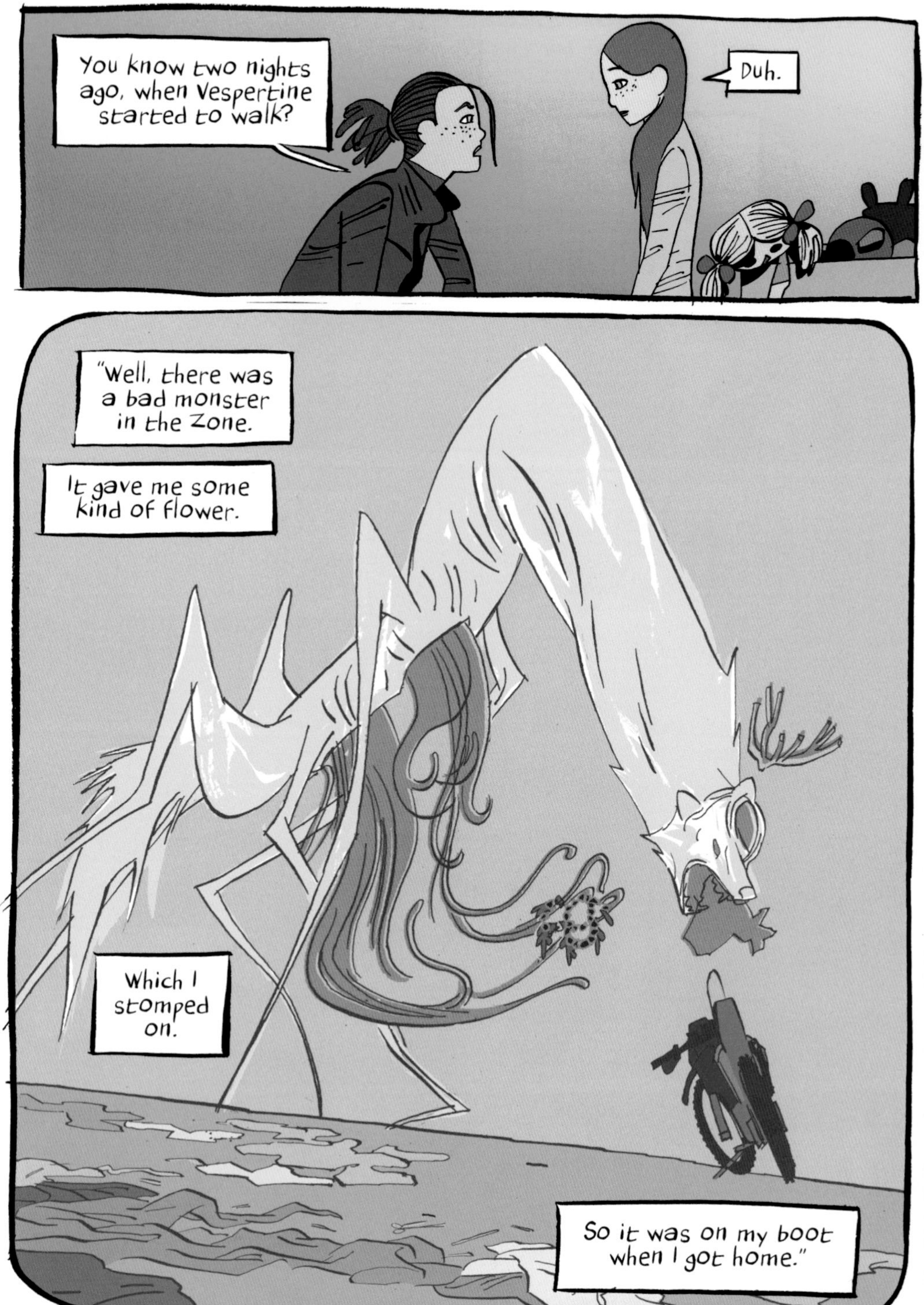
You know two nights ago, when Vespertine started to walk?
Duh.
"Well, there was a bad monster in the Zone.
It gave me some kind of flower.
Which I stomped on.
So it was on my boot when I got home."

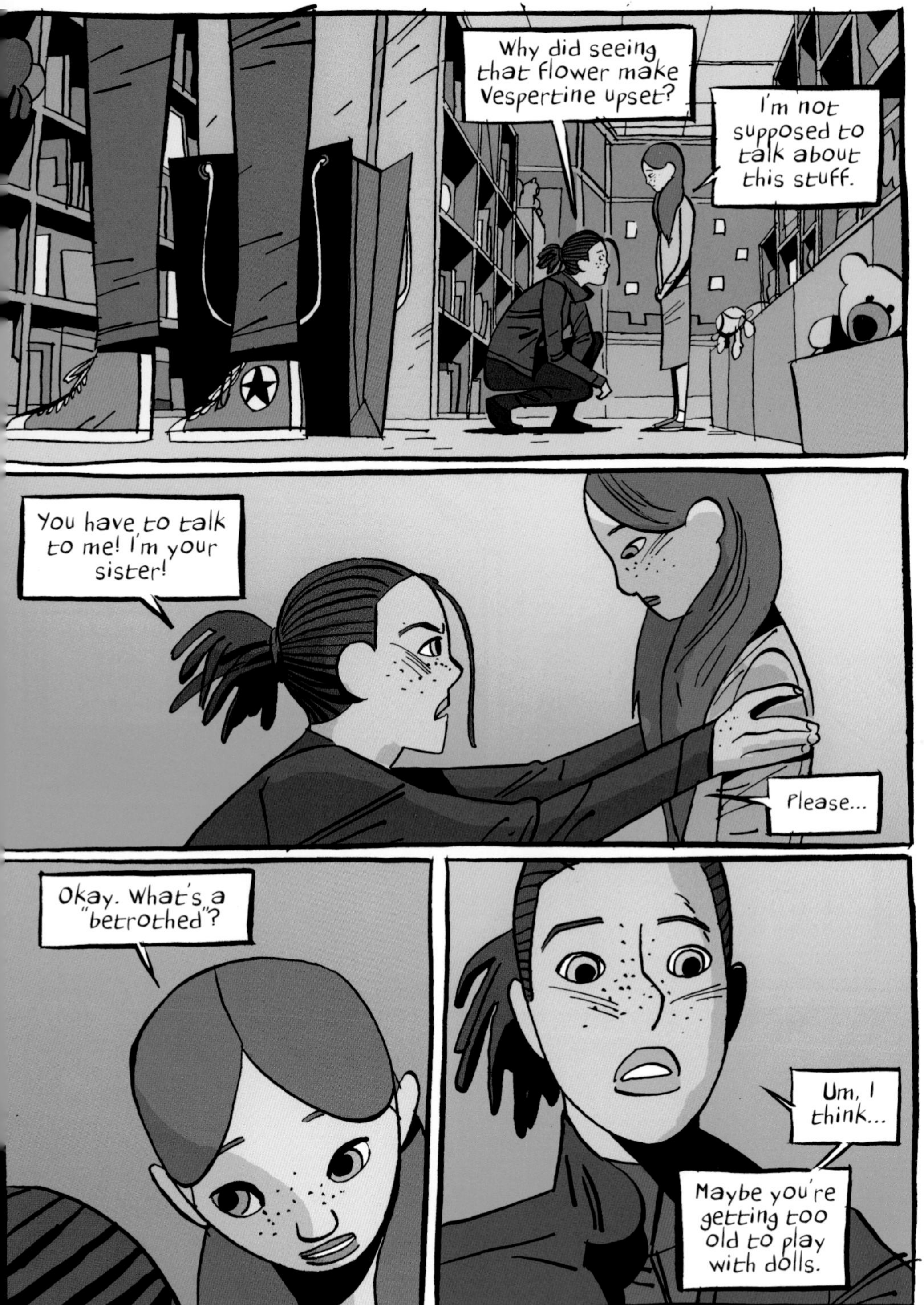
Why did seeing that flower make Vespertine upset?
I'm not supposed to talk about this stuff.
You have to talk to me! I'm your sister!
Please...
Okay. What's a "betrothed"?
Um, I think...
Maybe you're getting too old to play with dolls.

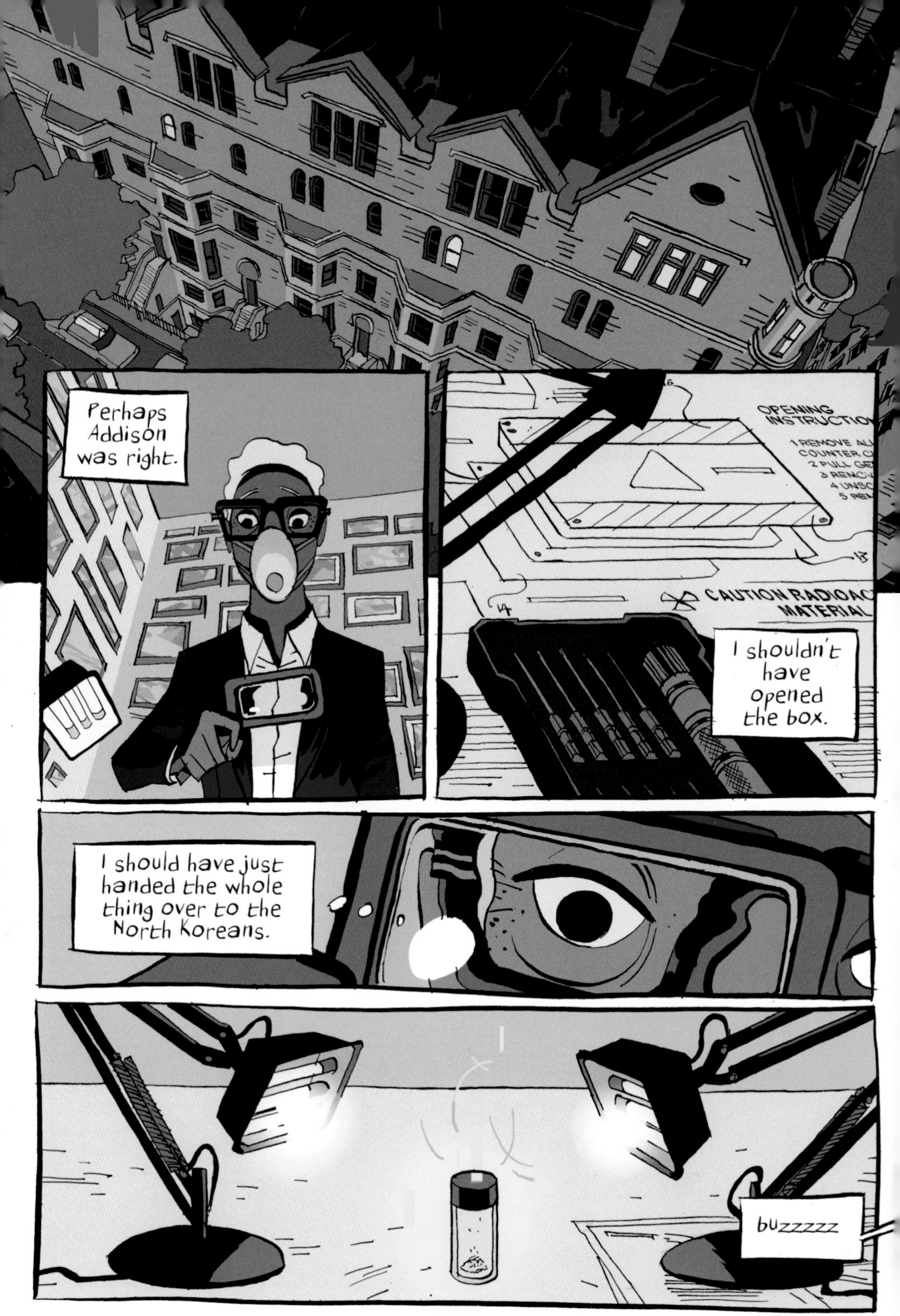
Perhaps Addison was right.
OPENING
CAUTION
MATERIAL
I shouldn't have opened the box.
I should have just handed the whole thing over to the North Koreans.
buzzzzz

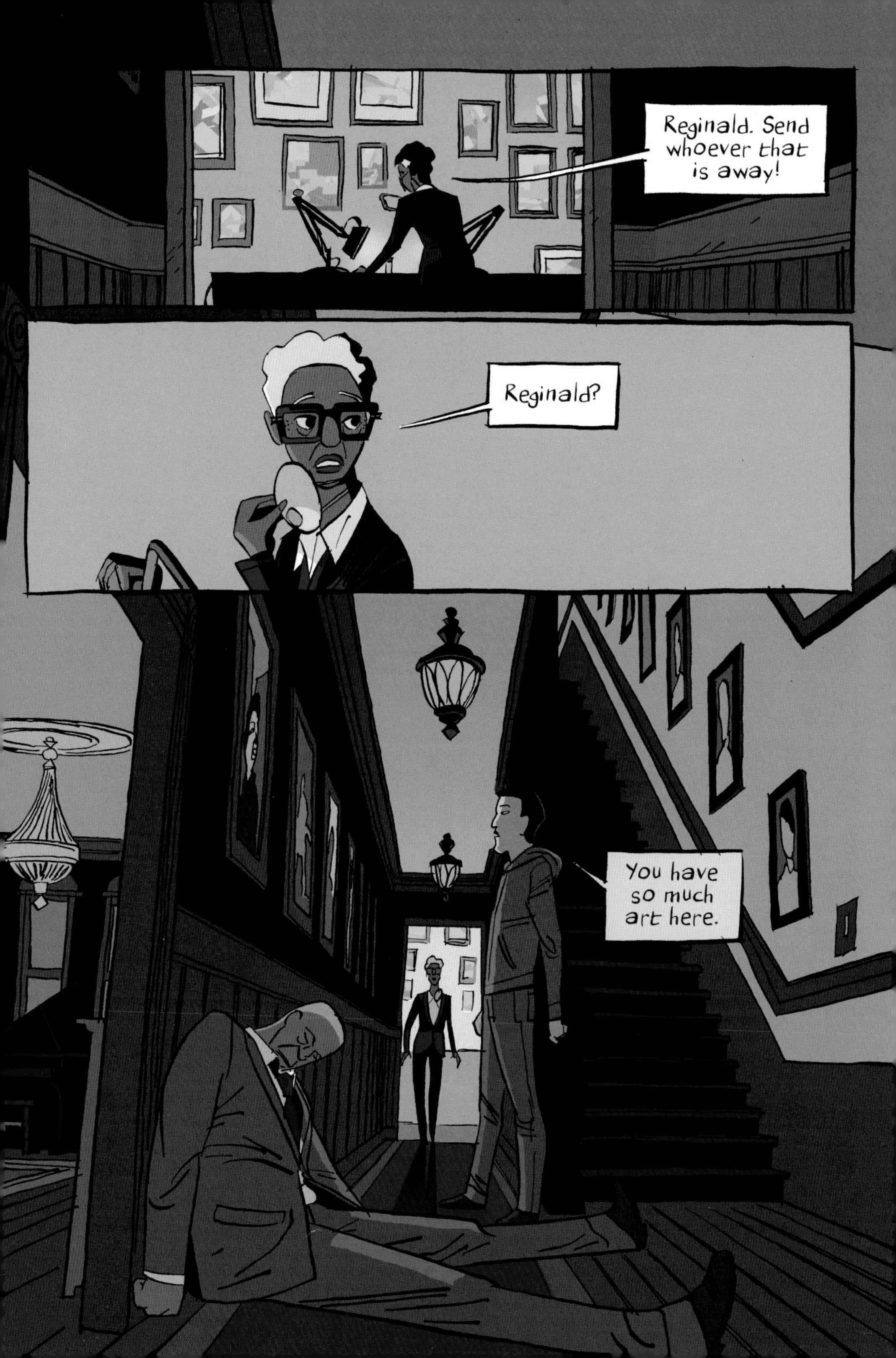
Reginald. Send whoever that is away!
Reginald?
You have so much art here.

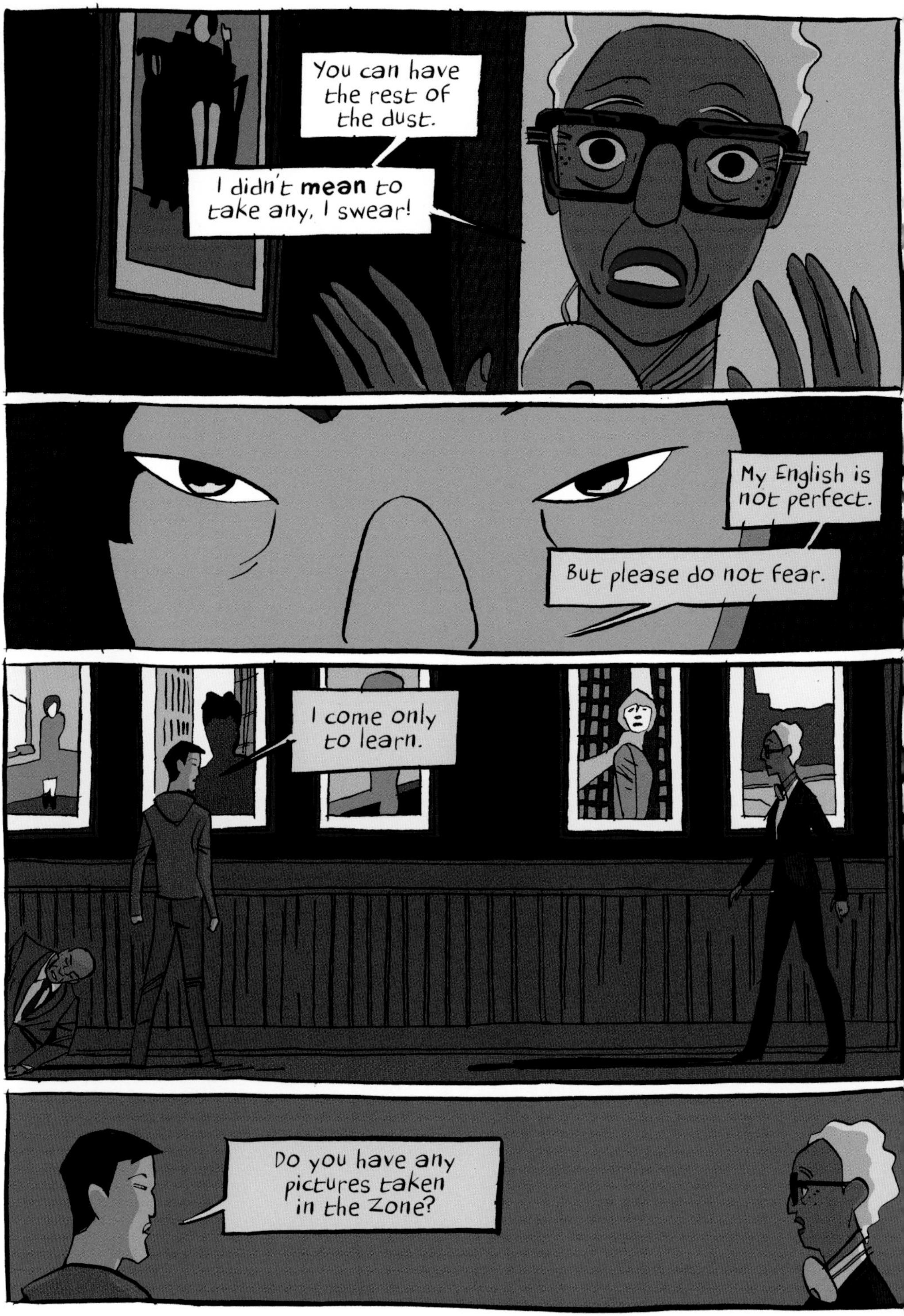
You can have the rest of the dust.
I didn't **mean** to take any, I swear!
My English is not perfect.
But please do not fear.
I come only to learn.
Do you have any pictures taken in the Zone?

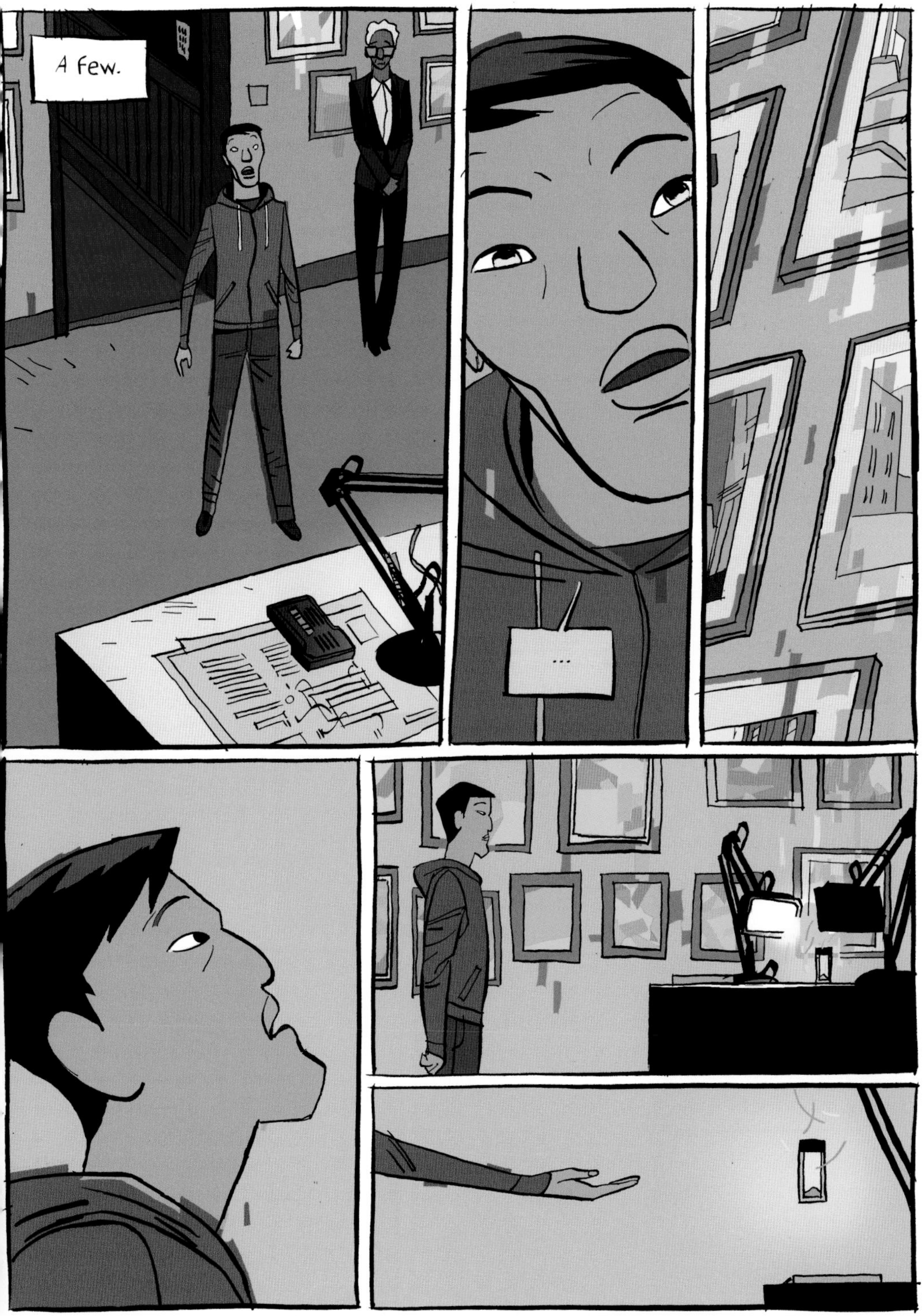
A few.
...

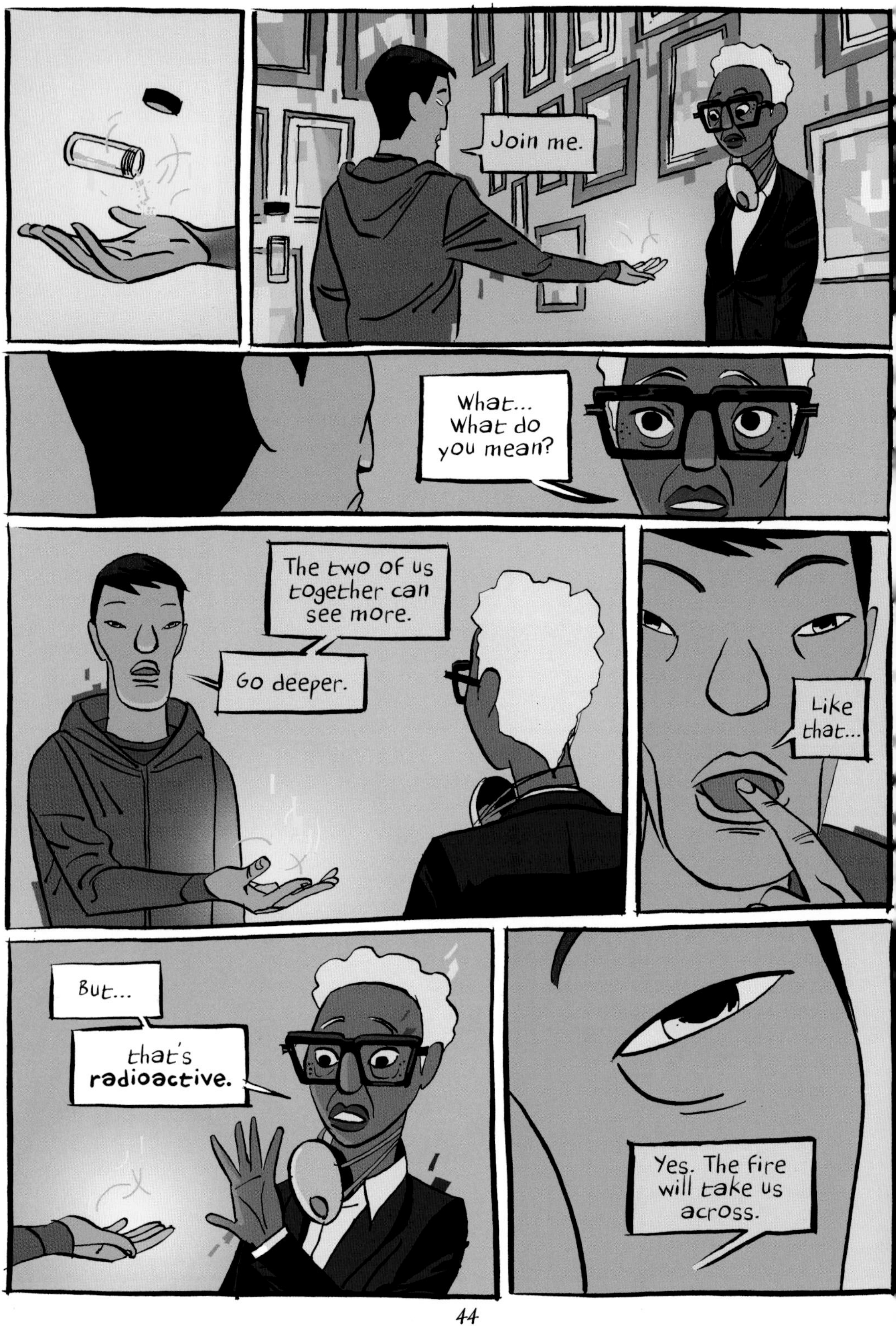
Join me.
What... What do you mean?
The two of us together can see more.
Go deeper.
Like that...
But...
that's **radioactive.**
Yes. The fire will take us across.

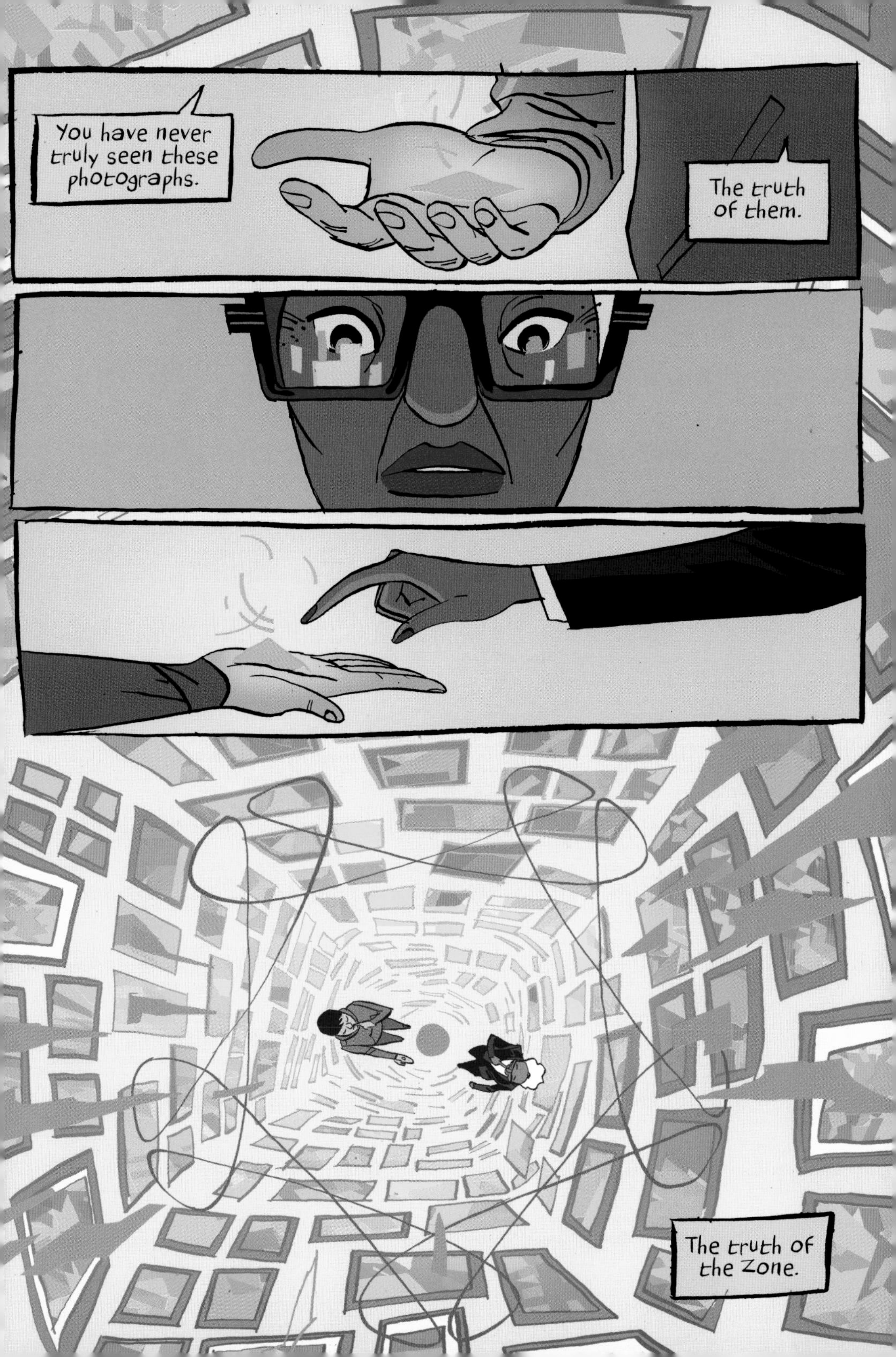
You have never truly seen these photographs.
The truth of them.
The truth of the Zone.

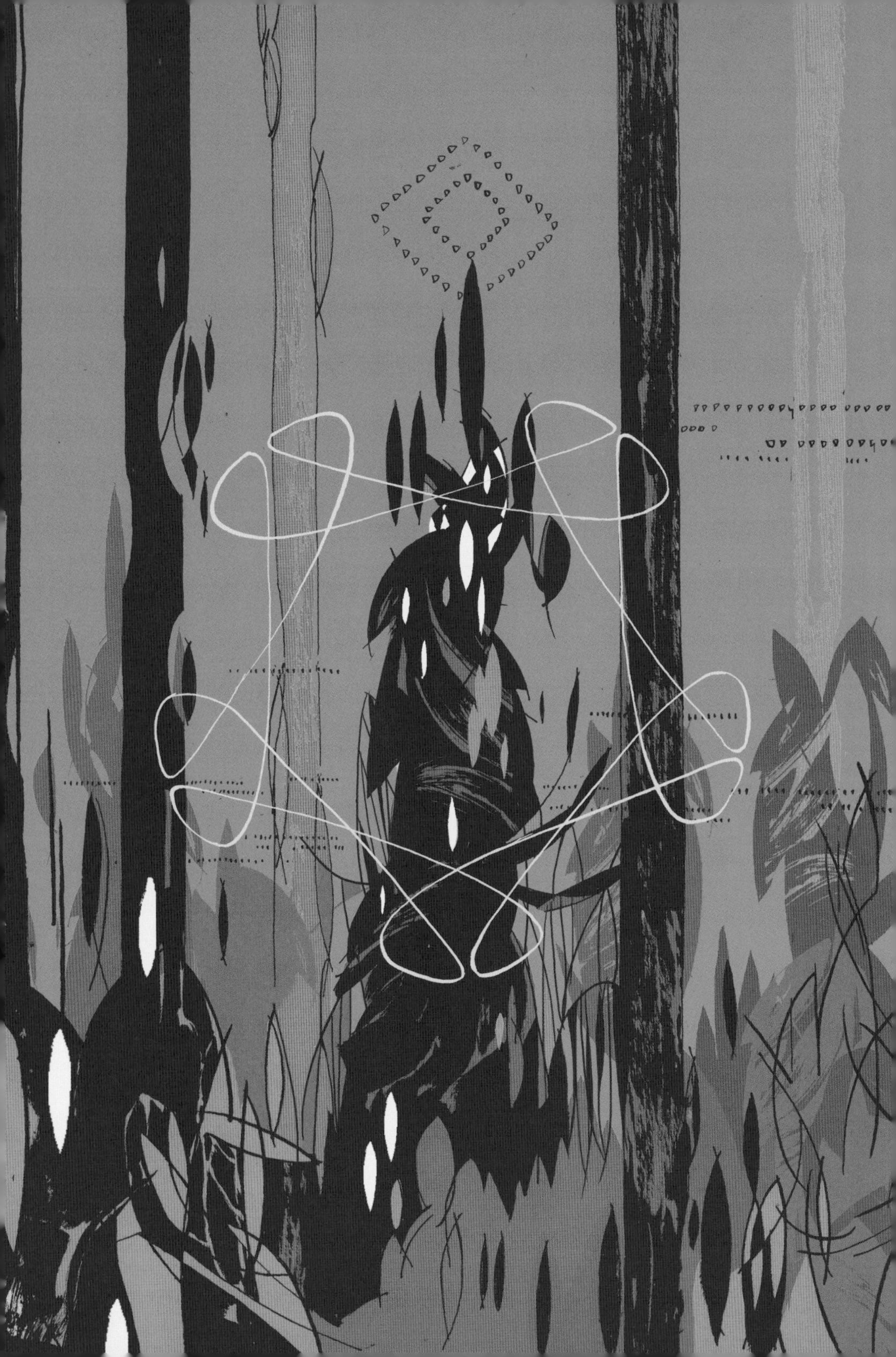

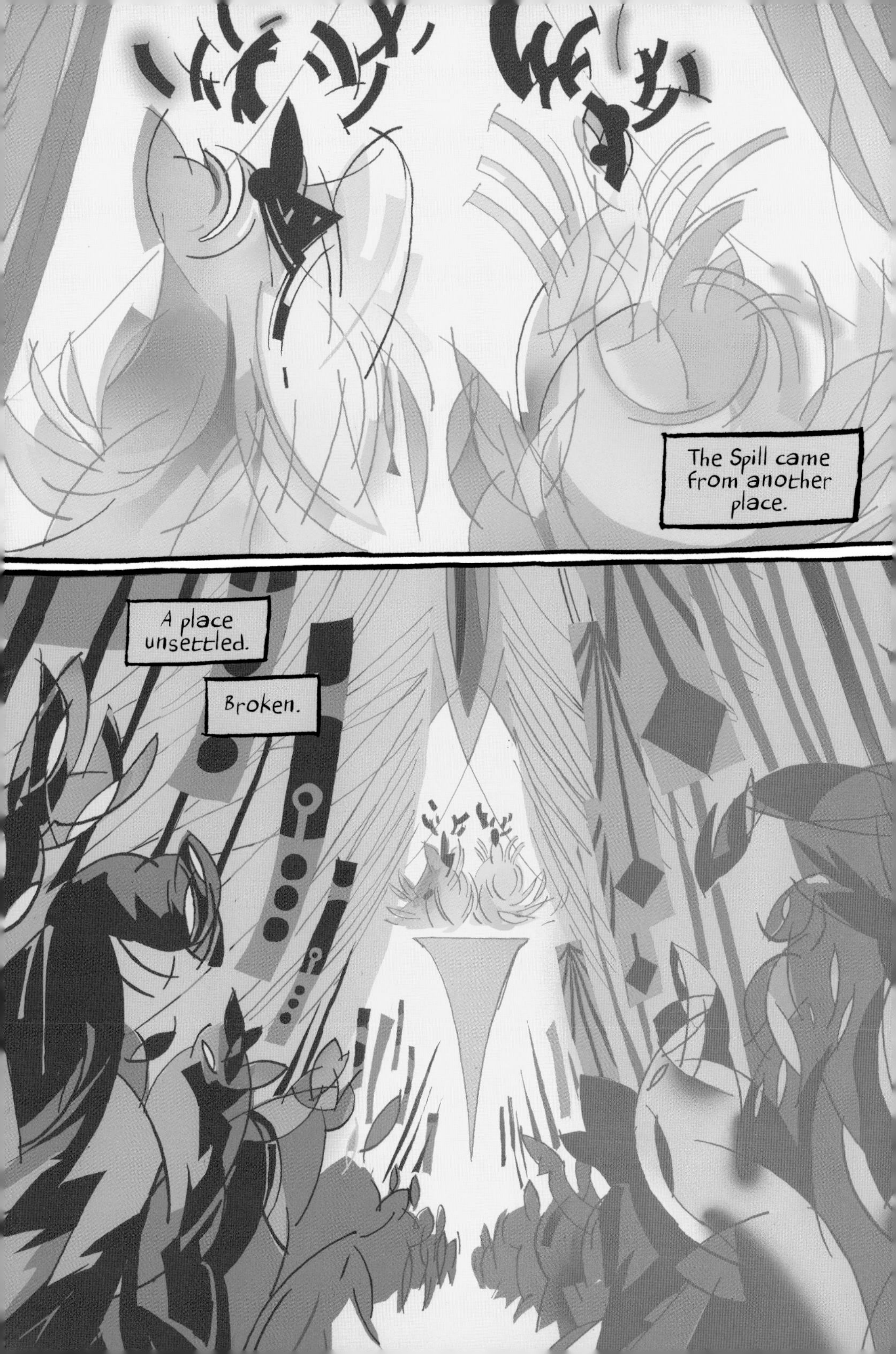
The Spill came from another place.
A place unsettled.
Broken.

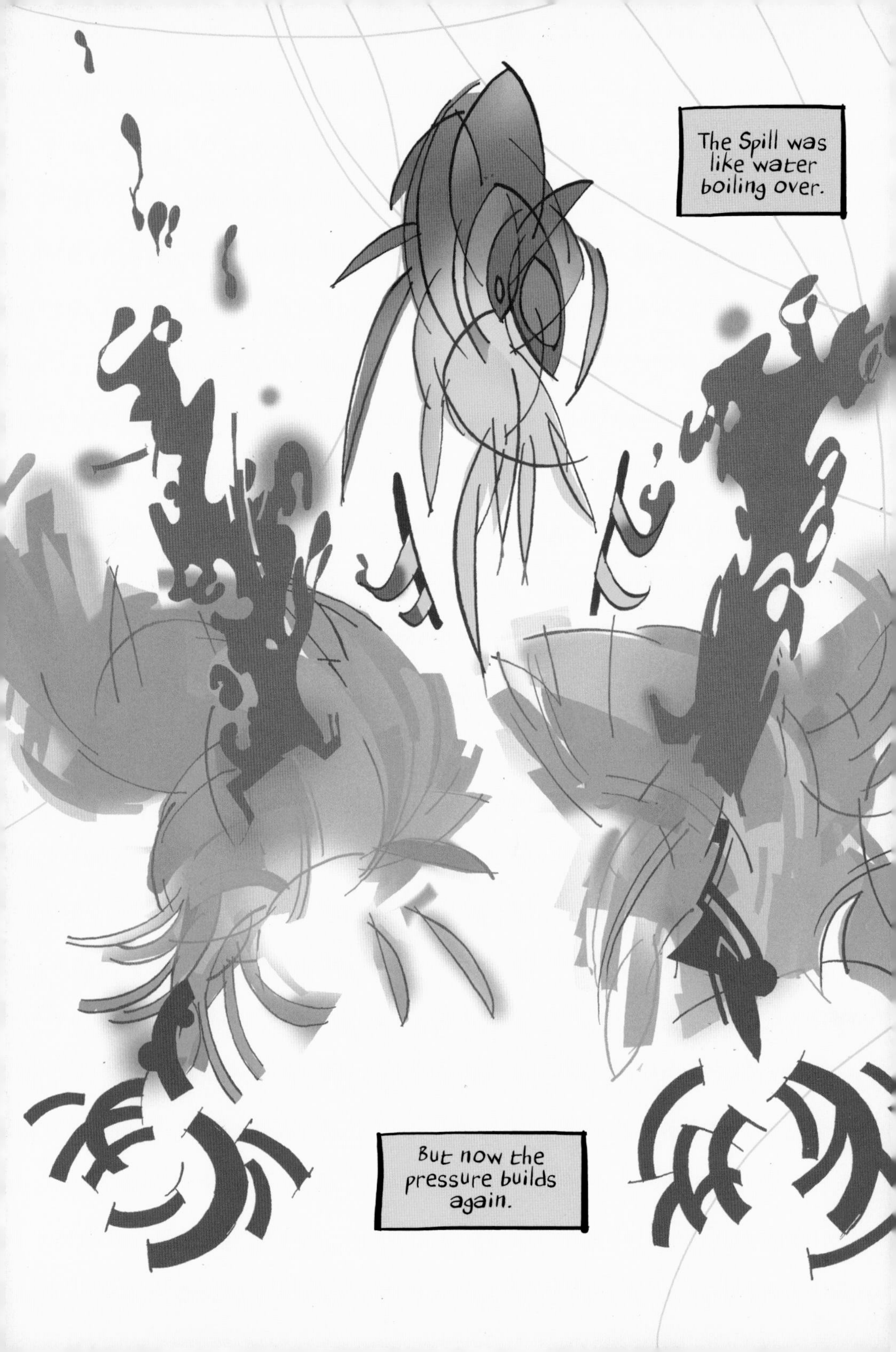
The Spill was like water boiling over.
But now the pressure builds again.

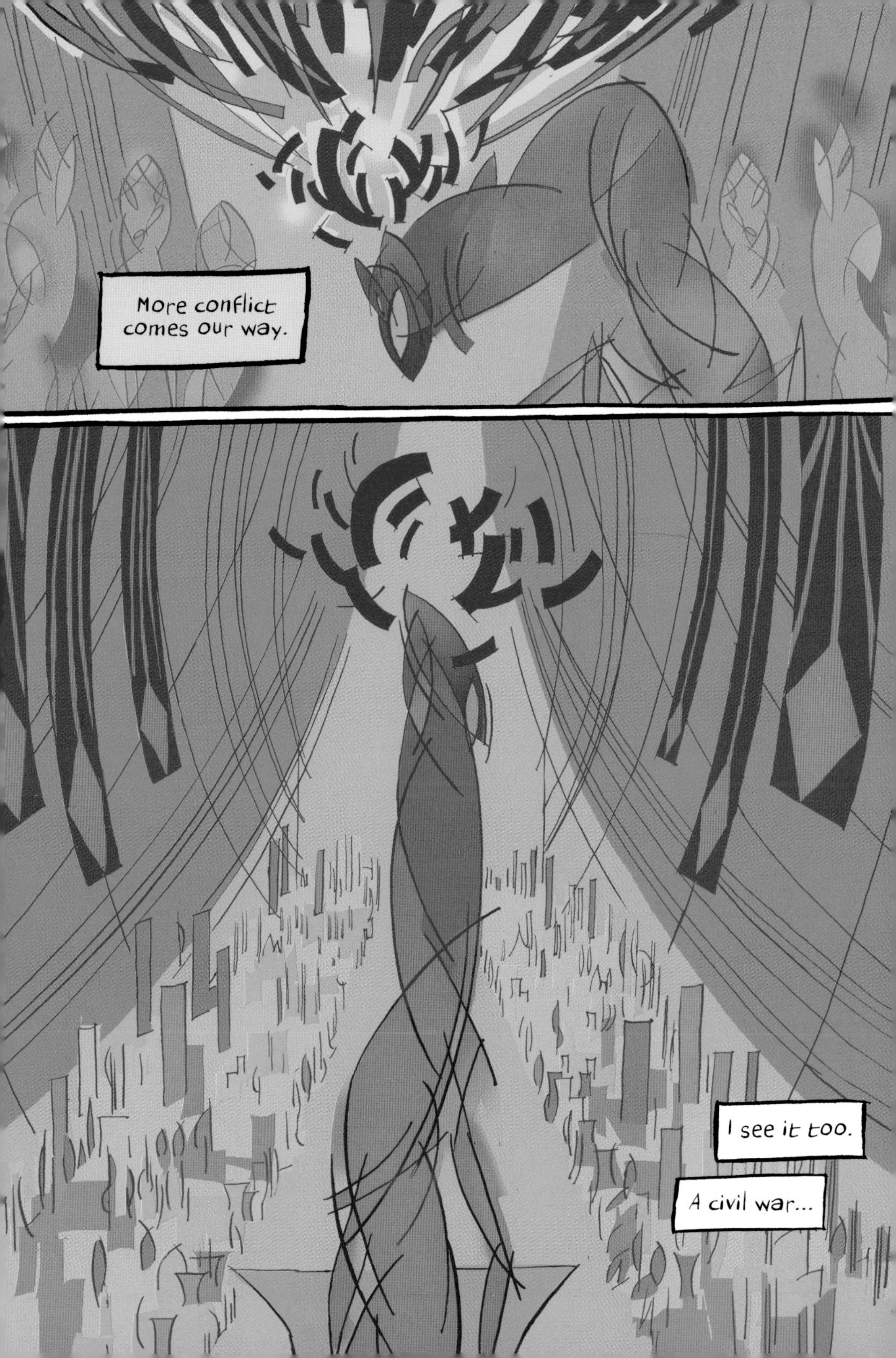
More conflict comes our way.
I see it too.
A civil war...

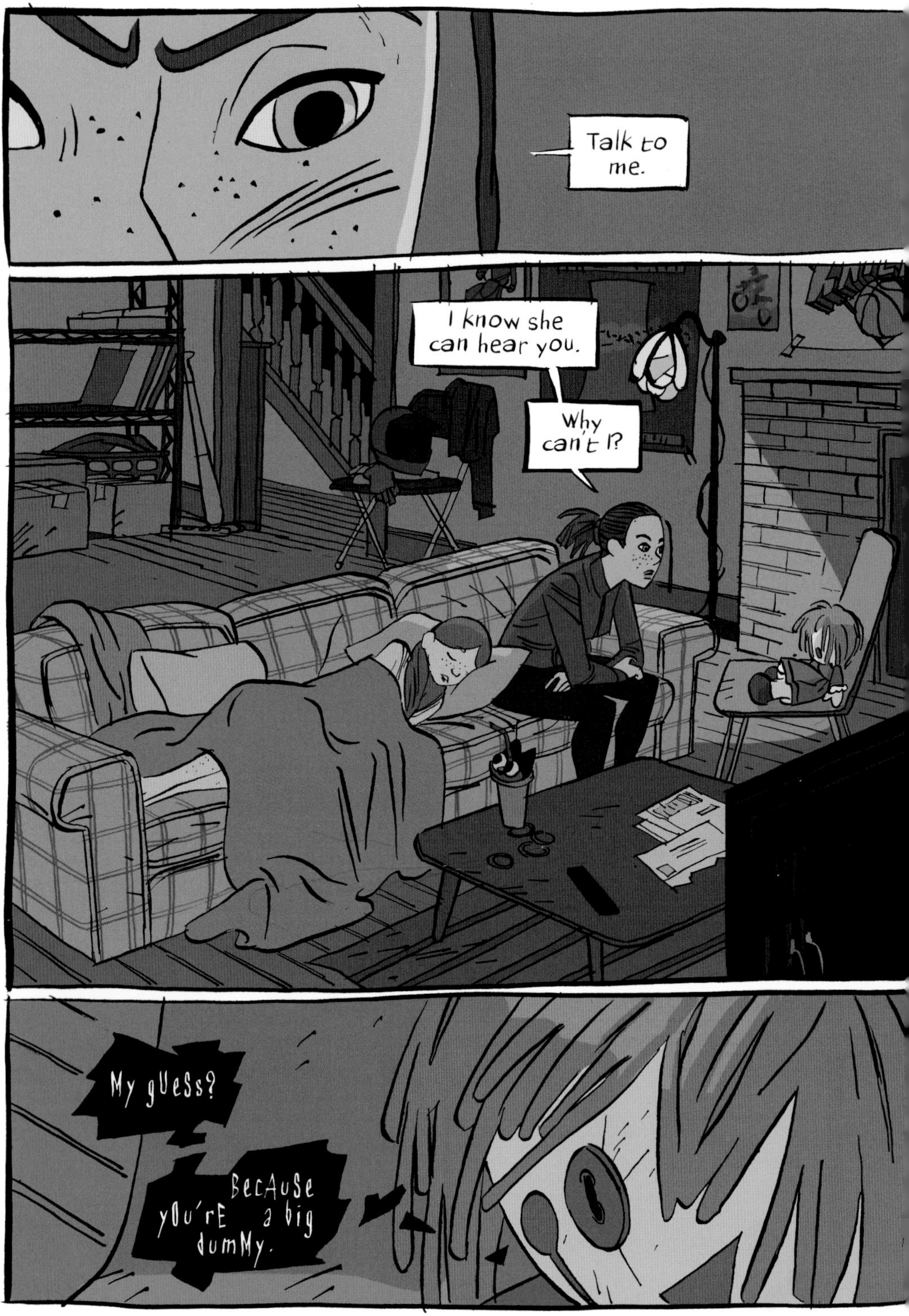
Talk to me.
I know she can hear you.
Why can't I?
My guess?
Because you're a big dummy.

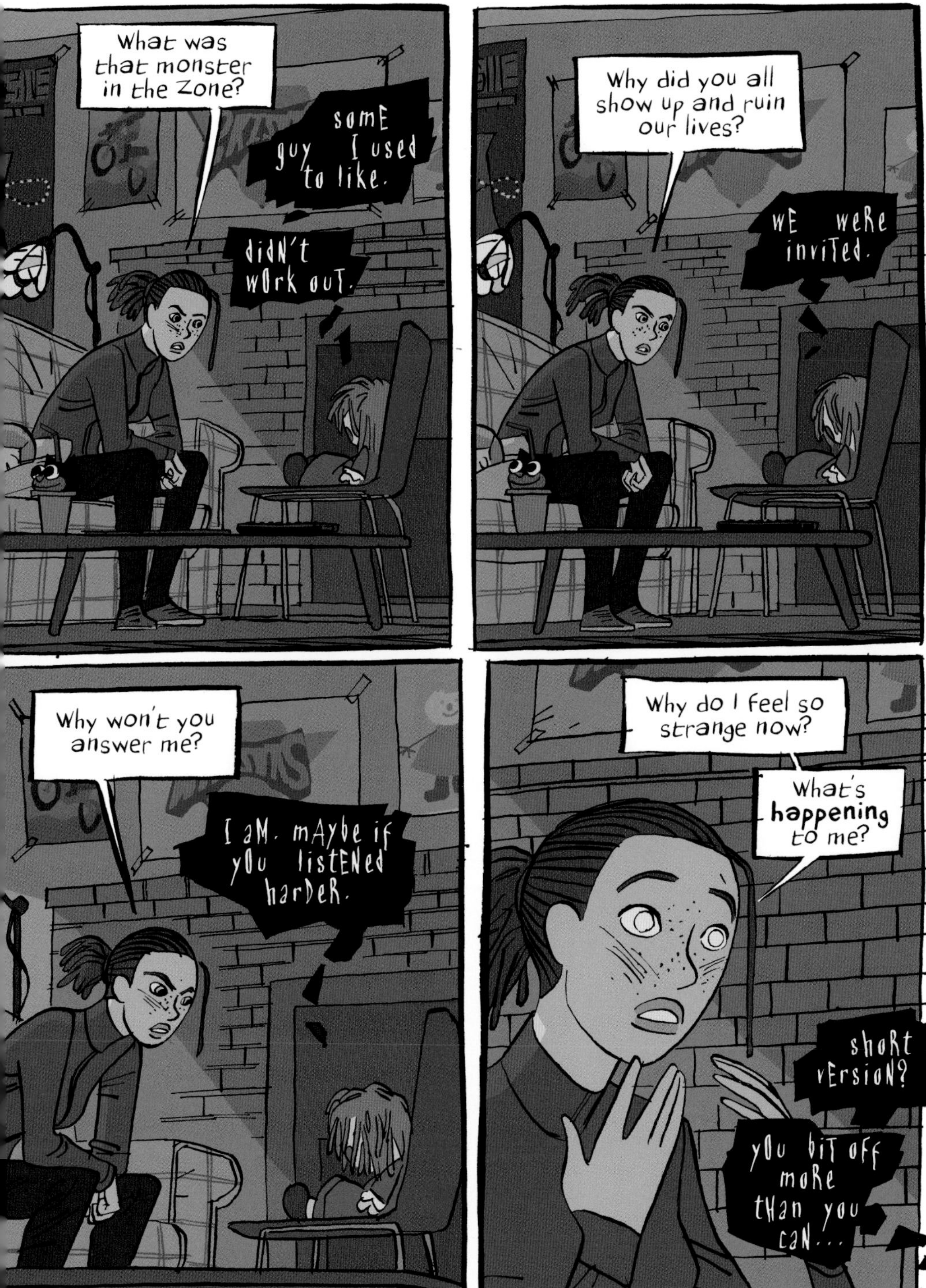
What was that monster in the Zone?
some guy I used to like.
didn't work out.
Why did you all show up and ruin our lives?
We were invited.
Why won't you answer me?
I am. maybe if you listened harder.
Why do I feel so strange now?
What's **happening** to me?
short version?
you bit off more than you can...

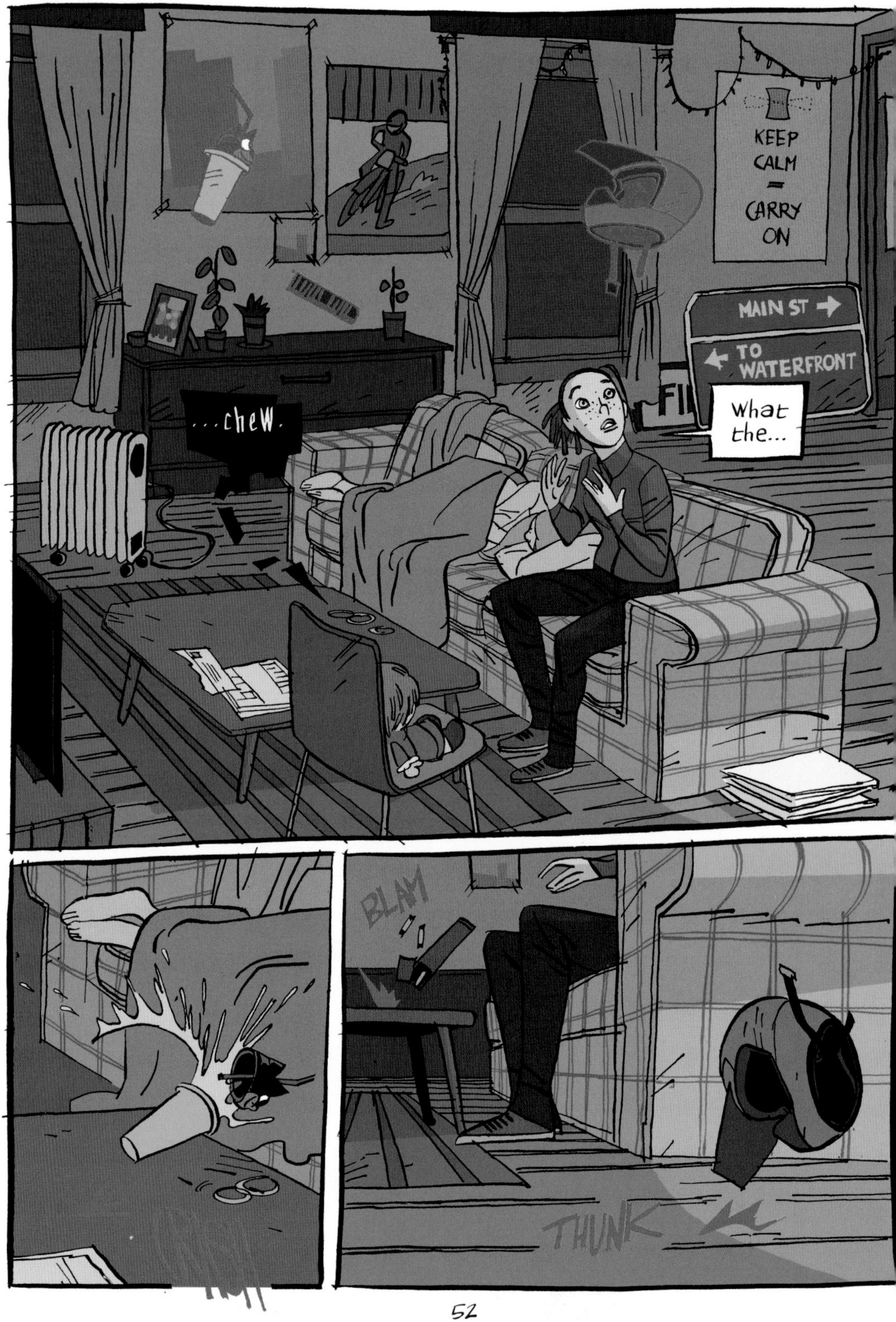
KEEP CALM = CARRY ON
MAIN ST
TO WATERFRONT
...chew.
What the...
BLAM
THUNK

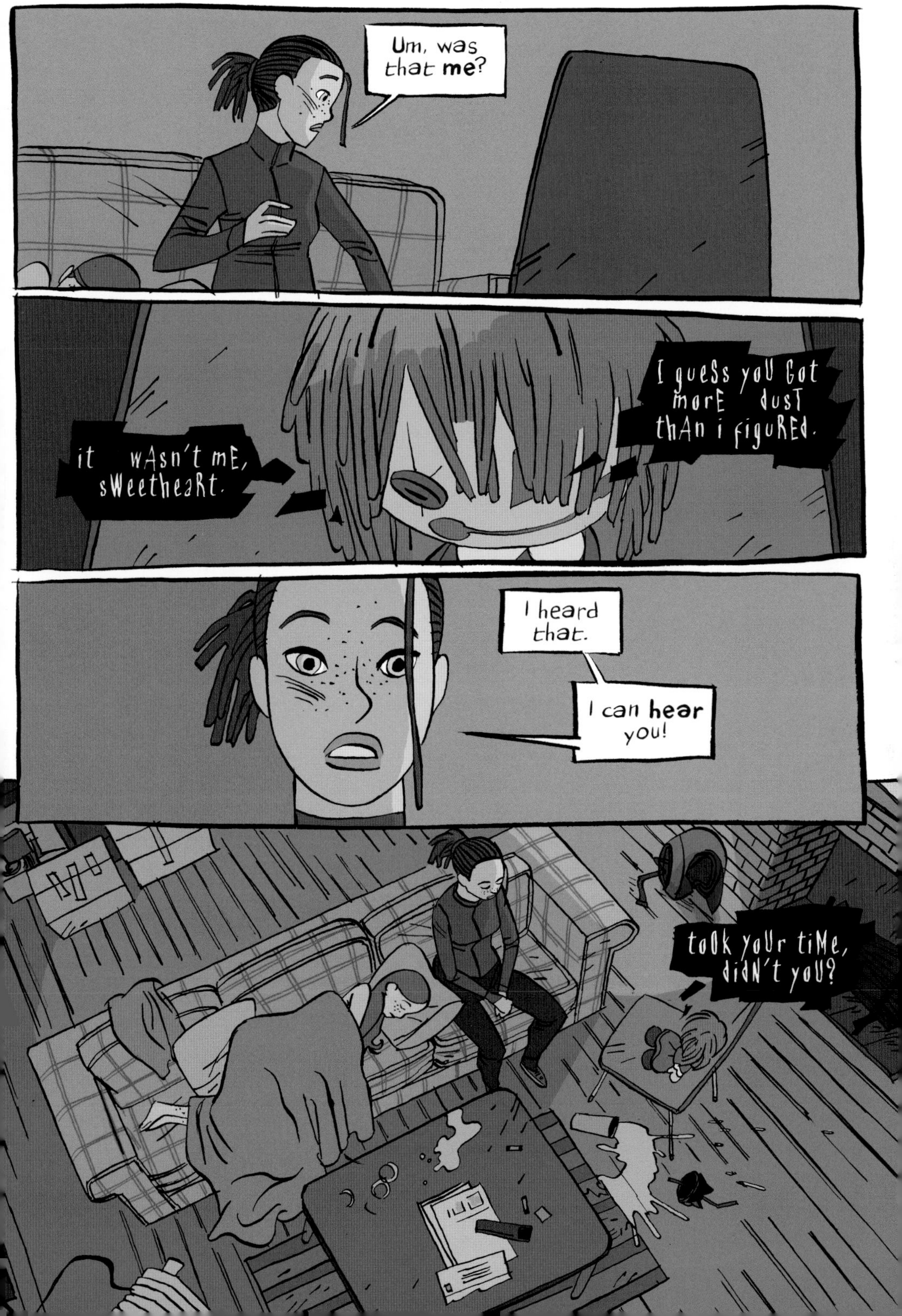
Um, was that me?
it wasn't me, sweetheart.
I guess you got more dust than i figured.
I heard that.
I can hear you!
took your time, didn't you?

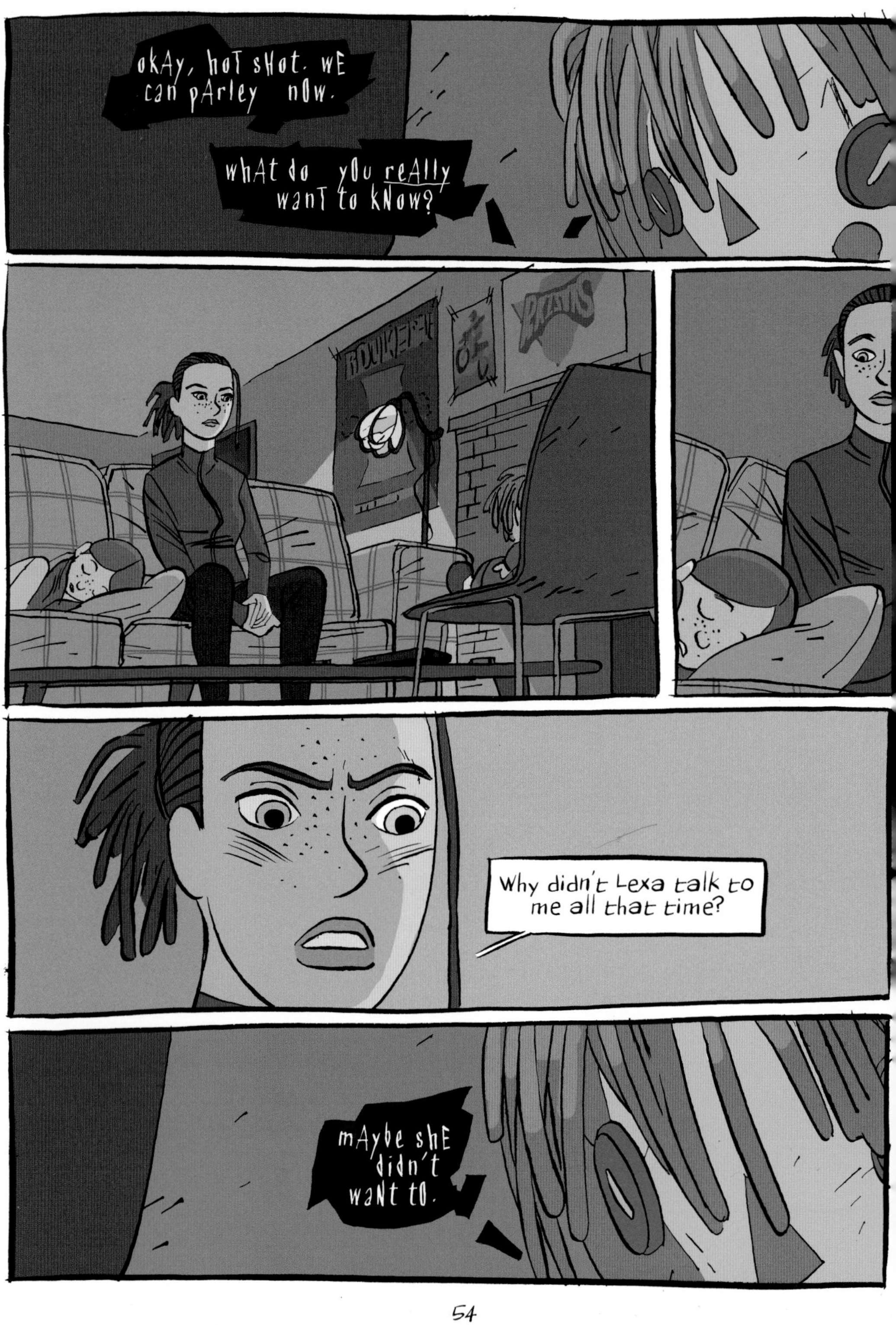
okAy, hot shot. wE can pArley now.
whAt do you reAlly want to kNow?
Why didn't Lexa talk to me all that time?
mAybe shE didn't wANt to.

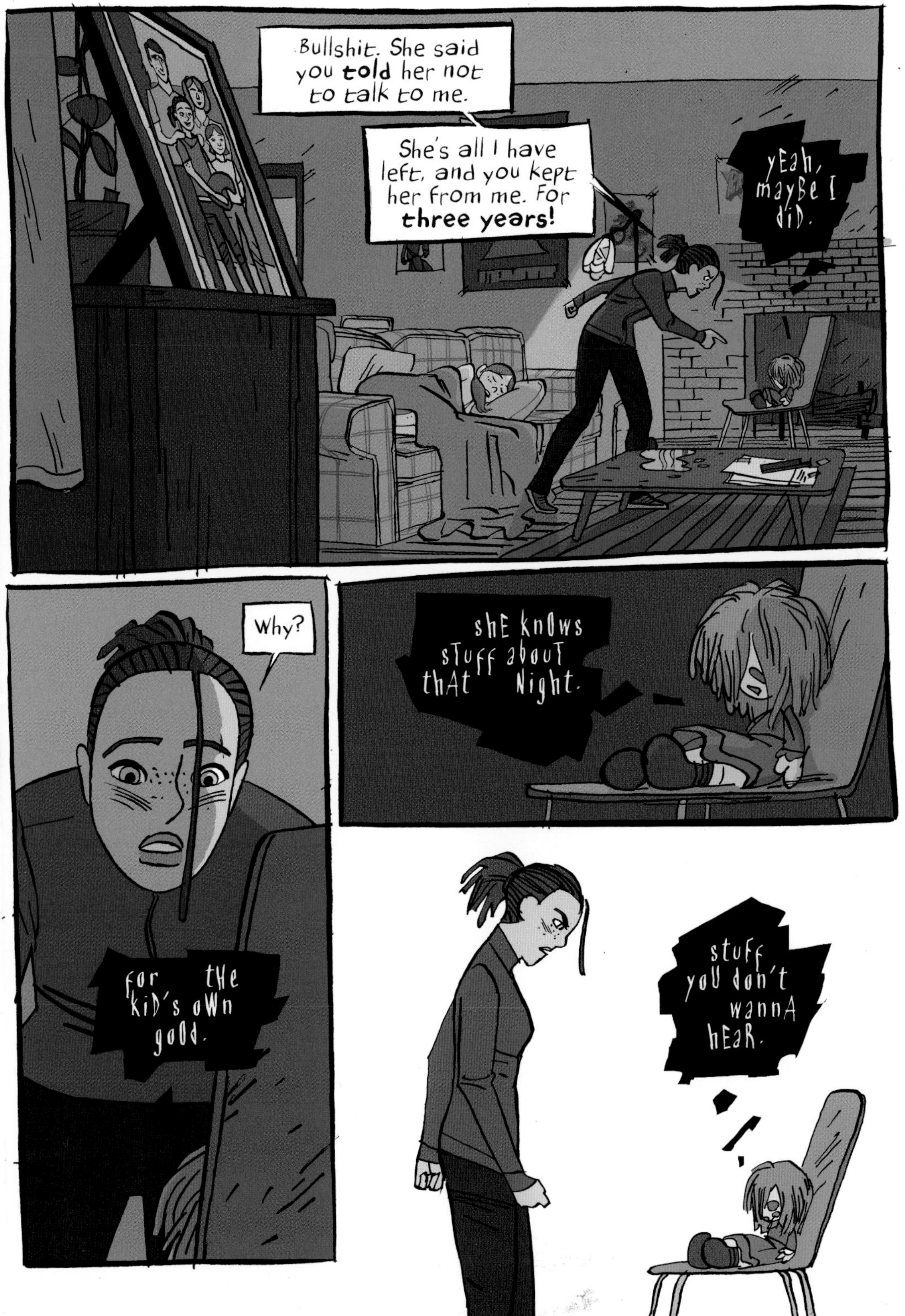
Bullshit. She said you **told** her not to talk to me.
She's all I have left, and you kept her from me. For **three years!**
yEah, maybE I diD.
Why?
shE knOws stUff abOuT thAt Night.
fOr thE kiD's oWn gOOd.
stuff yOU don't wannA hEaR.

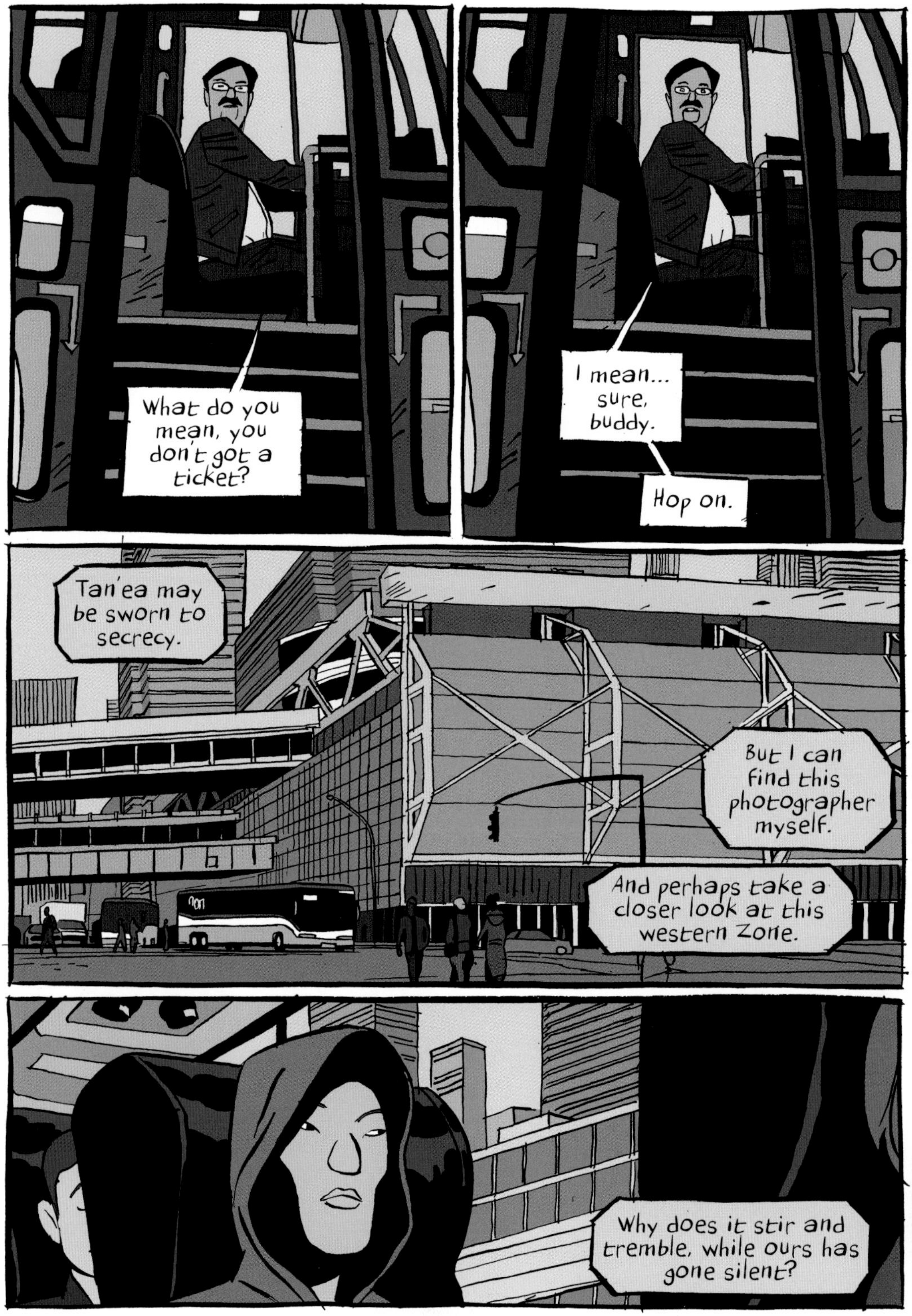
What do you mean, you don't got a ticket?
I mean... sure, buddy.
Hop on.
Tan'ea may be sworn to secrecy.
But I can find this photographer myself.
And perhaps take a closer look at this western Zone.
Why does it stir and tremble, while ours has gone silent?

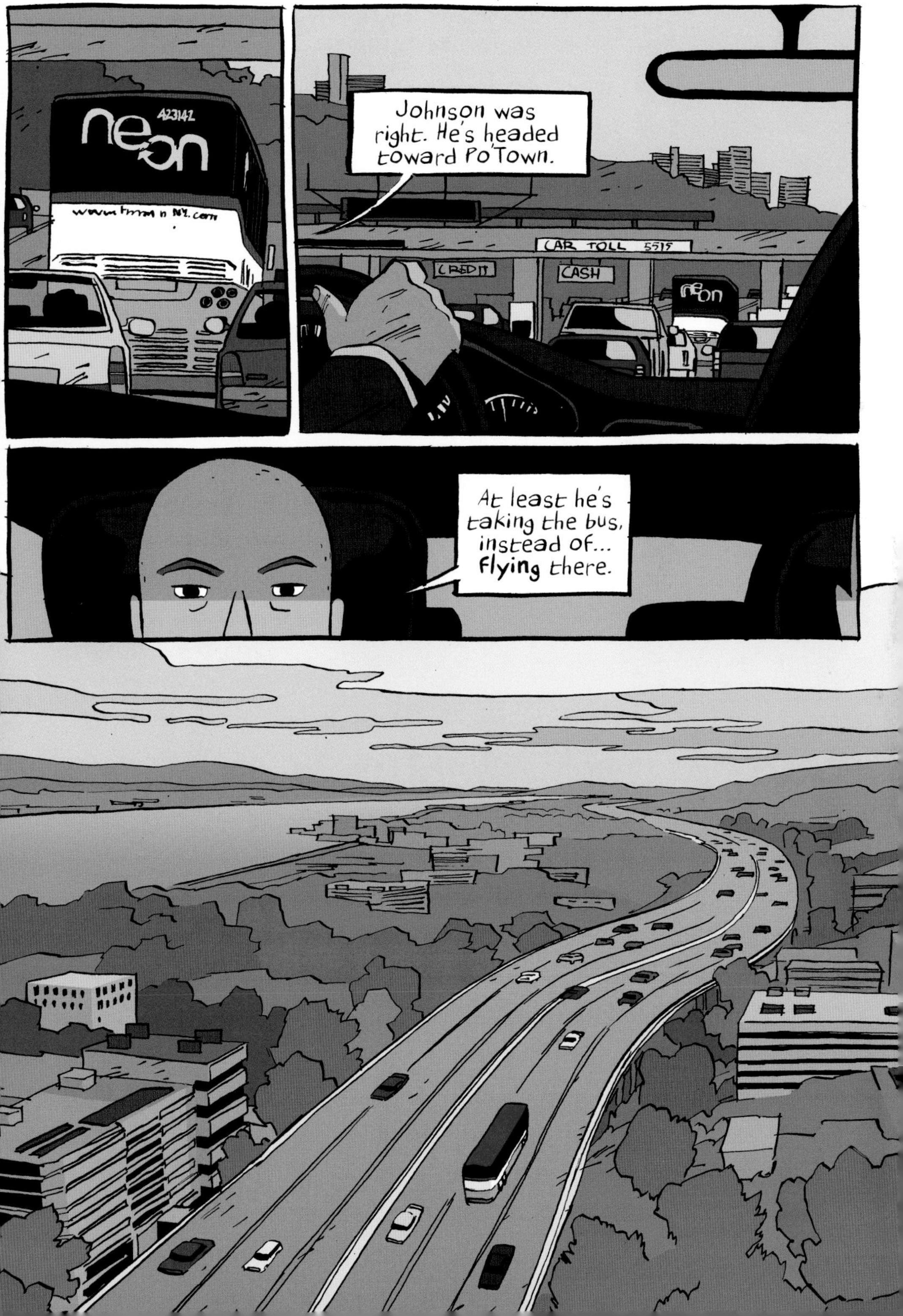
neon
423142
Johnson was right. He's headed toward Po'Town.
CAR TOLL 5515
CREDIT
CASH
neon
At least he's taking the bus, instead of... **Flying** there.

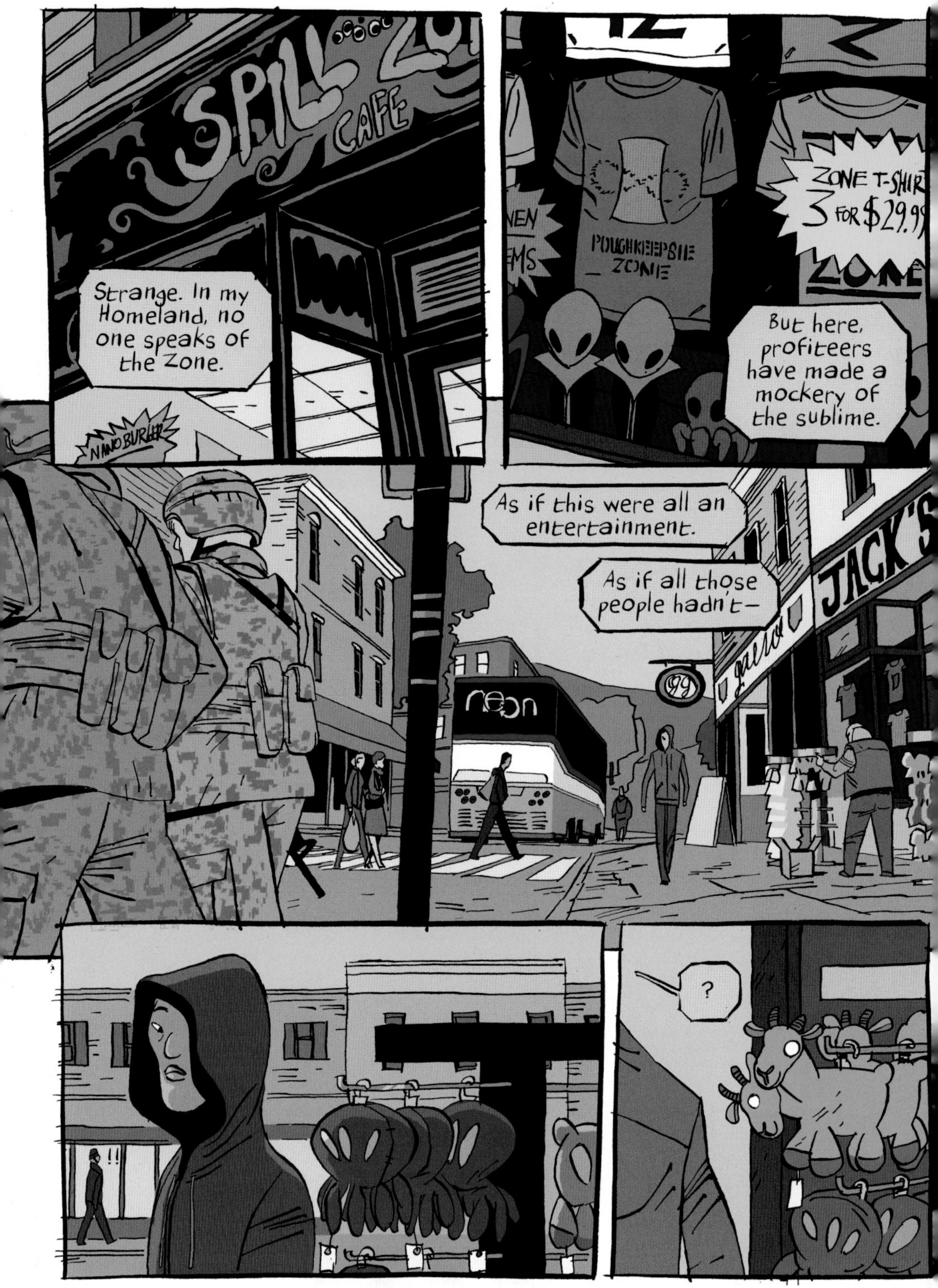
SPILL
CAFE
Strange. In my Homeland, no one speaks of the Zone.
NANO BURGER
POUGHKEEPSIE ZONE
ZONE T-SHIR
3 FOR $29.9
ZONE
But here, profiteers have made a mockery of the sublime.
As if this were all an entertainment.
As if all those people hadn't—
JACK'S
neon
99
!!
?

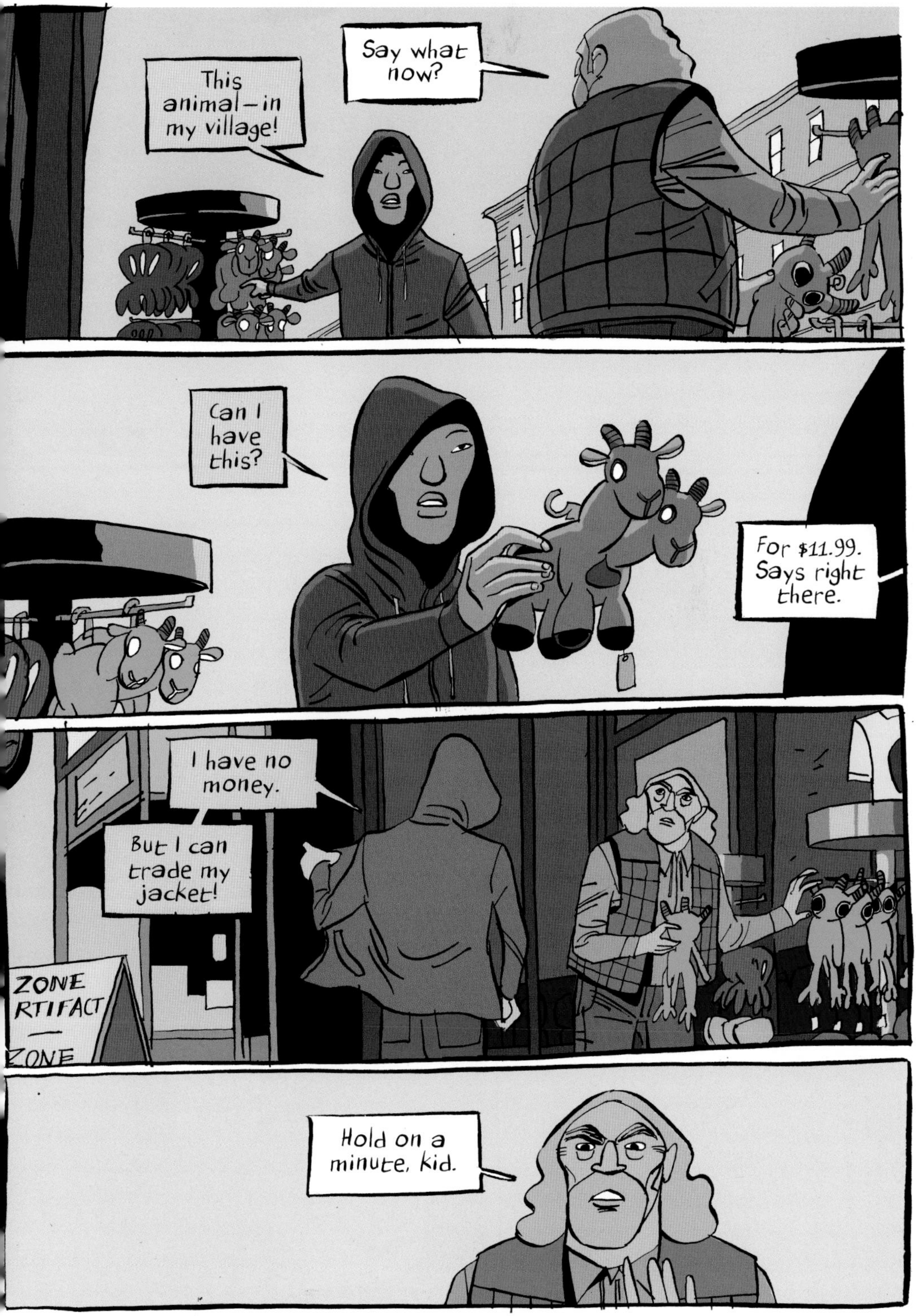
This animal—in my village!
Say what now?
Can I have this?
For $11.99. Says right there.
I have no money.
But I can trade my jacket!
ZONE
RTIFACT
—
ZONE
Hold on a minute, kid.

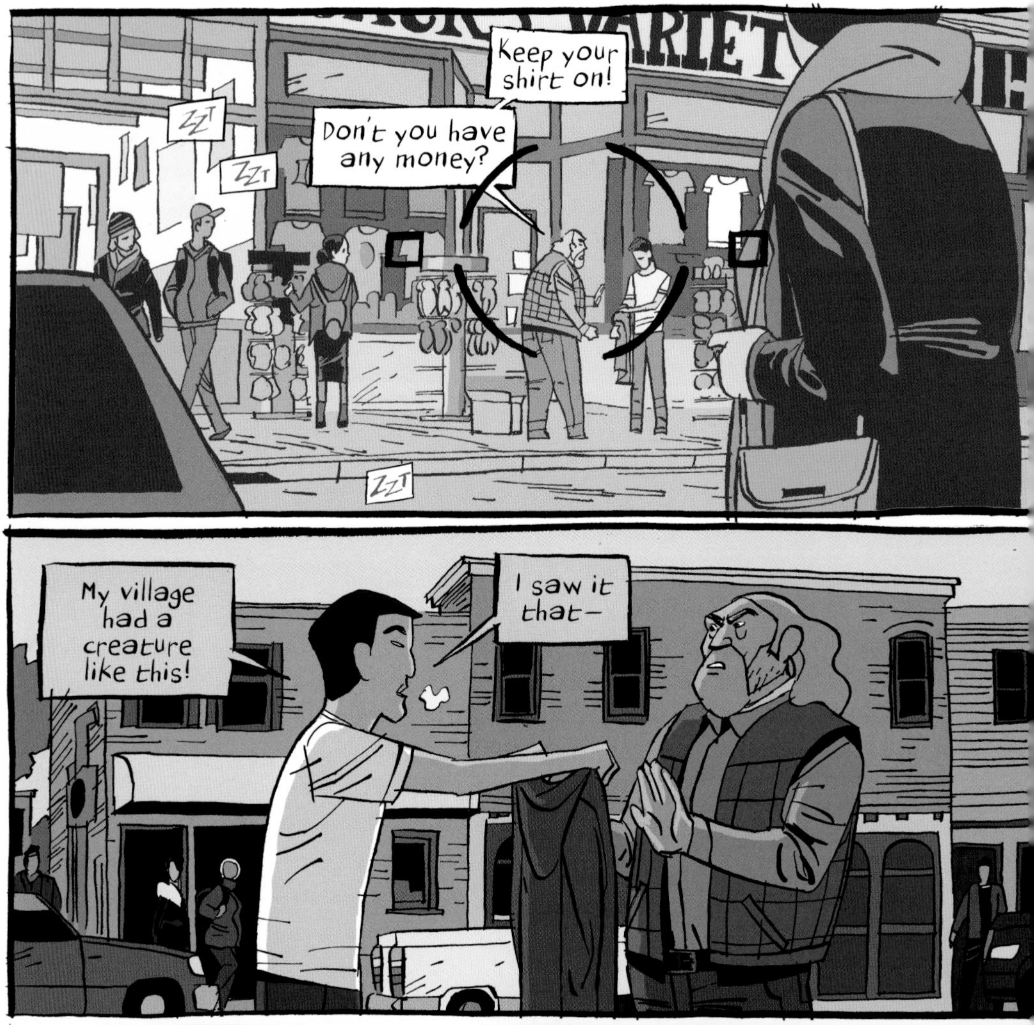
ZZT
ZZT
Keep your shirt on!
Don't you have any money?
ZZT
My village had a creature like this!
I saw it that—
—night.

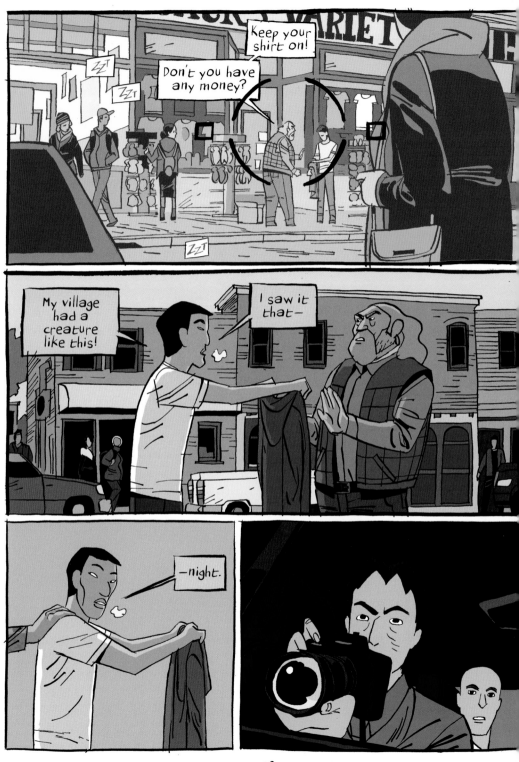

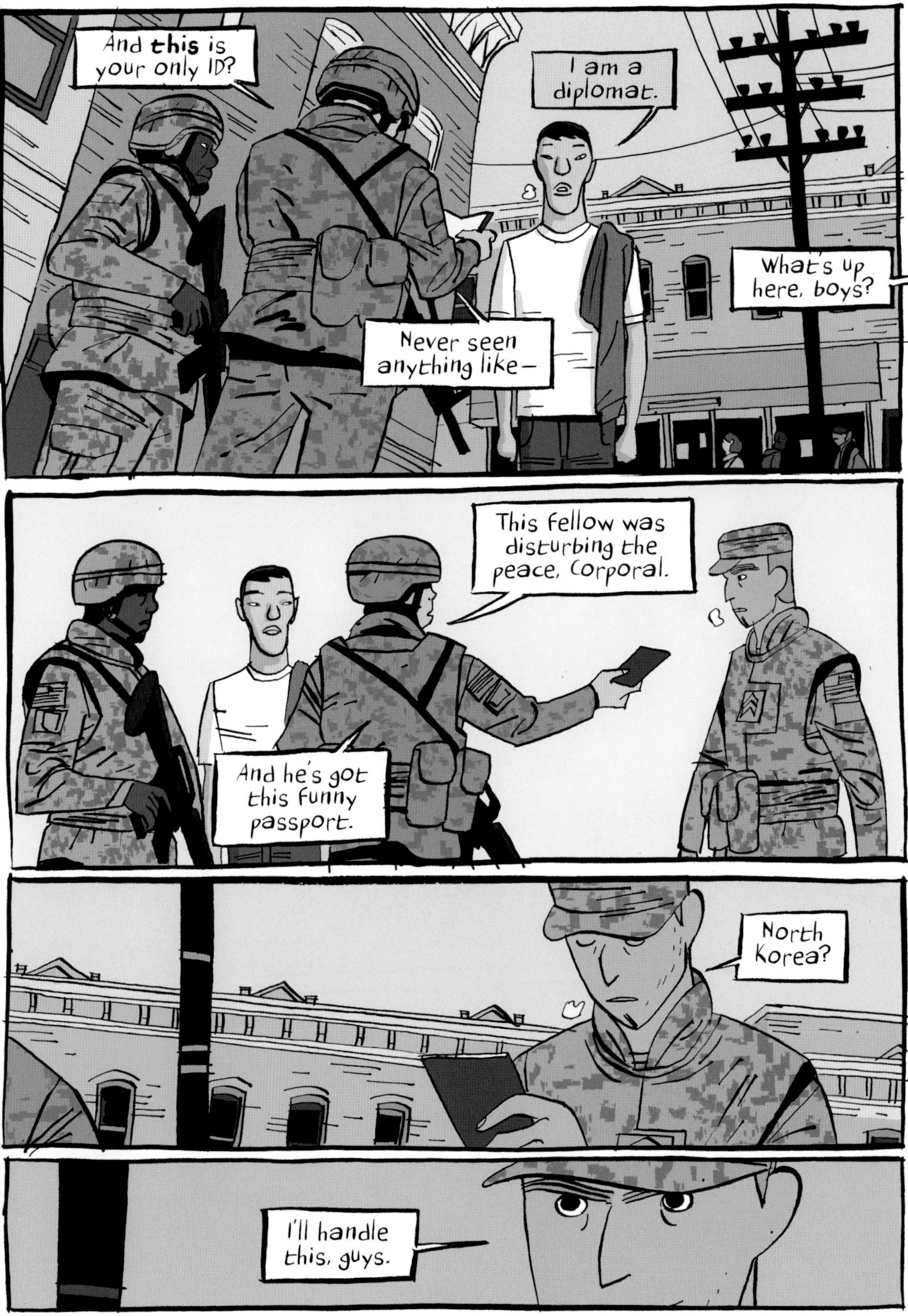
And this is your only ID?
I am a diplomat.
What's up here, boys?
Never seen anything like—
This fellow was disturbing the peace, Corporal.
And he's got this funny passport.
North Korea?
I'll handle this, guys.

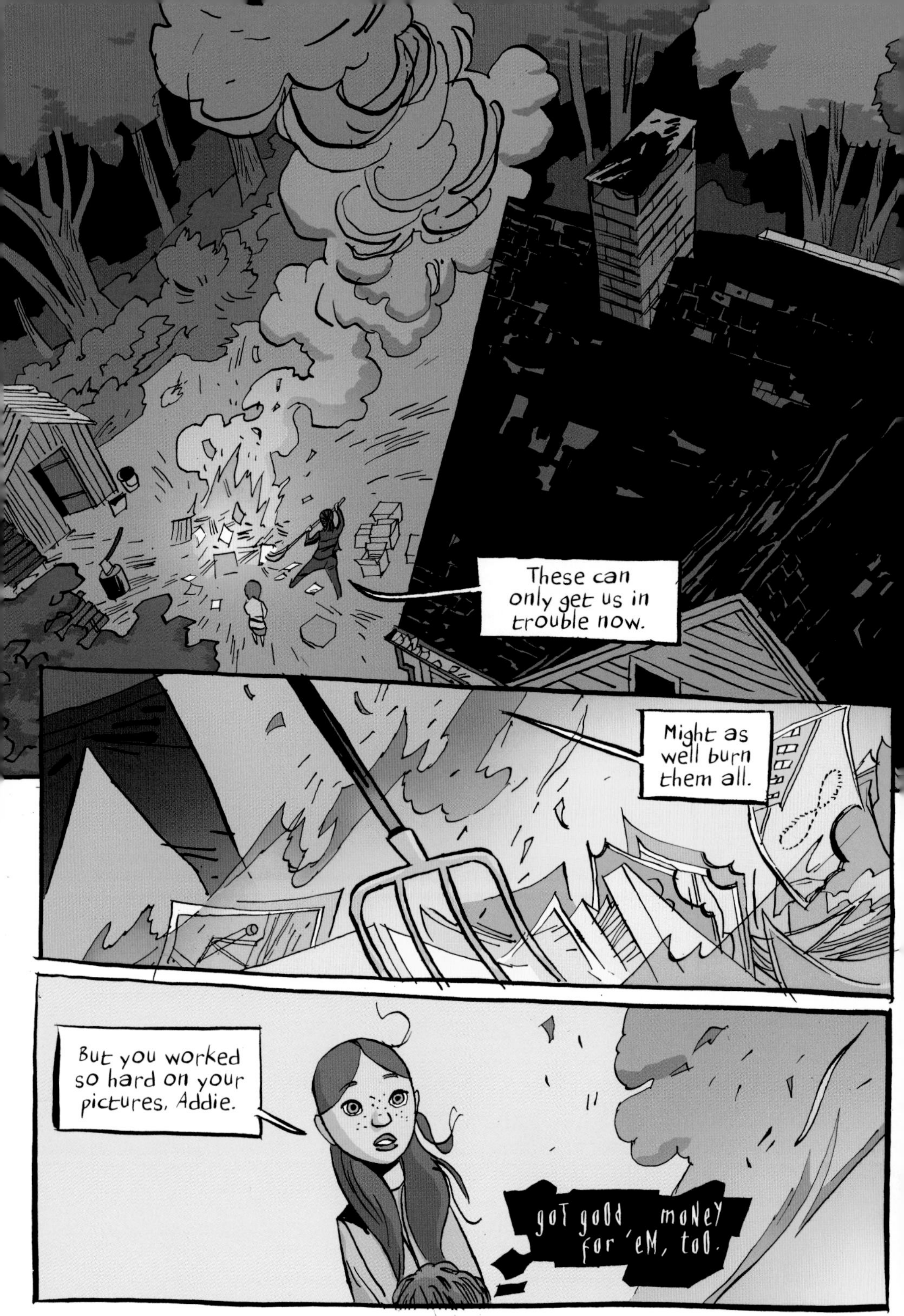
These can only get us in trouble now.
Might as well burn them all.
But you worked so hard on your pictures, Addie.
got good money for 'em, too.

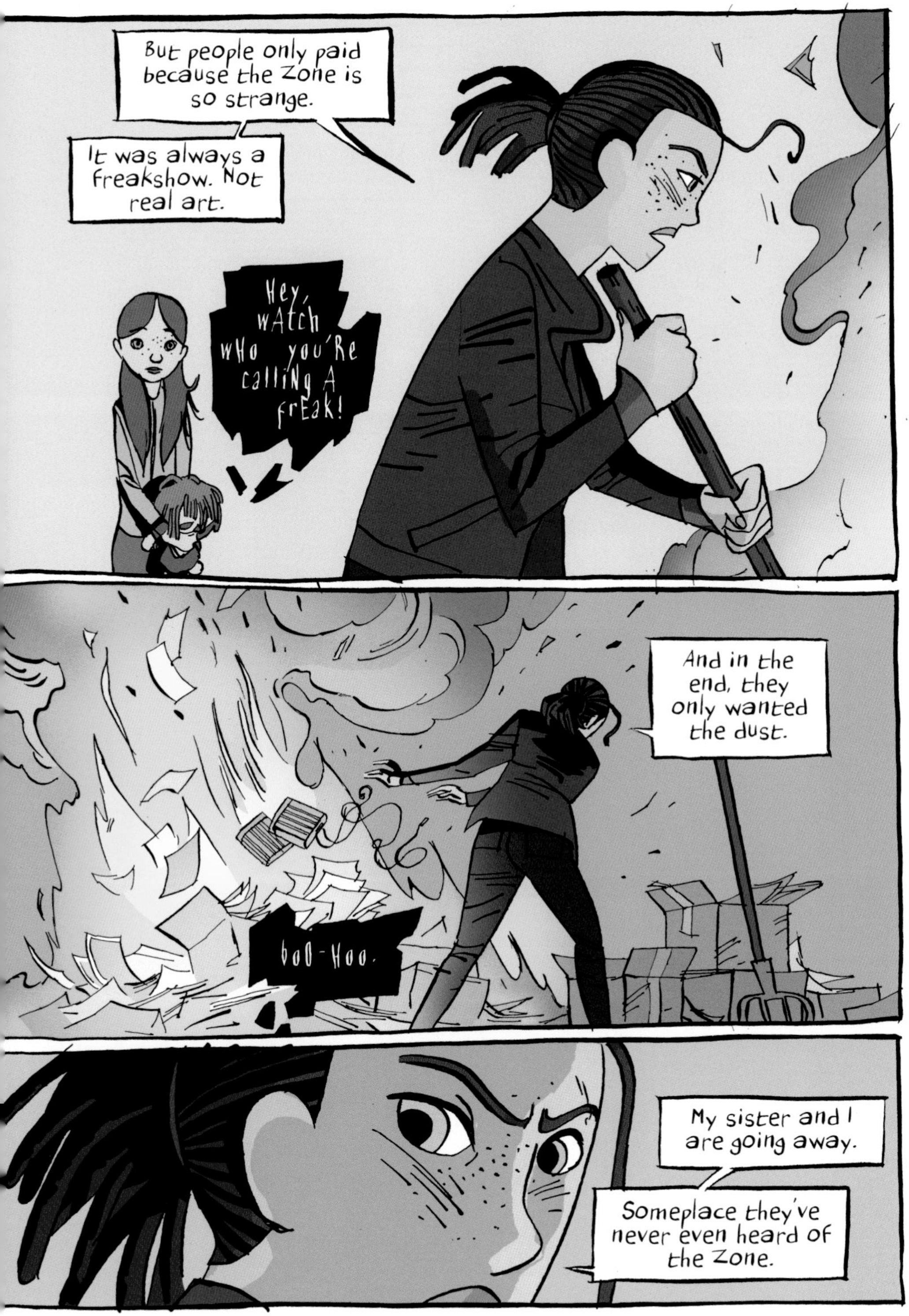

But people only paid because the Zone is so strange.
It was always a freakshow. Not real art.
Hey, watch who you're calling a freak!
And in the end, they only wanted the dust.
boo-hoo.
My sister and I are going away.
Someplace they've never even heard of the Zone.

64

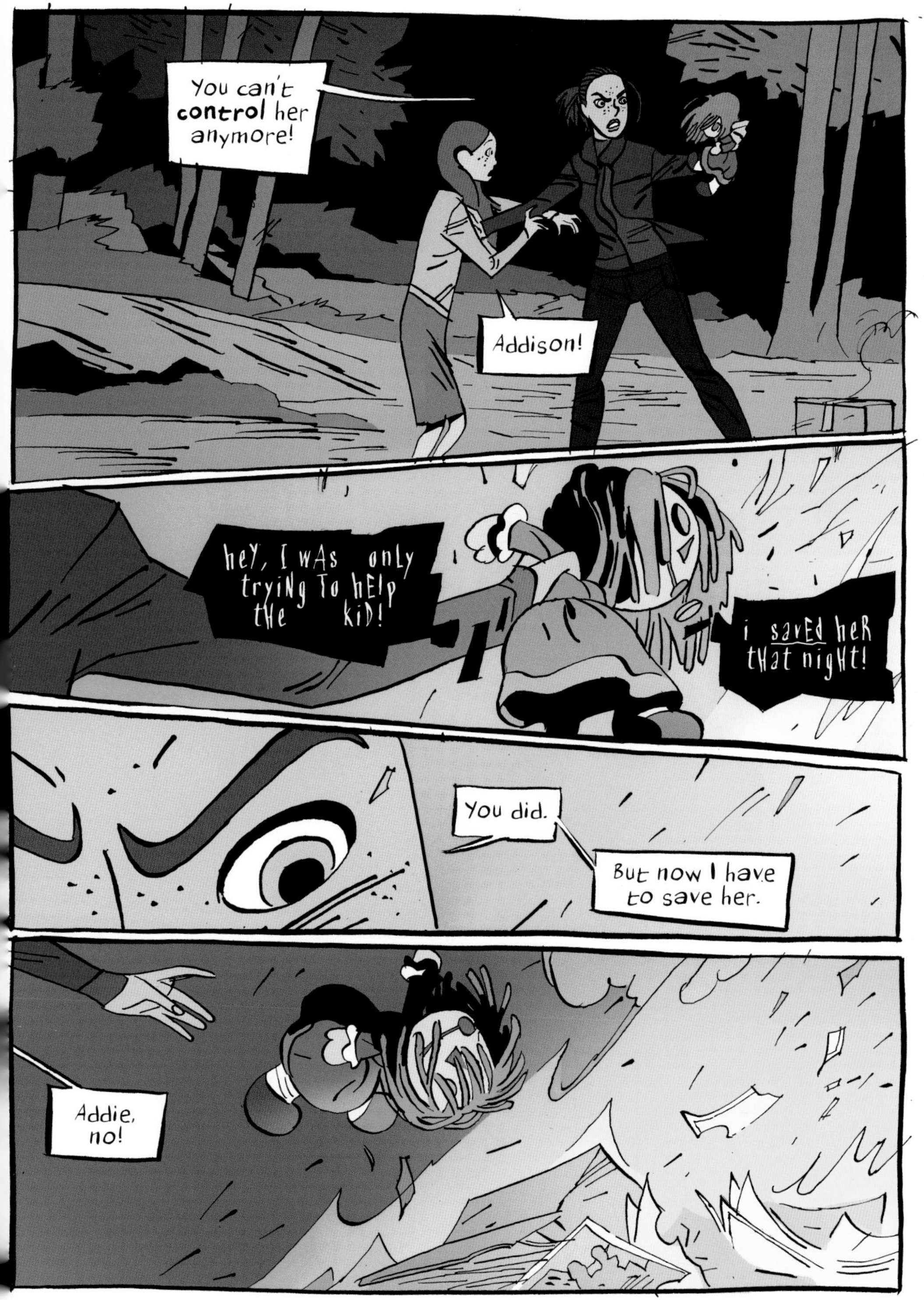
You can't **control** her anymore!
Addison!
hey, I wAs only trying to hElp the kid!
i saved her that night!
You did.
But now I have to save her.
Addie, no!

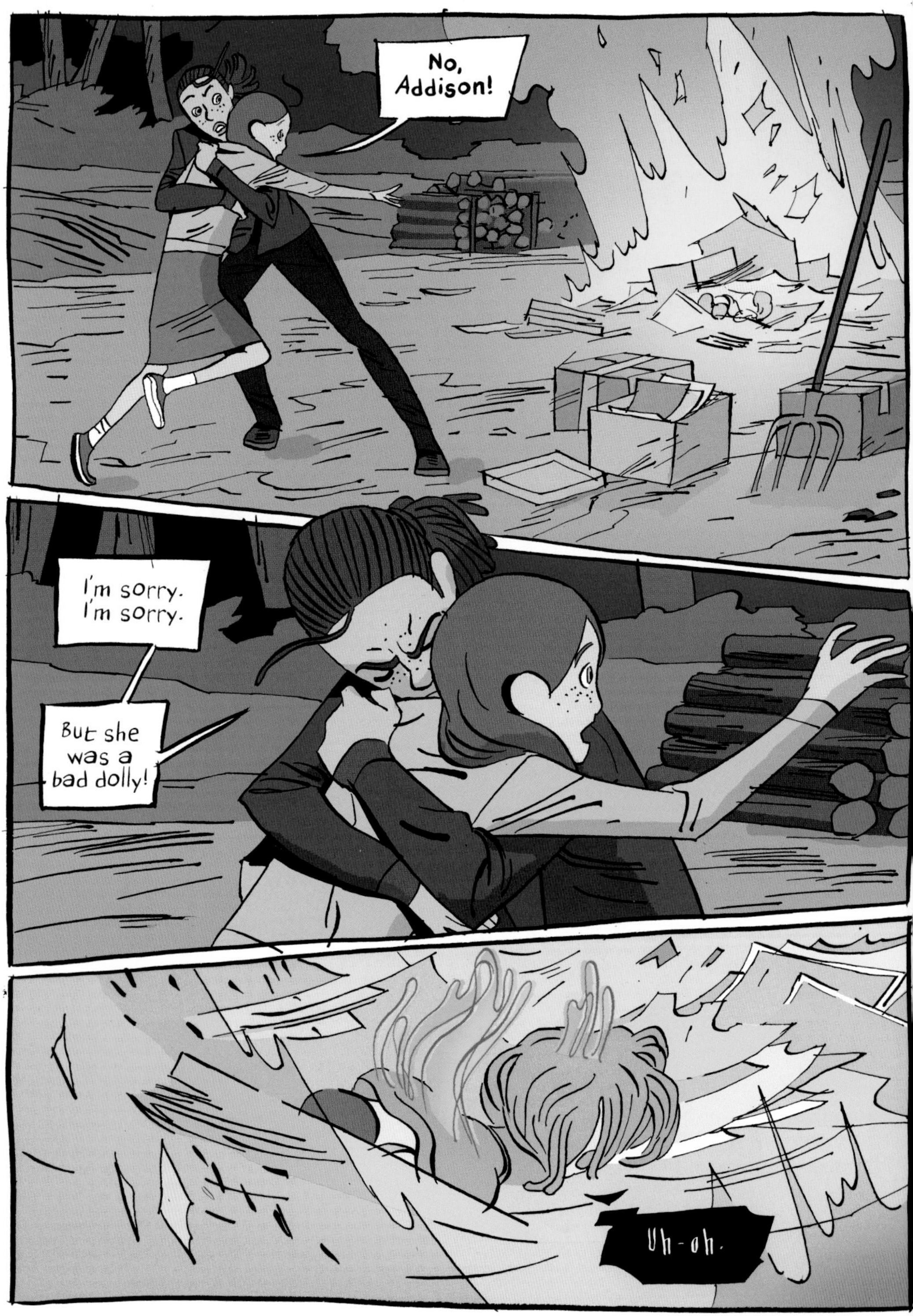
No, Addison!
I'm sorry. I'm sorry.
But she was a bad dolly!
Uh-oh.

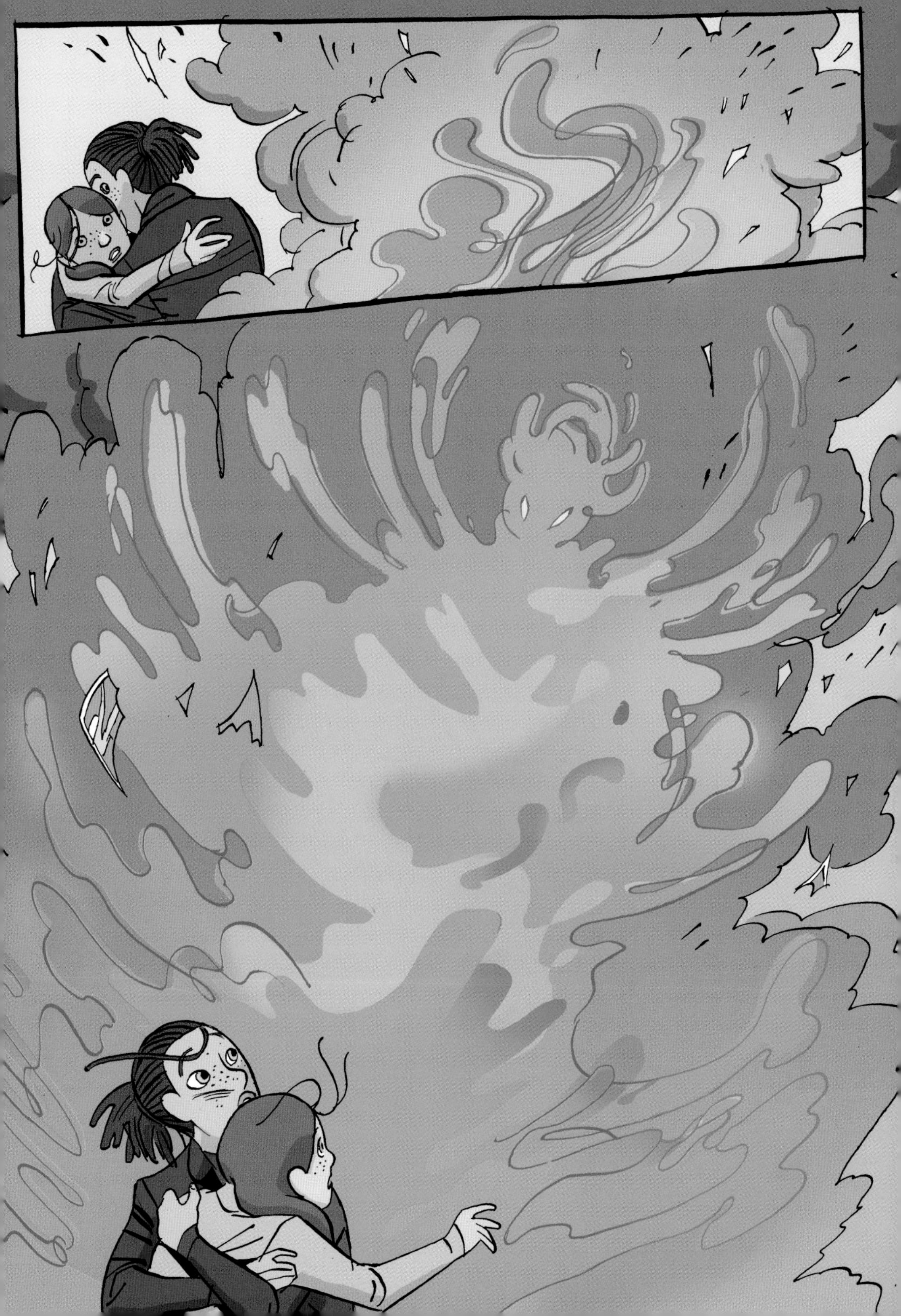

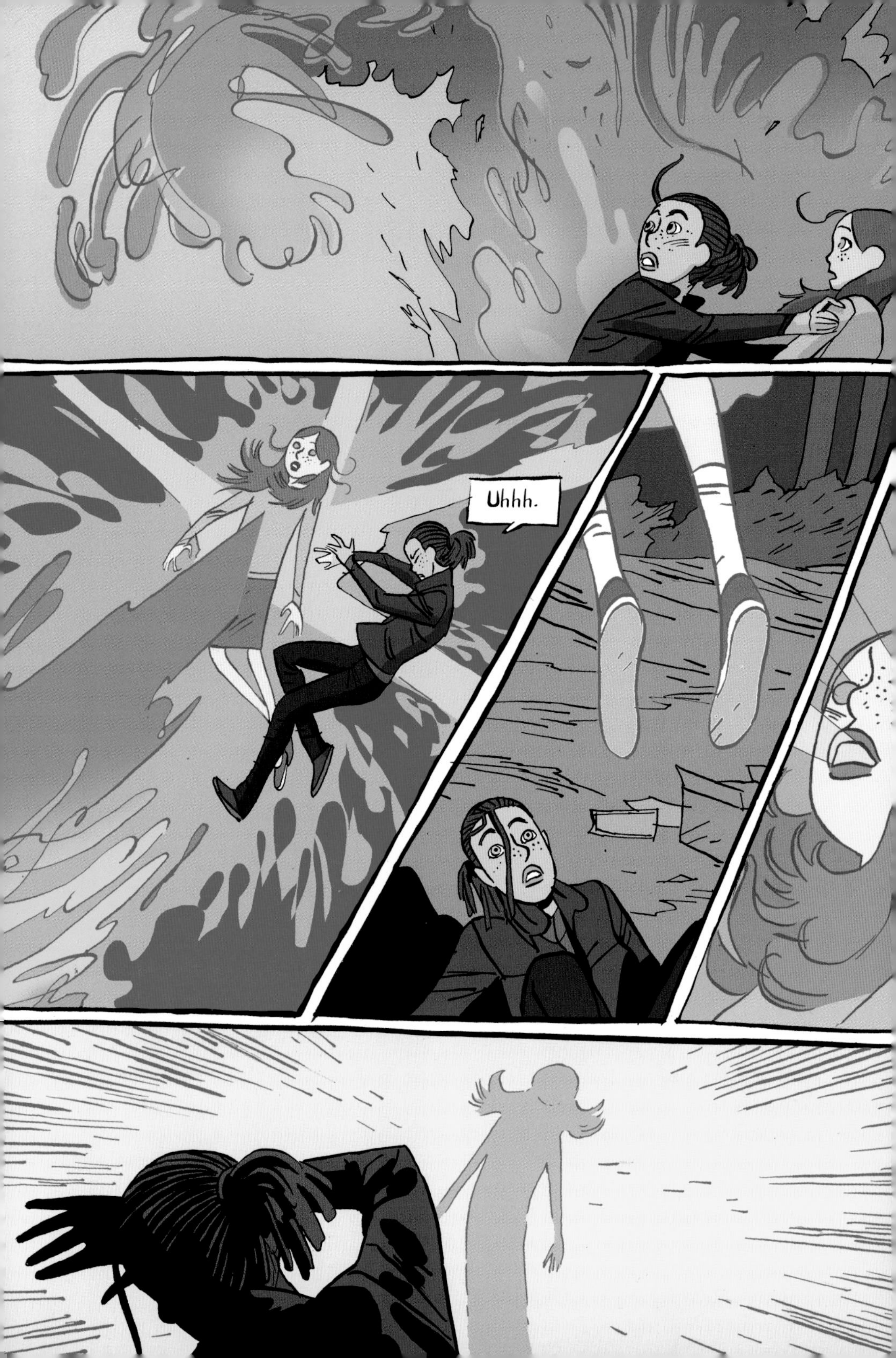
Uhhh.

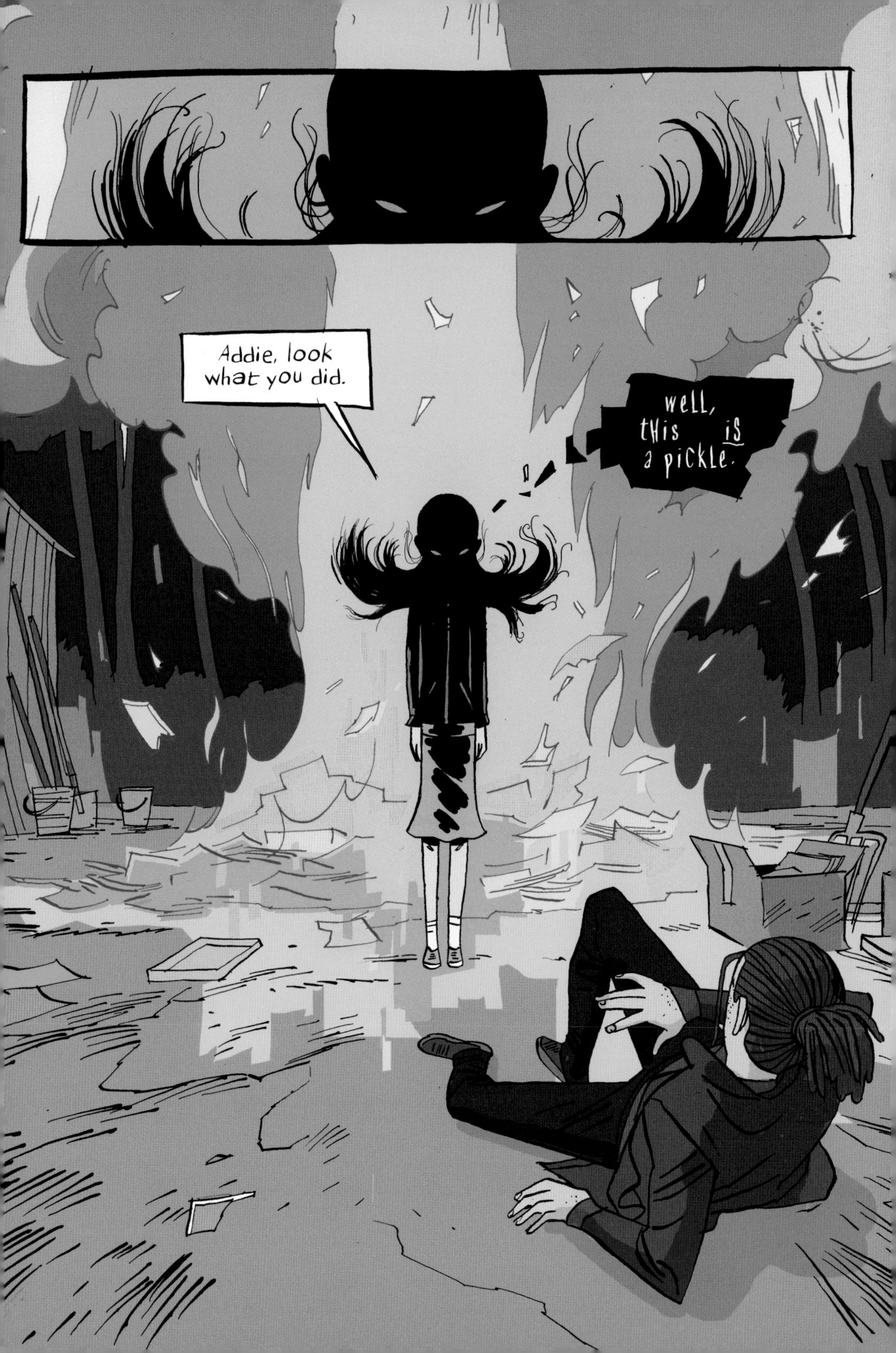

Addie, look what you did.
well, this is a pickle.

73

74

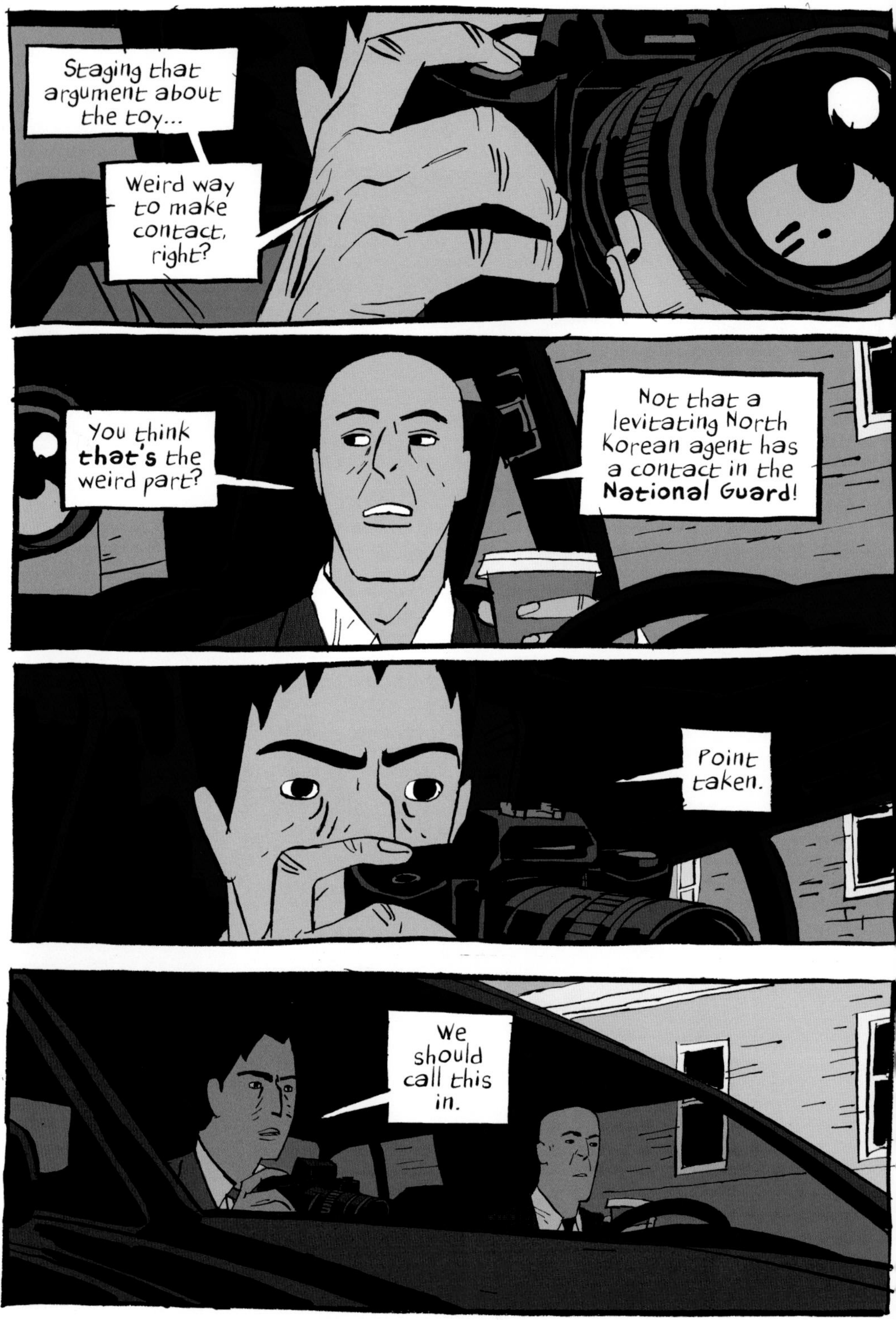

Staging that argument about the toy...
Weird way to make contact, right?
You think **that's** the weird part?
Not that a levitating North Korean agent has a contact in the **National Guard**!
Point taken.
We should call this in.

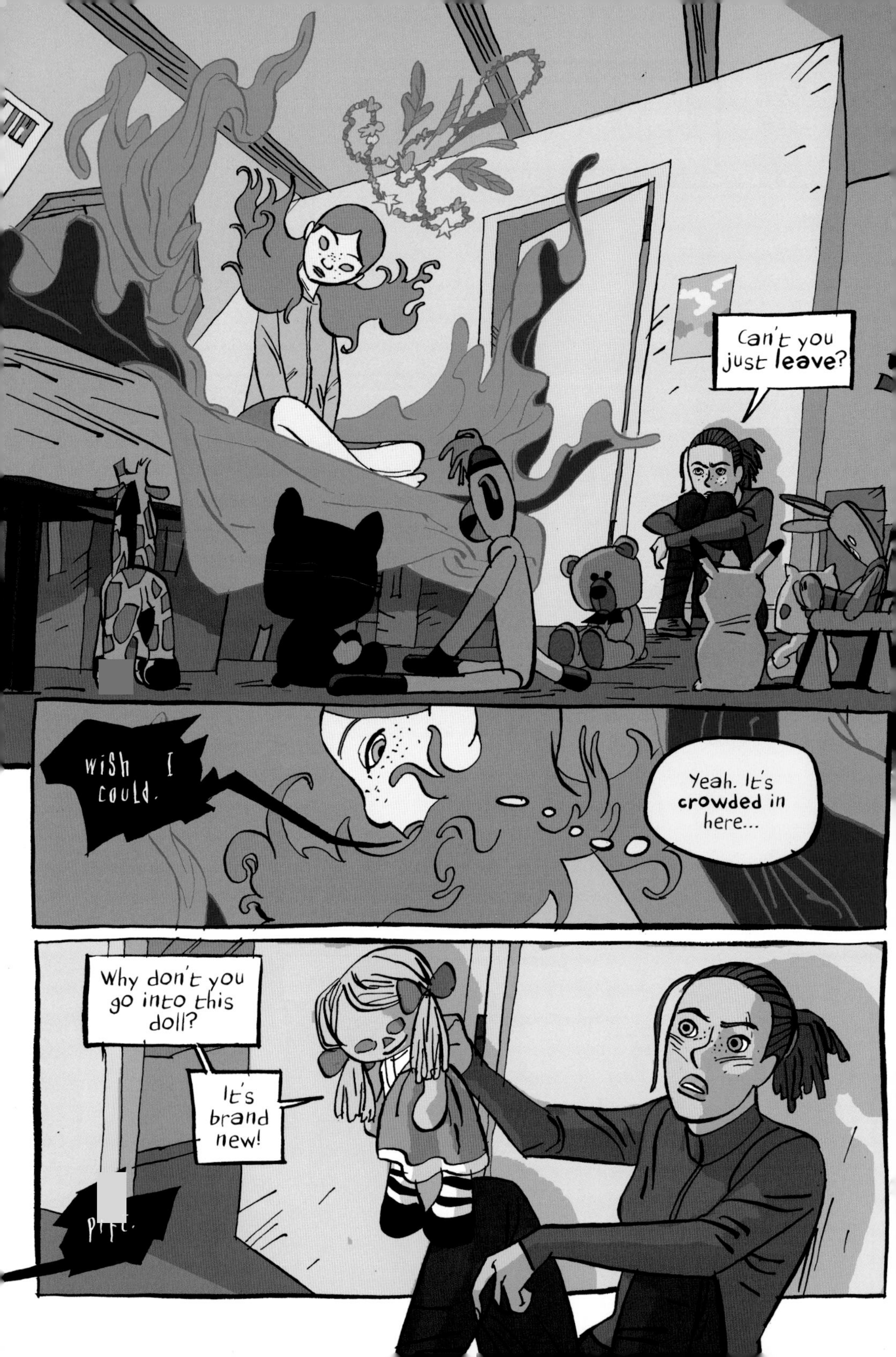
Can't you just leave?
wish I could.
Yeah. It's crowded in here...
Why don't you go into this doll?
It's brand new!
pfft.

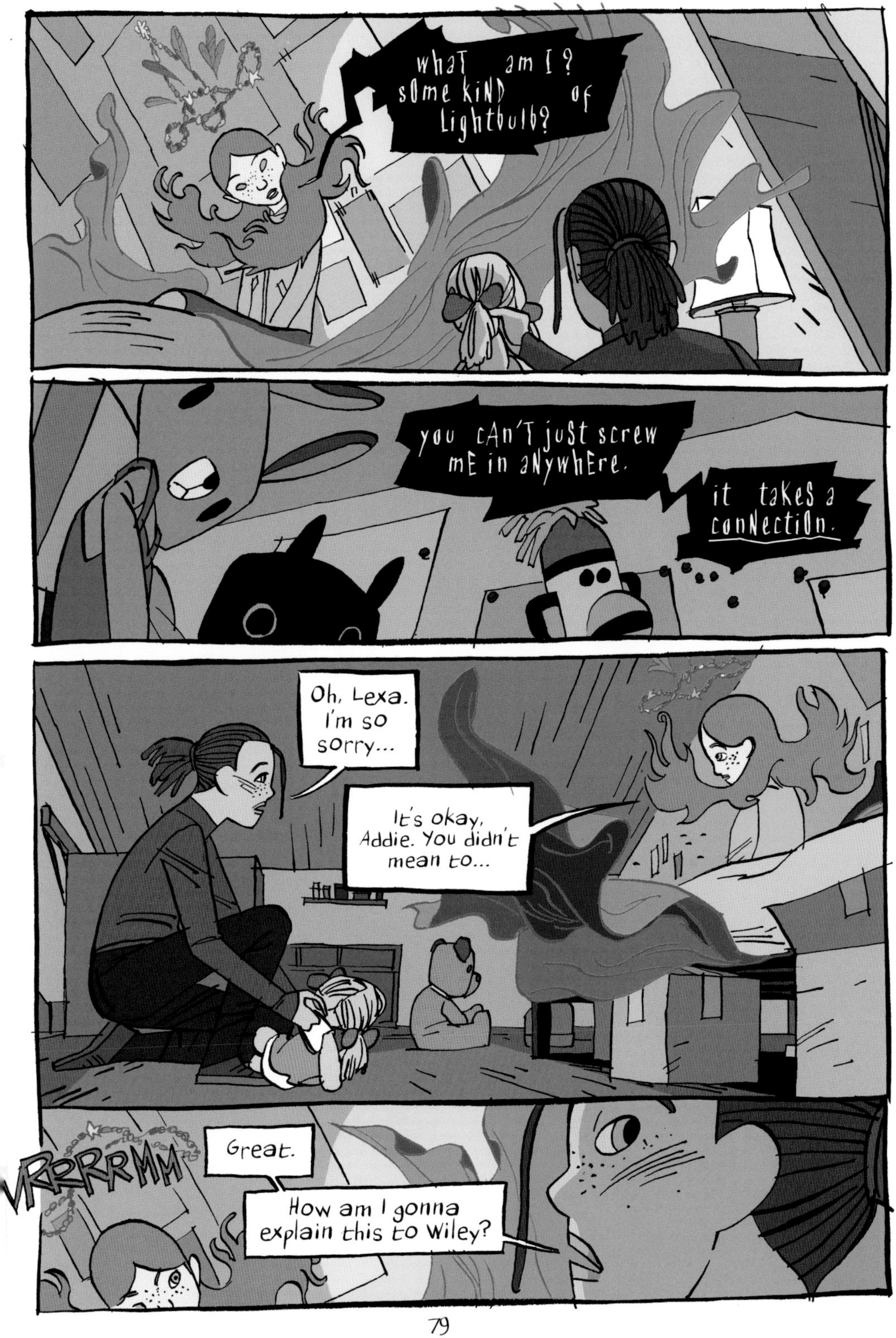
what am I? some kind of lightbulb?
you can't just screw me in anywhere.
it takes a connection.
Oh, Lexa. I'm so sorry...
It's okay, Addie. You didn't mean to...
VRRRRRMM
Great.
How am I gonna explain this to Wiley?

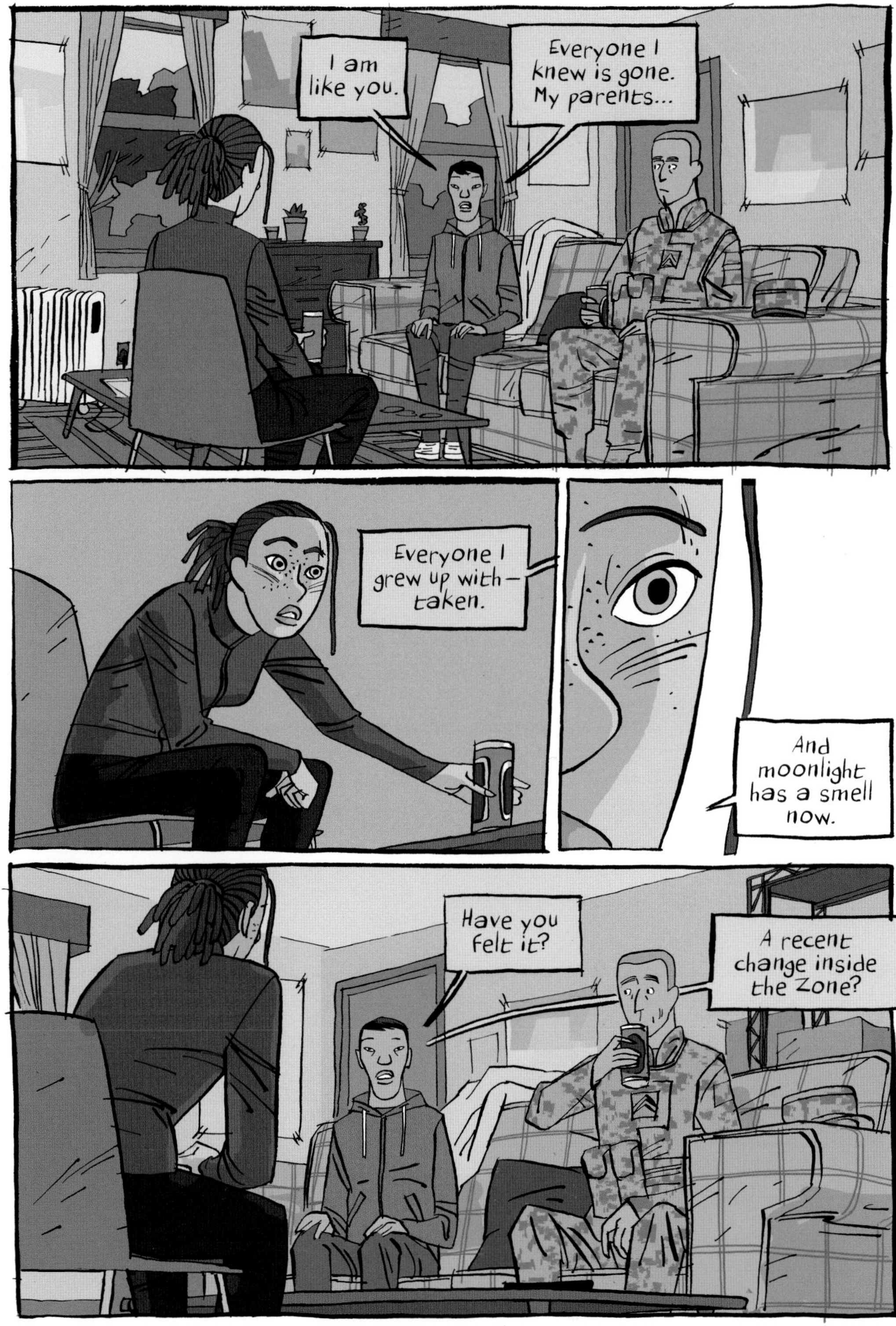
I am like you.
Everyone I knew is gone. My parents...
Everyone I grew up with— taken.
And moonlight has a smell now.
Have you felt it?
A recent change inside the Zone?

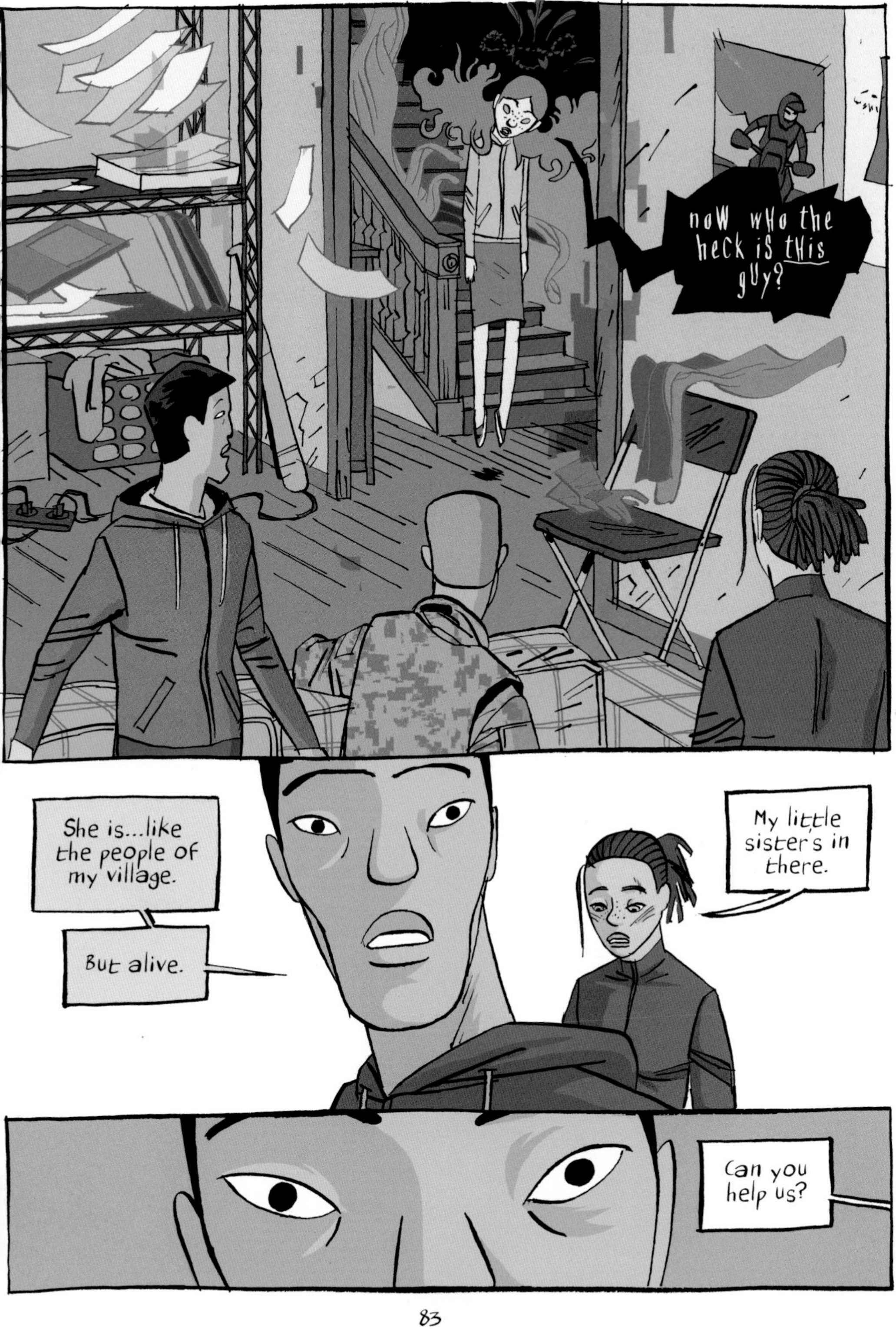
now who the heck is this guy?
She is...like the people of my village.
But alive.
My little sister's in there.
Can you help us?

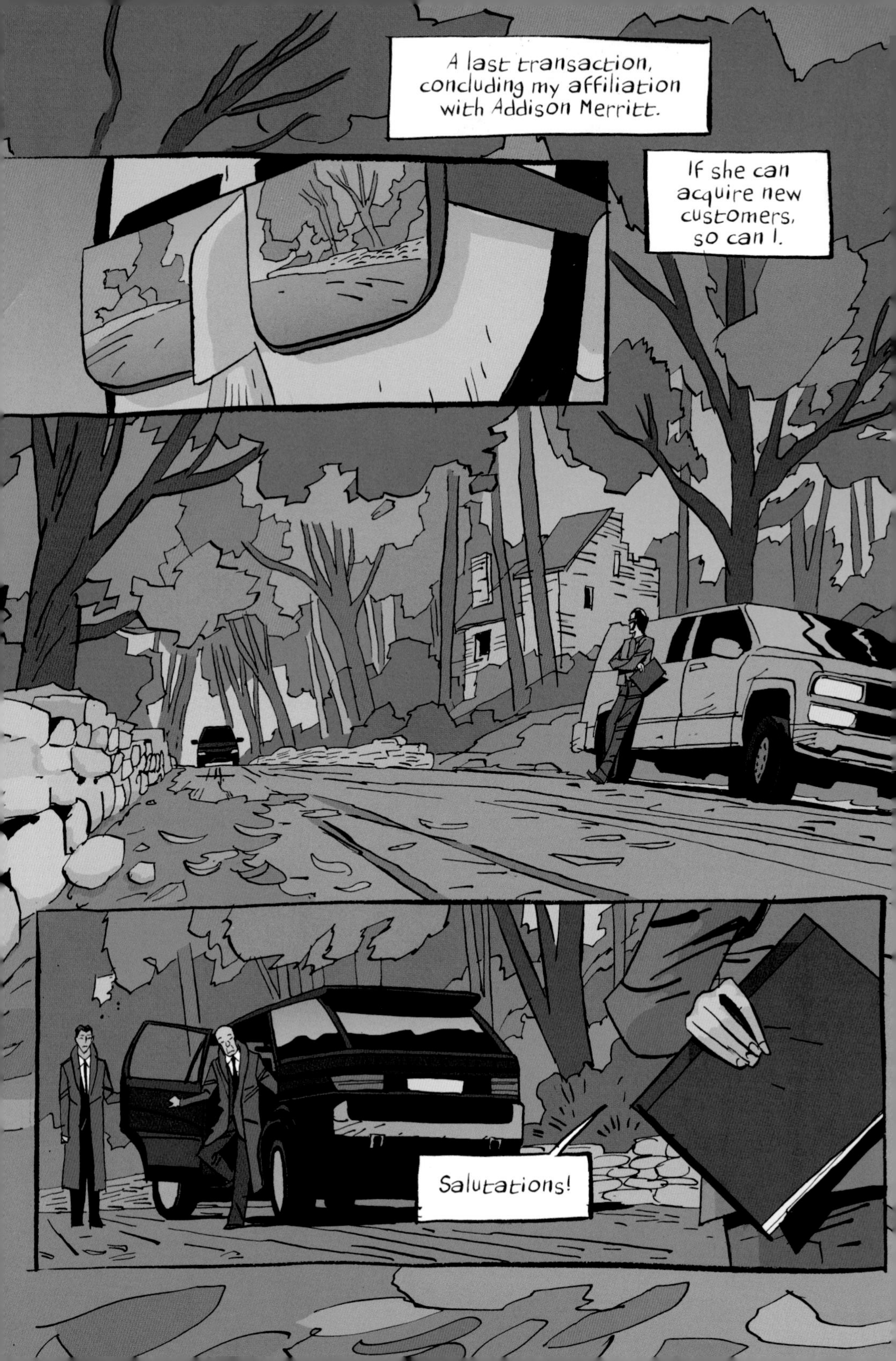
A last transaction, concluding my affiliation with Addison Merritt.
If she can acquire new customers, so can I.
Salutations!

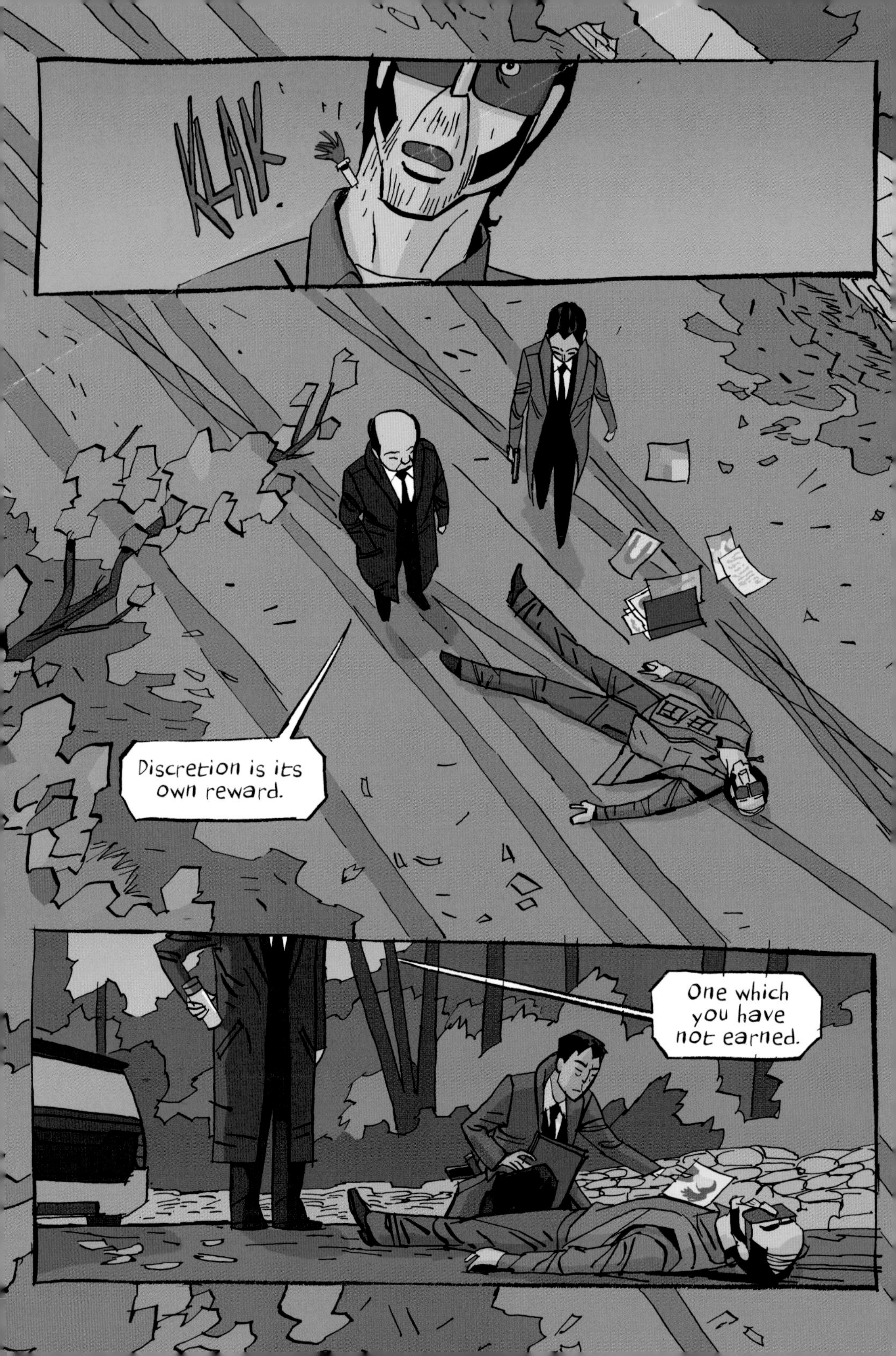
KLAK
Discretion is its own reward.
One which you have not earned.

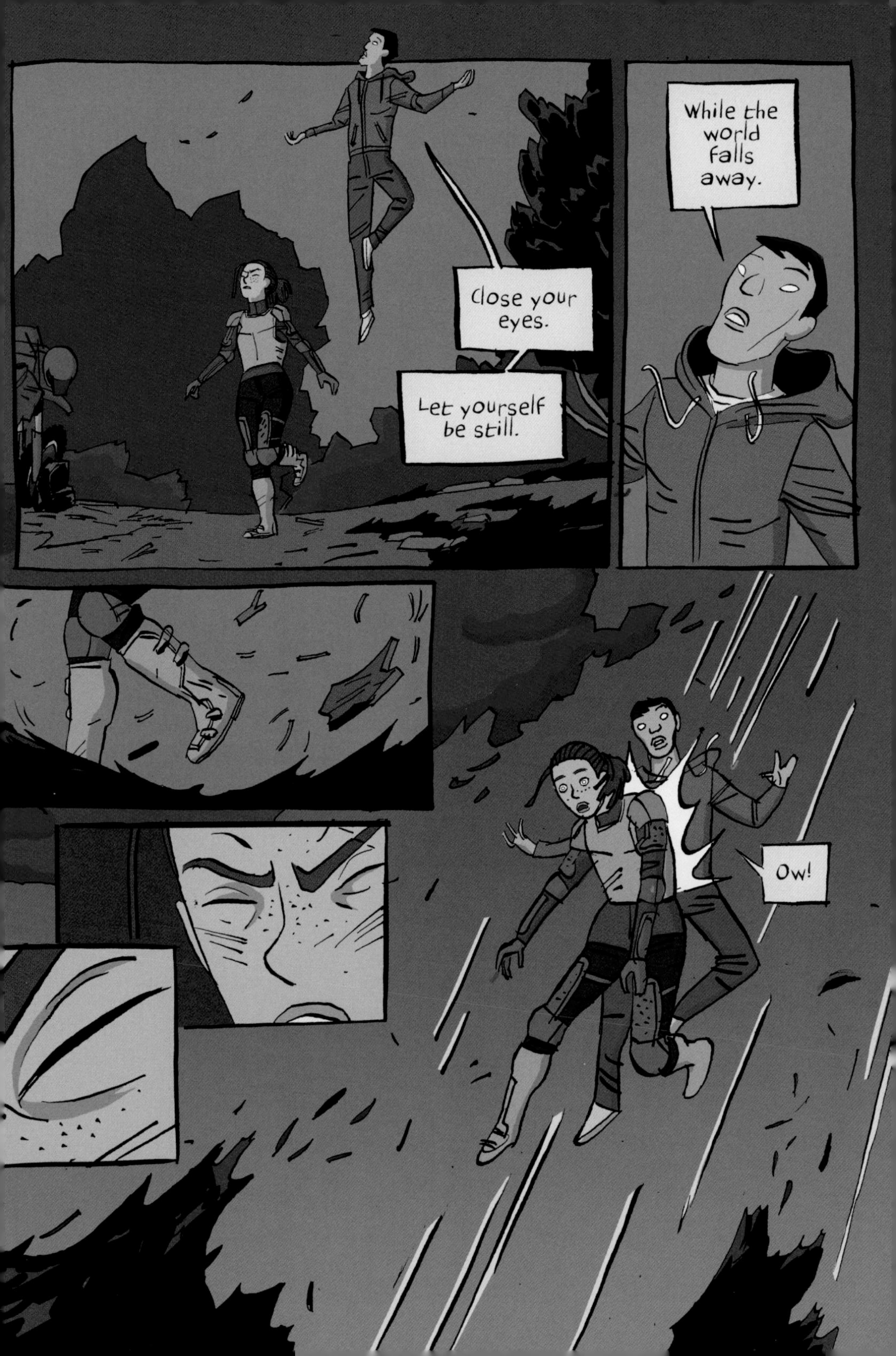
Close your eyes.
Let yourself be still.
While the world falls away.
Ow!

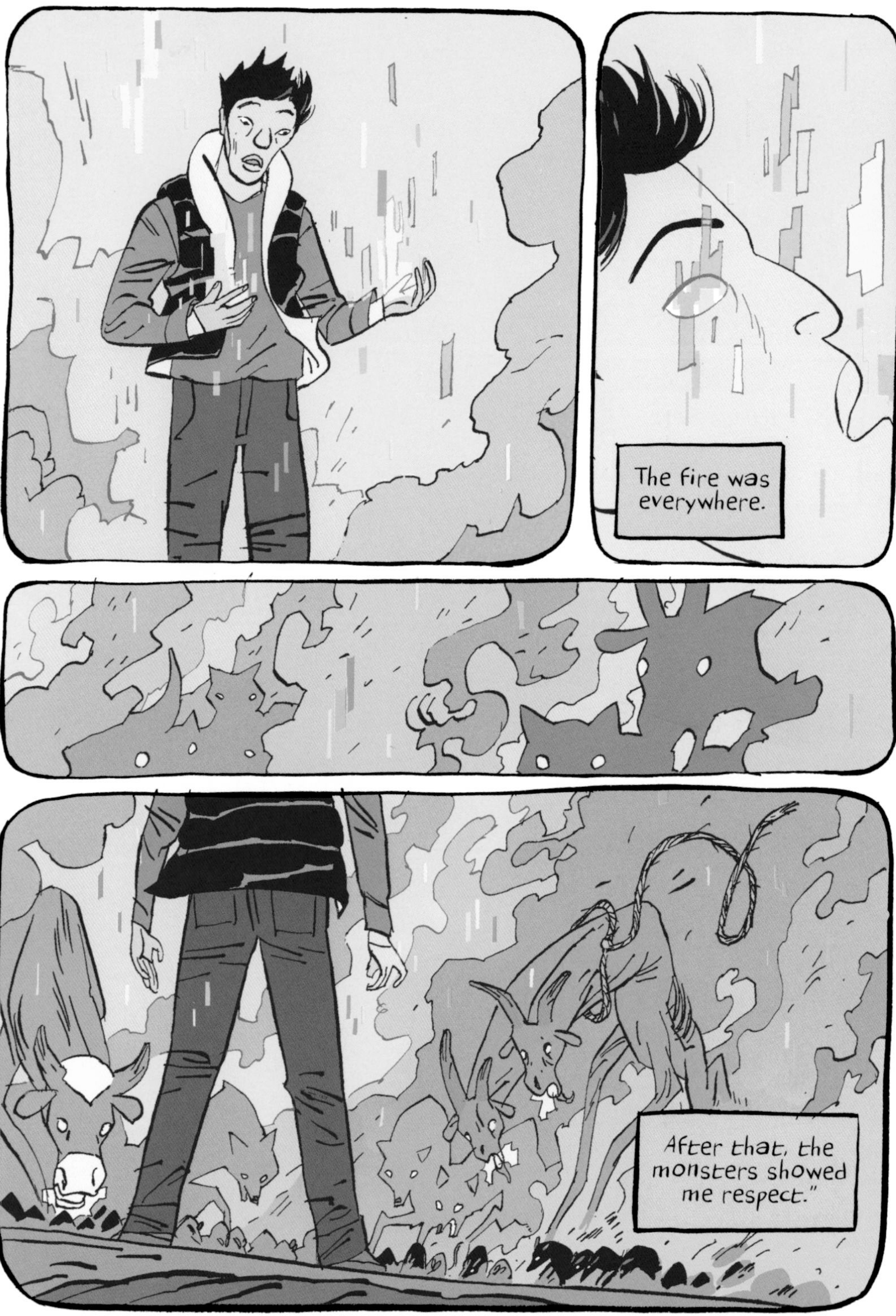
The fire was everywhere.
After that, the monsters showed me respect."

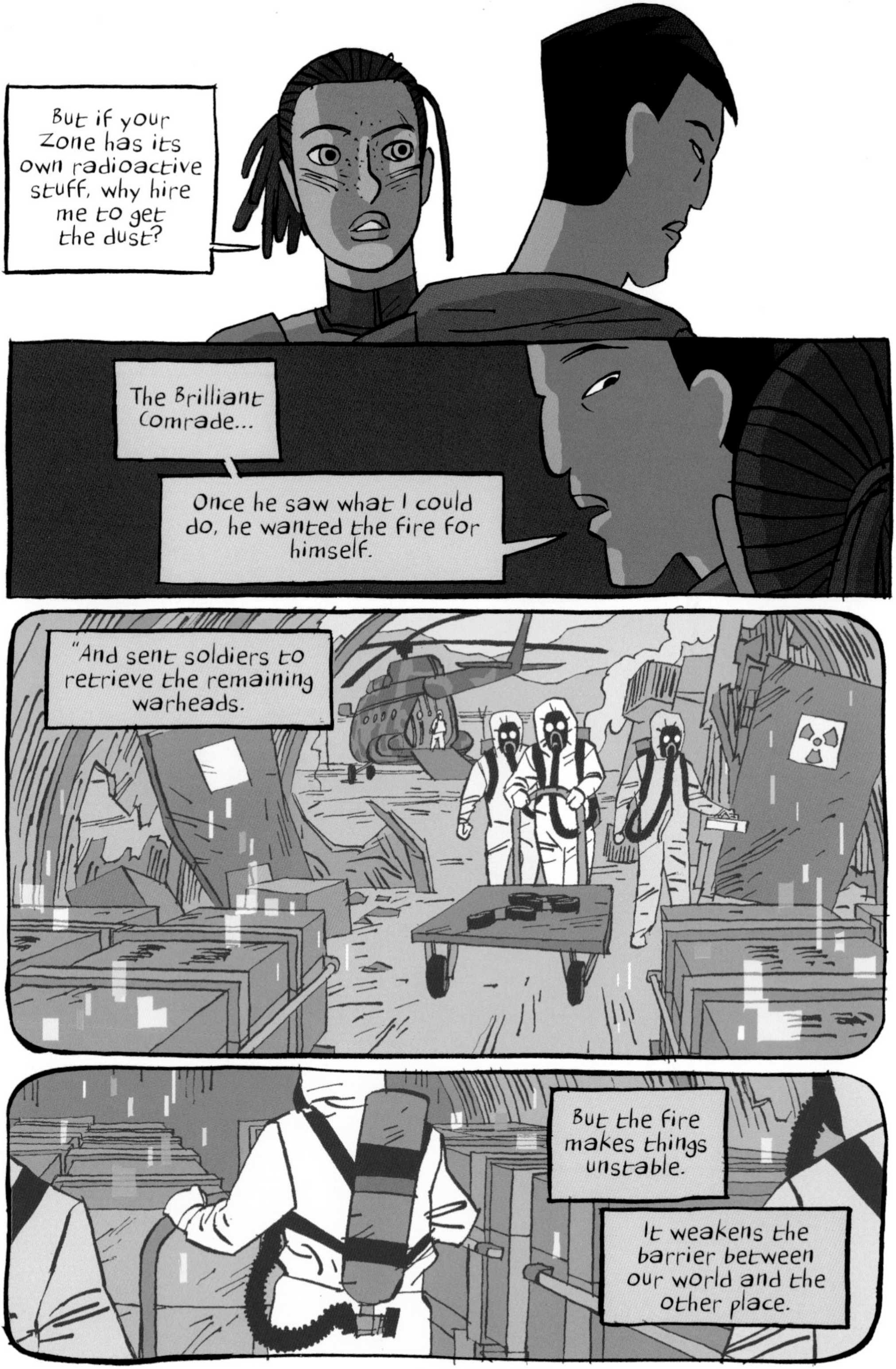
But if your Zone has its own radioactive stuff, why hire me to get the dust?
The Brilliant Comrade...
Once he saw what I could do, he wanted the fire for himself.
"And sent soldiers to retrieve the remaining warheads.
But the fire makes things unstable.
It weakens the barrier between our world and the other place.

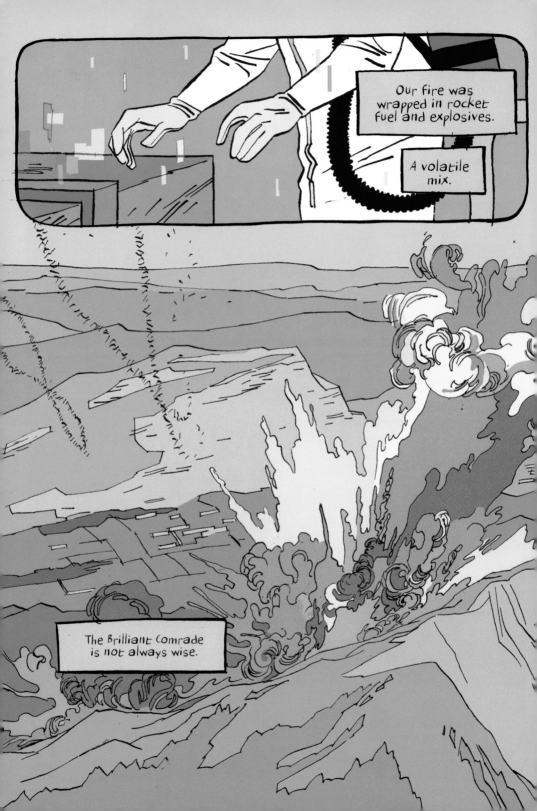

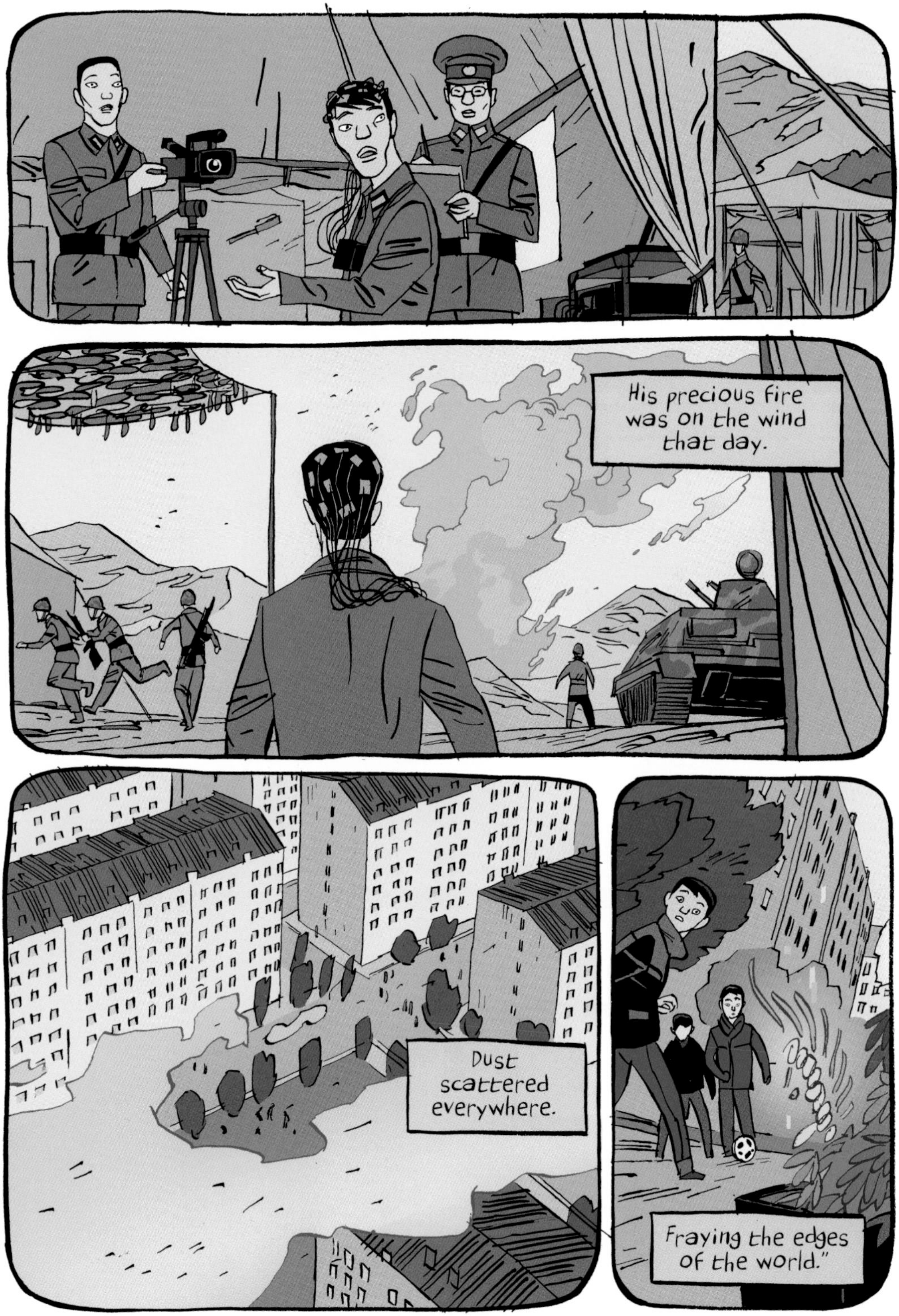
His precious fire was on the wind that day.
Dust scattered everywhere.
Fraying the edges of the world."

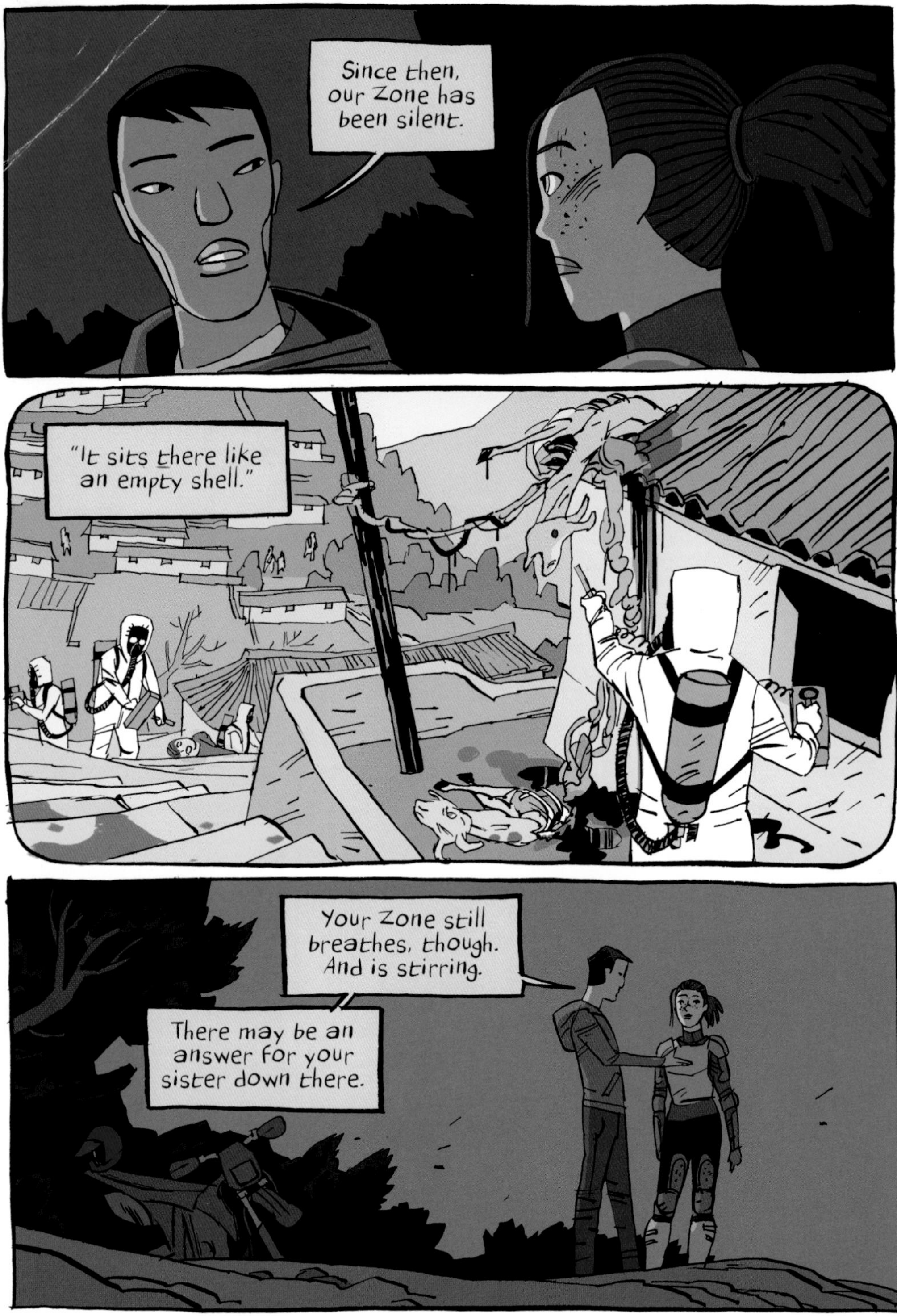
Since then, our Zone has been silent.
"It sits there like an empty shell."
Your Zone still breathes, though. And is stirring.
There may be an answer for your sister down there.

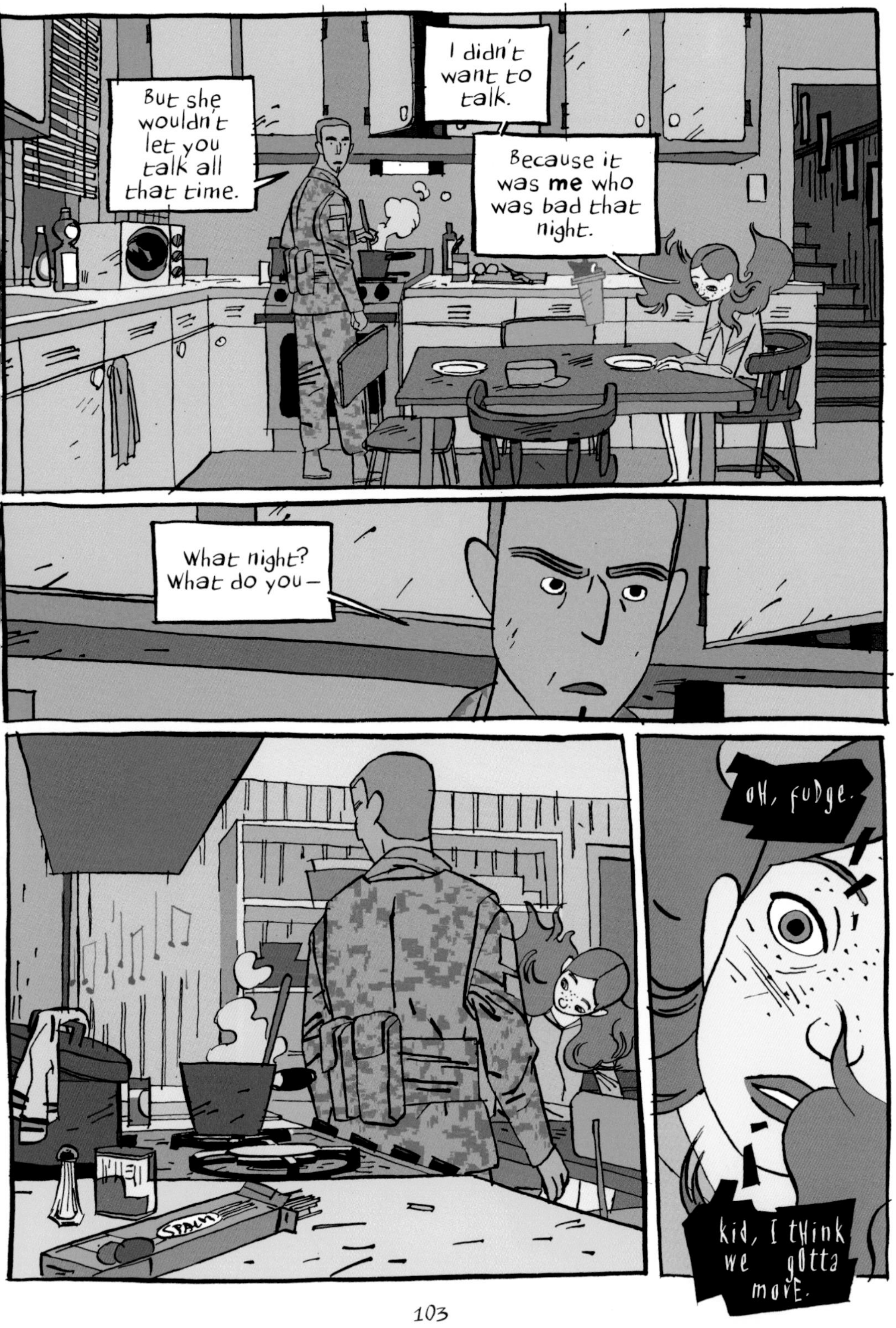
But she wouldn't let you talk all that time.
I didn't want to talk.
Because it was **me** who was bad that night.
What night? What do you—
OH, FUDGE.
KID, I THINK WE GOTTA MOVE.

104

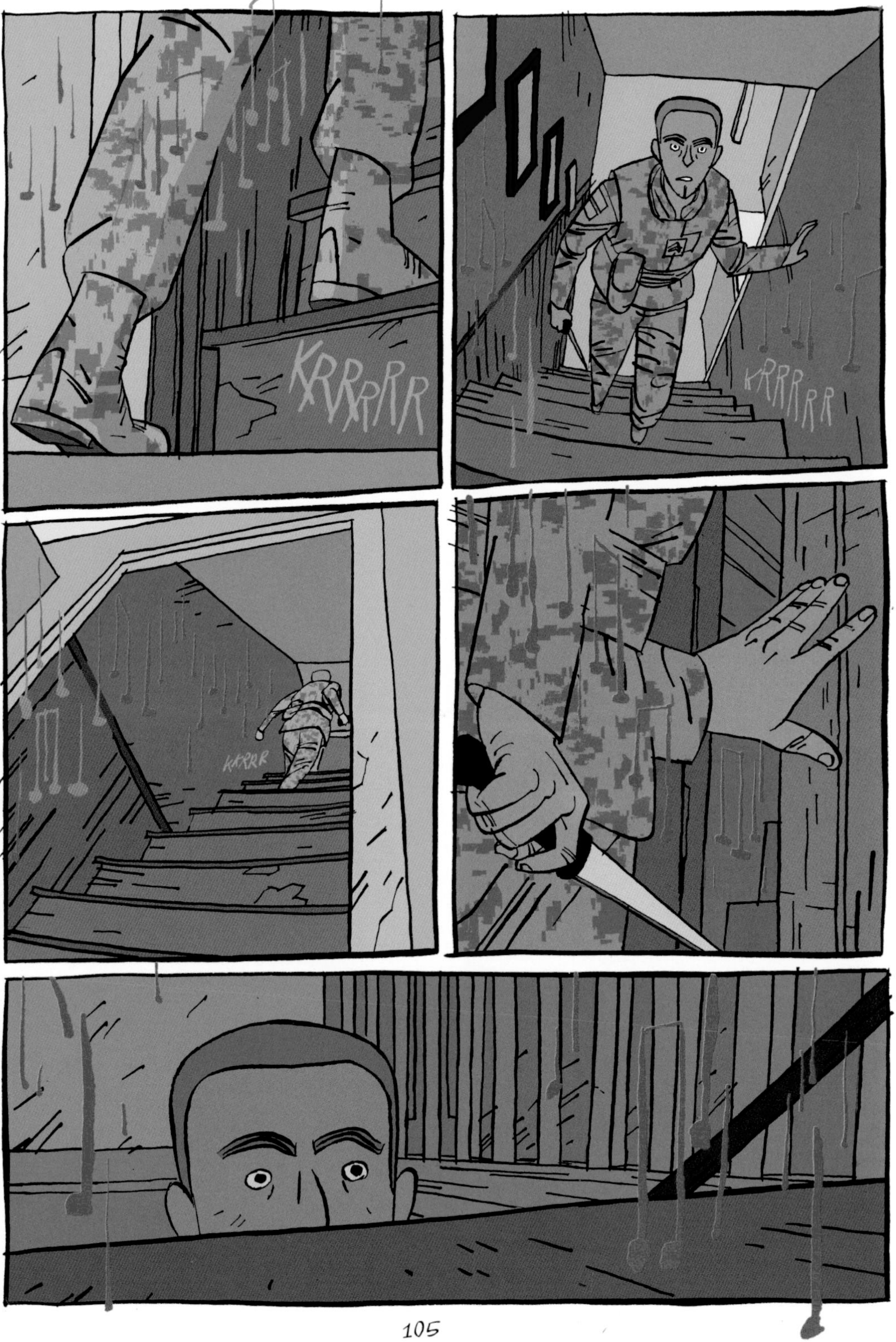
KRRRRRR
KRRRRRR
KRRRR

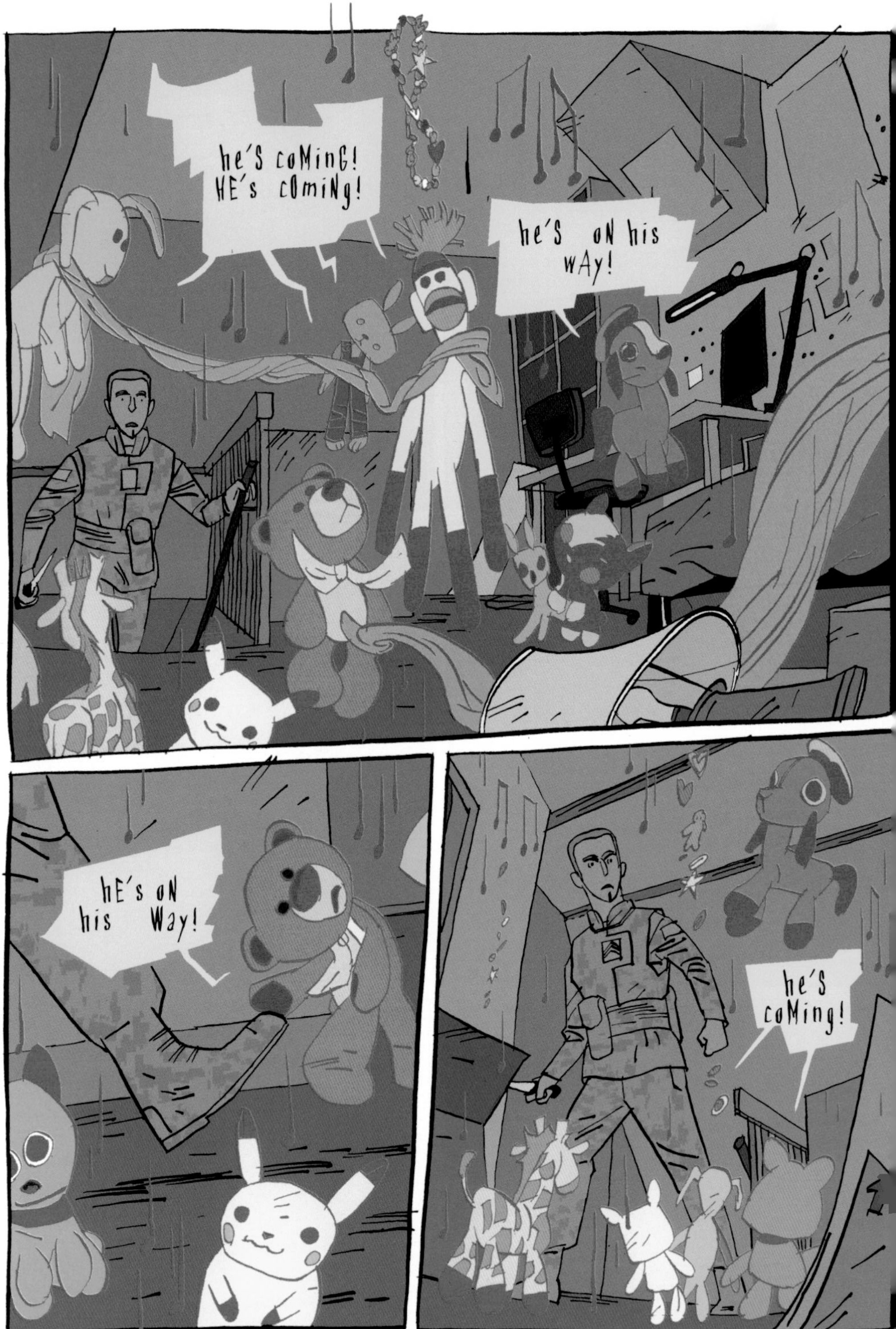
he's coMinG! HE's cOMiNg!
he's oN his wAy!
hE's oN his Way!
he's coMing!

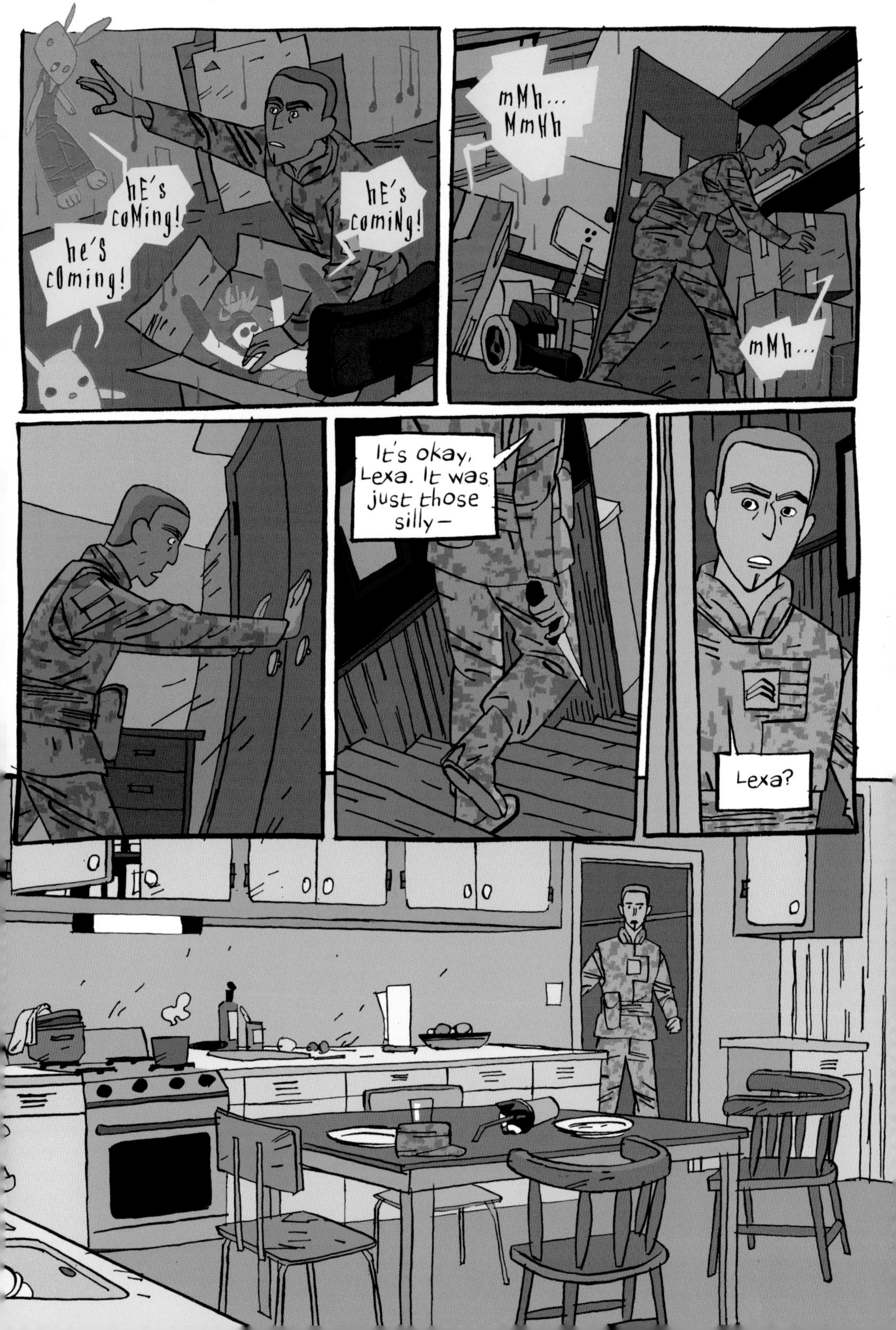
hE's coMing!
he's coming!
hE's coMiNg!
mMh... MmHh
mMh...
It's okay, Lexa. It was just those silly—
Lexa?

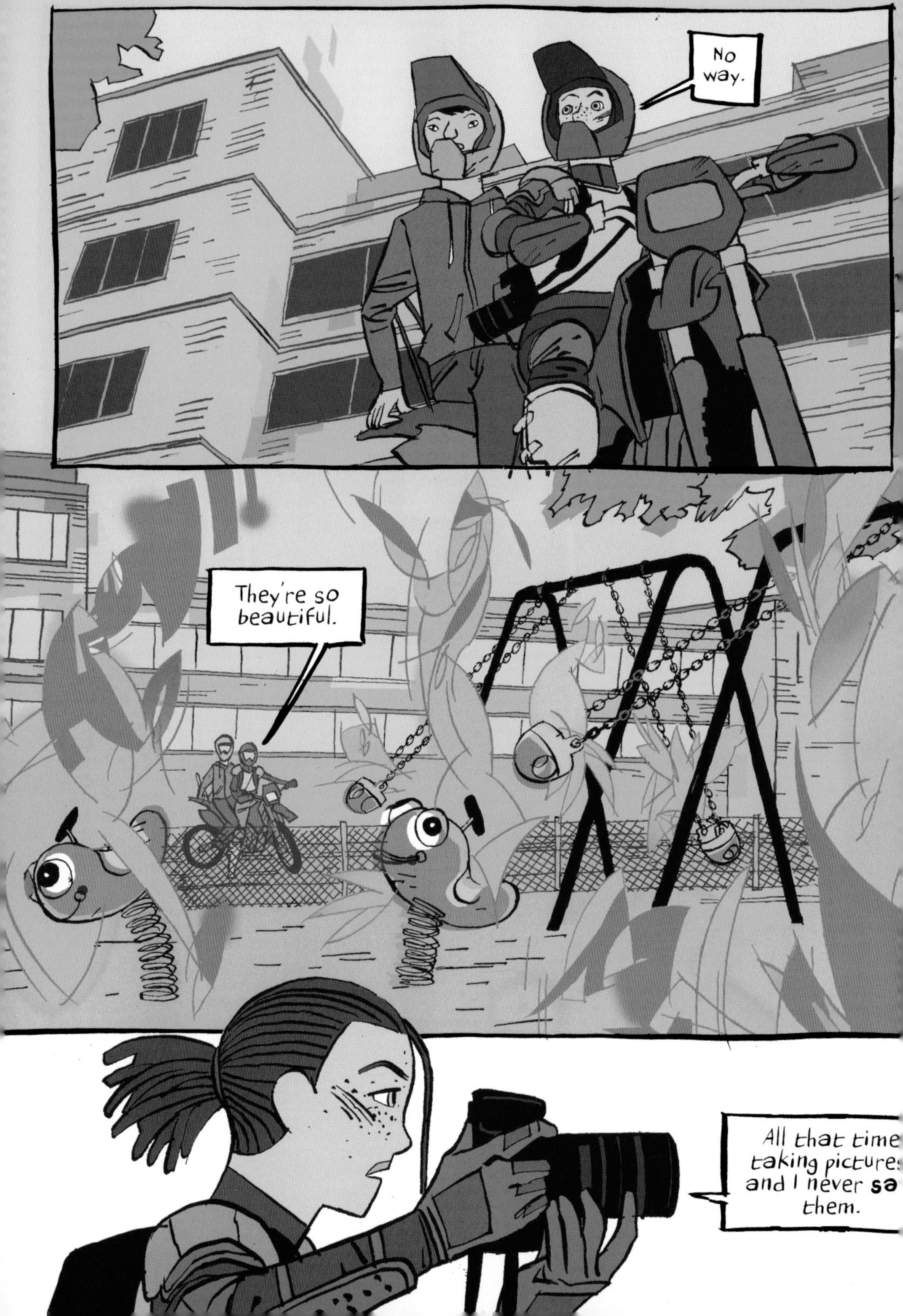
No way.
They're so beautiful.
All that time taking pictures and I never sa them.

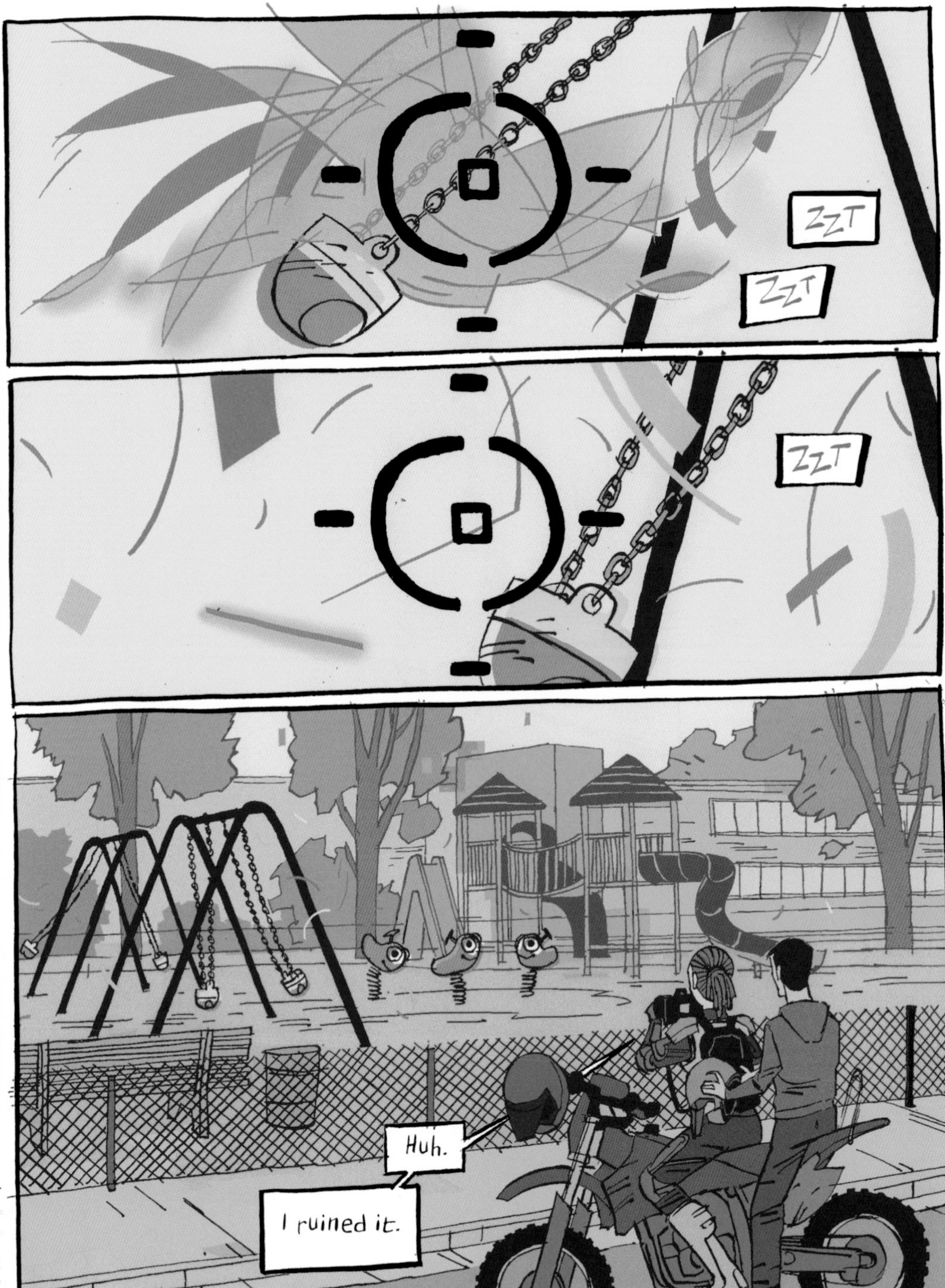
ZZT
ZZT
ZZT
Huh.
I ruined it.

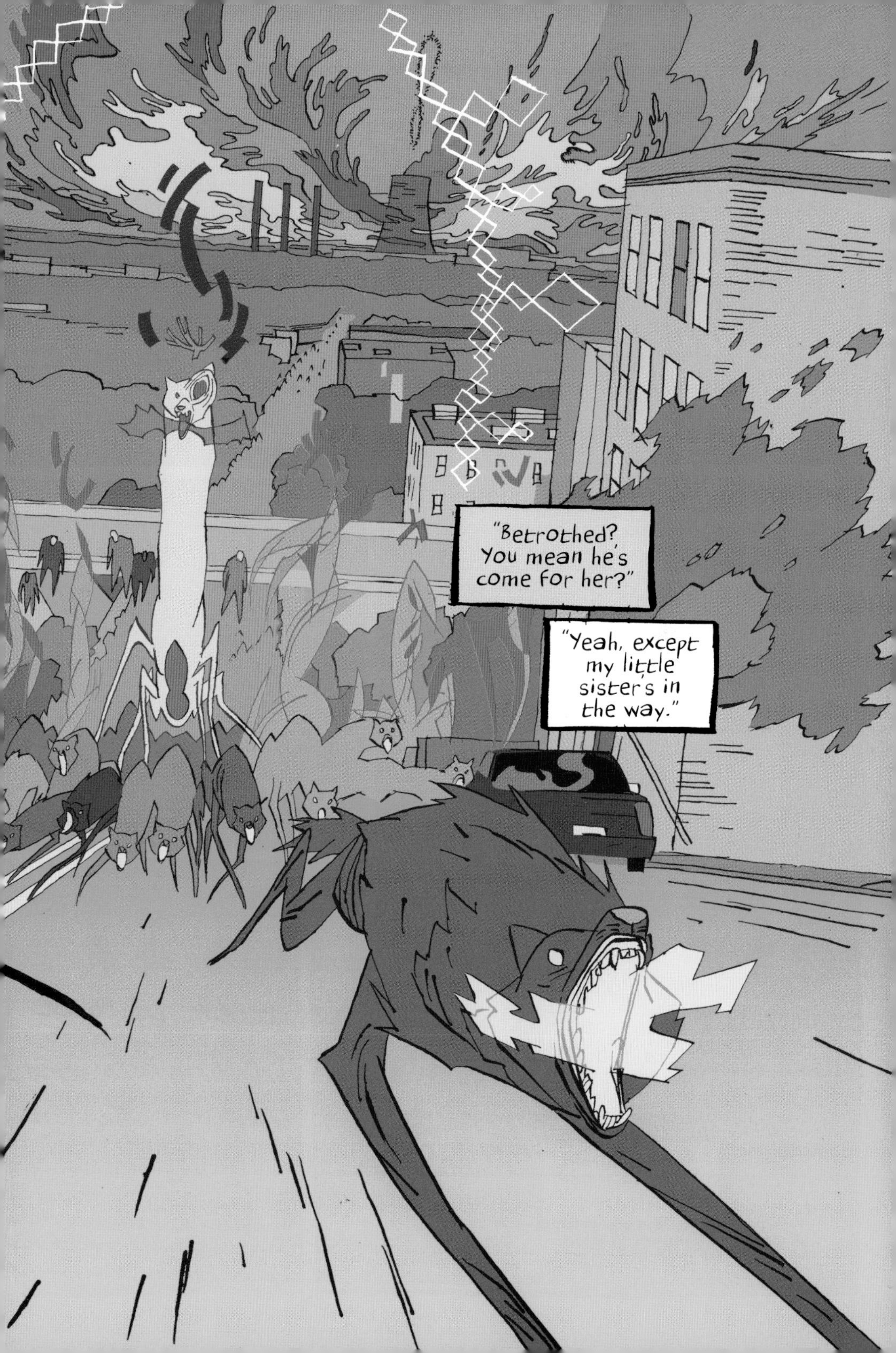
"Betrothed? You mean he's come for her?"
"Yeah, except my little sister's in the way."

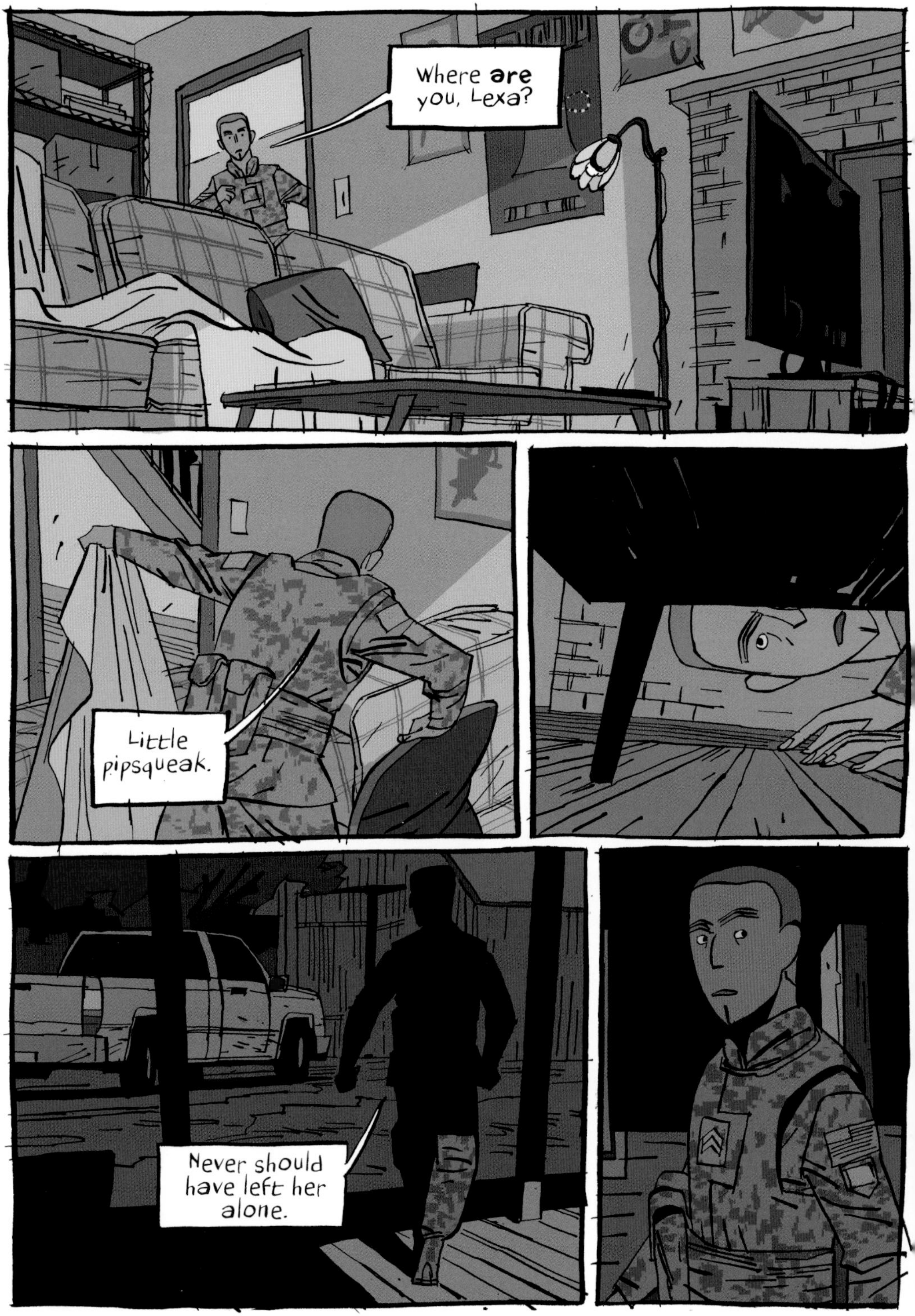
Where **are** you, Lexa?
Little pipsqueak.
Never should have left her alone.

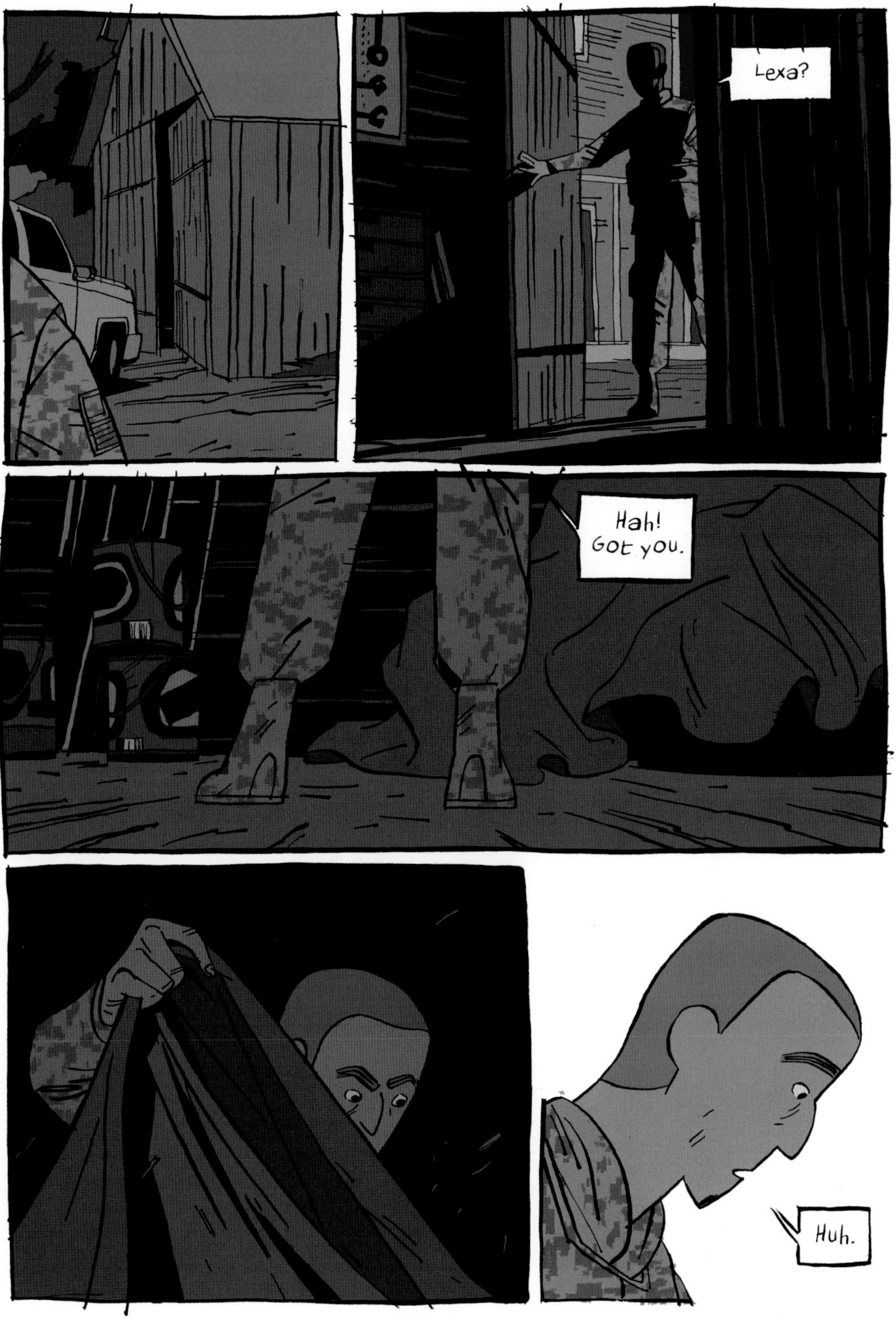
Lexa?
Hah! Got you.
Huh.

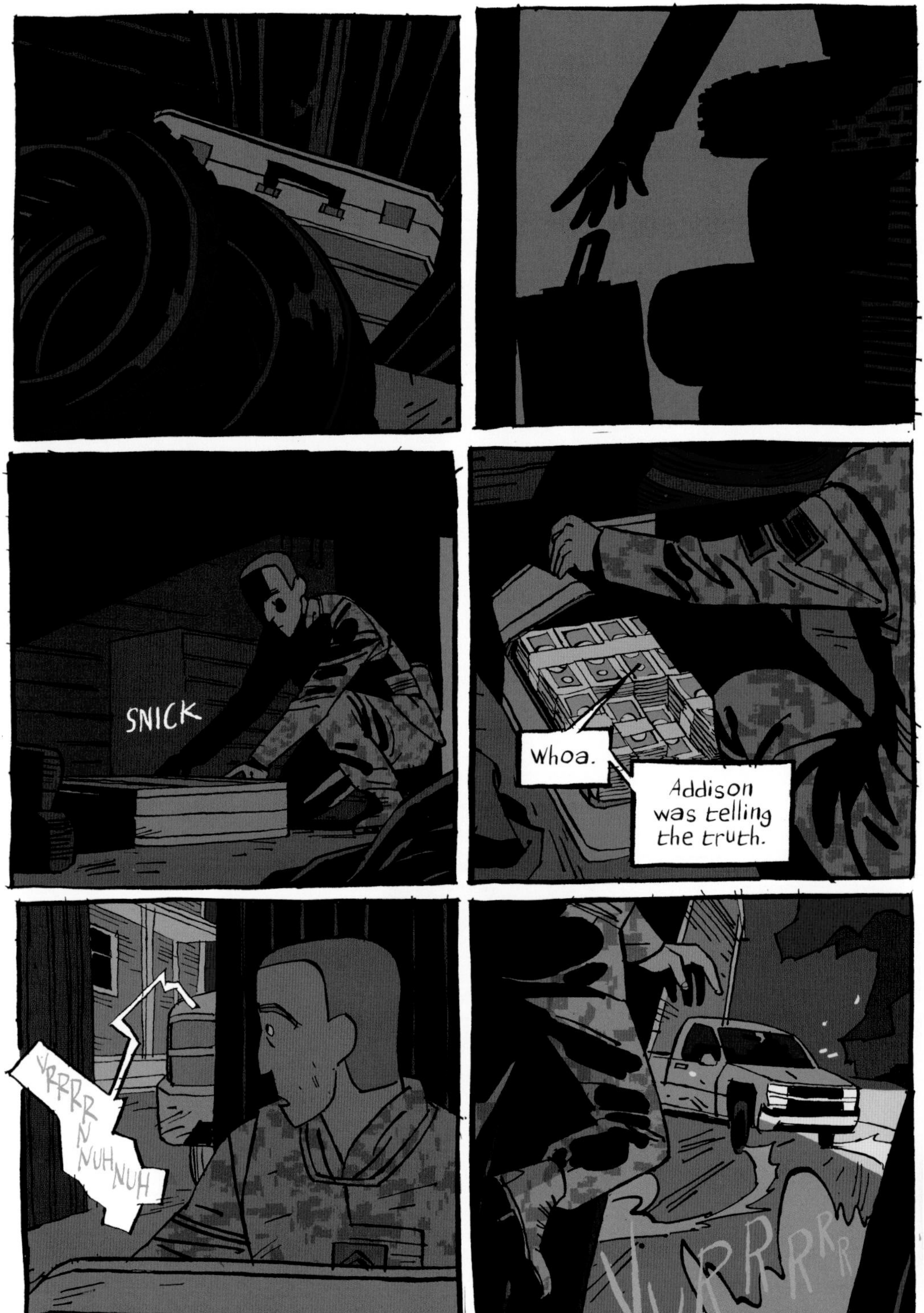
SNICK
Whoa.
Addison was telling the truth.
VRRRR NNUHNUH
VVRRRRR

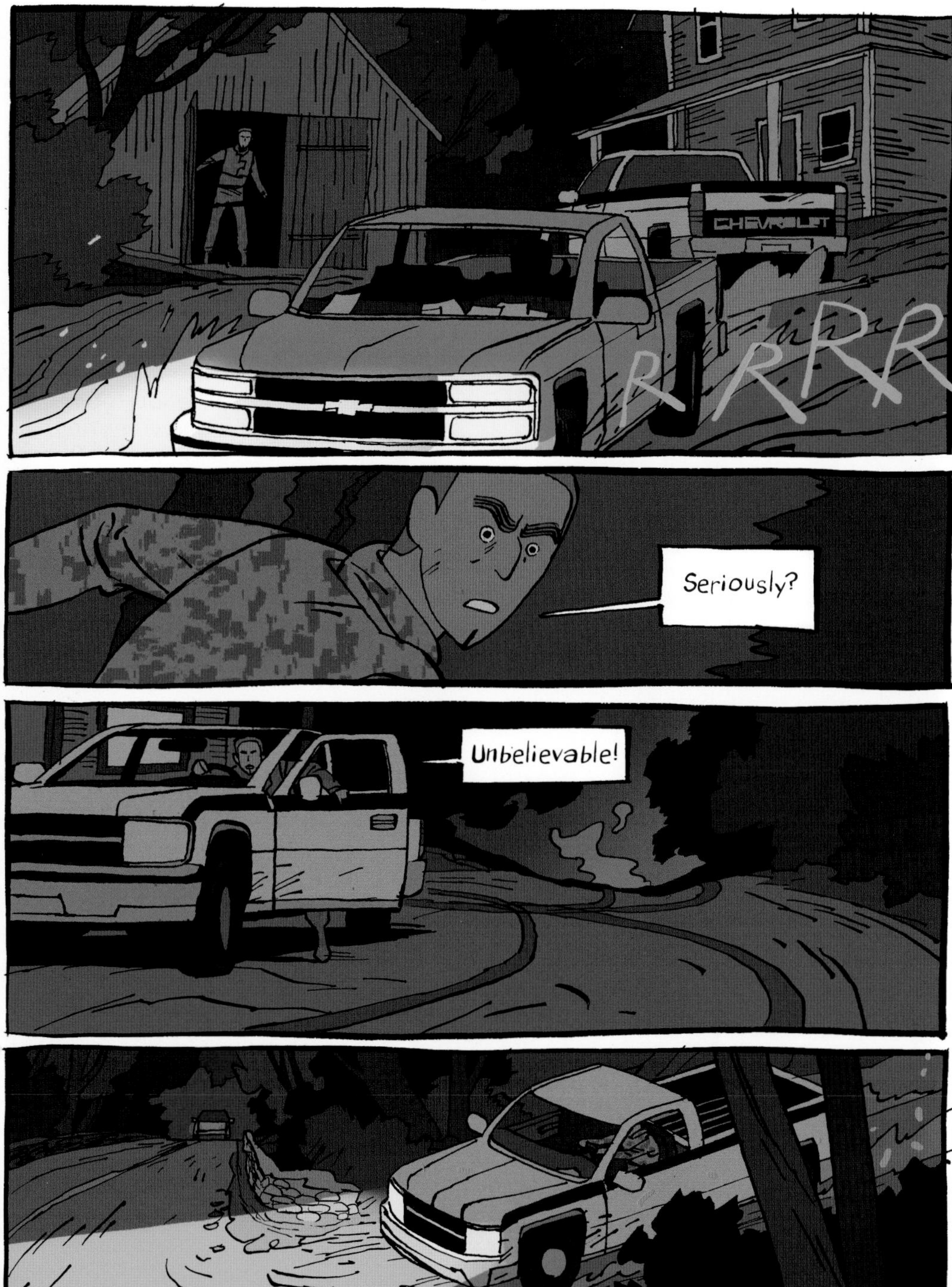
CHEVROLET
RRRR
Seriously?
Unbelievable!

118

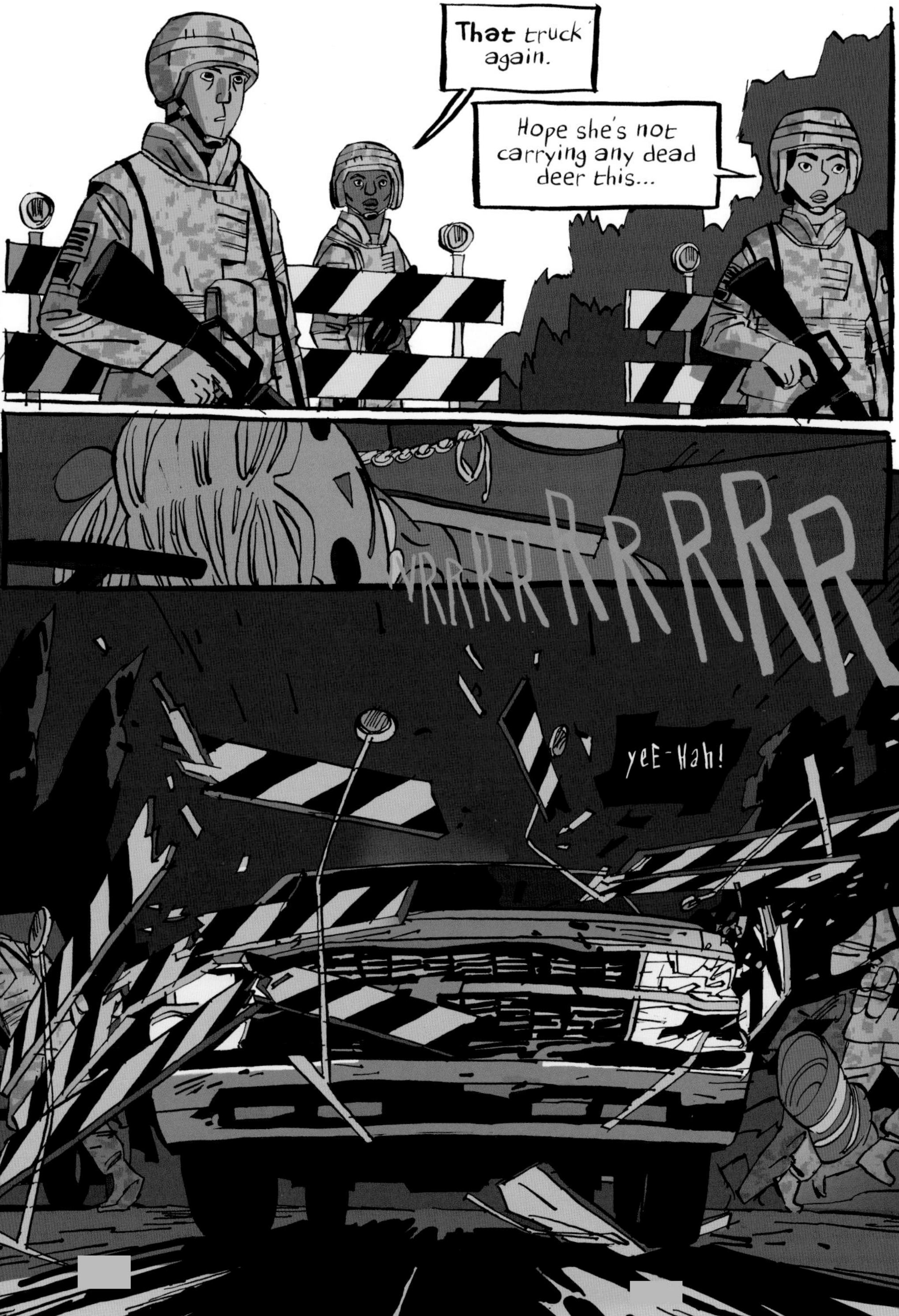
That truck again.
Hope she's not carrying any dead deer this...
VRRRRRRRRRR
yeE-Hah!

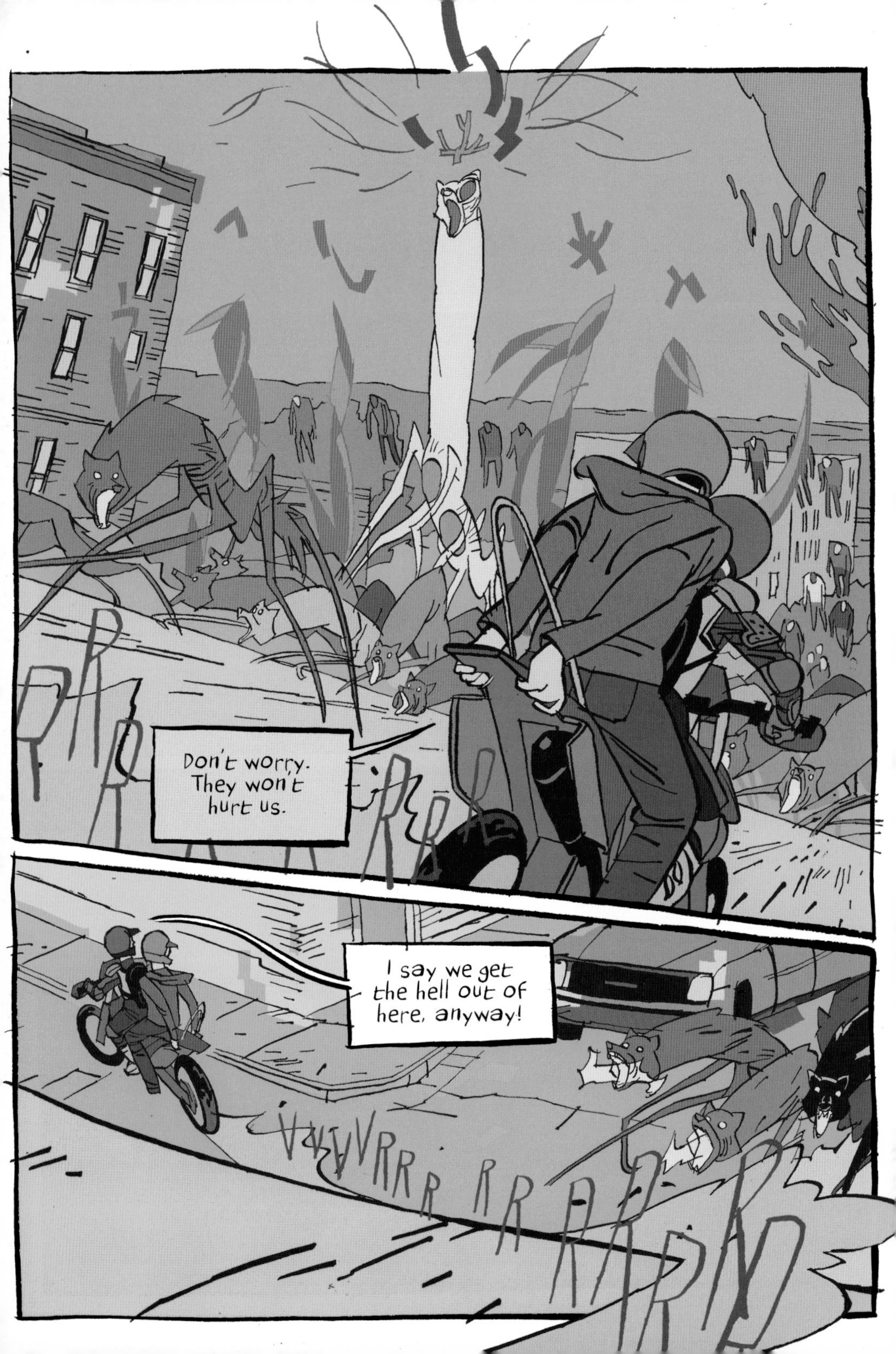
Don't worry. They won't hurt us.
I say we get the hell out of here, anyway!

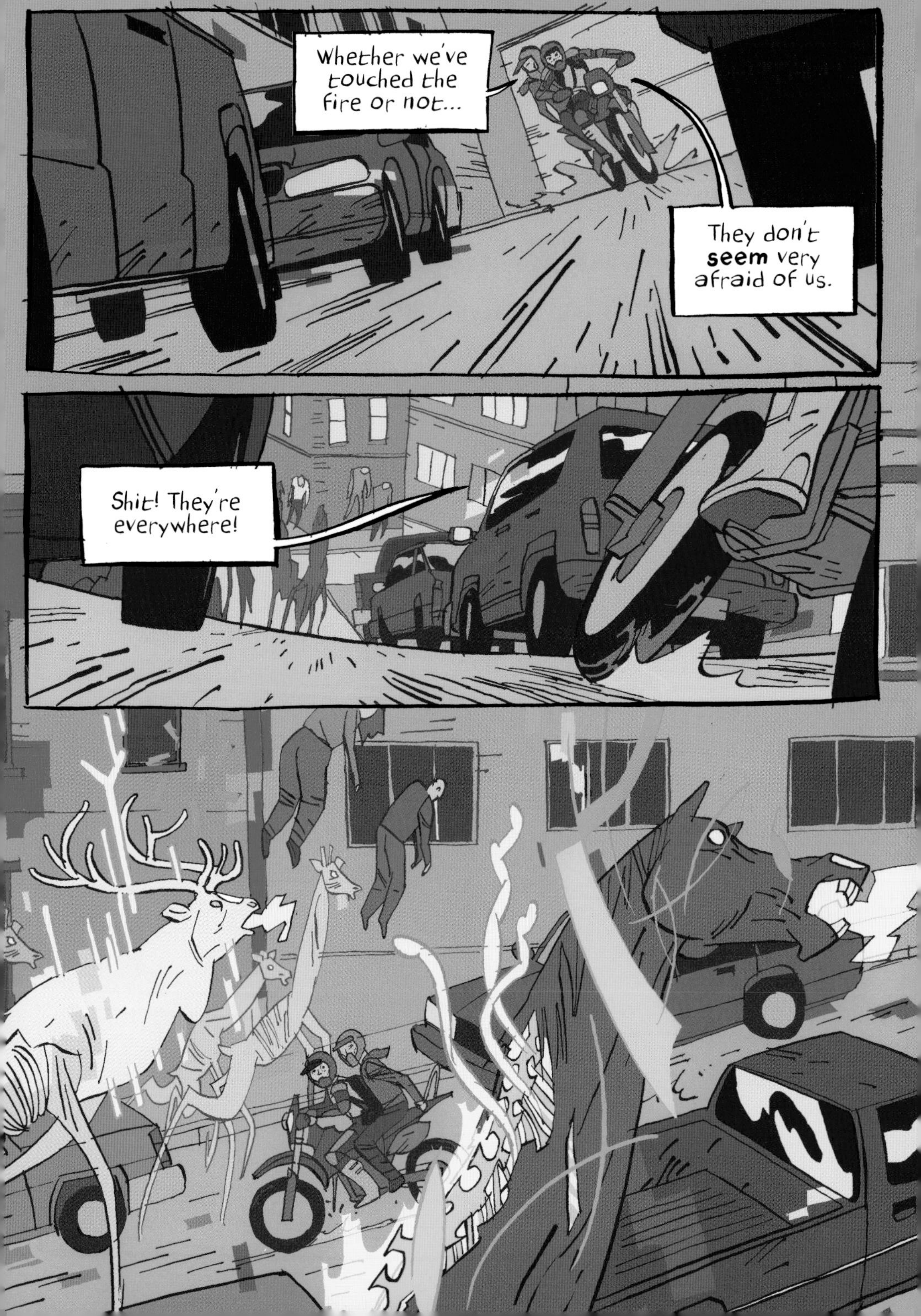
Whether we've touched the fire or not...
They don't **seem** very afraid of us.
Shit! They're everywhere!

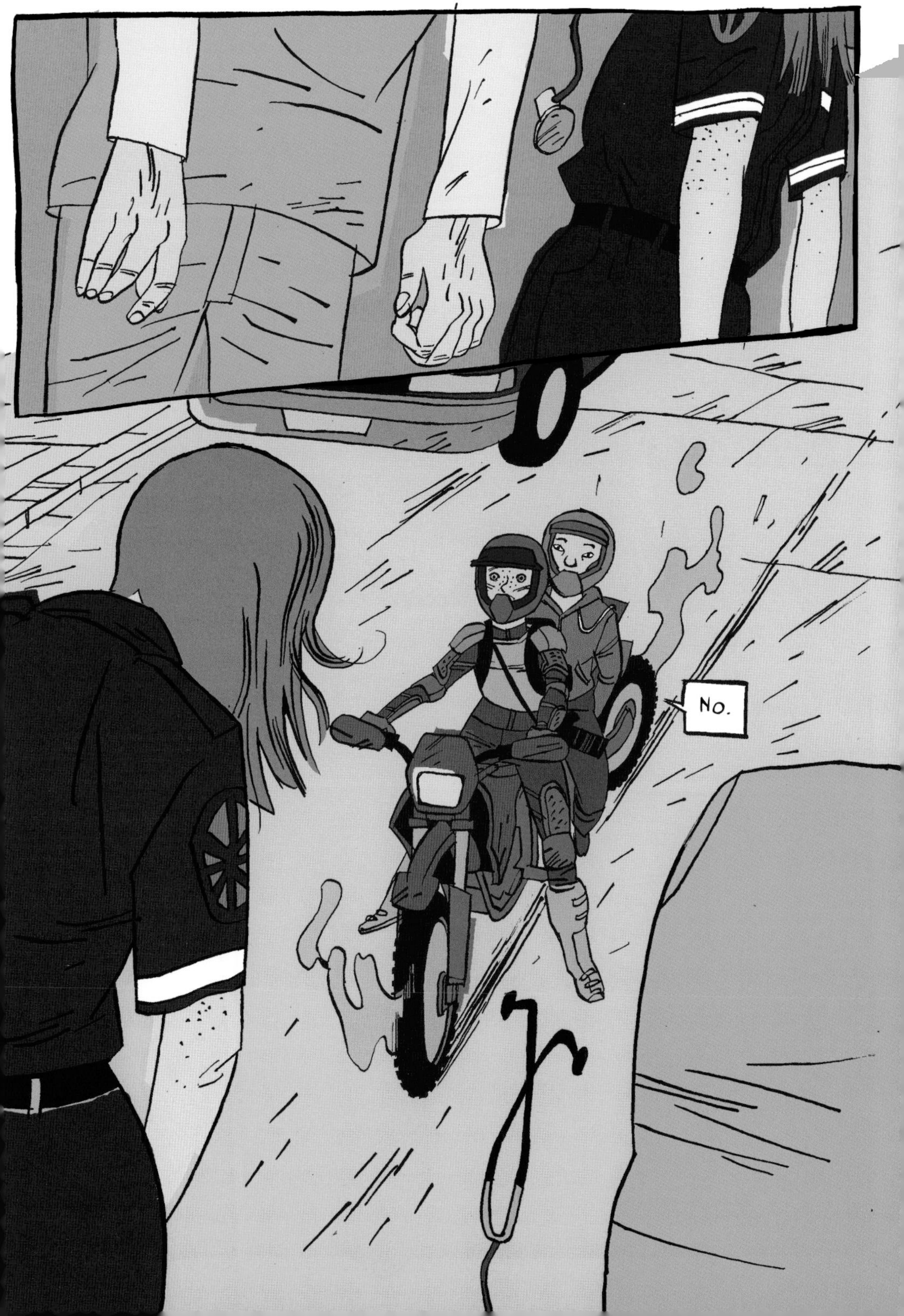
NO.

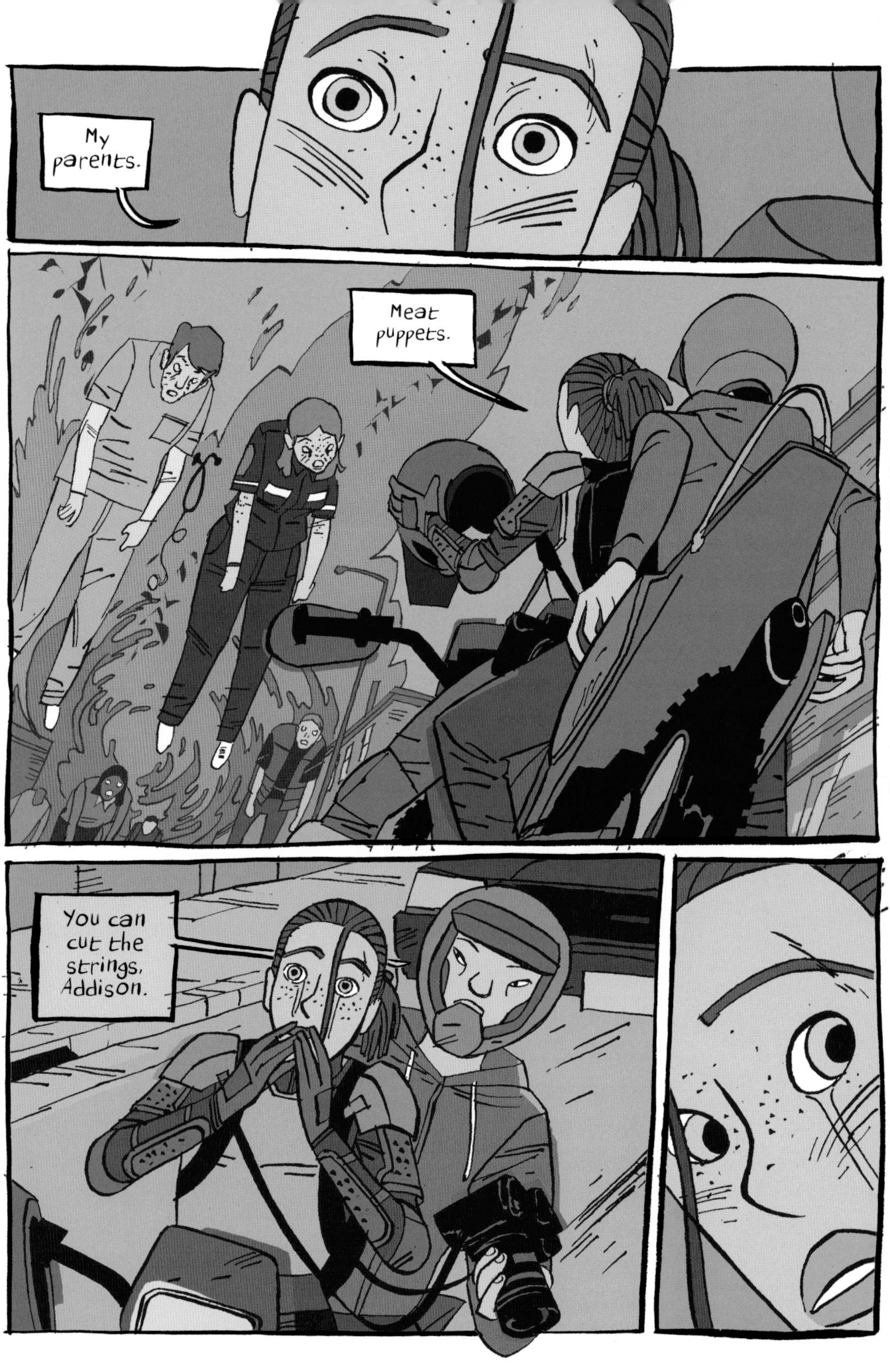
My parents.
Meat puppets.
You can cut the strings, Addison.

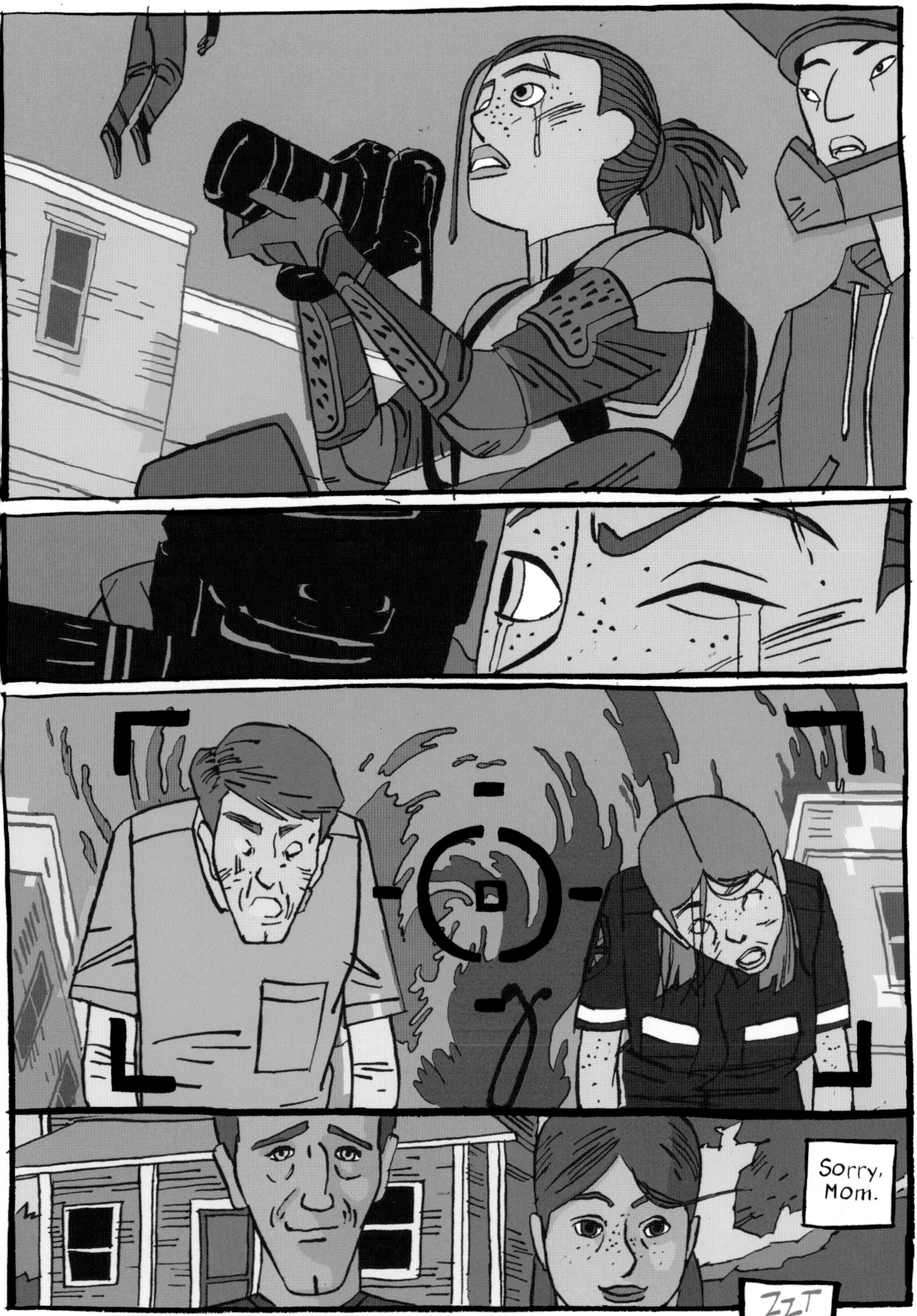
Sorry, Mom.
ZZT

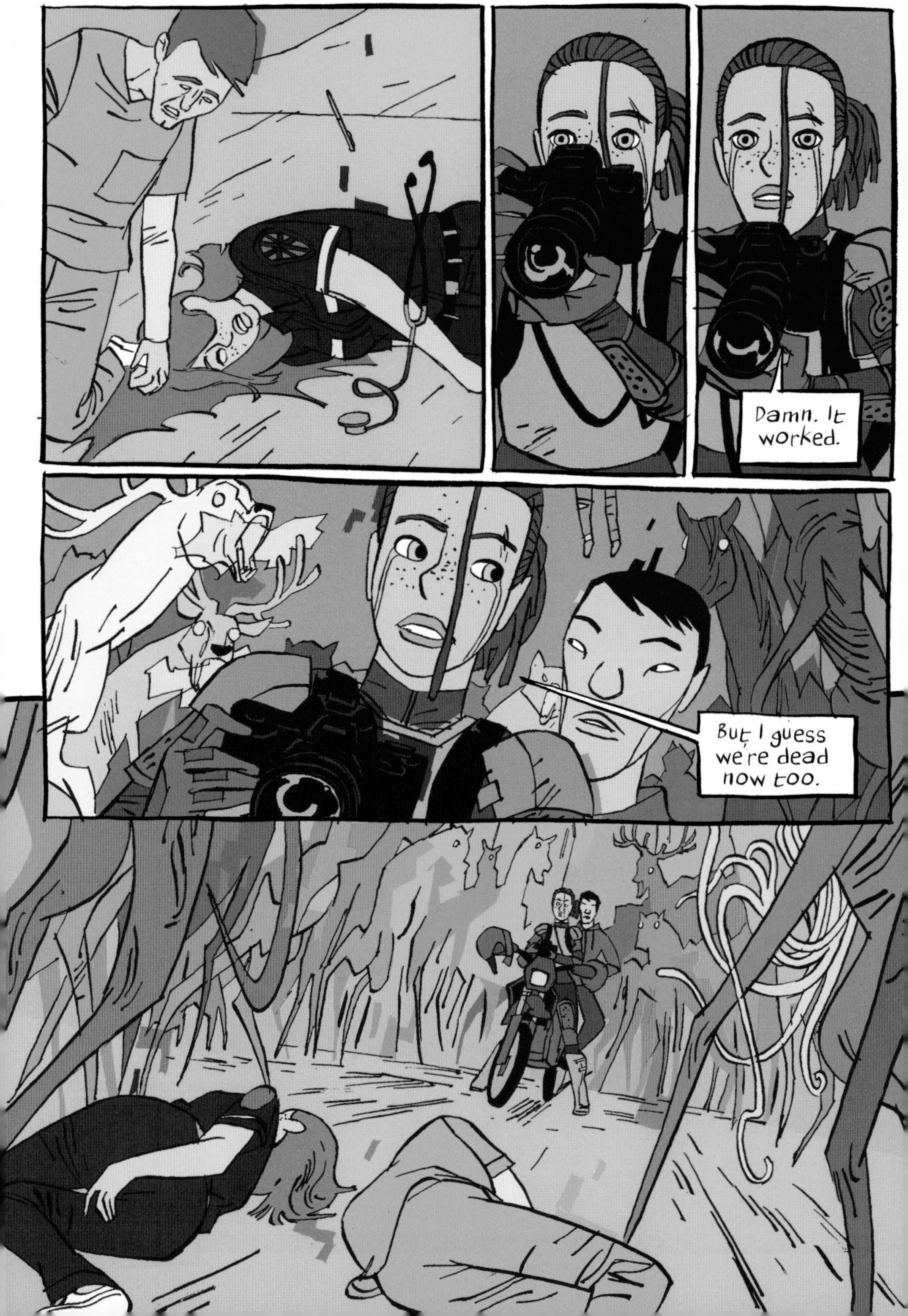

Damn. It worked.
But I guess we're dead now too.

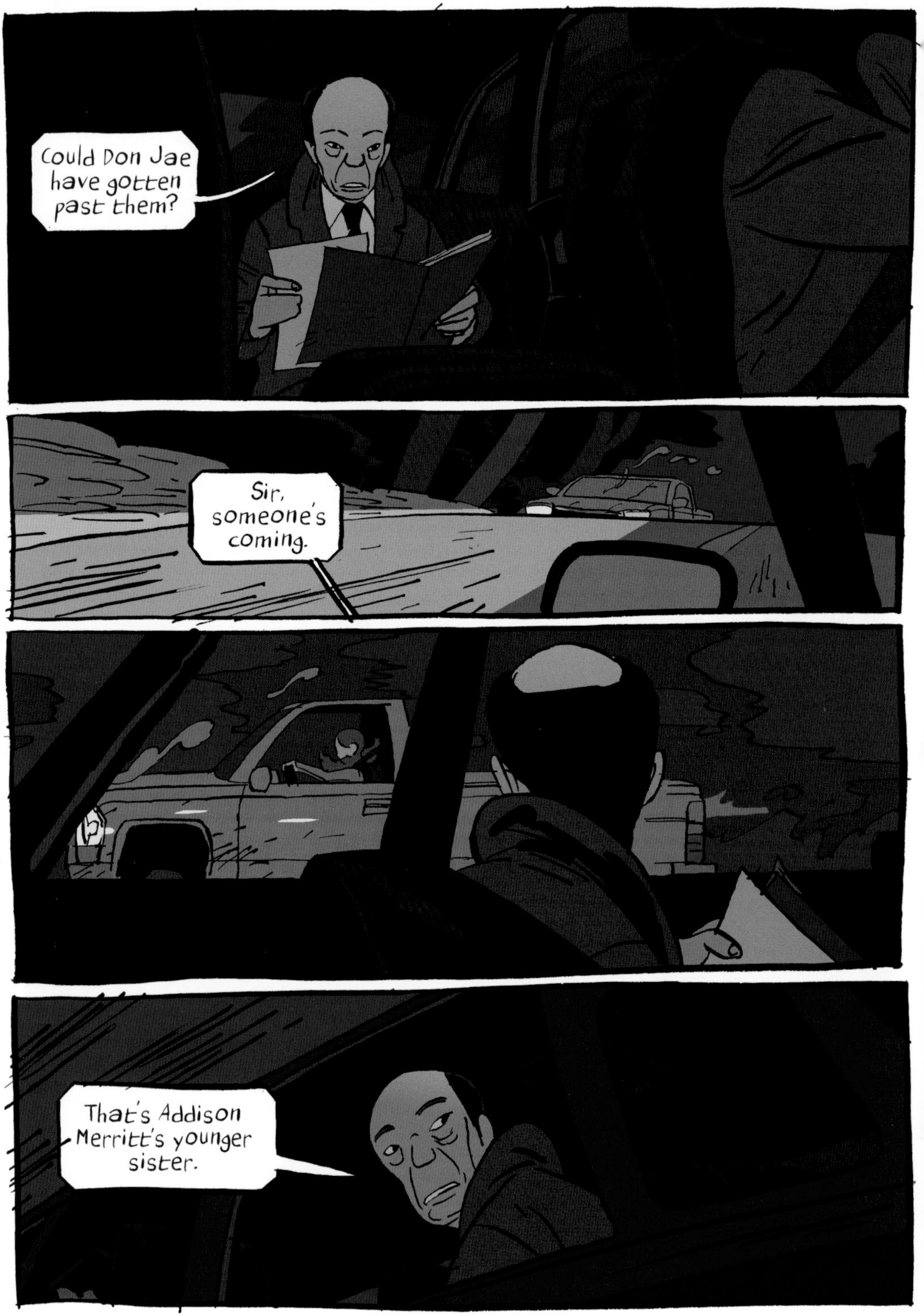

Could Don Jae have gotten past them?
Sir, someone's coming.
That's Addison Merritt's younger sister.

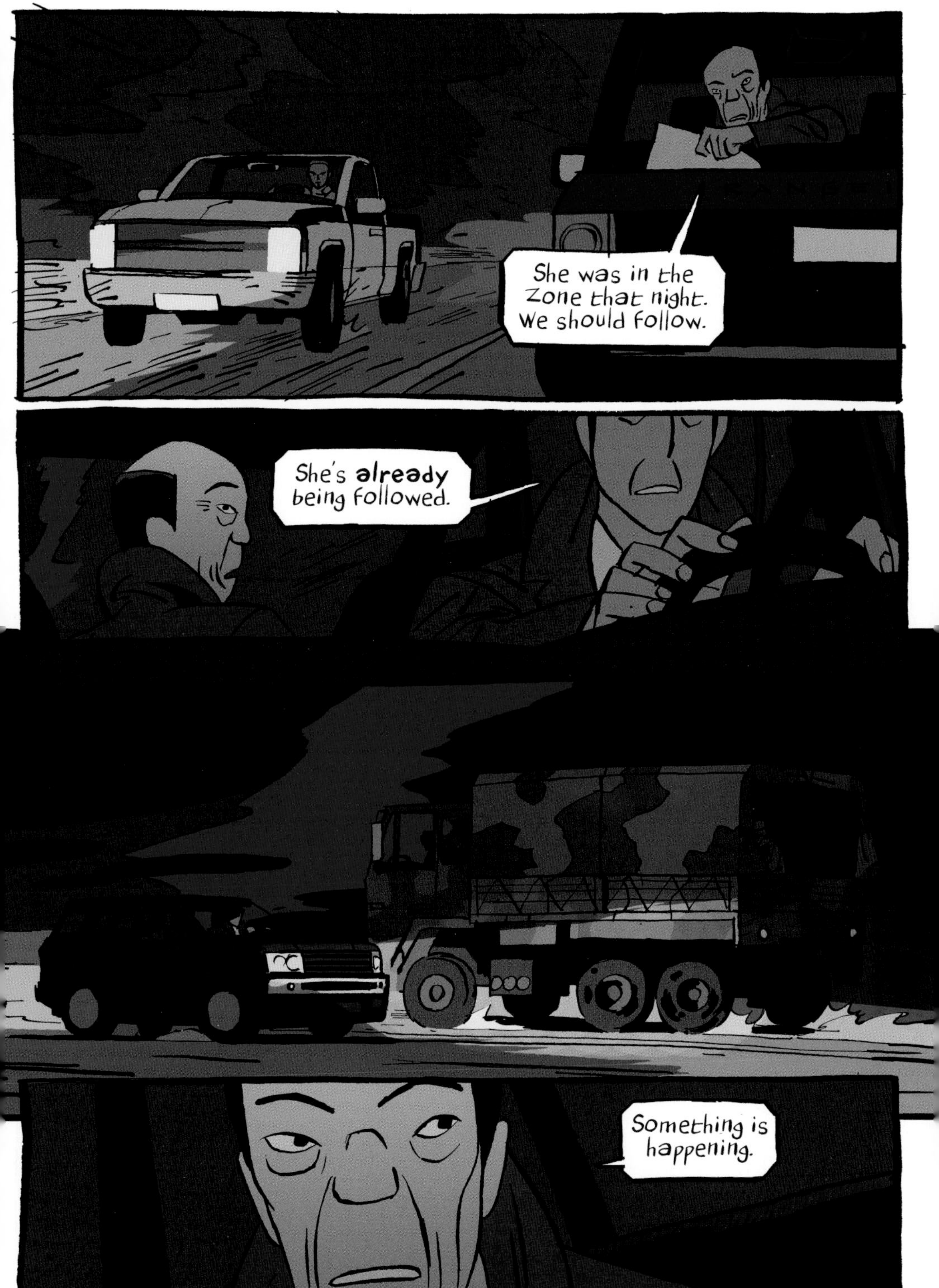
She was in the Zone that night. We should follow.
She's **already** being followed.
Something is happening.

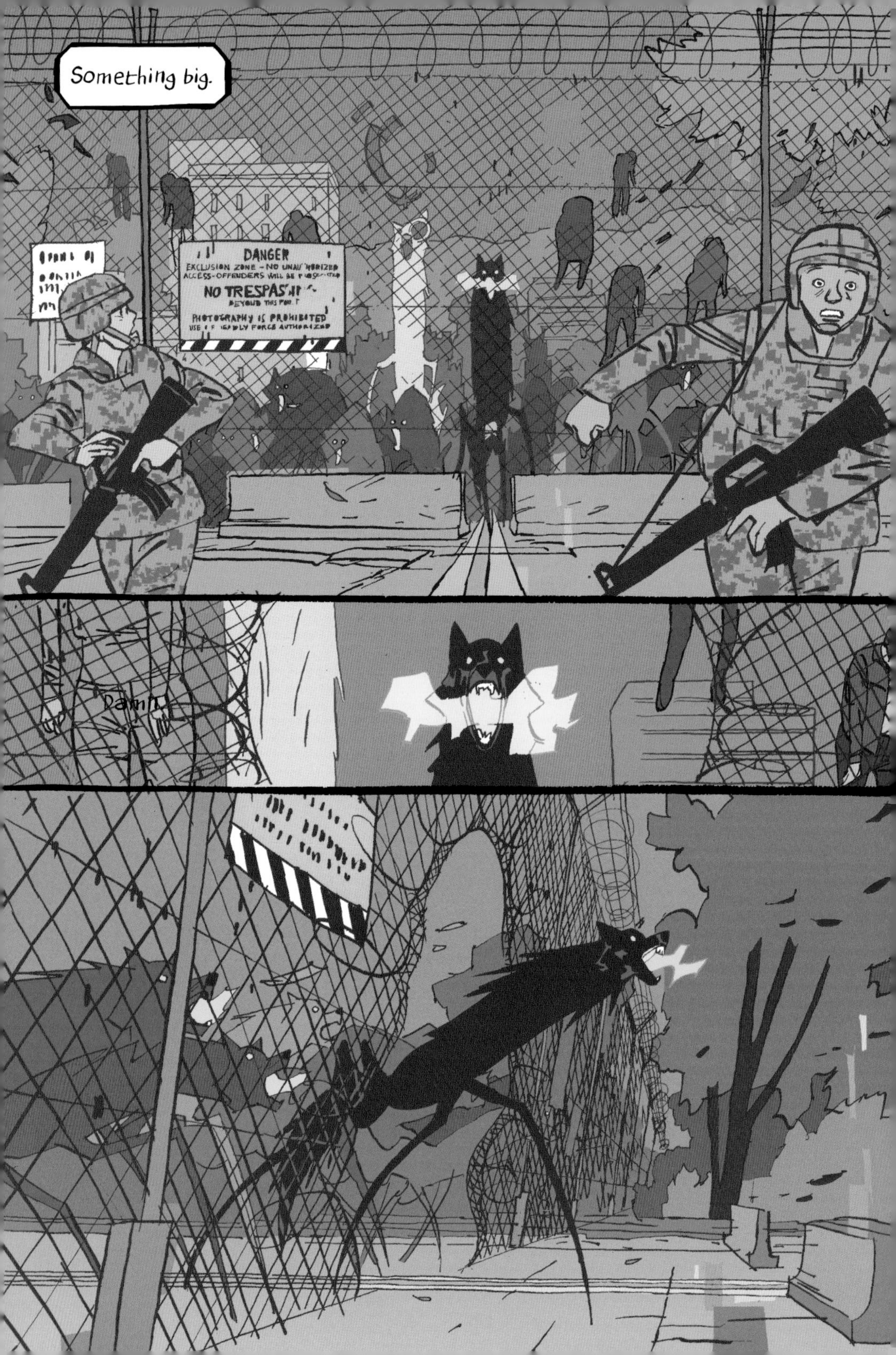
Something big.
DANGER
EXCLUSION ZONE - NO UNAU'HORIZED
ACCESS - OFFENDERS WILL BE
NO TRESPAS
PHOTOGRAPHY IS PROHIBITED
Damn.

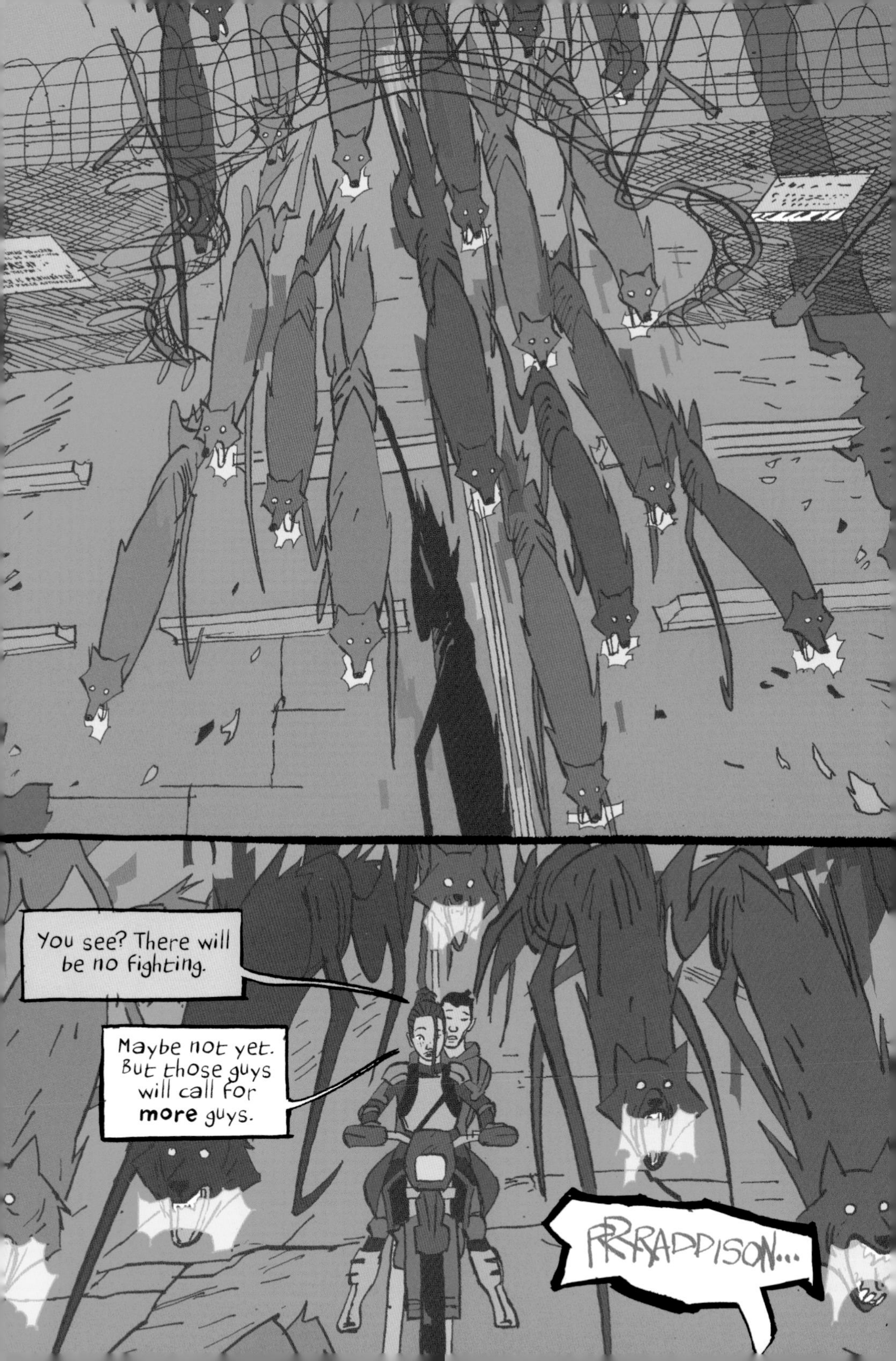
You see? There will be no fighting.
Maybe not yet. But those guys will call for **more** guys.
RRRRADDISON...

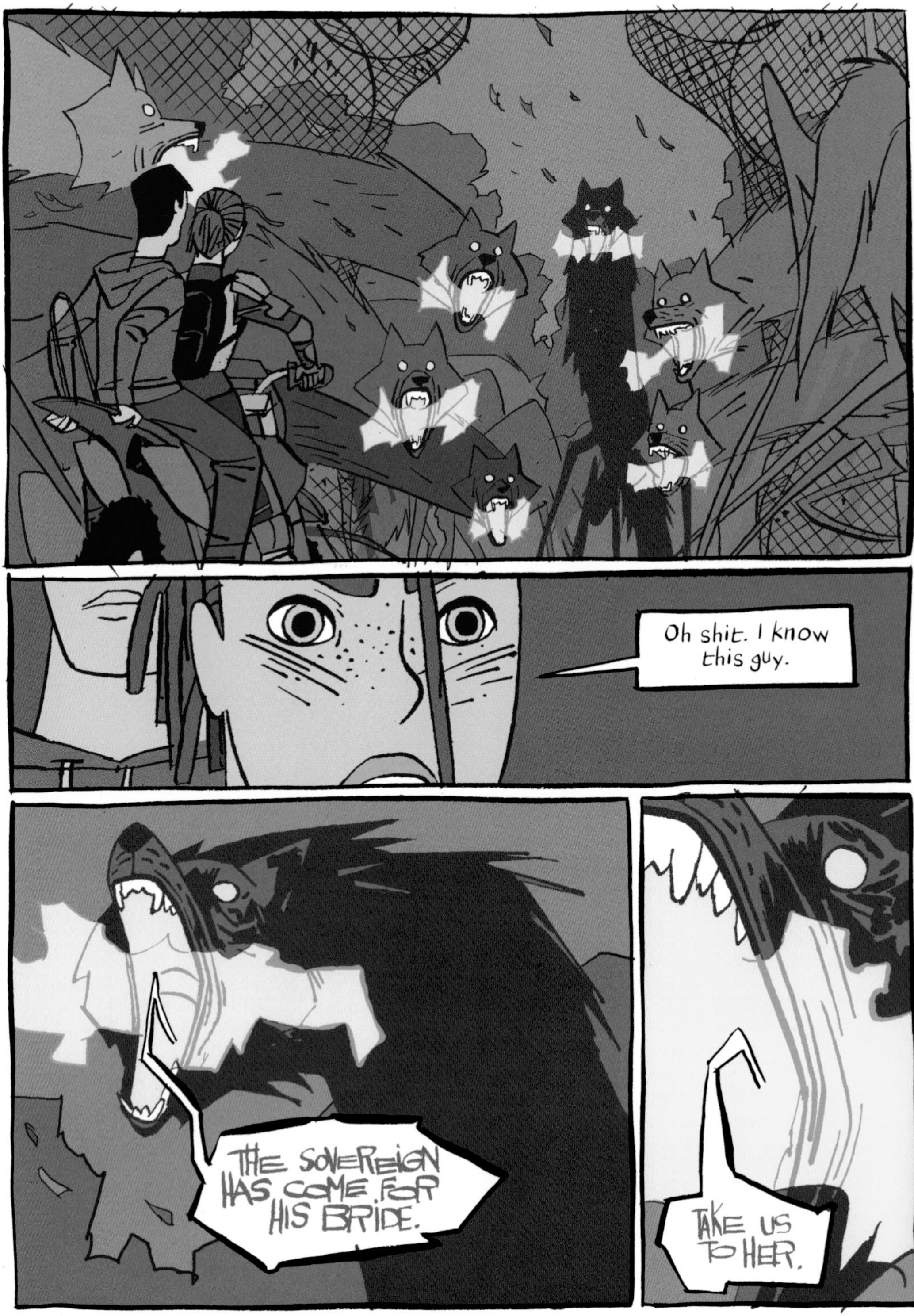
Oh shit. I know this guy.
THE SOVEREIGN HAS COME FOR HIS BRIDE.
TAKE US TO HER.

141

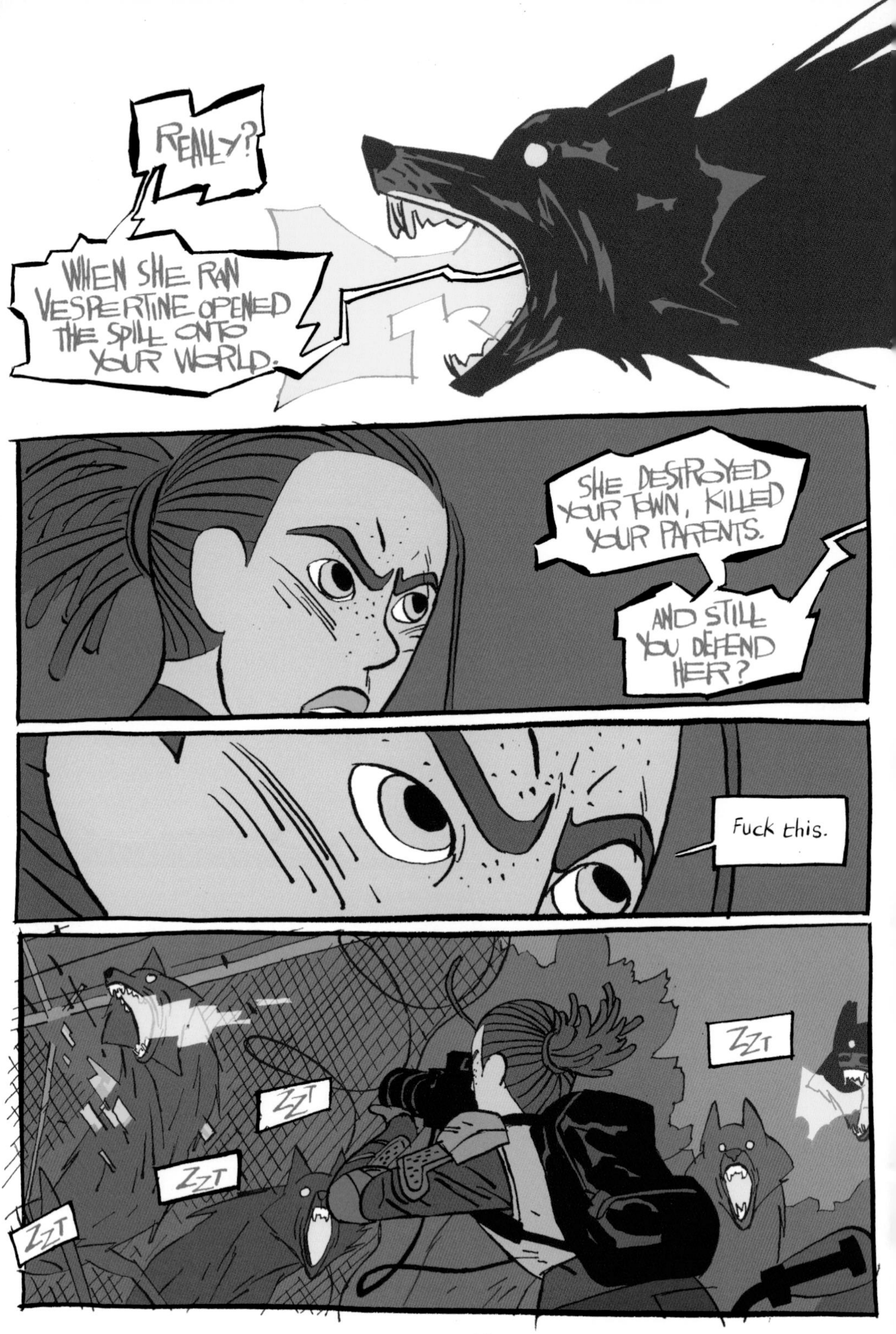
REALLY?
WHEN SHE RAN VESPERTINE OPENED THE SPILL ONTO YOUR WORLD.
SHE DESTROYED YOUR TOWN, KILLED YOUR PARENTS.
AND STILL YOU DEFEND HER?
Fuck this.
ZZT
ZZT
ZZT
ZZT

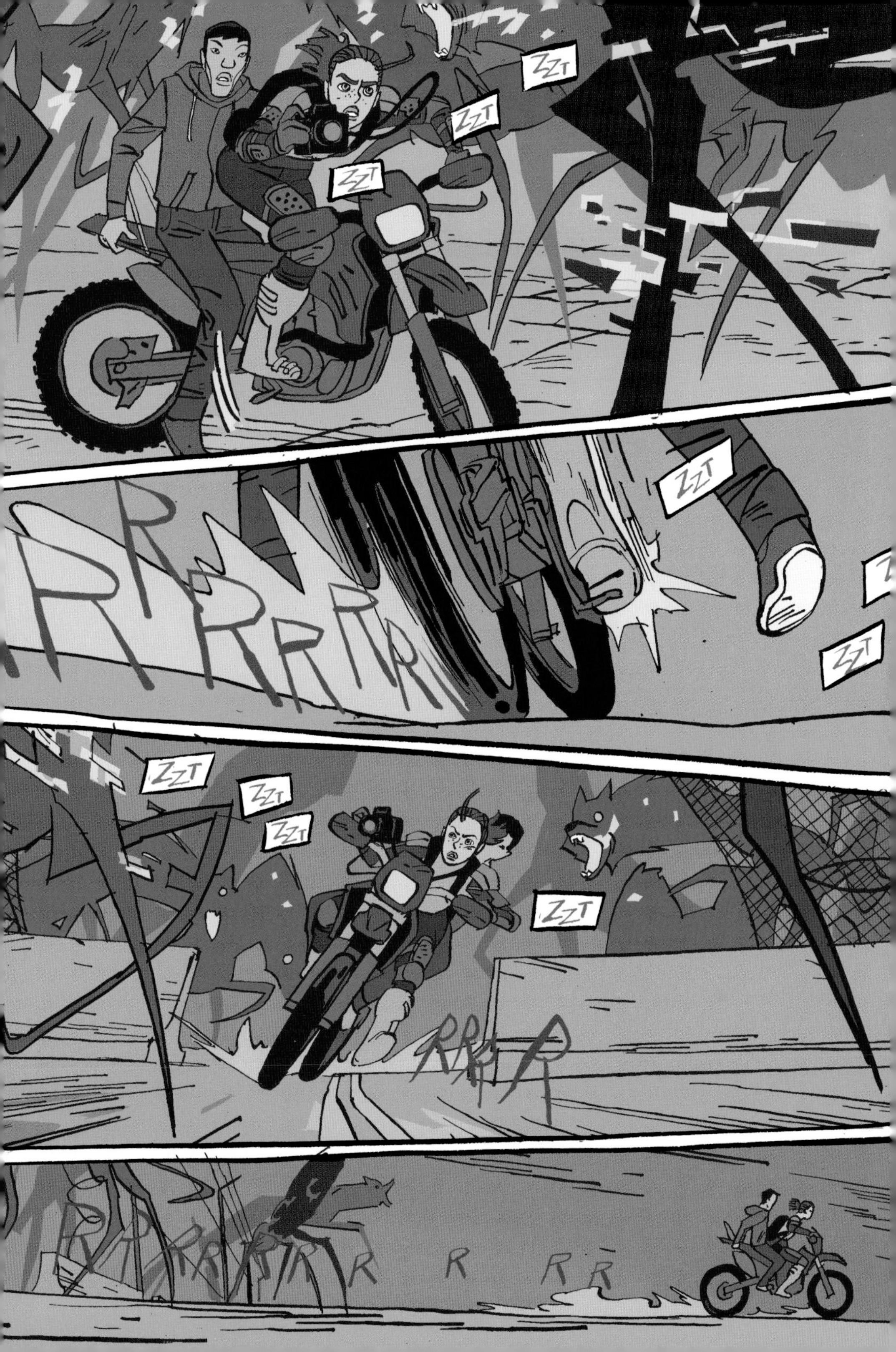

ZZT
ZZT
ZZT
RRRRRRRR
ZZT
ZZT
ZZT
ZZT
ZZT
ZZT
RRRR
RRRRRRRR R R R R

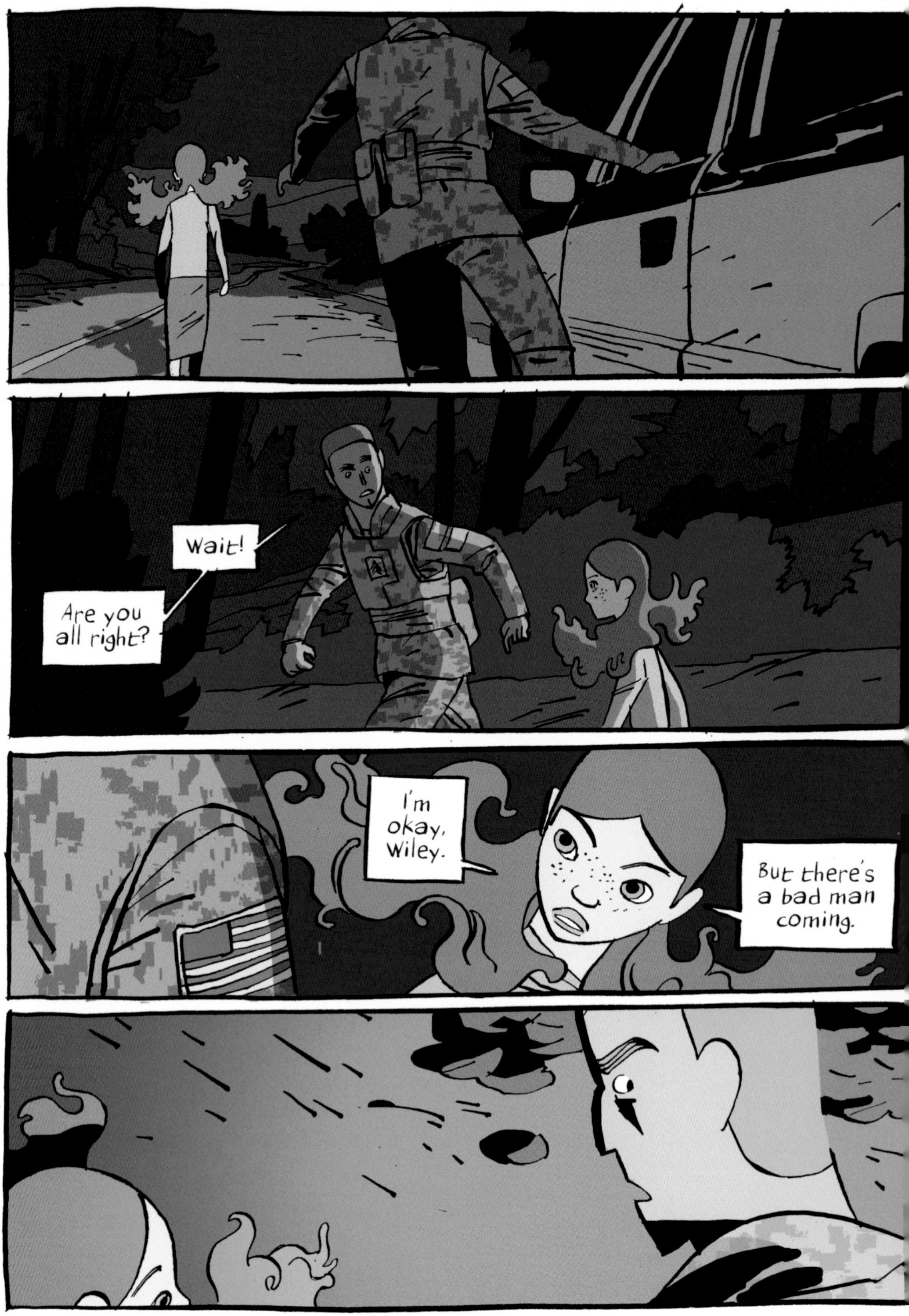
Wait!
Are you all right?
I'm okay, Wiley.
But there's a bad man coming.

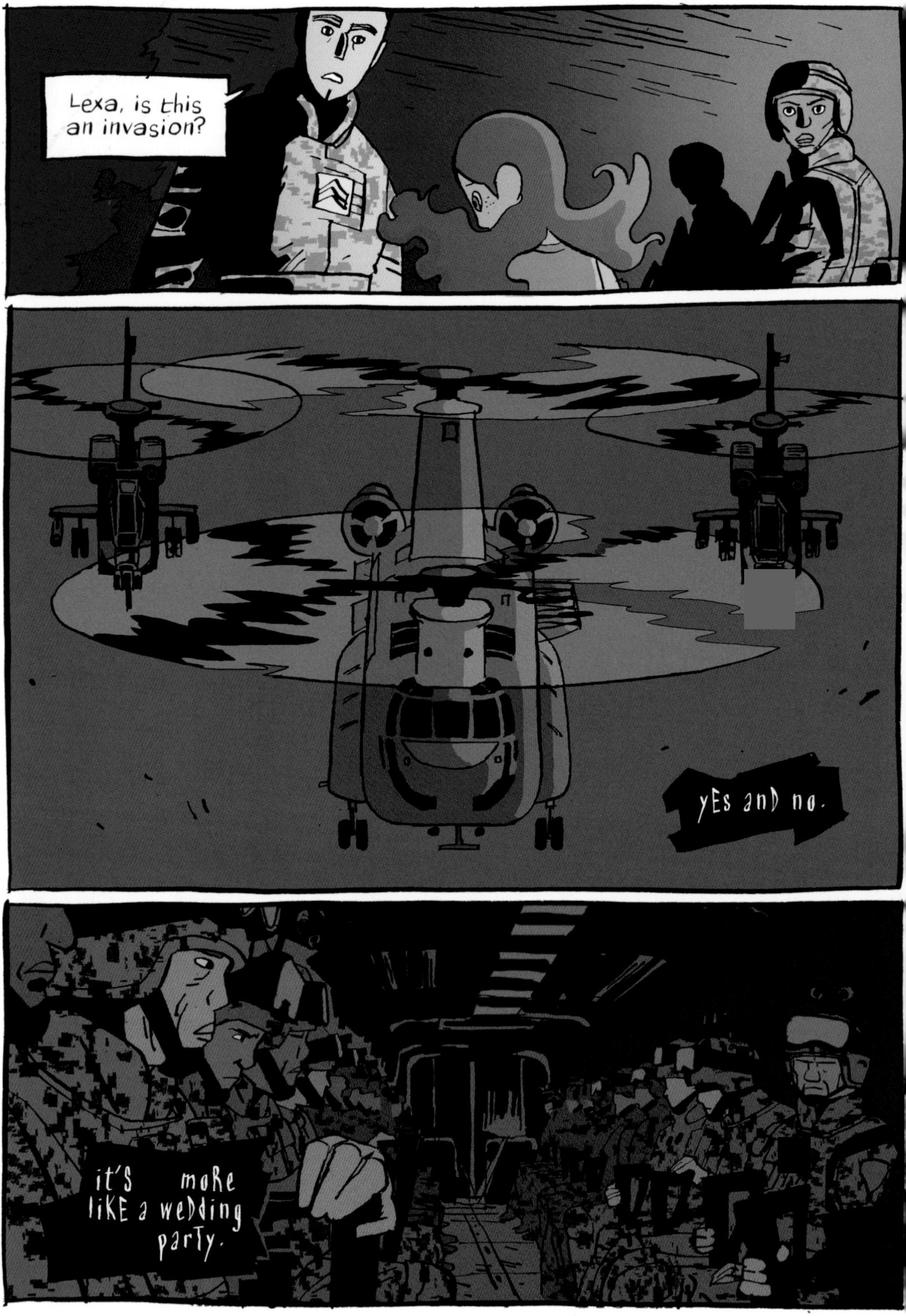
Lexa, is this an invasion?
yEs anD no.
it'S more liKE a weDDing party.

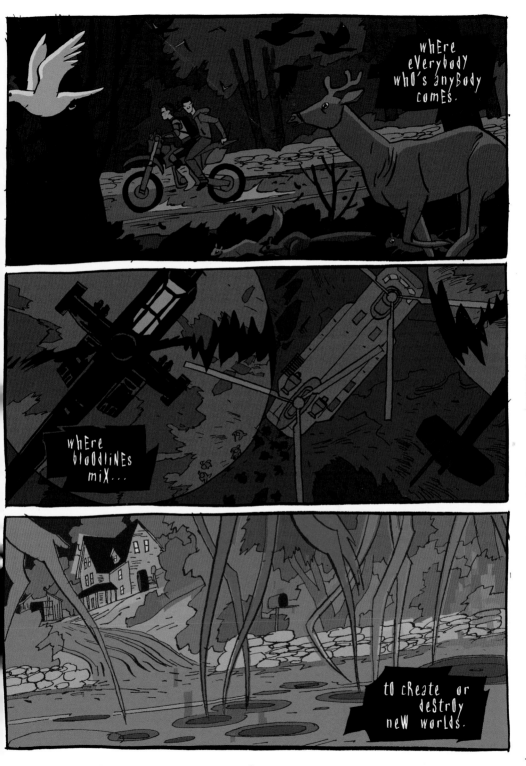

wHEre
eVerybody
whO's anyBody
comEs.

whEre
blOOdliNEs
miX...

tO cReate or
deStrOy
neW worlds.

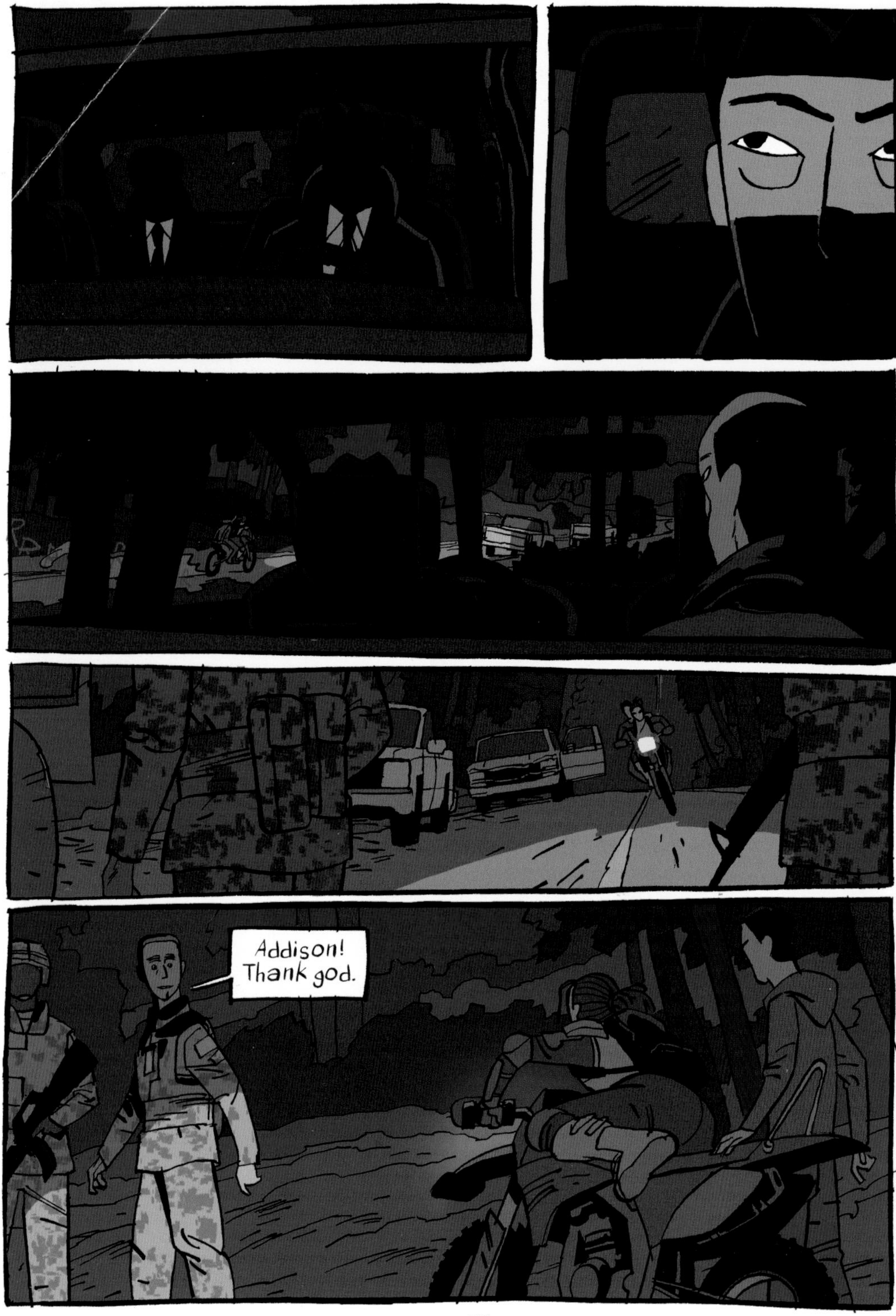
Addison! Thank god.

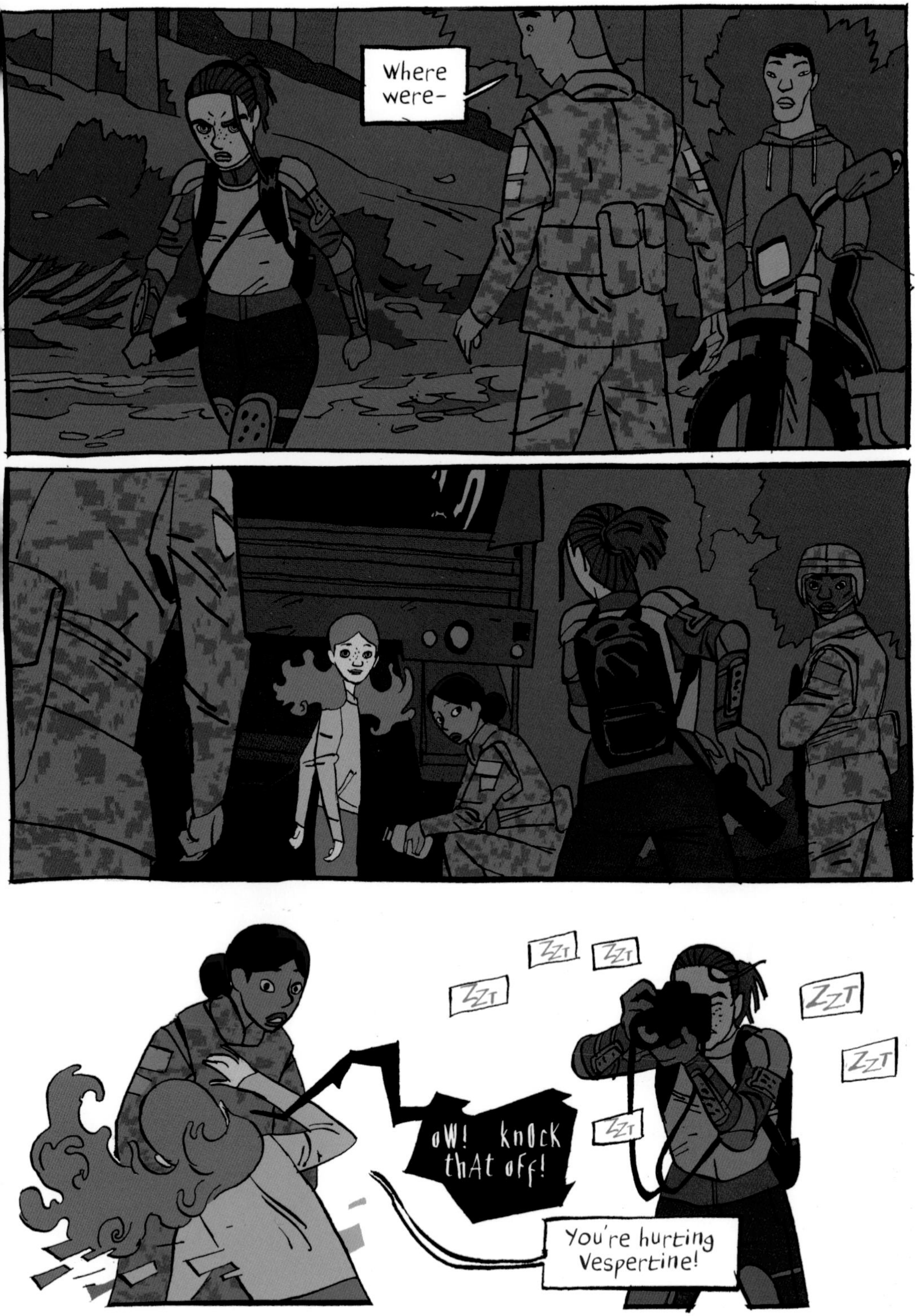
Where were-
ZZT
ZZT
ZZT
ZZT
ZZT
ZZT
OW! KNOCK THAT OFF!
You're hurting Vespertine!

152

154

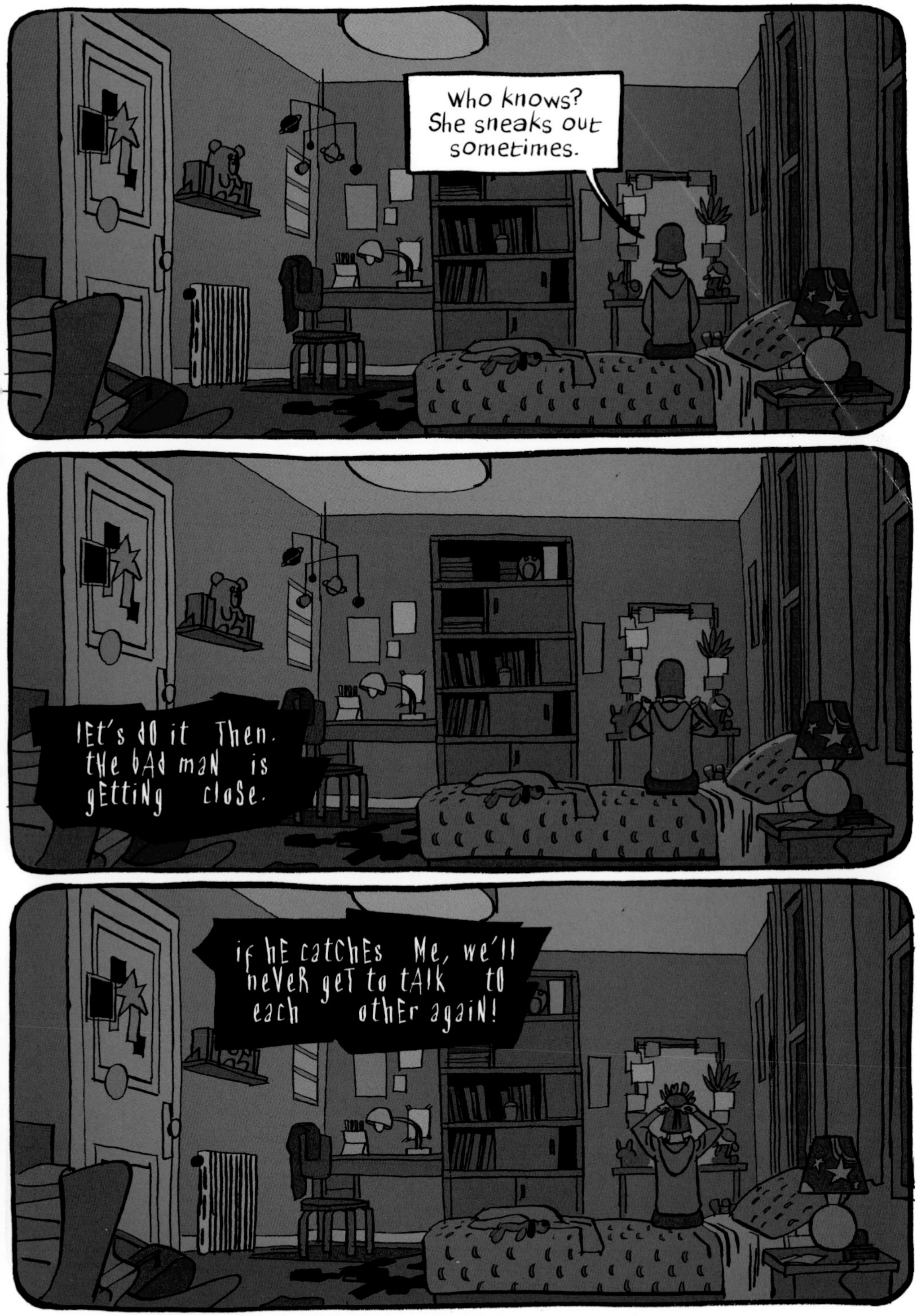

Who knows? She sneaks out sometimes.
lEt's dO it Then. tHe bAd maN is gEtting close.
if hE catcHes Me, we'll neVeR get to tAlk to each otHEr agaiN!

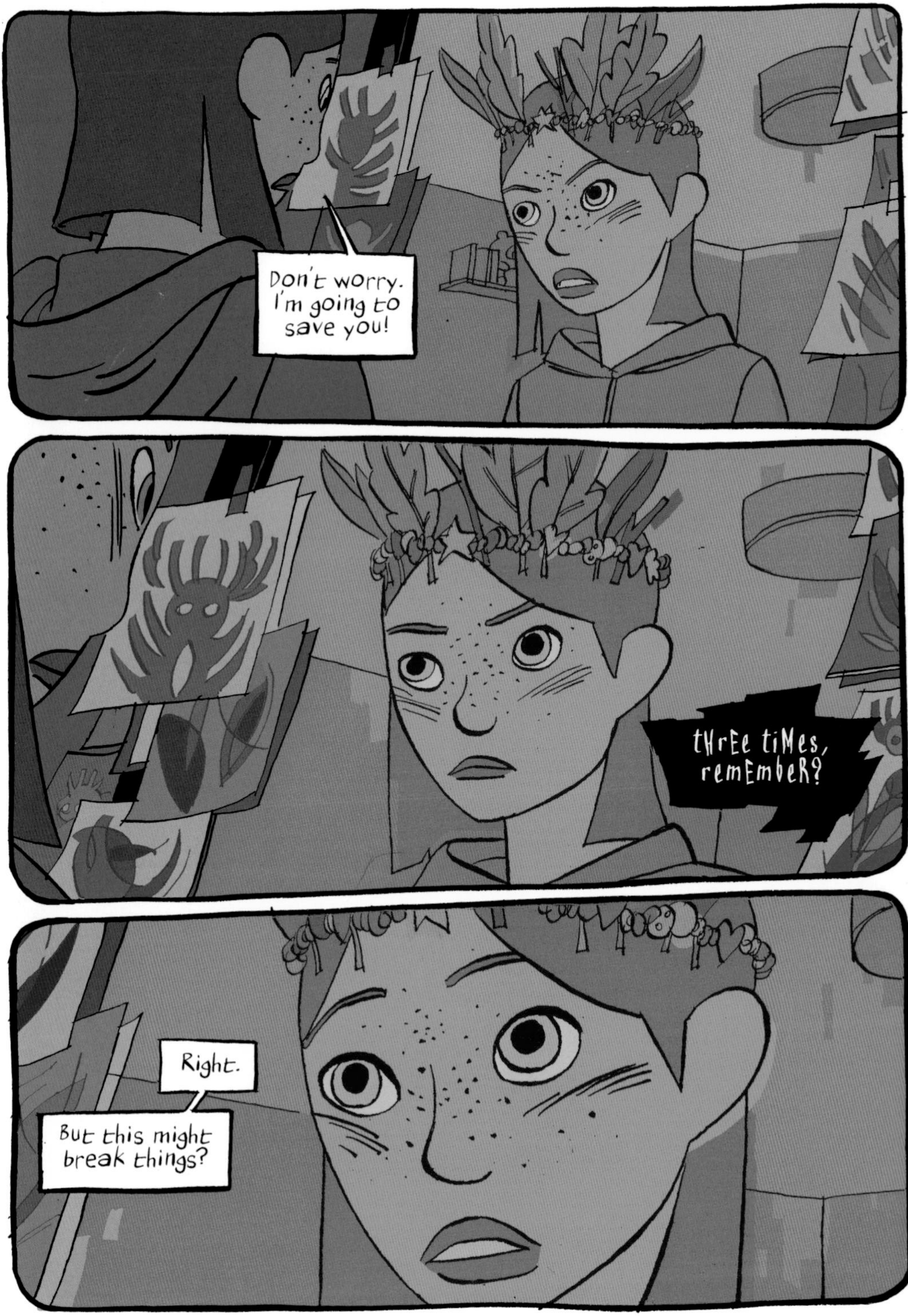
Don't worry. I'm going to save you!
tHrEe tiMes, remEmbeR?
Right.
But this might break things?

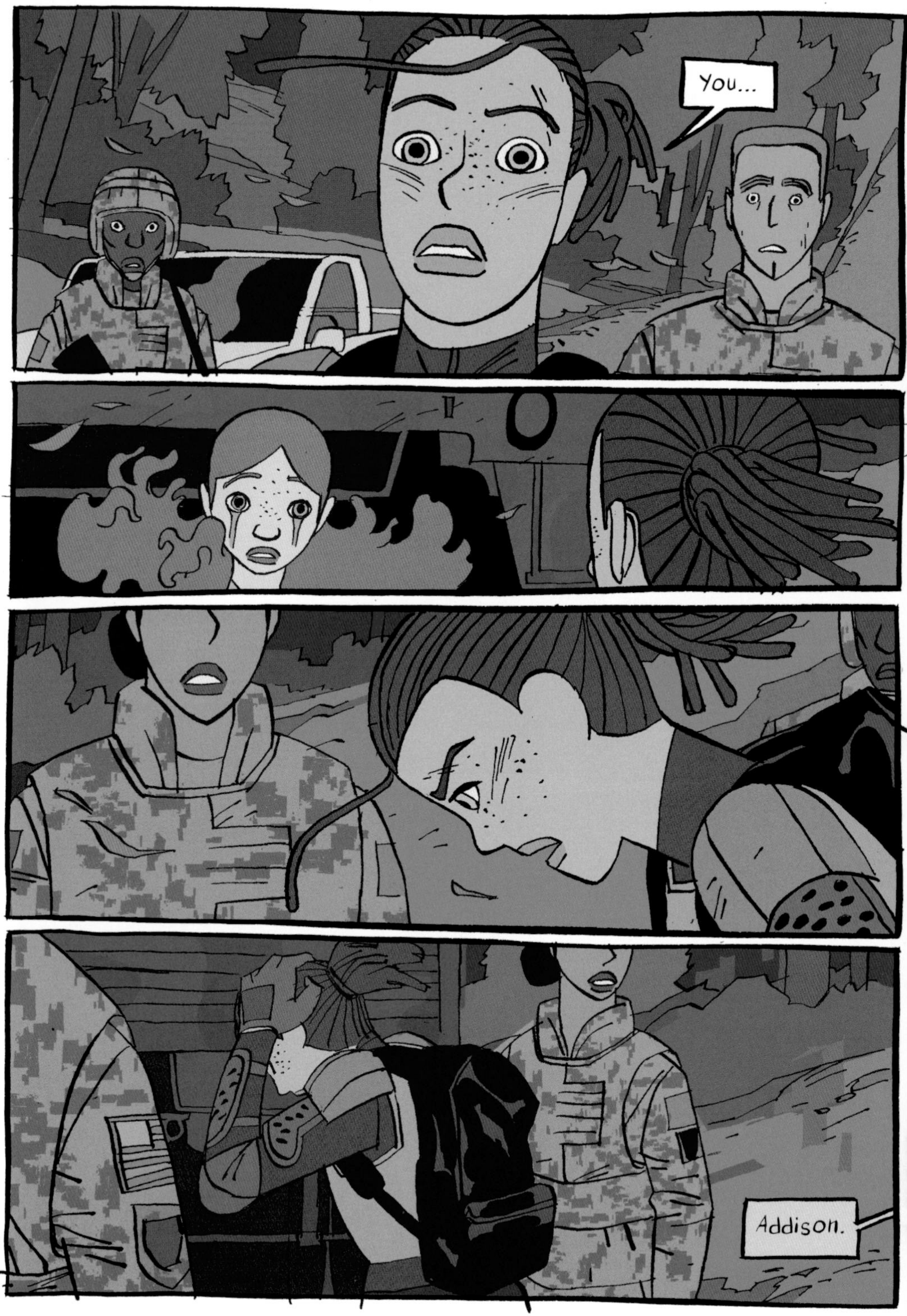
You...
Addison.

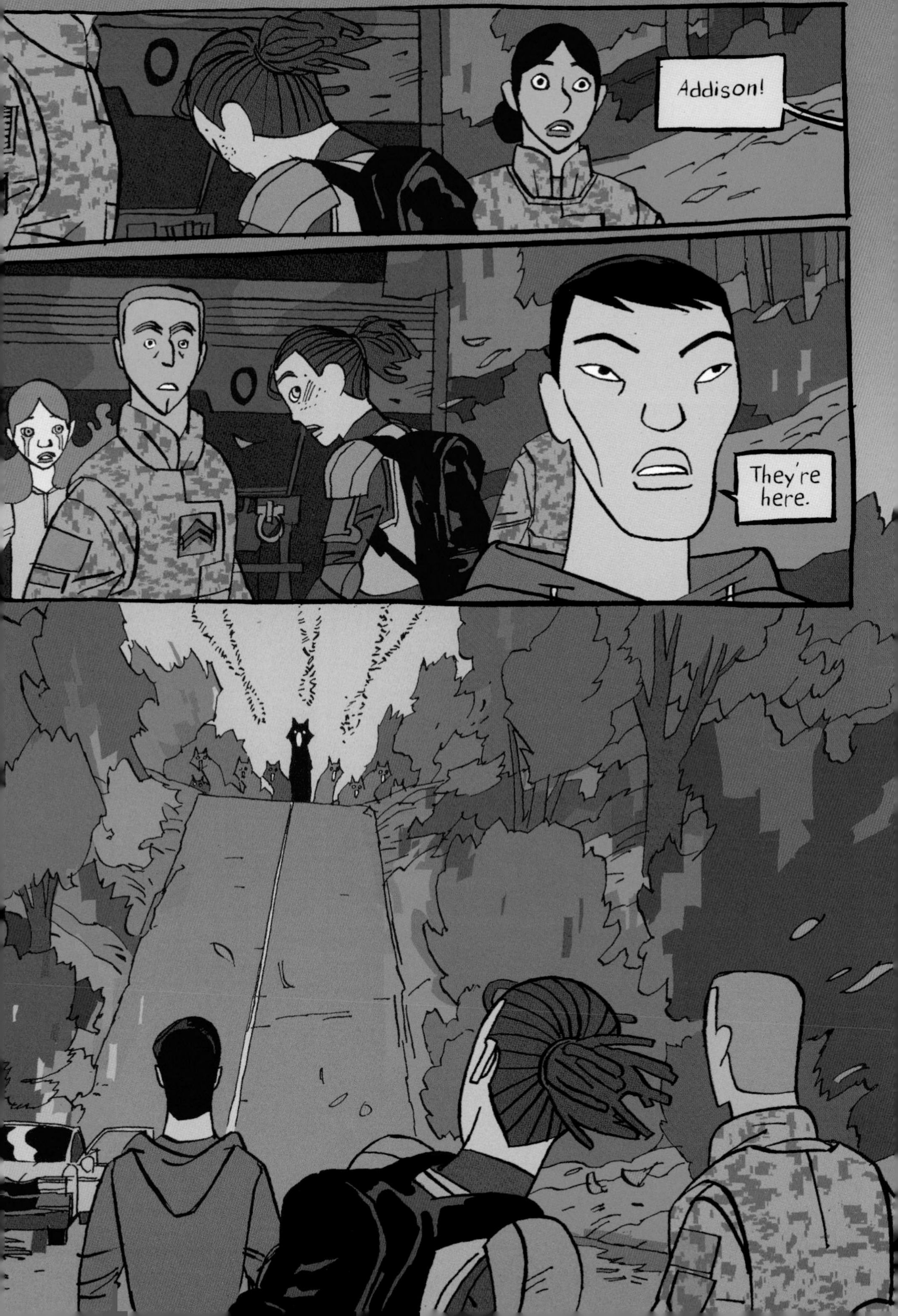
Addison!
They're here.

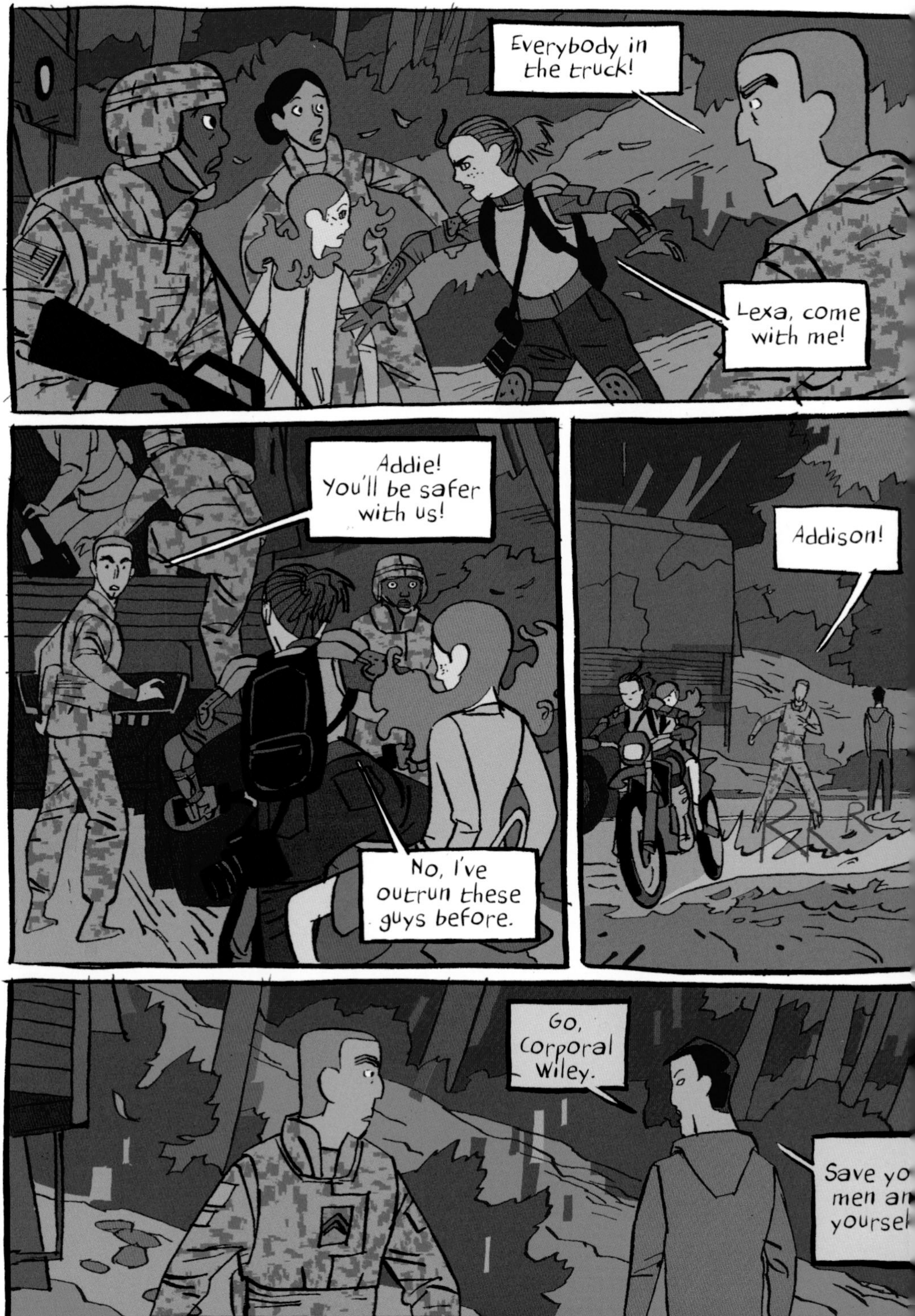

Everybody in the truck!
Lexa, come with me!
Addie! You'll be safer with us!
No, I've outrun these guys before.
Addison!
RRRR
Go, Corporal Wiley.

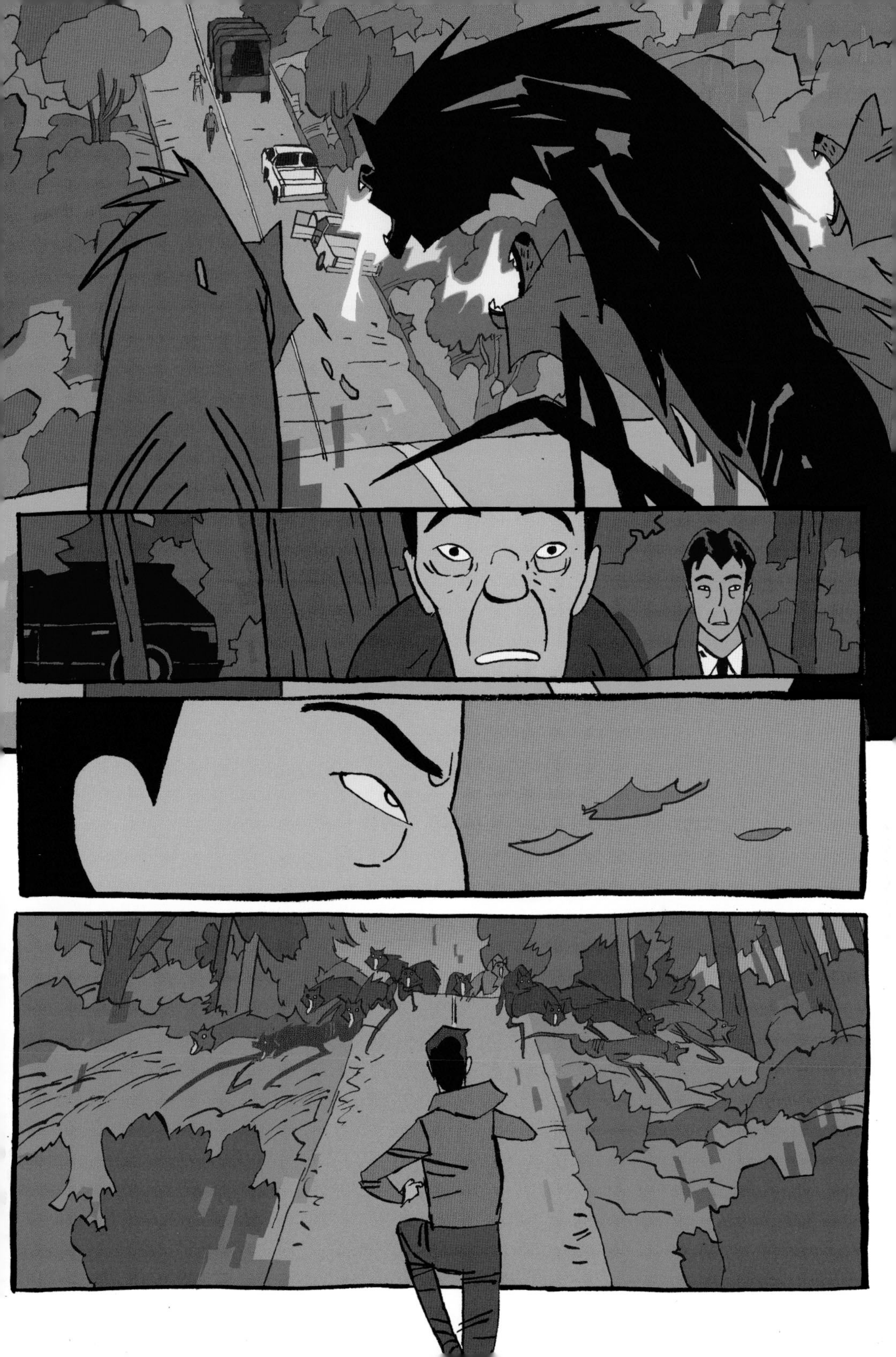

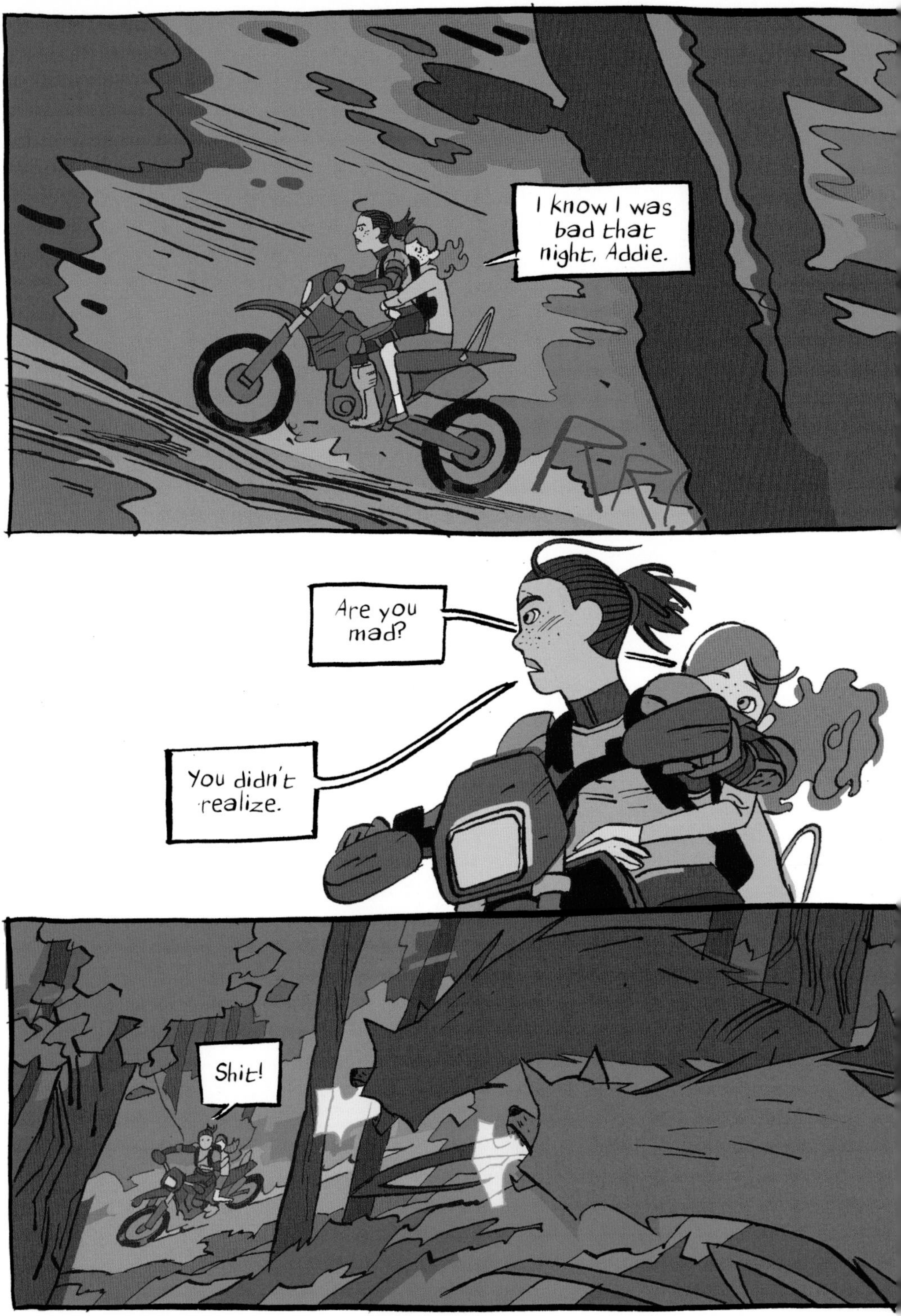
I know I was bad that night, Addie.
Are you mad?
You didn't realize.
Shit!

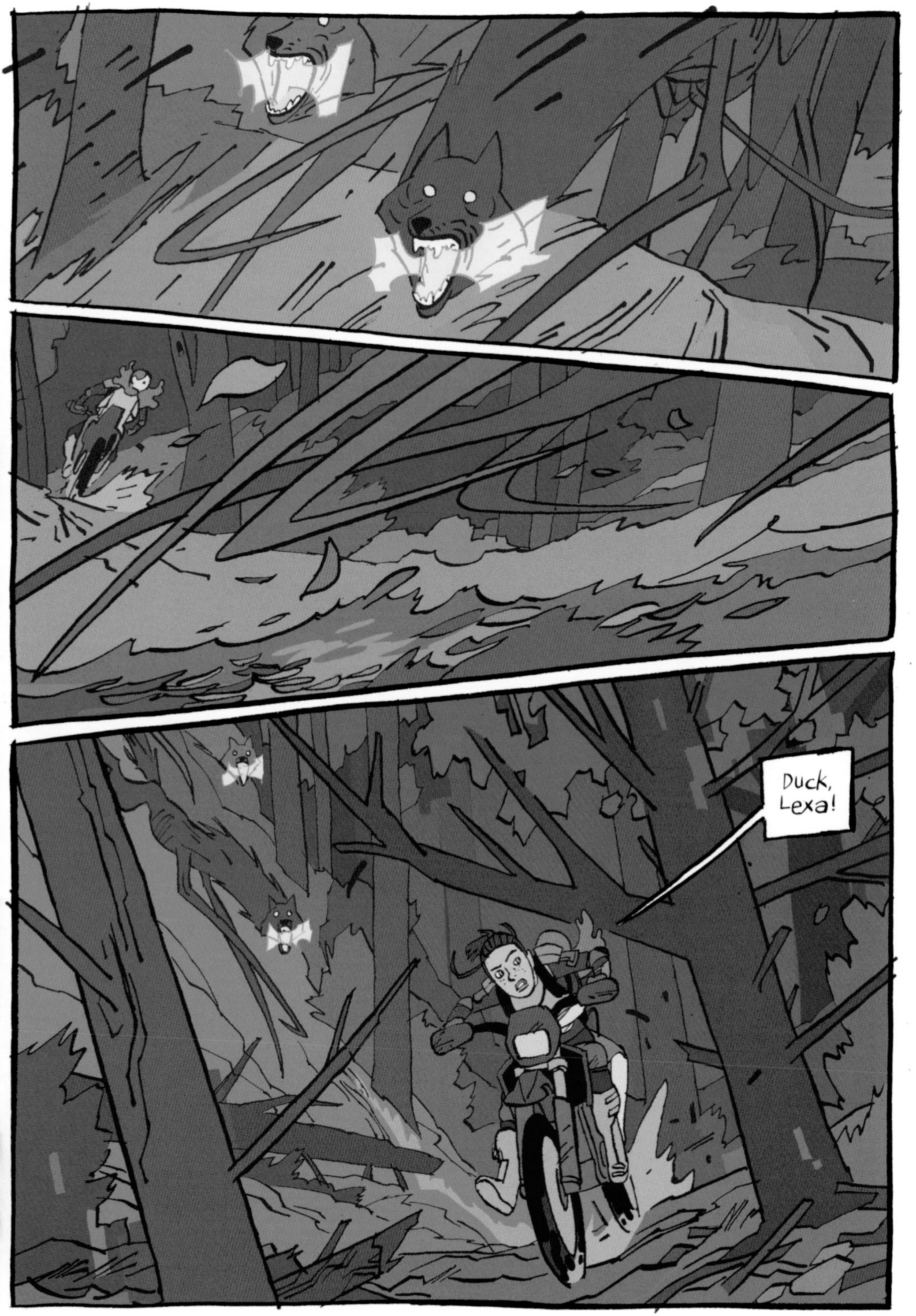
Duck, Lexa!

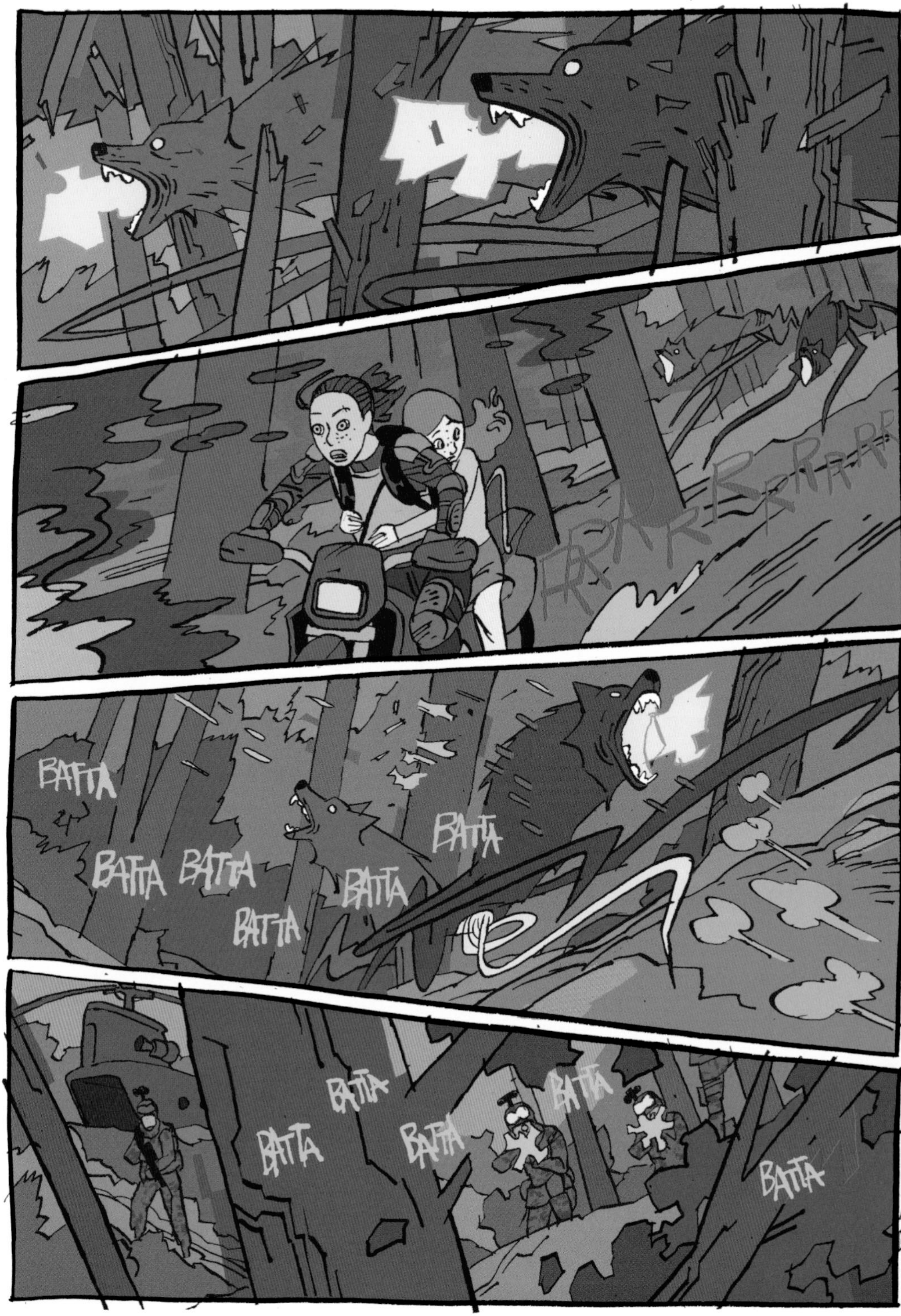
RRRARRRRRRRRRR
BATTA
BATTA
BATTA
BATTA
BATTA
BATTA
BATTA
BATTA
BATTA
BATTA
BATTA

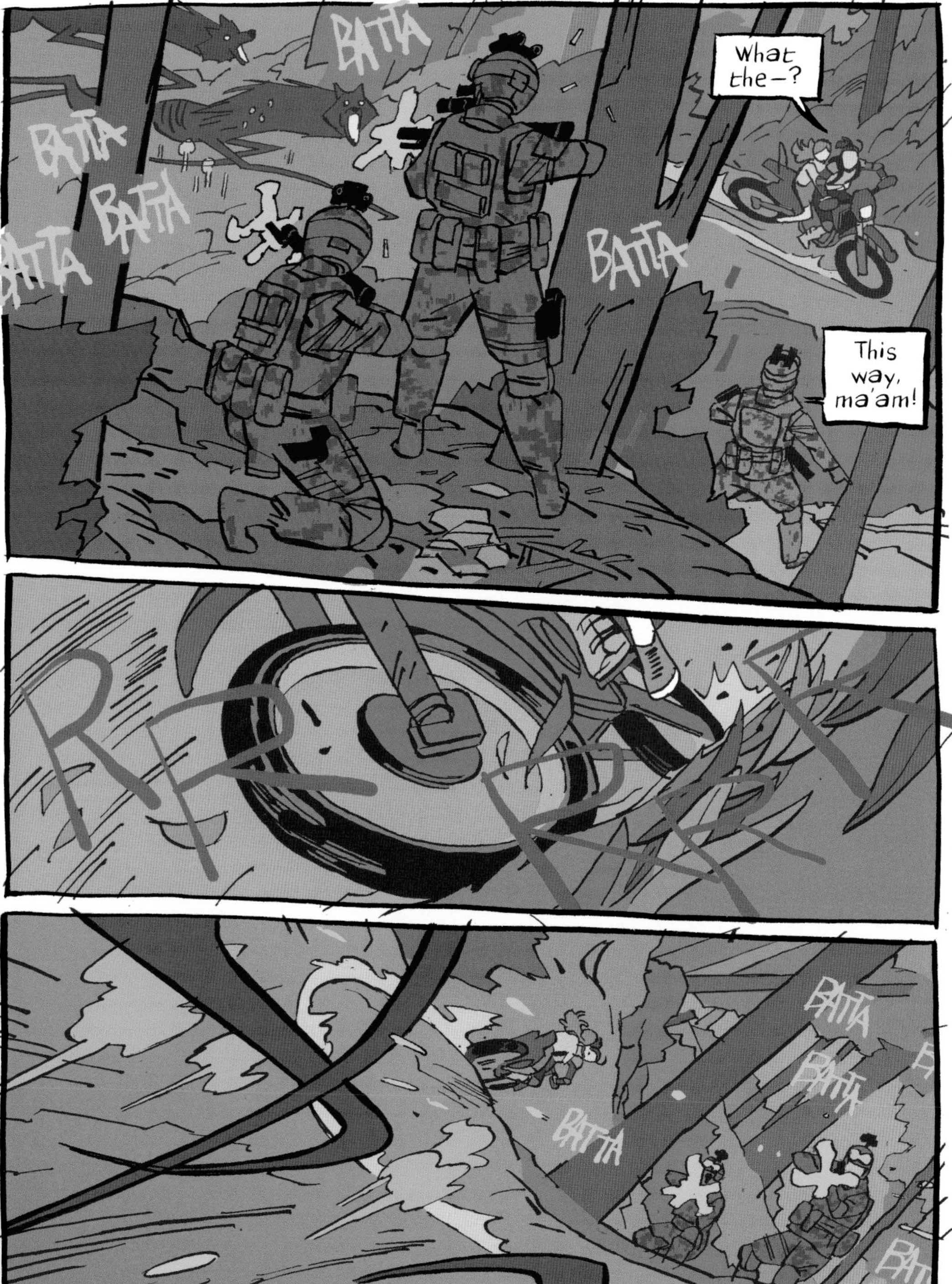
BATTA
BATTA
BATTA
BATTA
BATTA
What the–?
This way, ma'am!
BATTA
BATTA
BATTA
BATTA

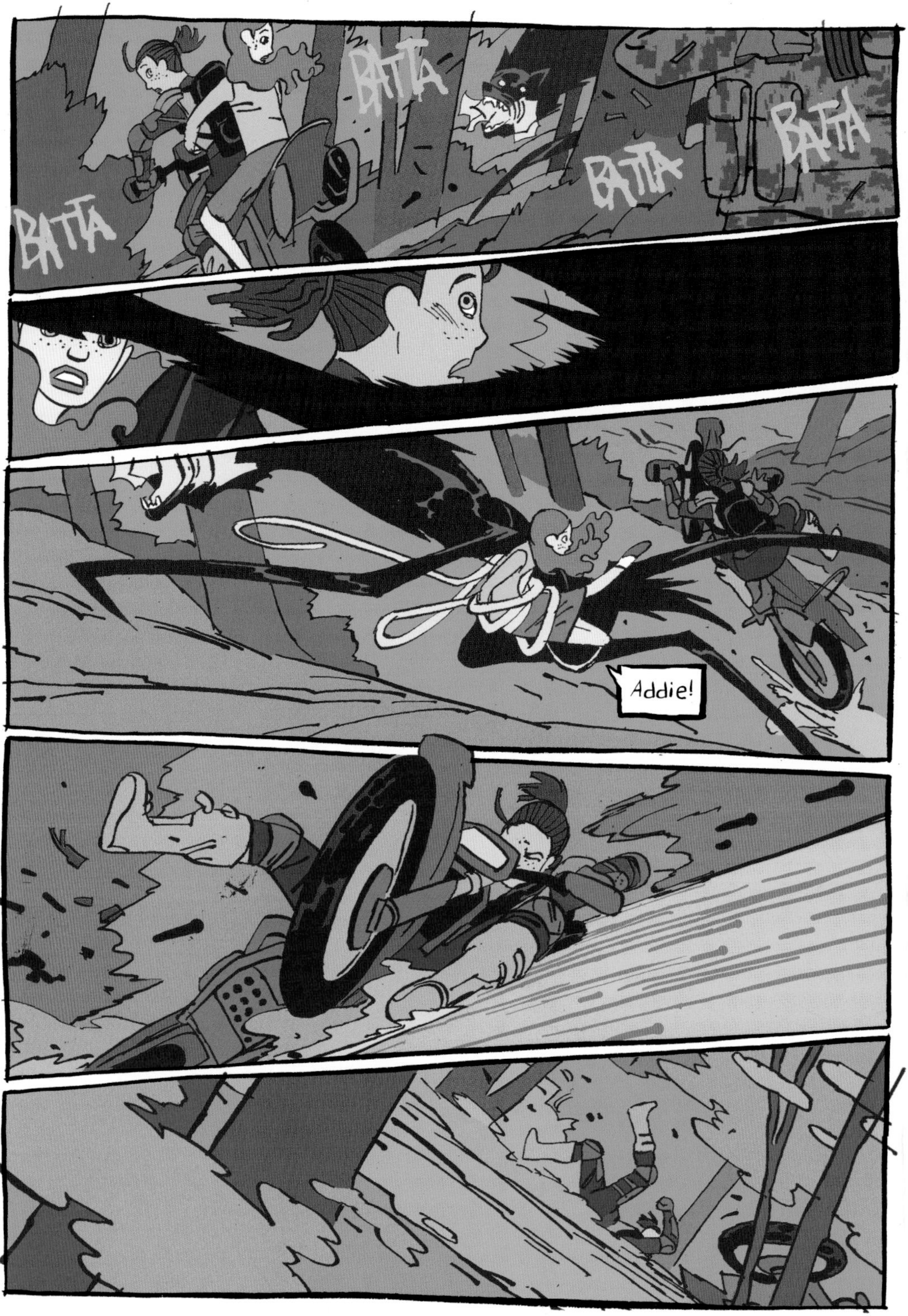
BATTA
BATTA
BATTA
BATTA
Addie!

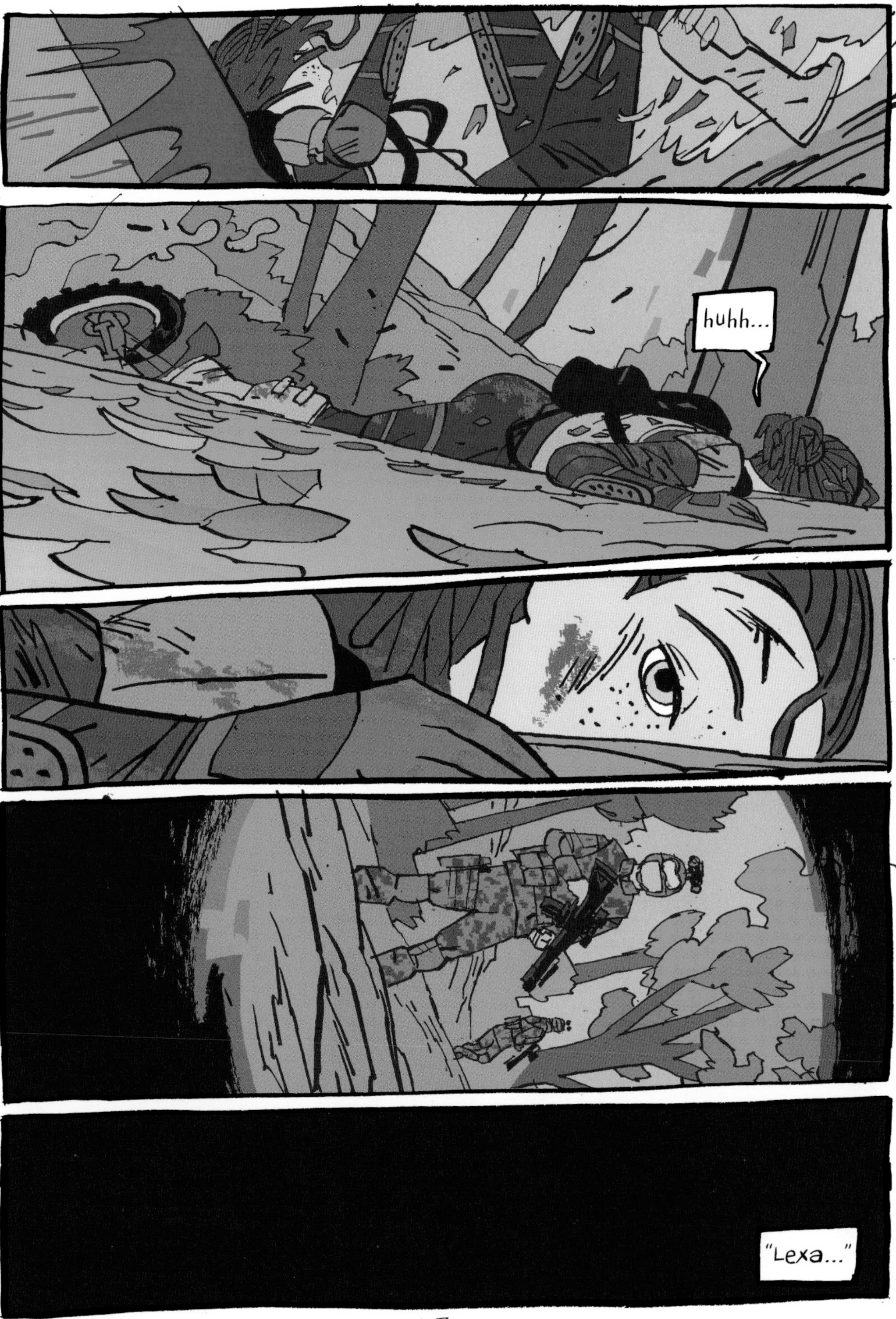
huhh...
"Lexa..."

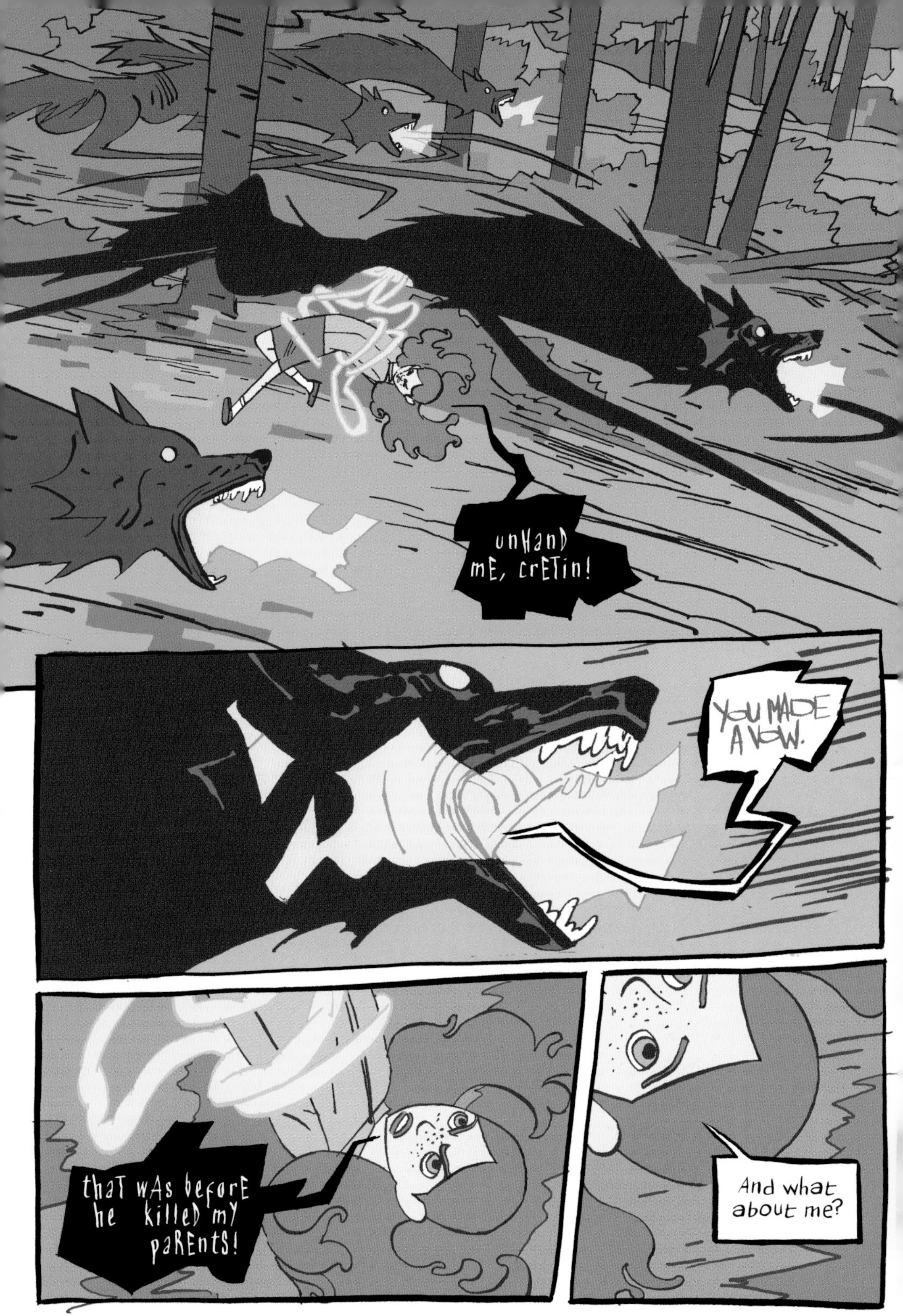
UNHAND ME, CRETIN!
YOU MADE A VOW.
THAT WAS BEFORE HE KILLED MY PARENTS!
And what about me?

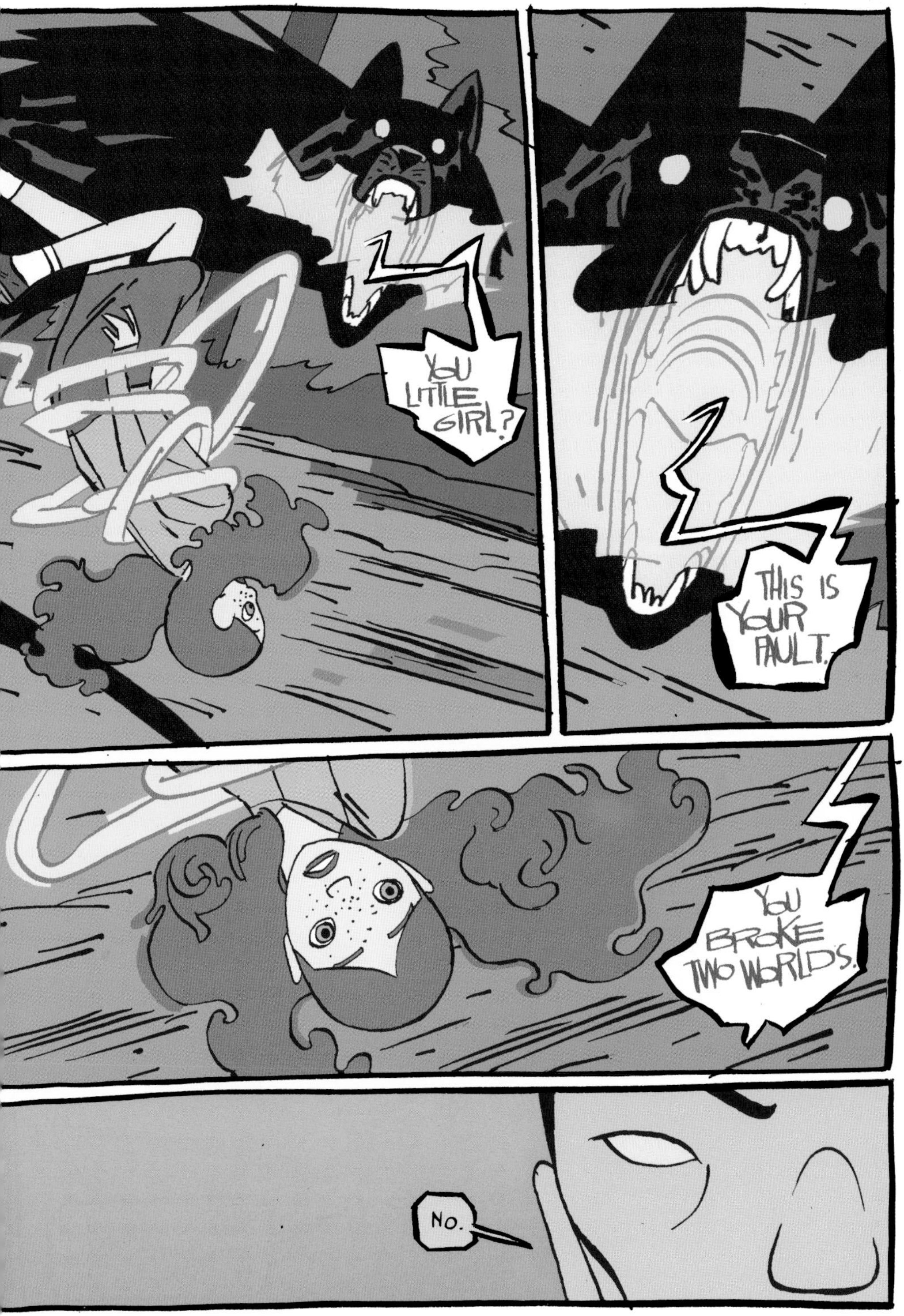
YOU LITTLE GIRL?
THIS IS YOUR FAULT.
YOU BROKE TWO WORLDS.
NO.

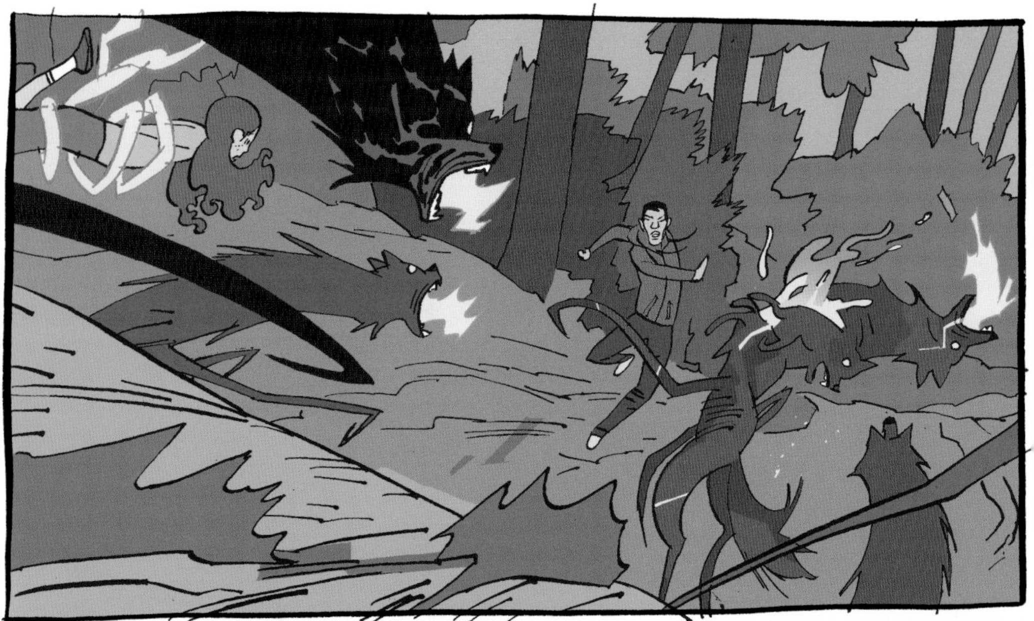

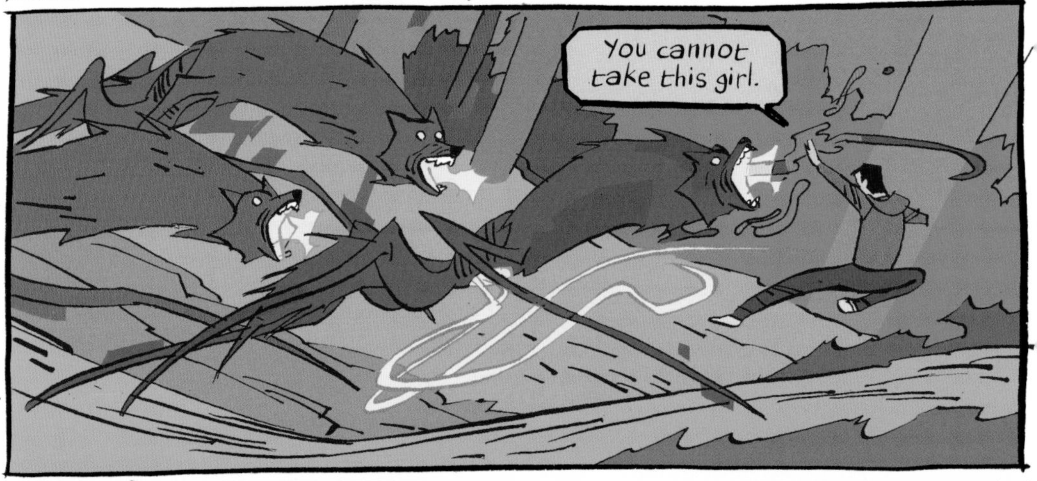
You cannot take this girl.

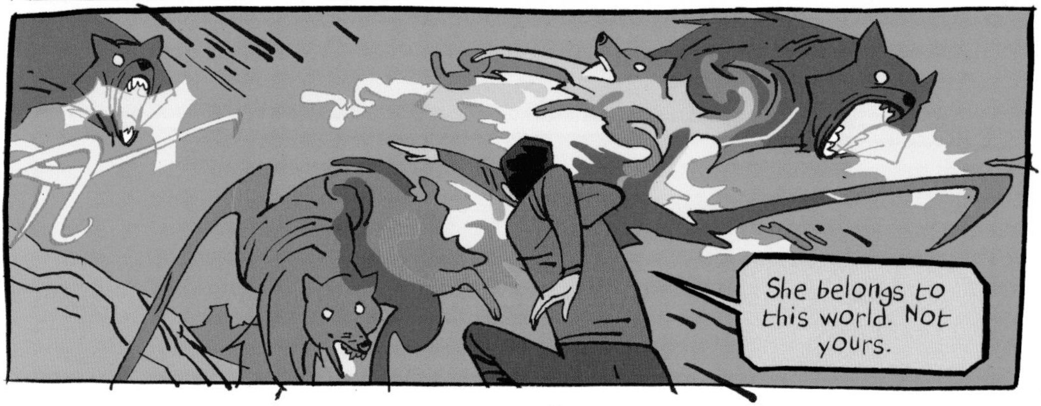
She belongs to this world. Not yours.

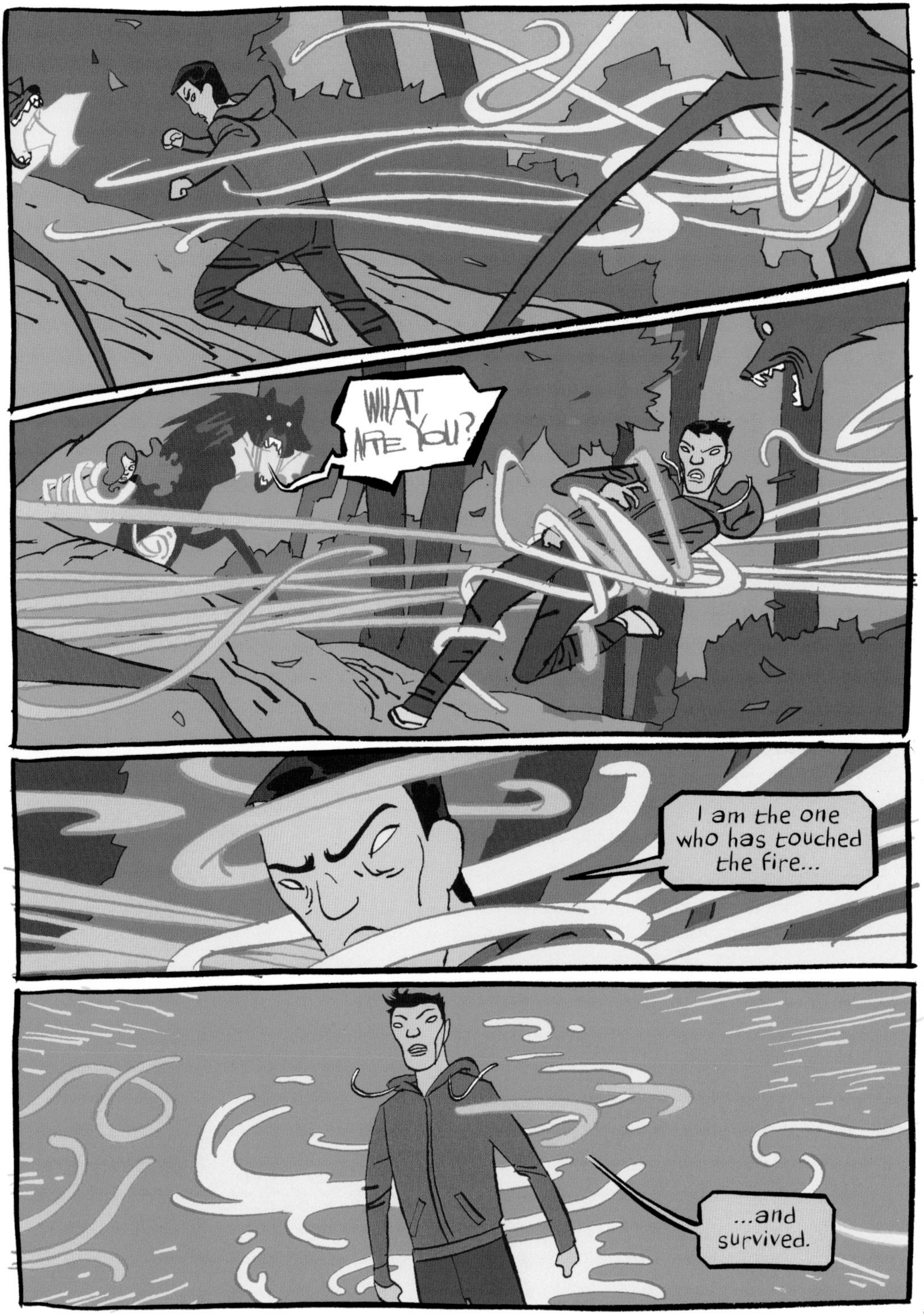
WHAT ARE YOU?
I am the one who has touched the fire...
...and survived.

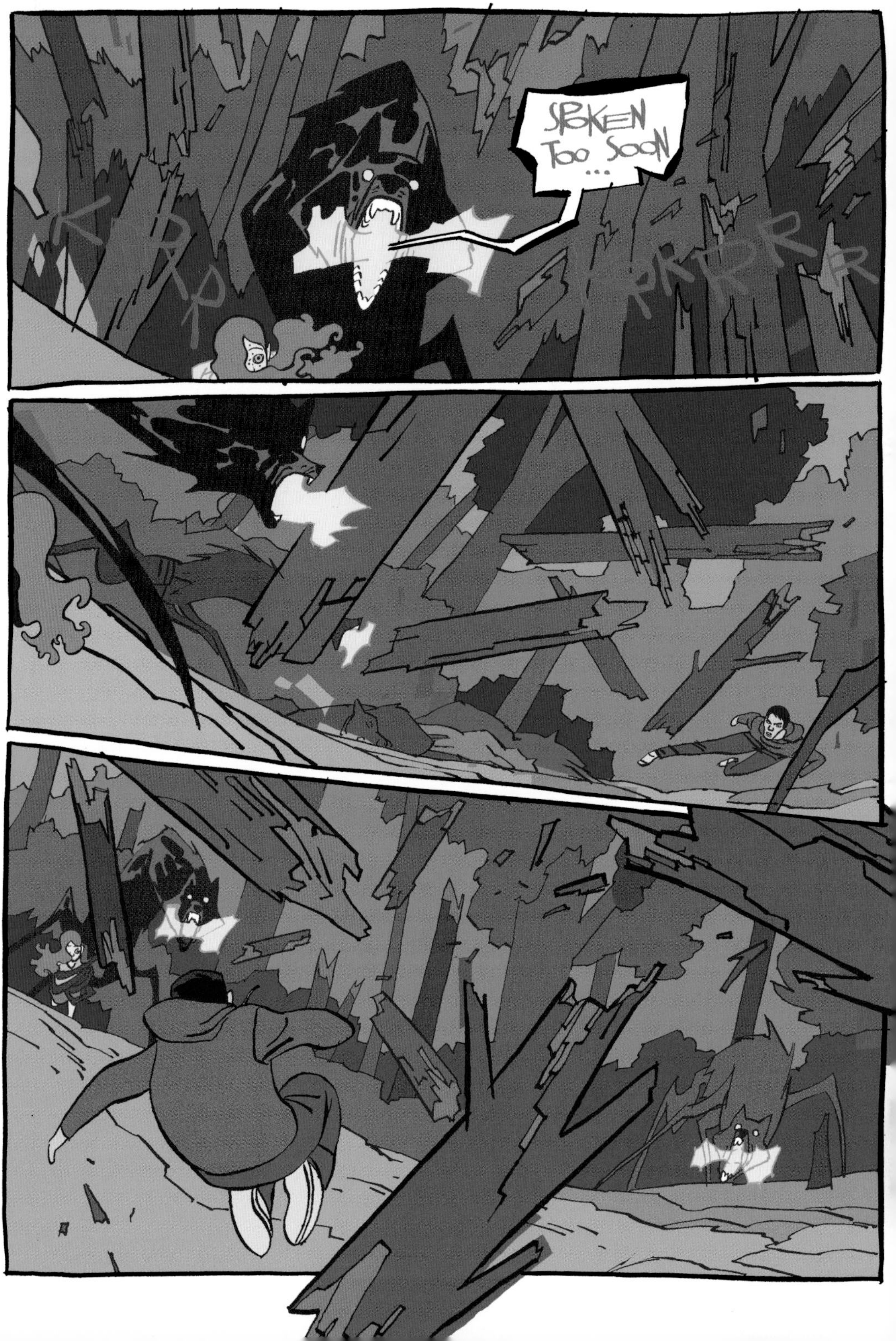
SPOKEN TOO SOON ...
KRRR
KRRRRRRR

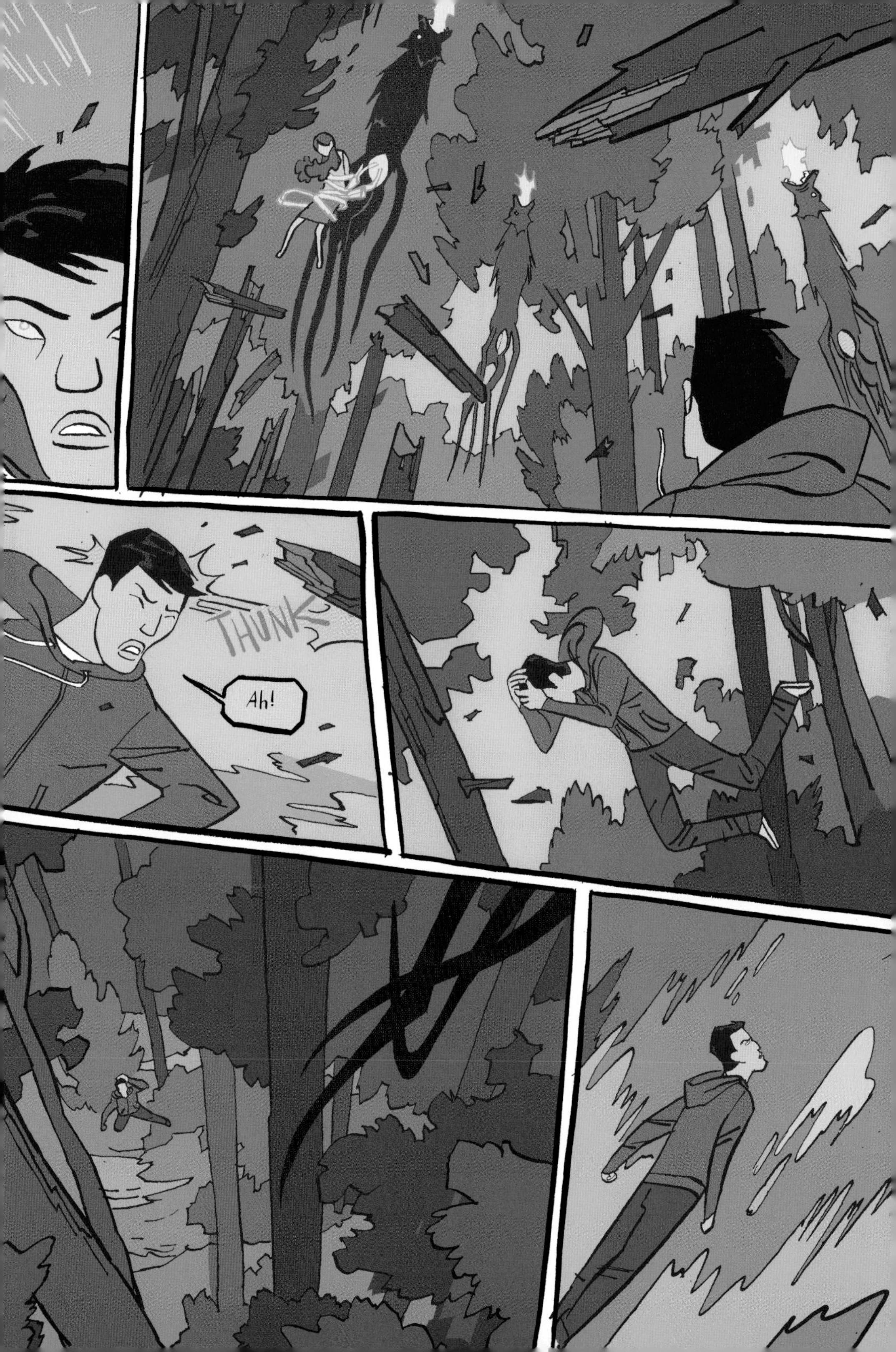
THUNK
Ah!

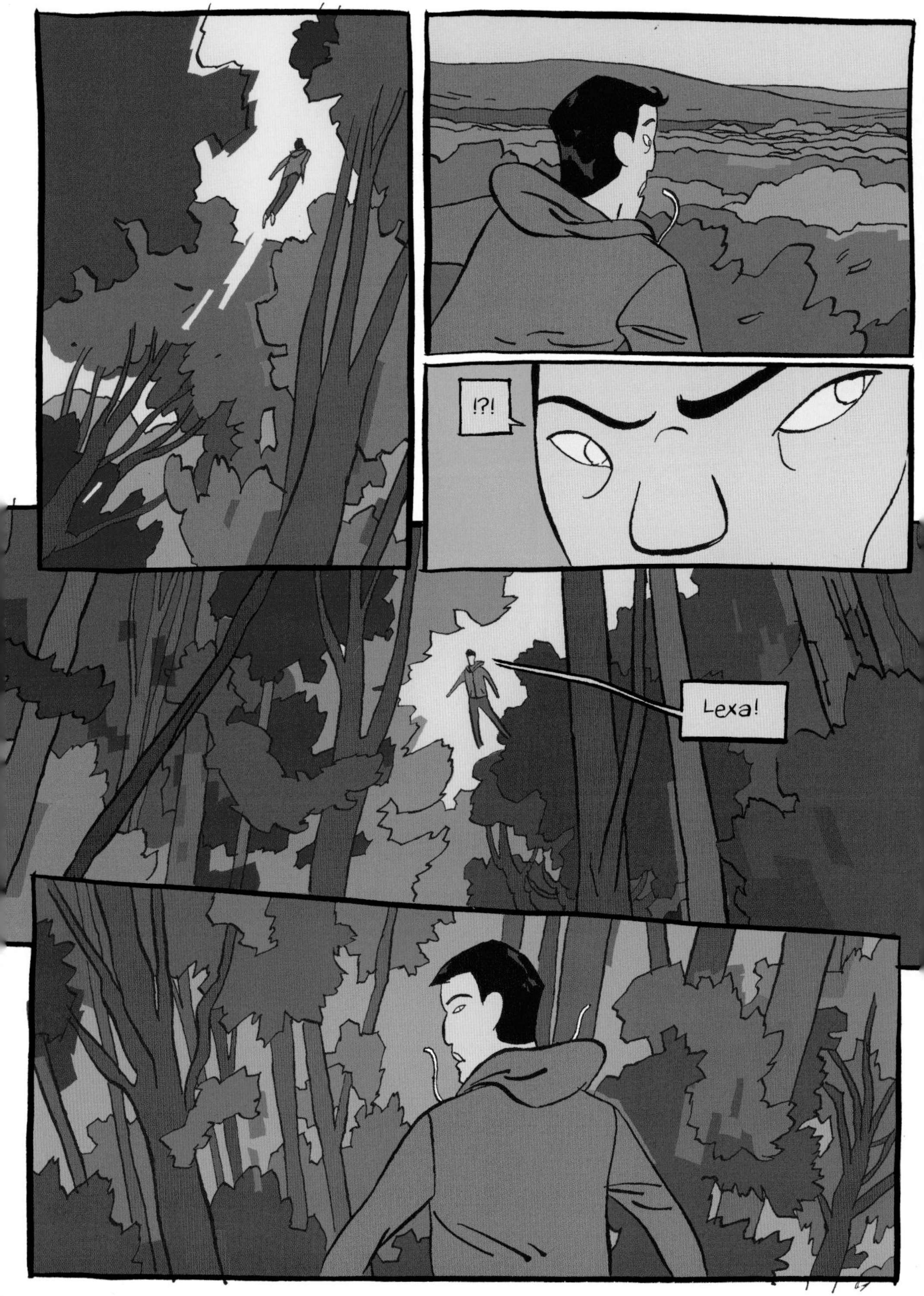
!?!
Lexa!

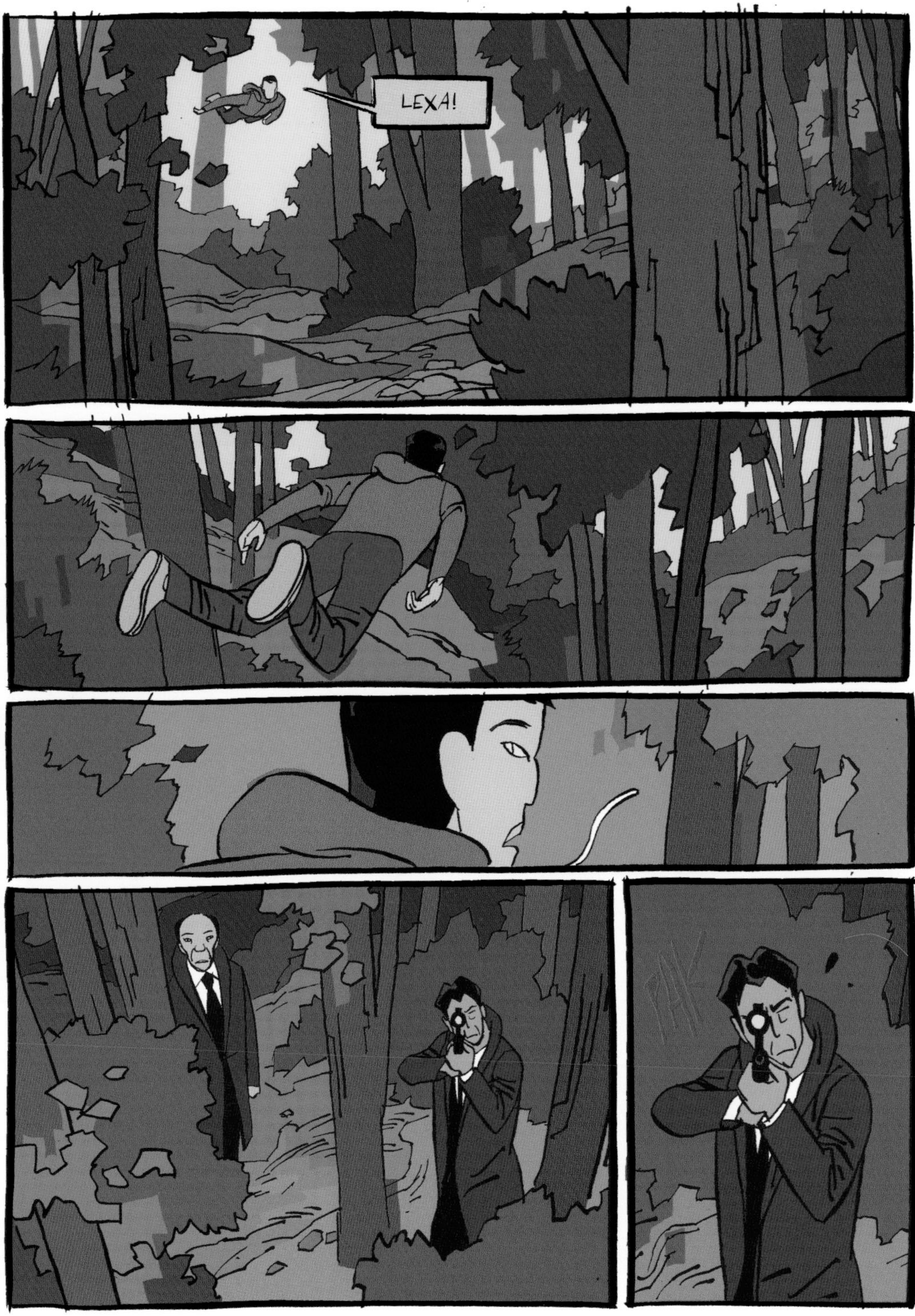
LEXA!

176

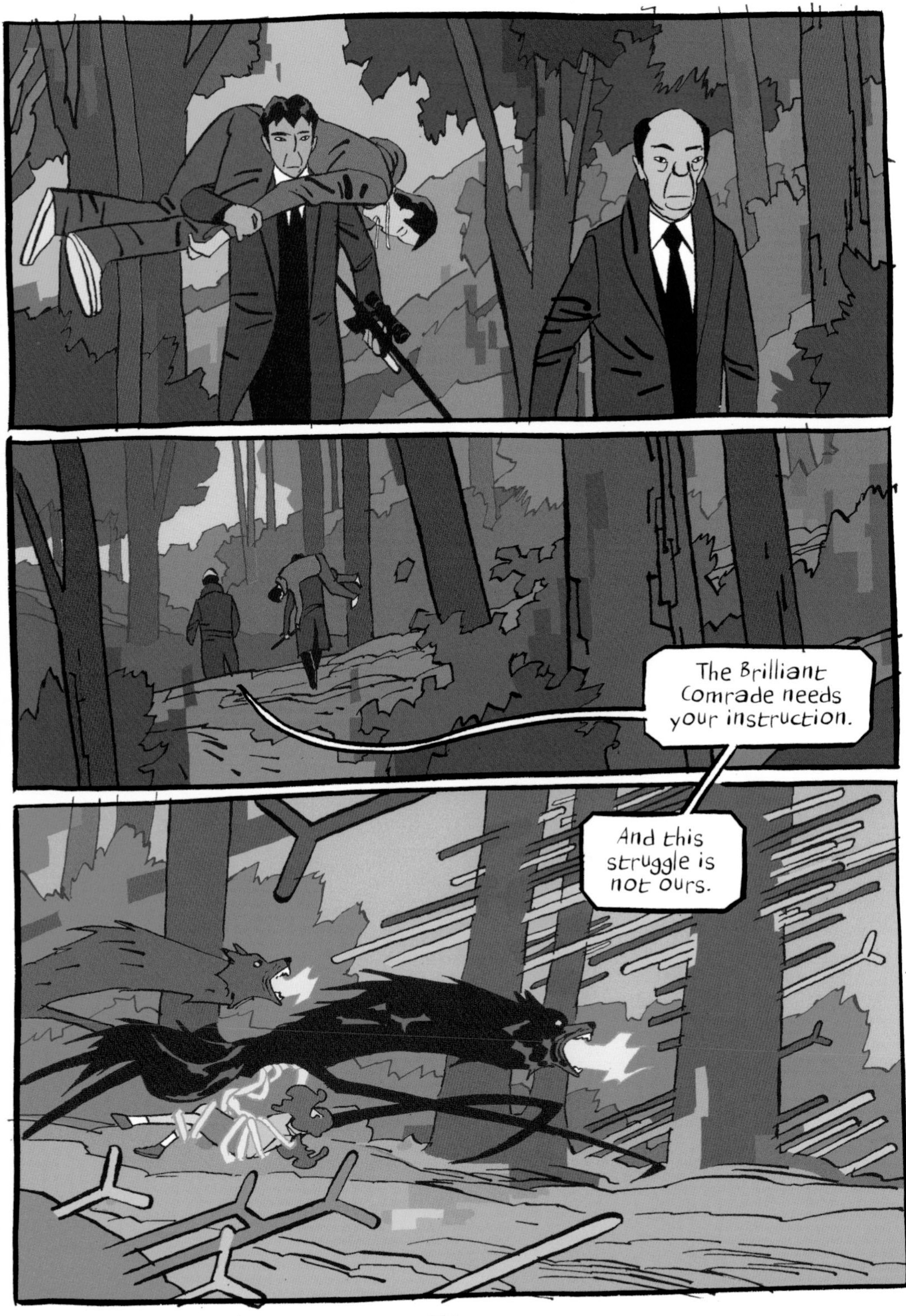
The Brilliant Comrade needs your instruction.
And this struggle is not ours.

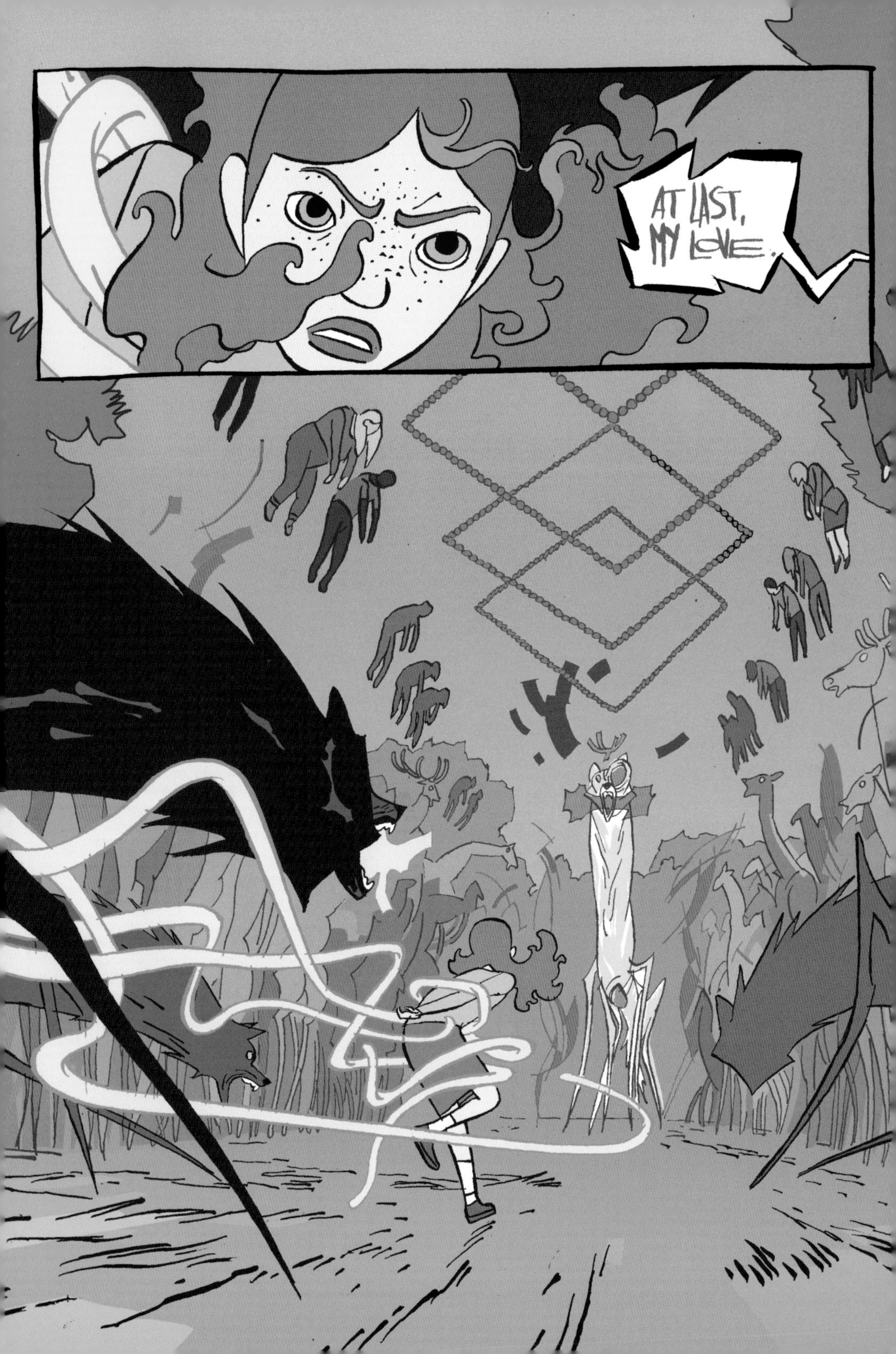
AT LAST, MY LOVE.

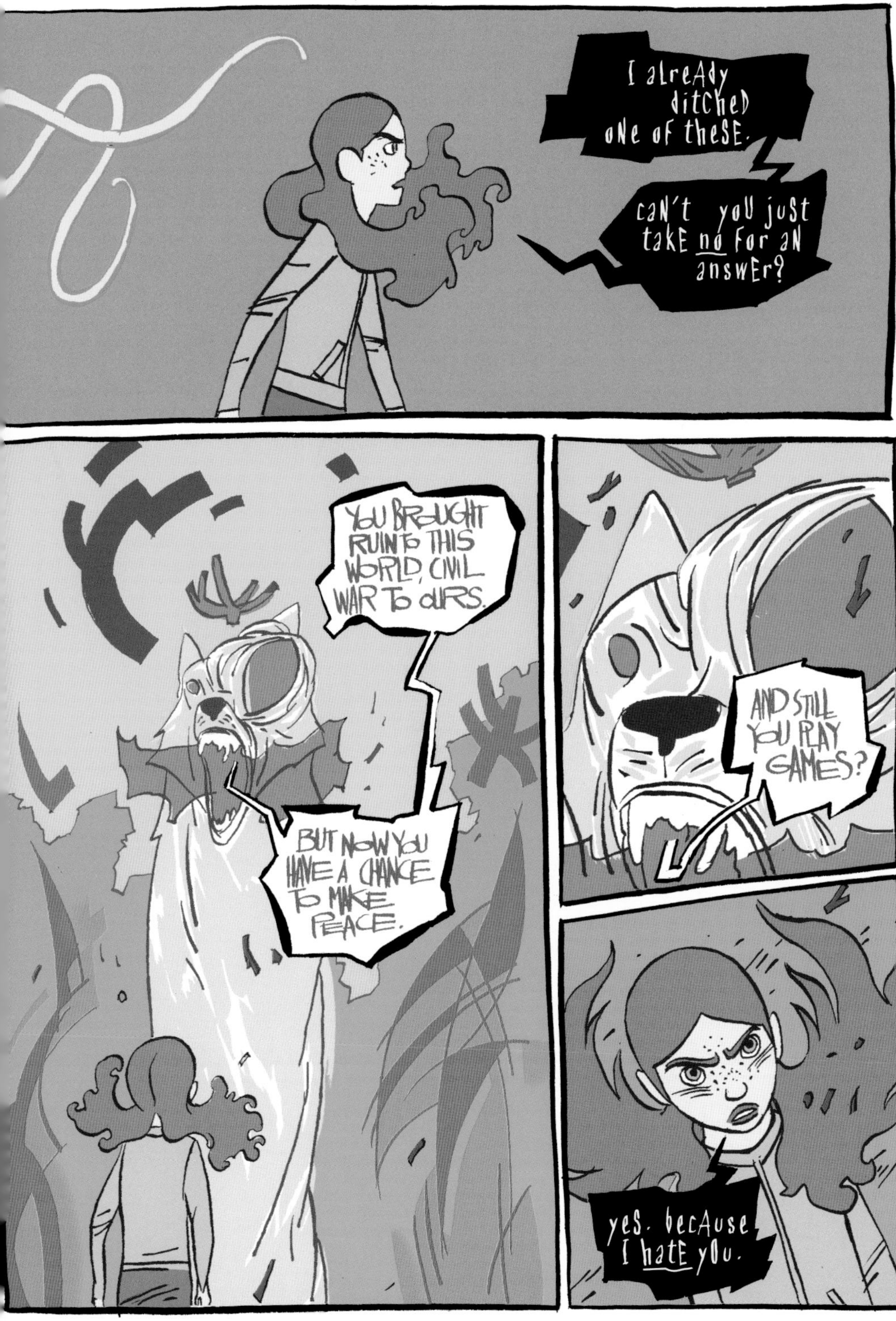
I already ditched one of these.
can't you just take no for an answer?
YOU BROUGHT RUIN TO THIS WORLD, CIVIL WAR TO OURS.
BUT NOW YOU HAVE A CHANCE TO MAKE PEACE.
AND STILL YOU PLAY GAMES?
yes. because I hate you.

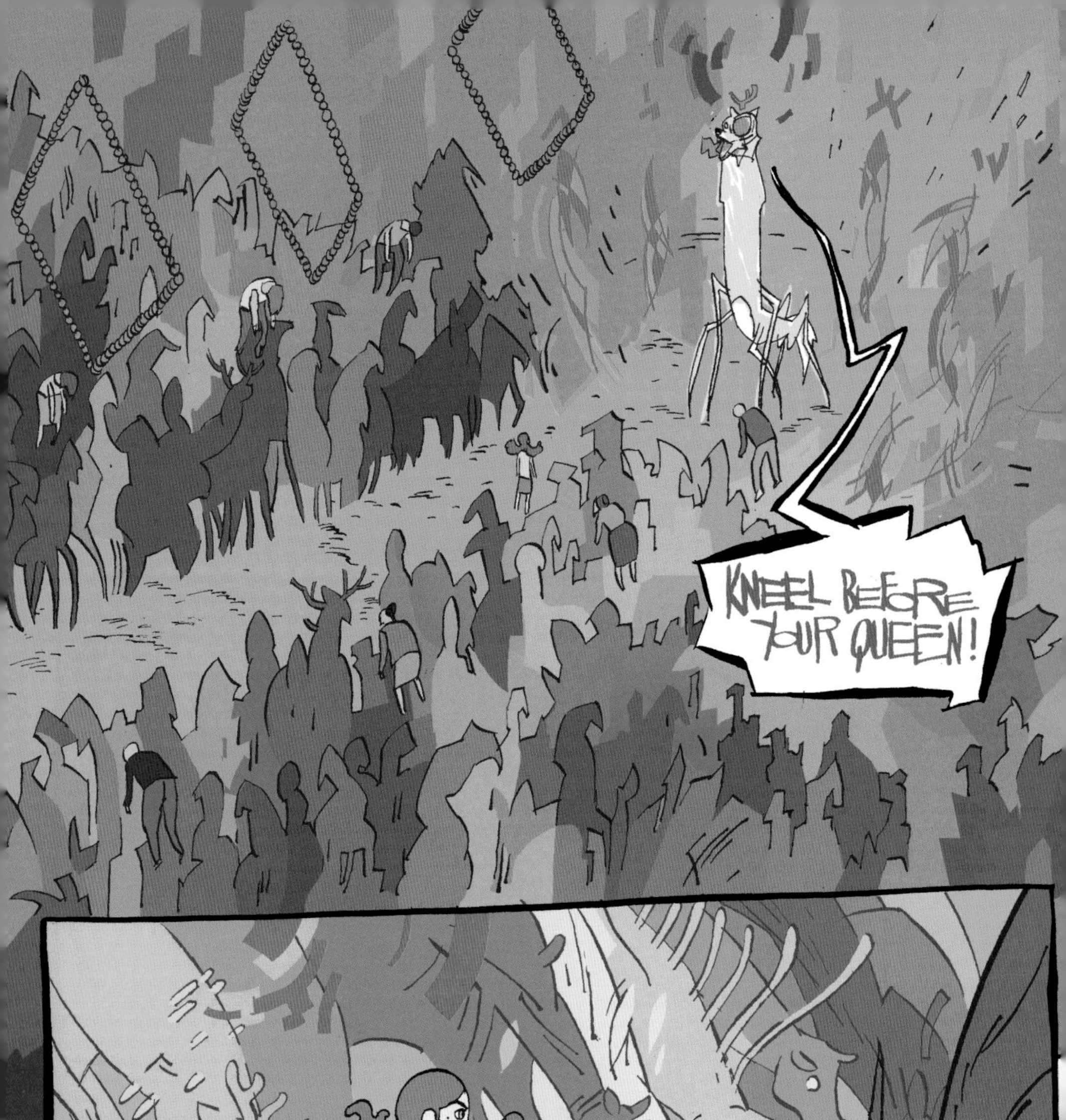
KNEEL BEFORE YOUR QUEEN!

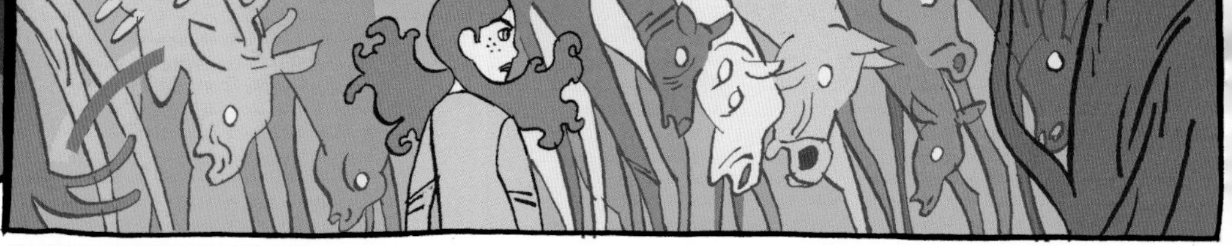

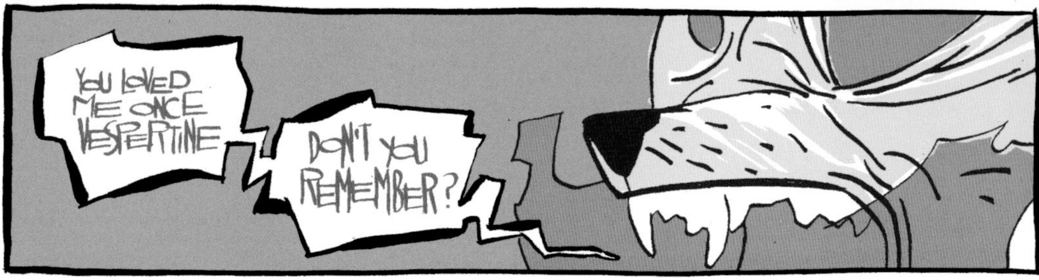
YOU LOVED ME ONCE VESPERTINE
DON'T YOU REMEMBER?

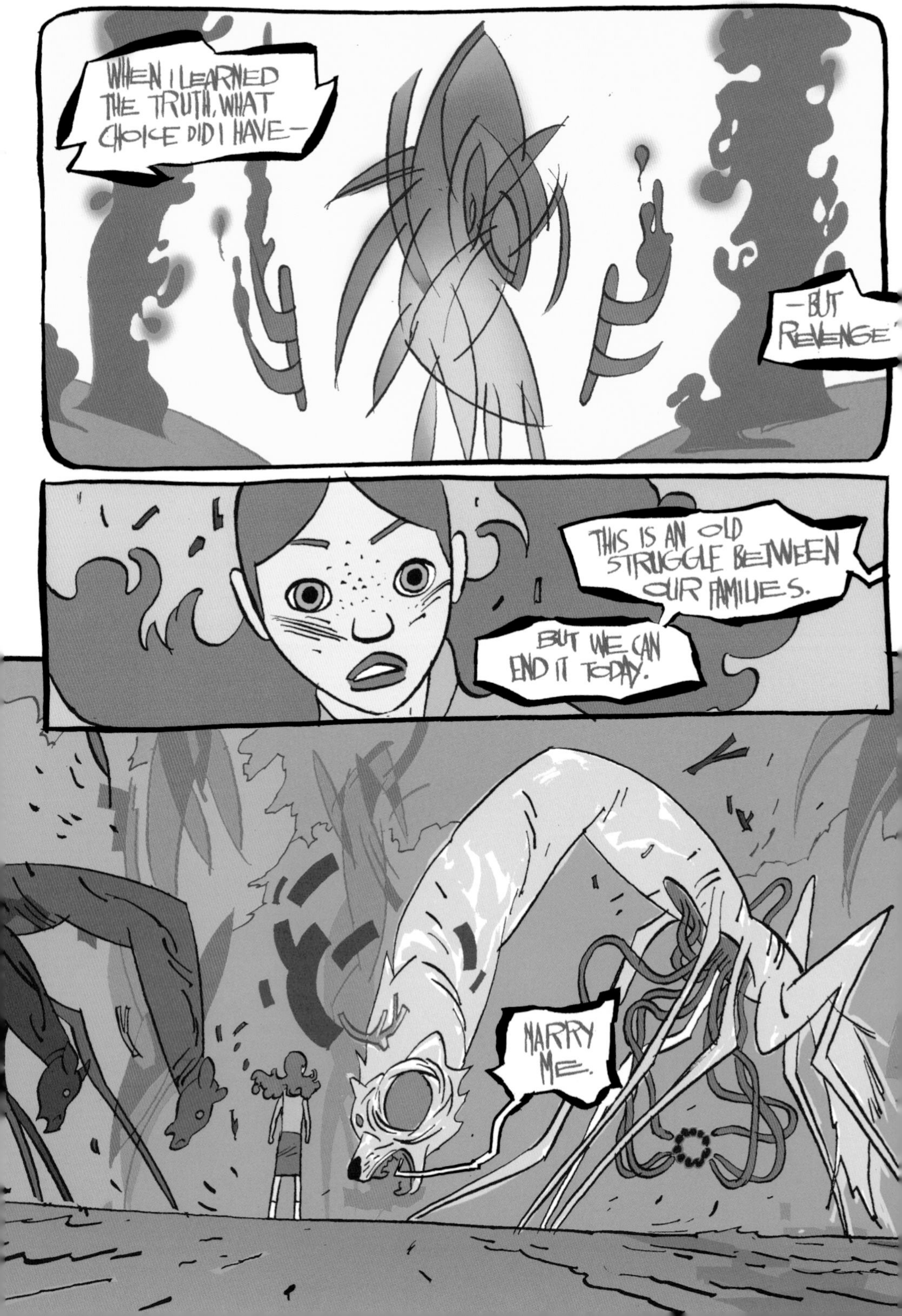
WHEN I LEARNED THE TRUTH, WHAT CHOICE DID I HAVE—
—BUT REVENGE?
THIS IS AN OLD STRUGGLE BETWEEN OUR FAMILIES.
BUT WE CAN END IT TODAY.
MARRY ME.

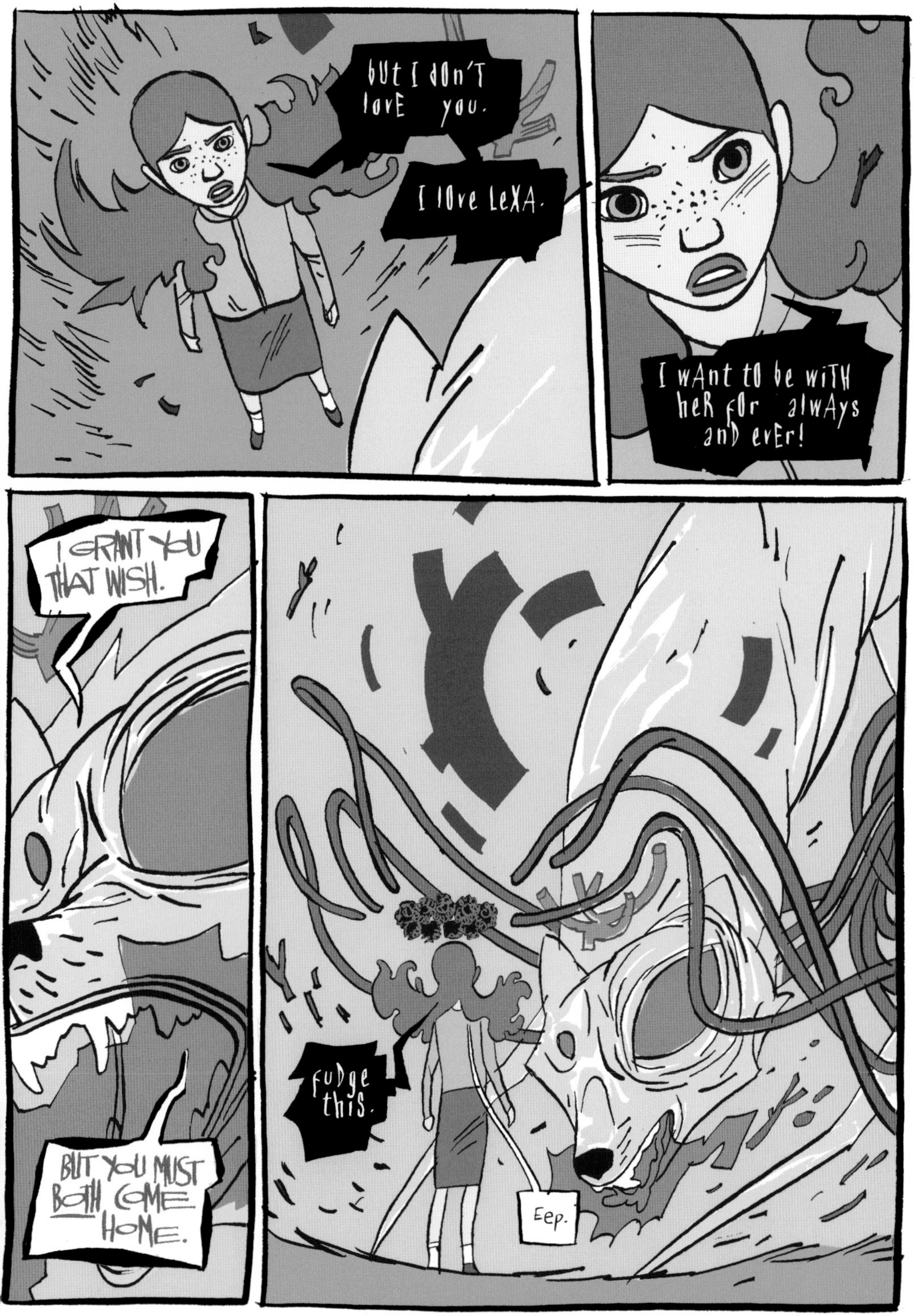
but I don't love you.
I love Lexa.
I want to be with her for always and ever!
I GRANT YOU THAT WISH.
BUT YOU MUST BOTH COME HOME.
Fudge this.
Eep.

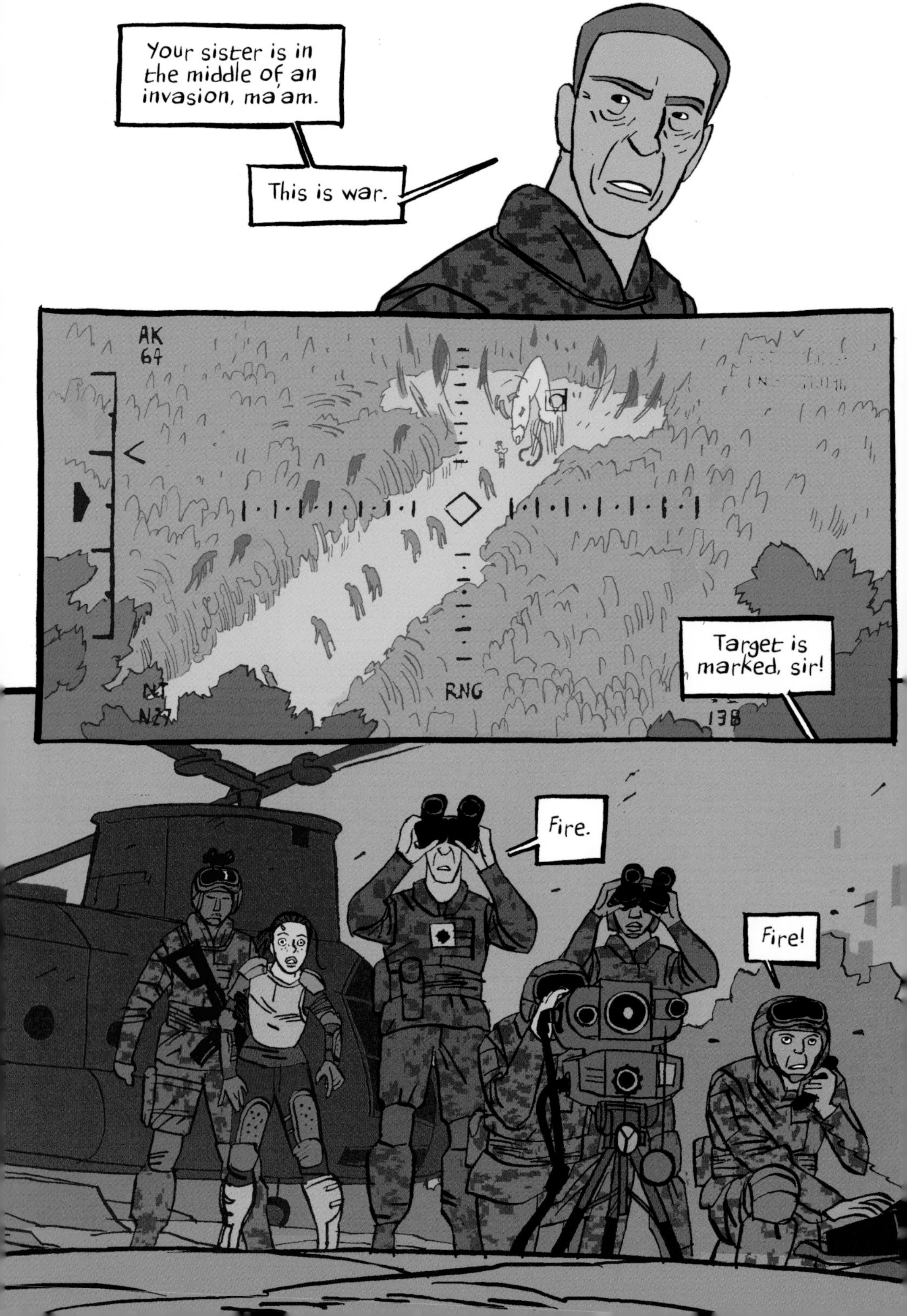
Your sister is in the middle of an invasion, ma'am.
This is war.
AK
64
RNG
138
Target is marked, sir!
Fire.
Fire!

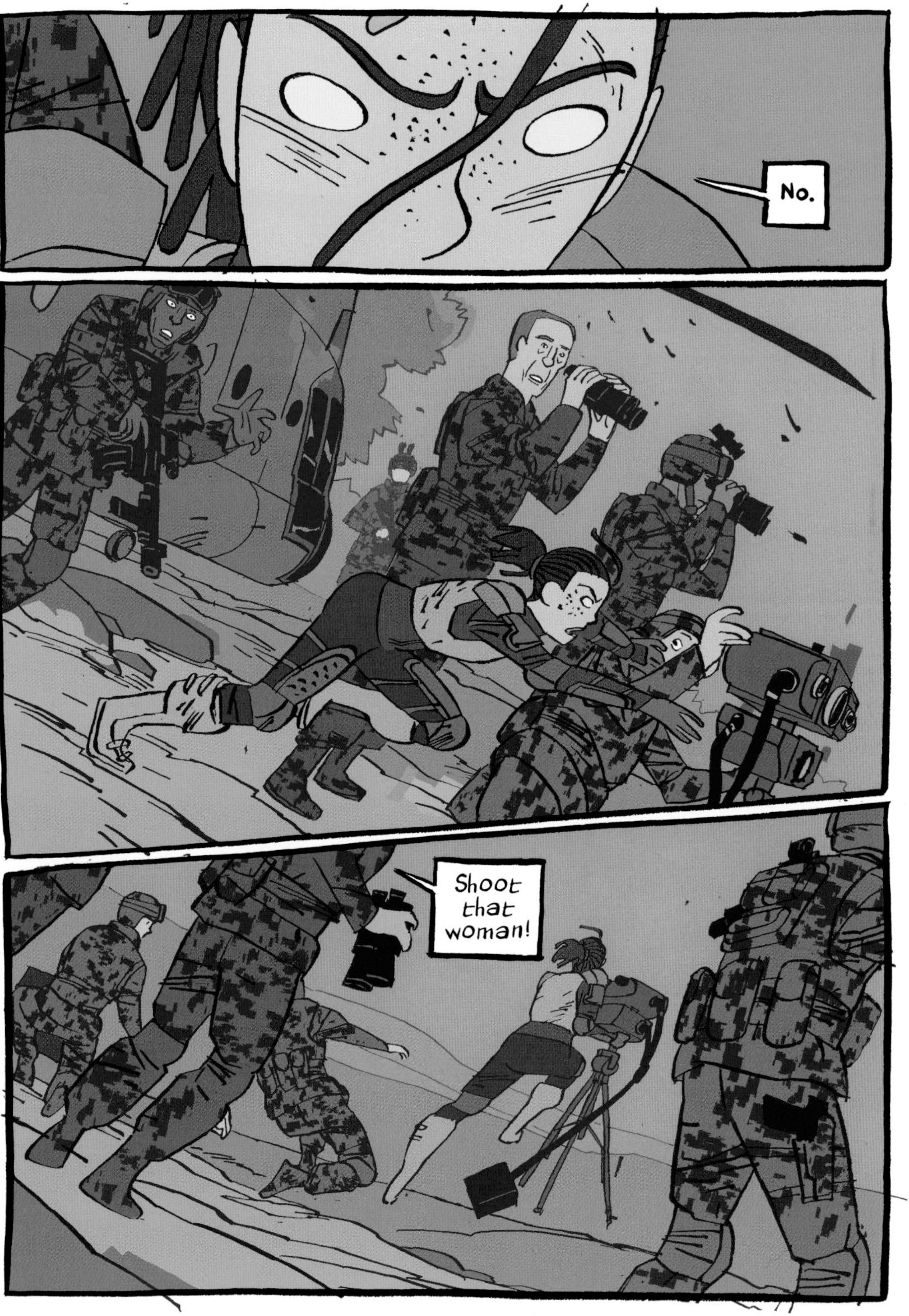
No.
Shoot that woman!

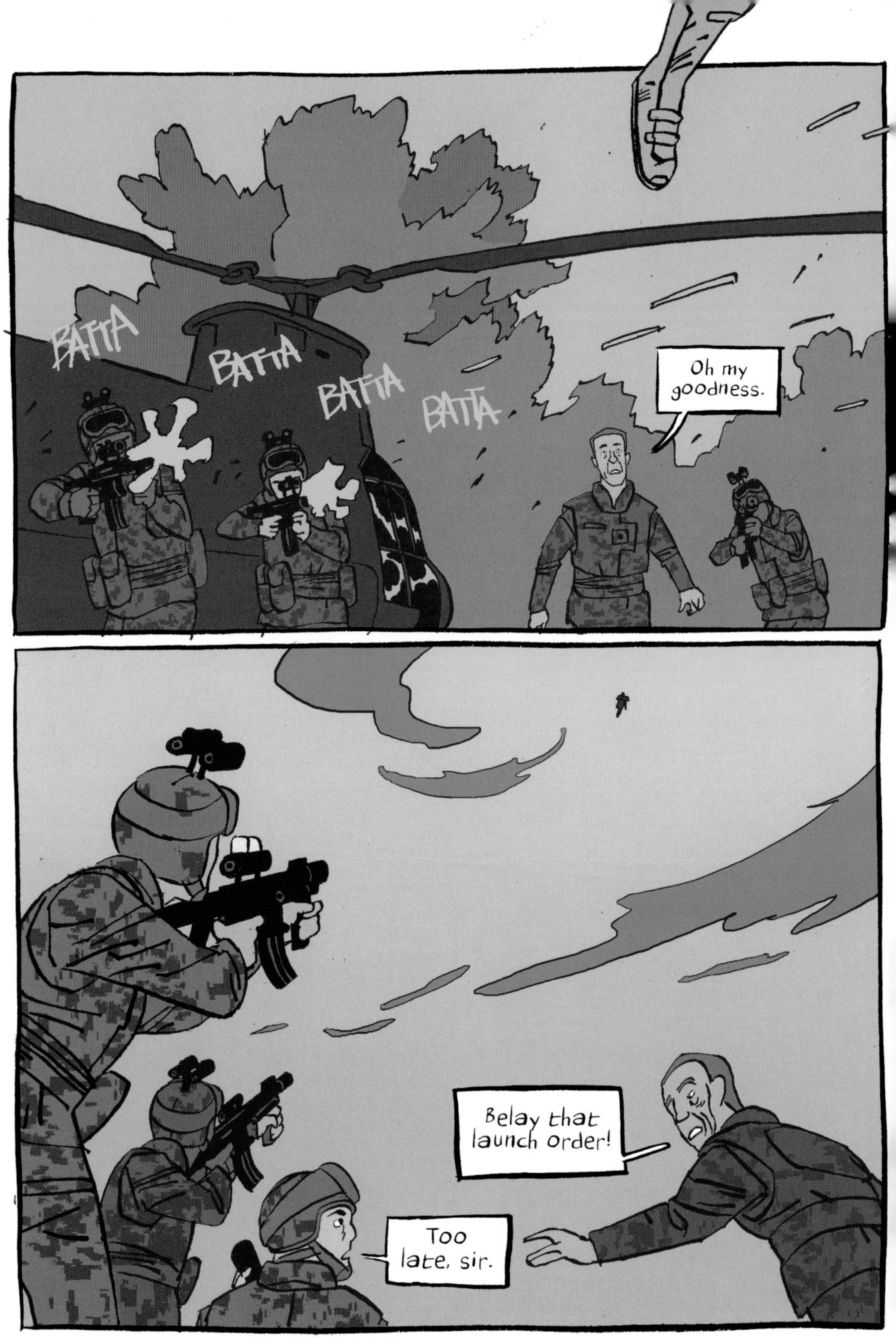
BATTA
BATTA
BATTA
BATTA
Oh my goodness.
Belay that launch order!
Too late, sir.

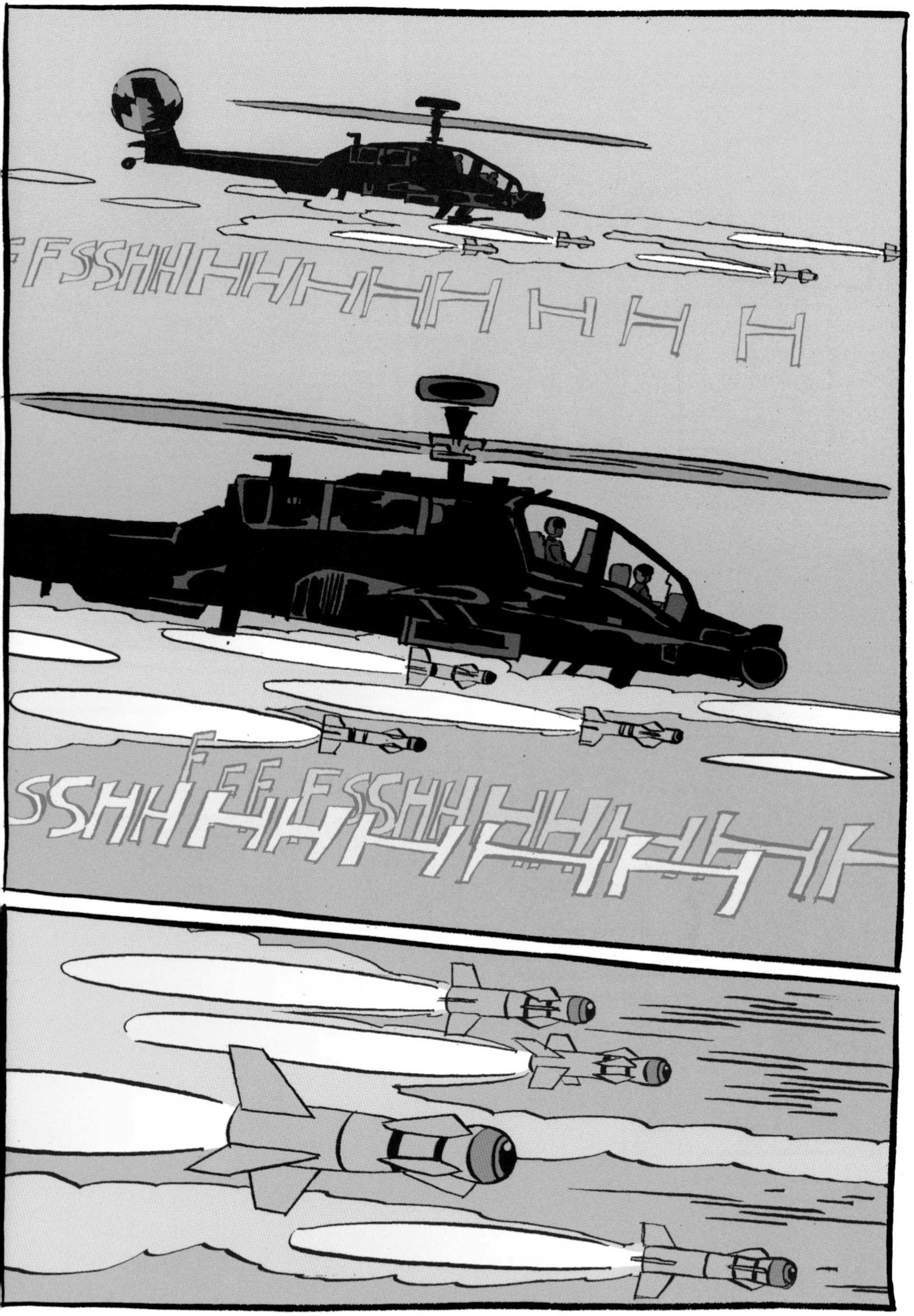
FFSSHHHHHHHHHHH
FFFSSHHHHHHHHHHHH

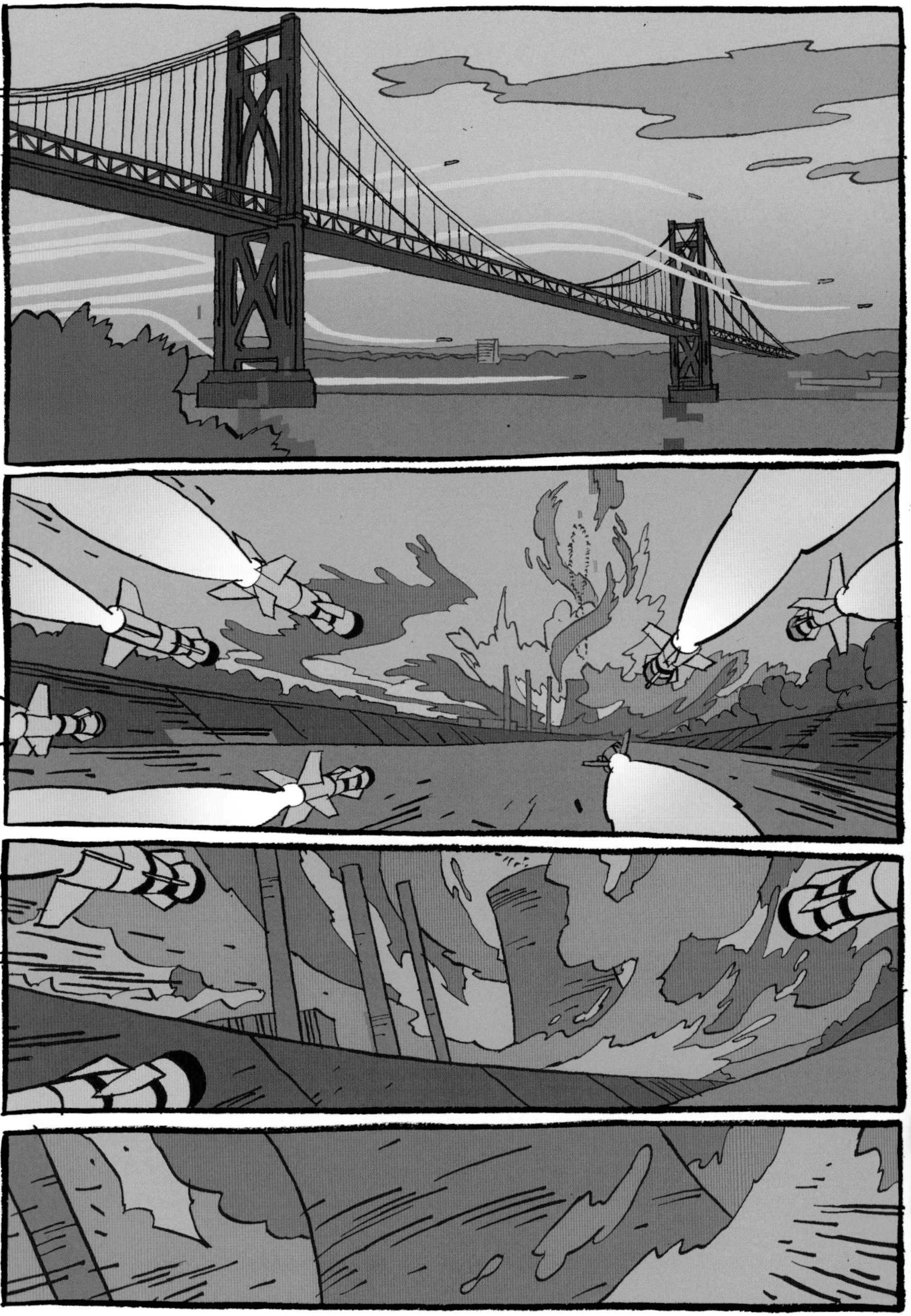

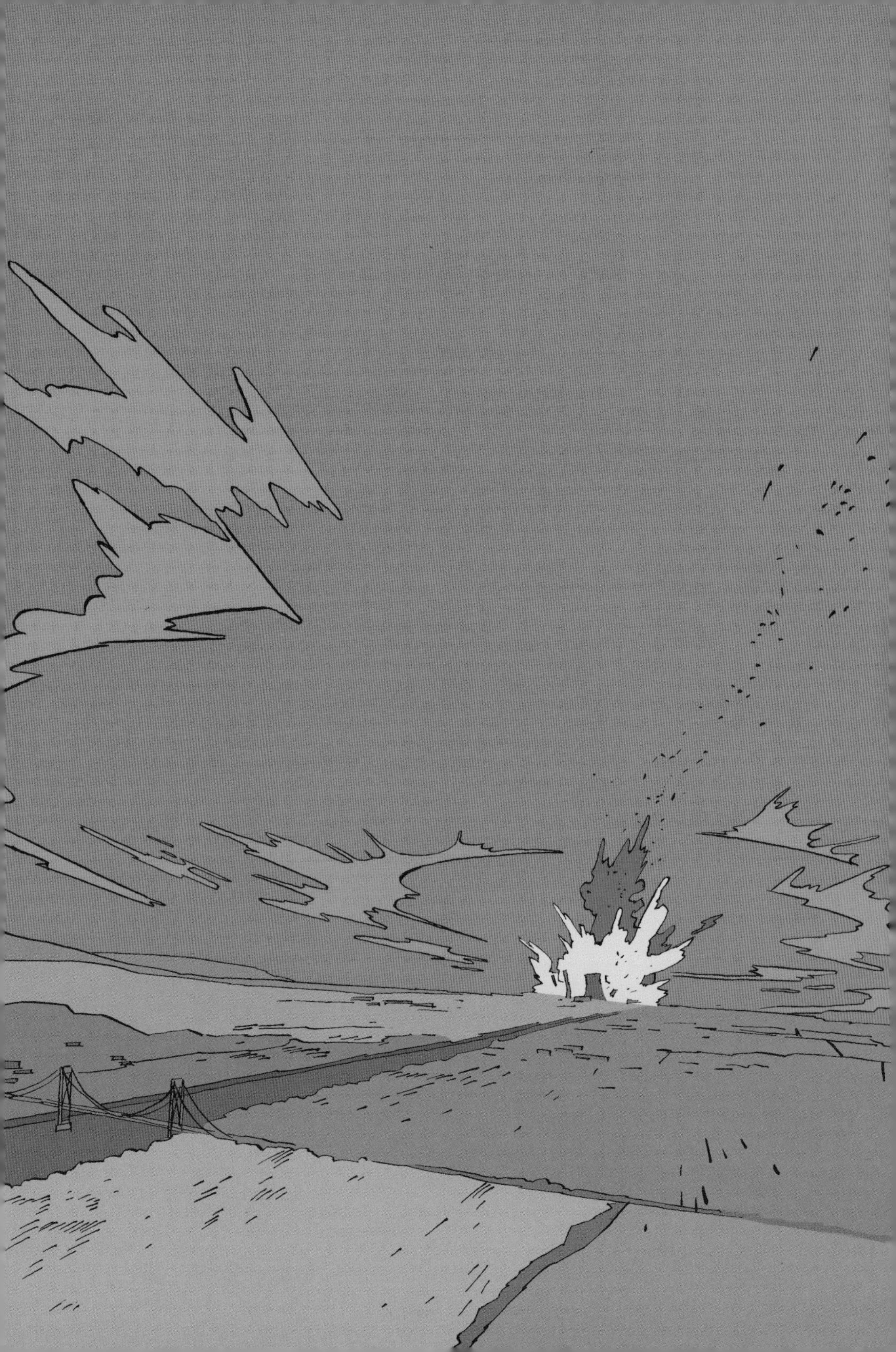

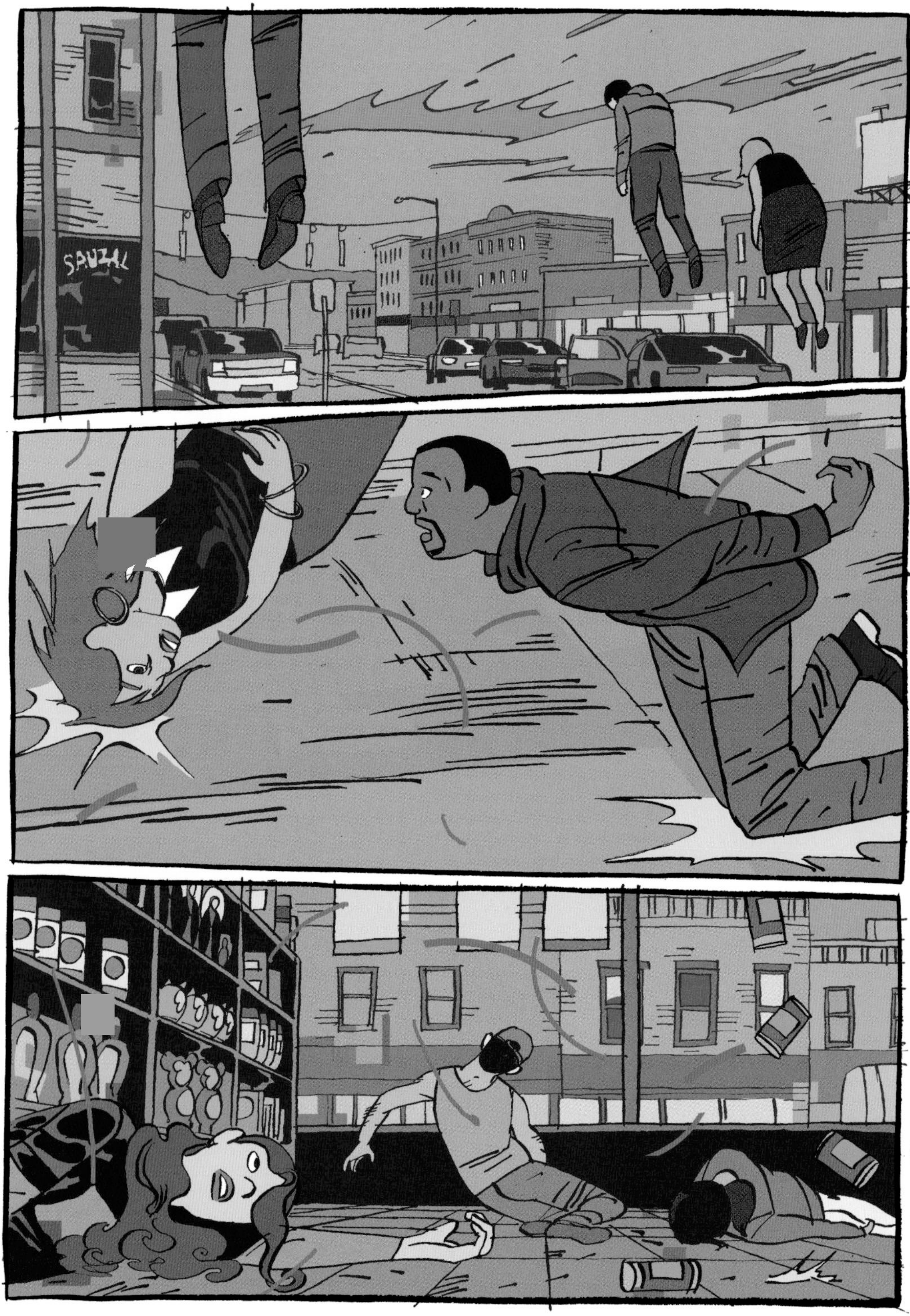
SAUZAL

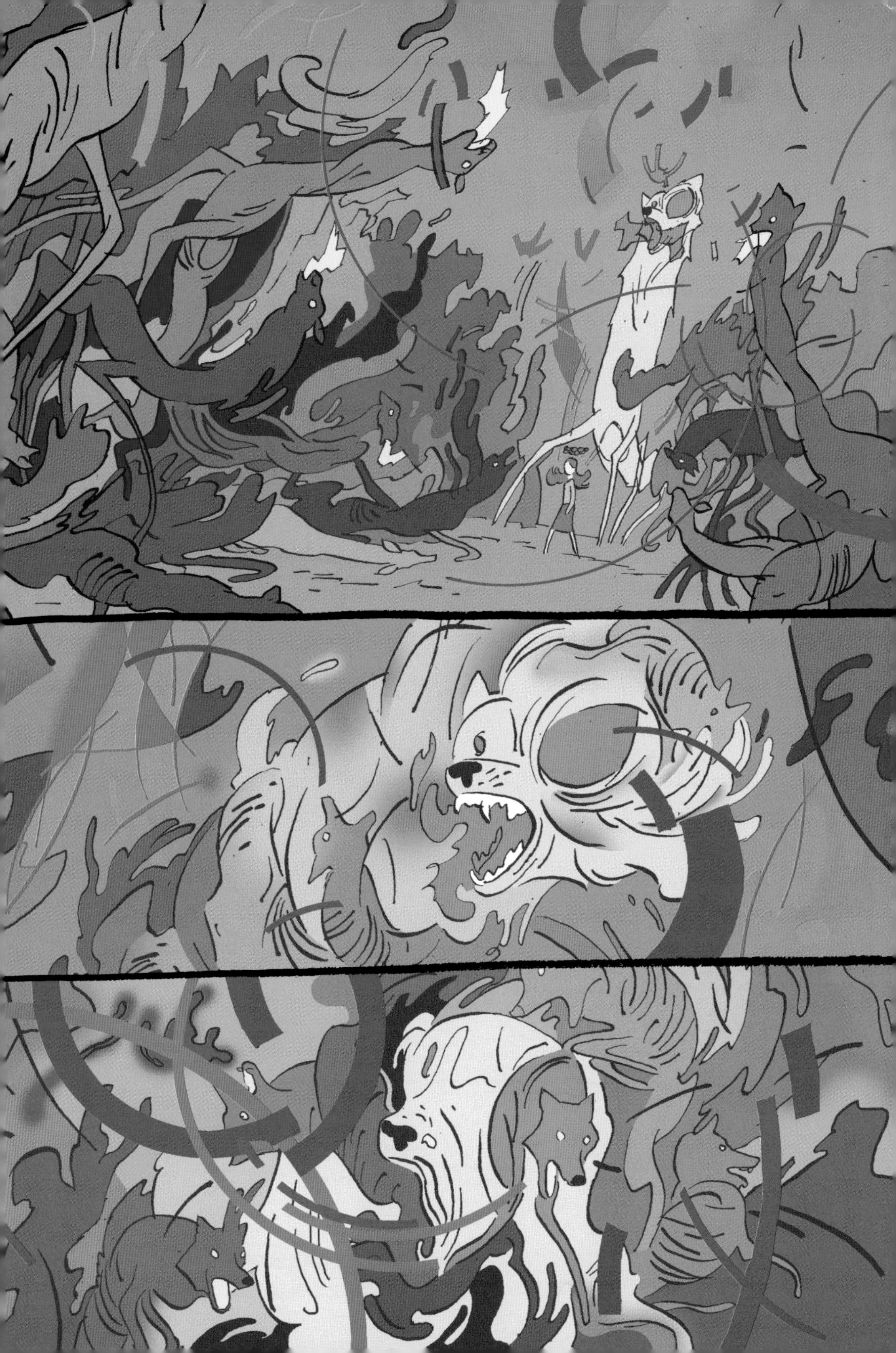

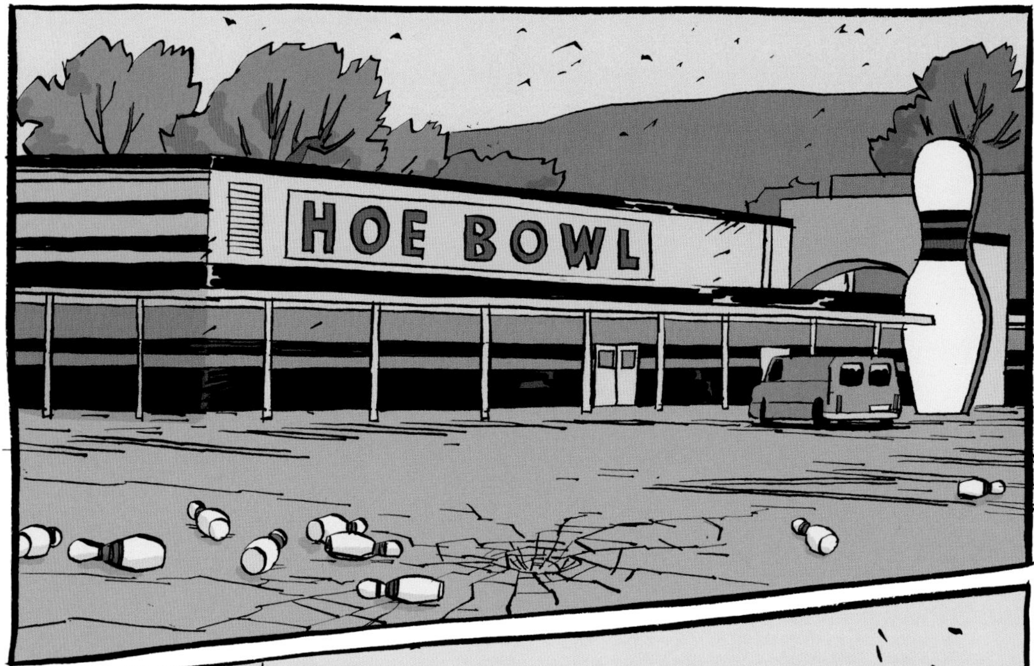
HOE BOWL

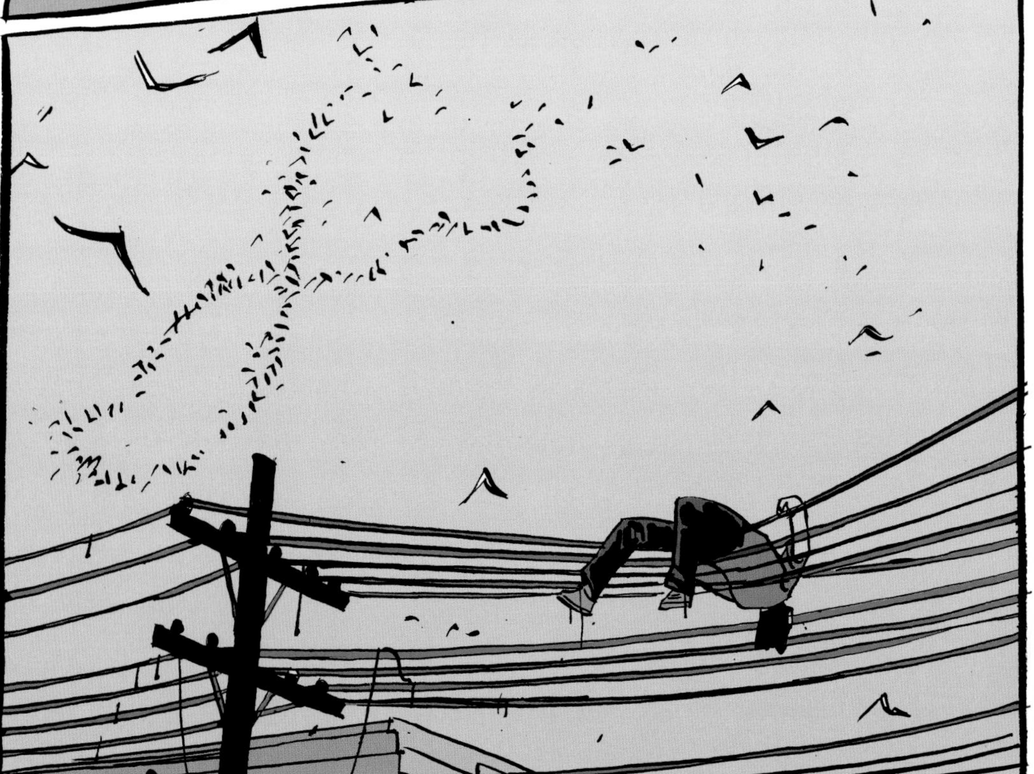

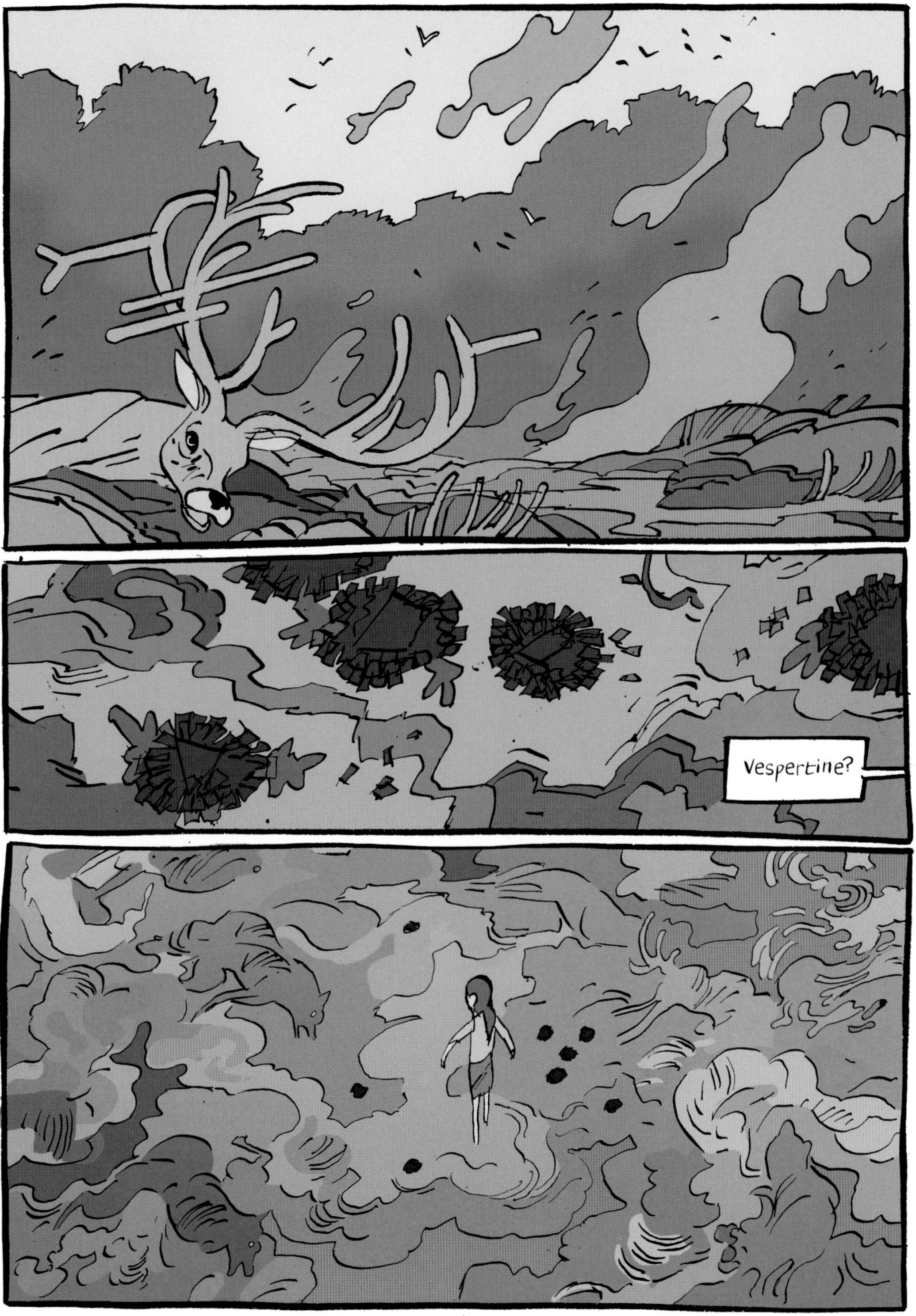
Vespertine?

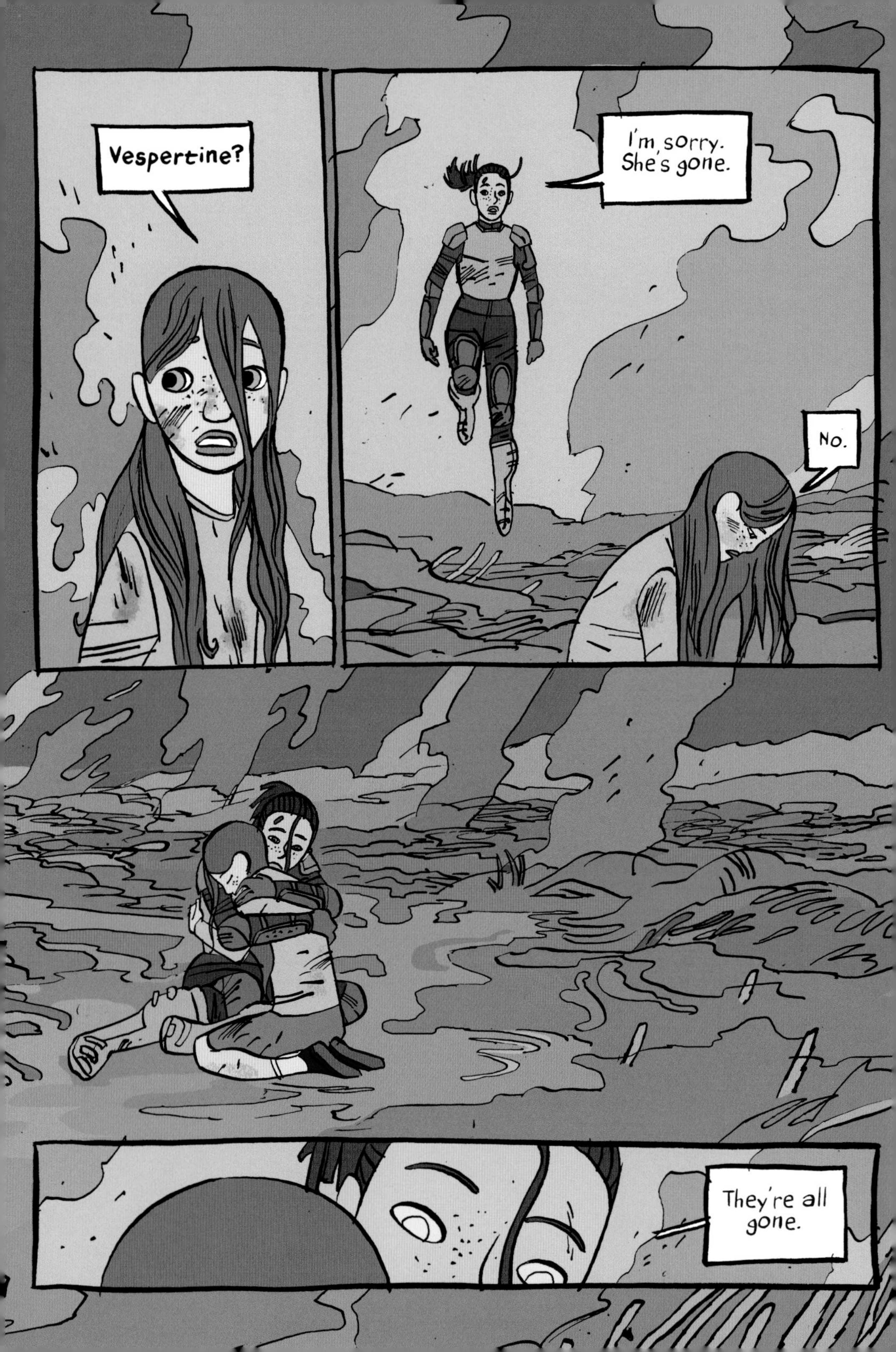
Vespertine?
I'm sorry. She's gone.
No.
They're all gone.

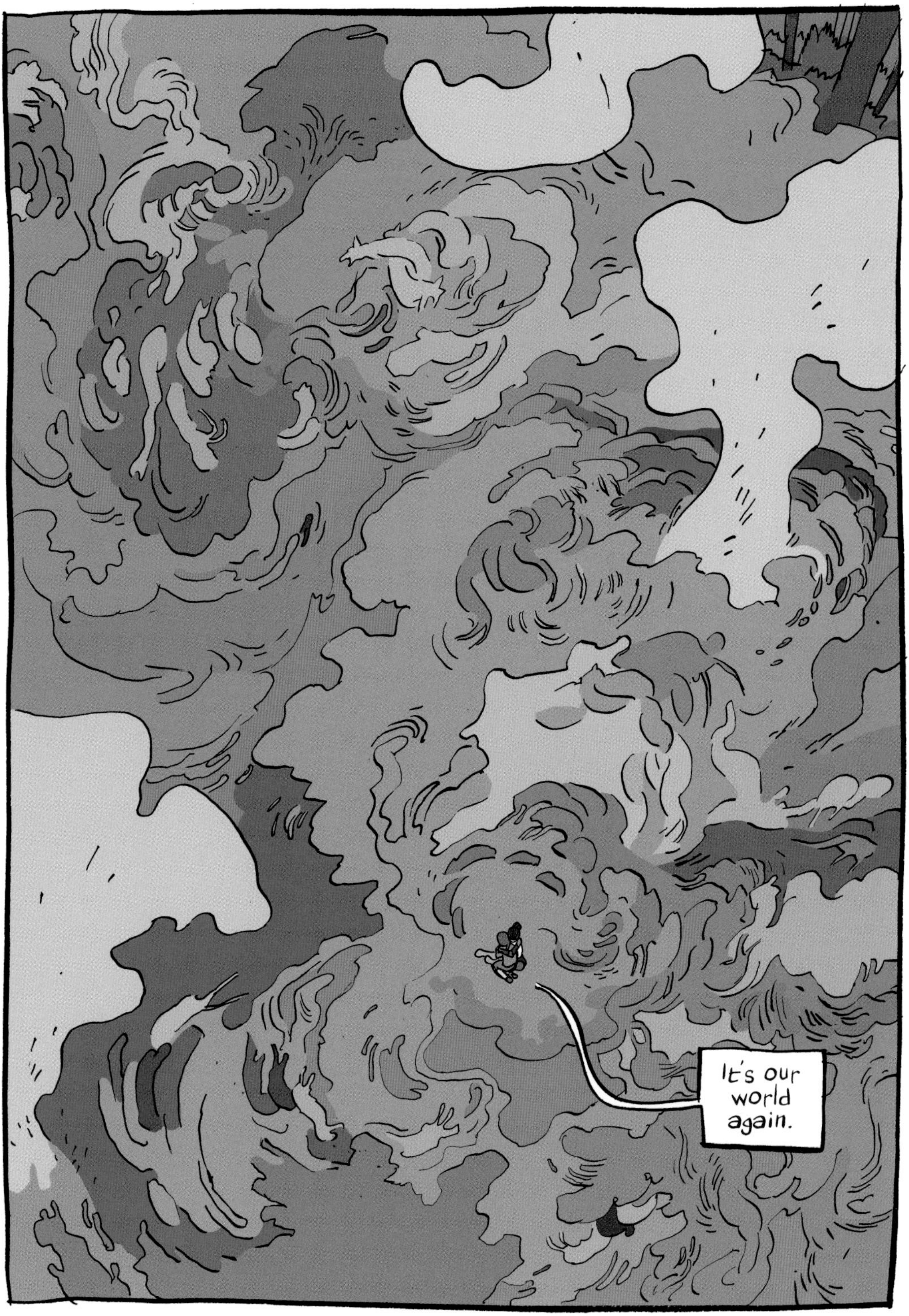
It's our world again.

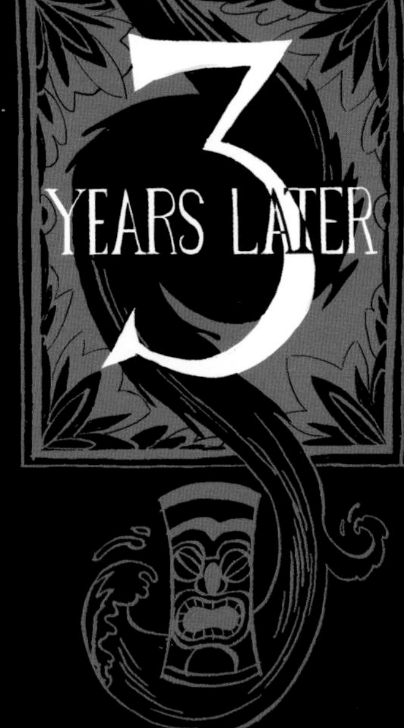
3 YEARS LATER

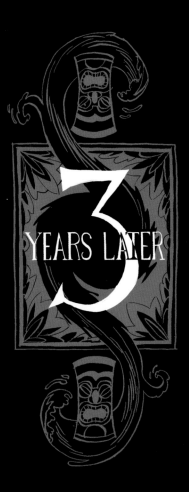

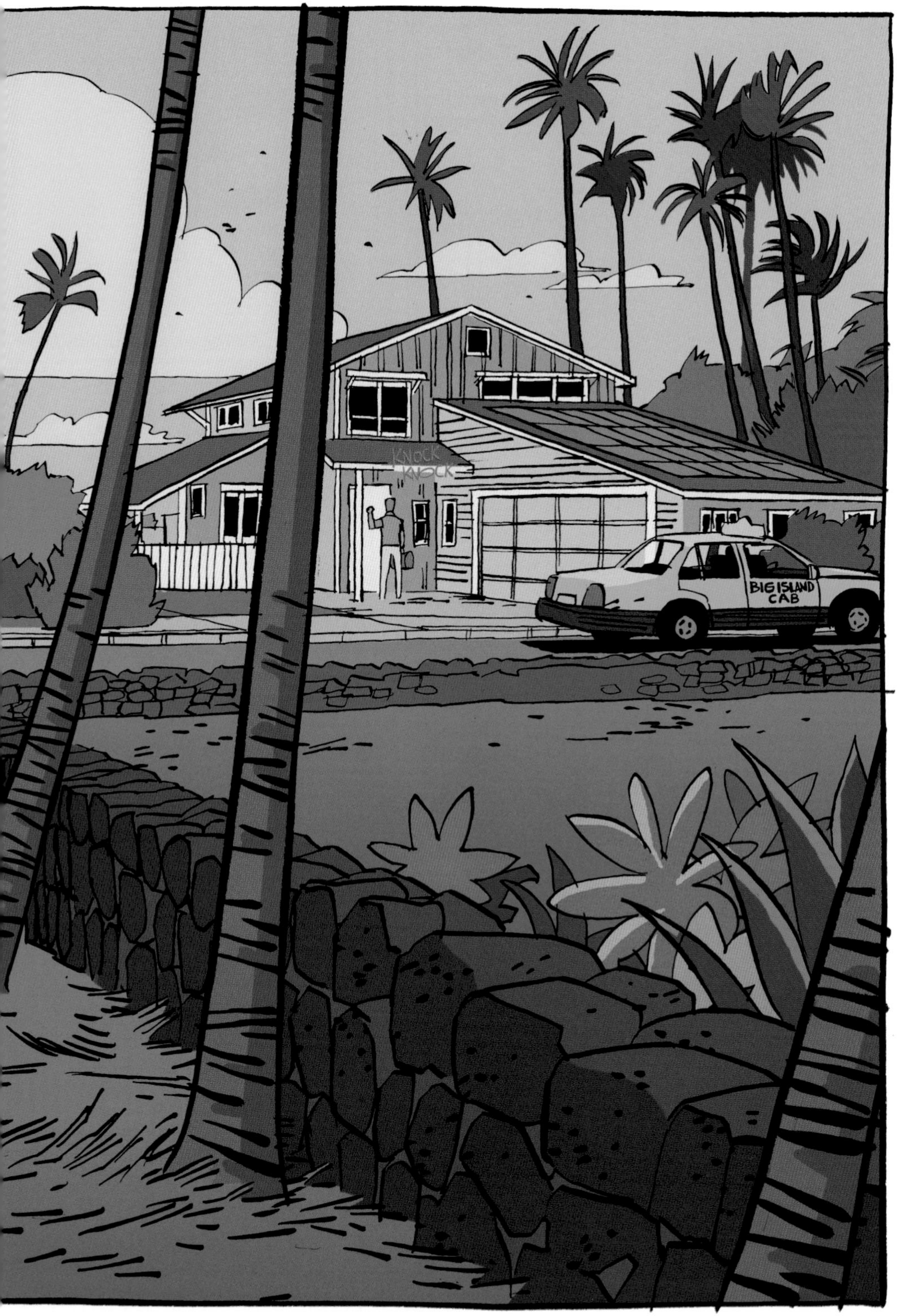
KNOCK
KNOCK
BIG ISLAND
CAB

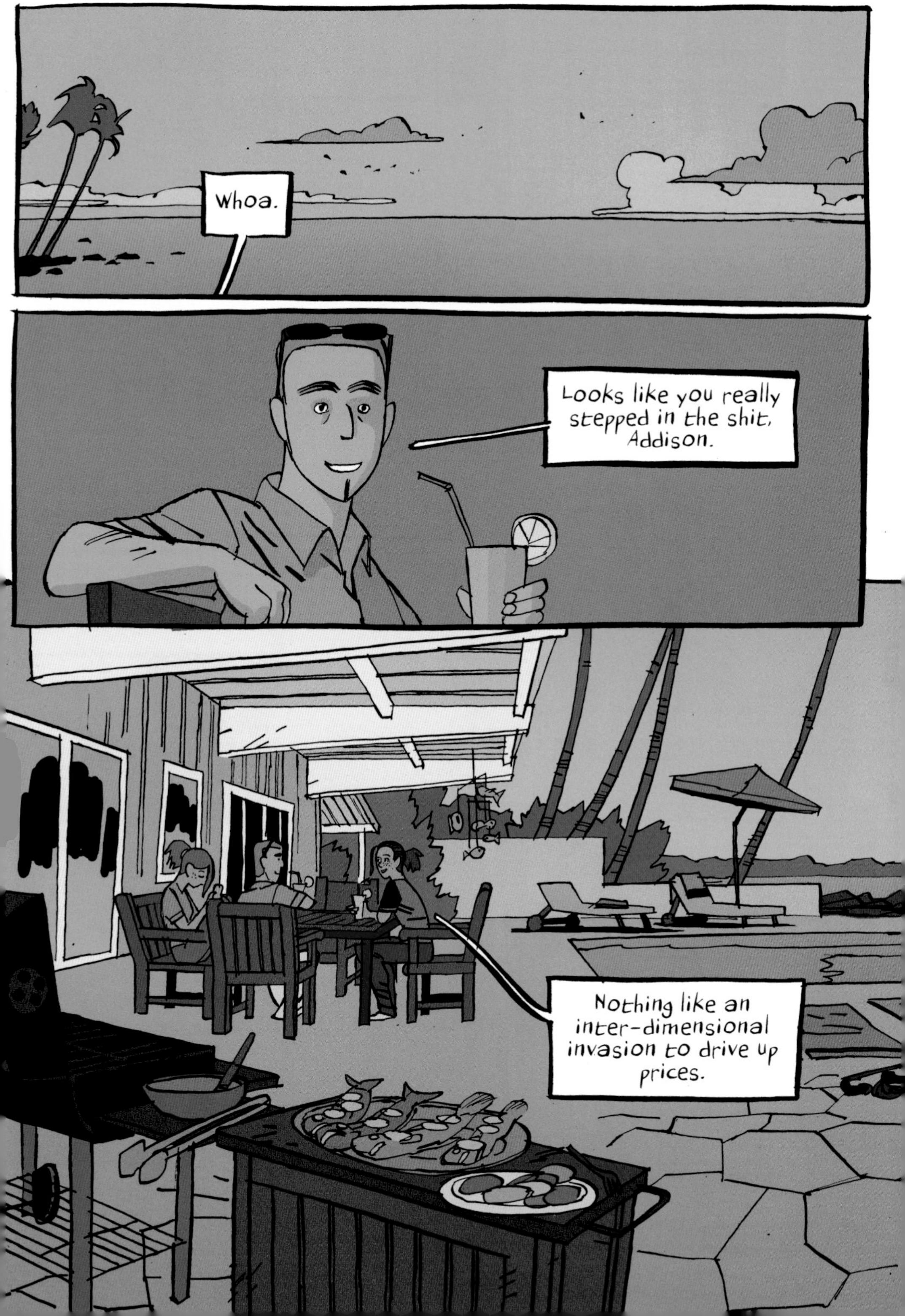
Whoa.
Looks like you really stepped in the shit, Addison.
Nothing like an inter-dimensional invasion to drive up prices.

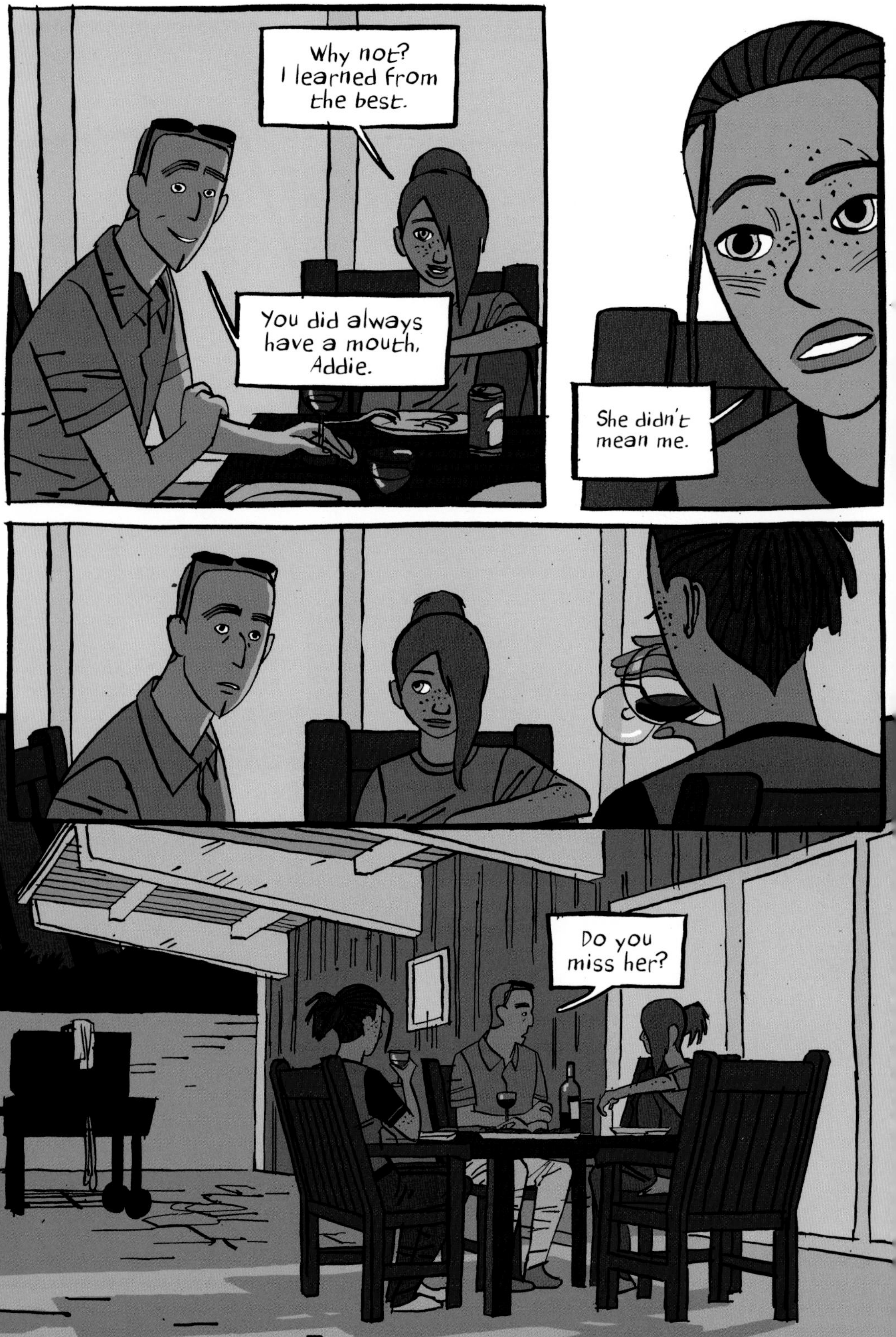
Why not? I learned from the best.
You did always have a mouth, Addie.
She didn't mean me.
Do you miss her?

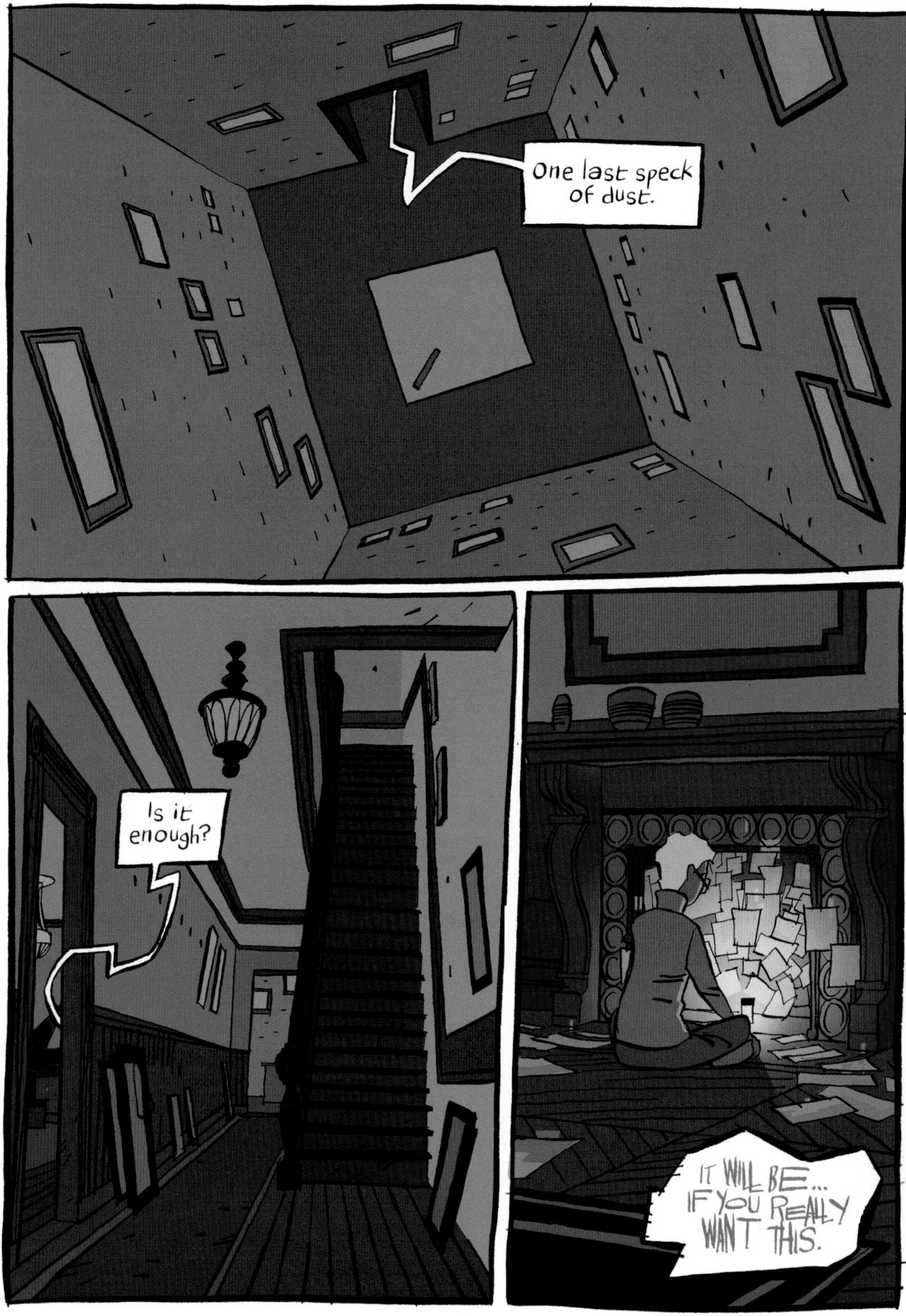
One last speck of dust.
Is it enough?
IT WILL BE... IF YOU REALLY WANT THIS.

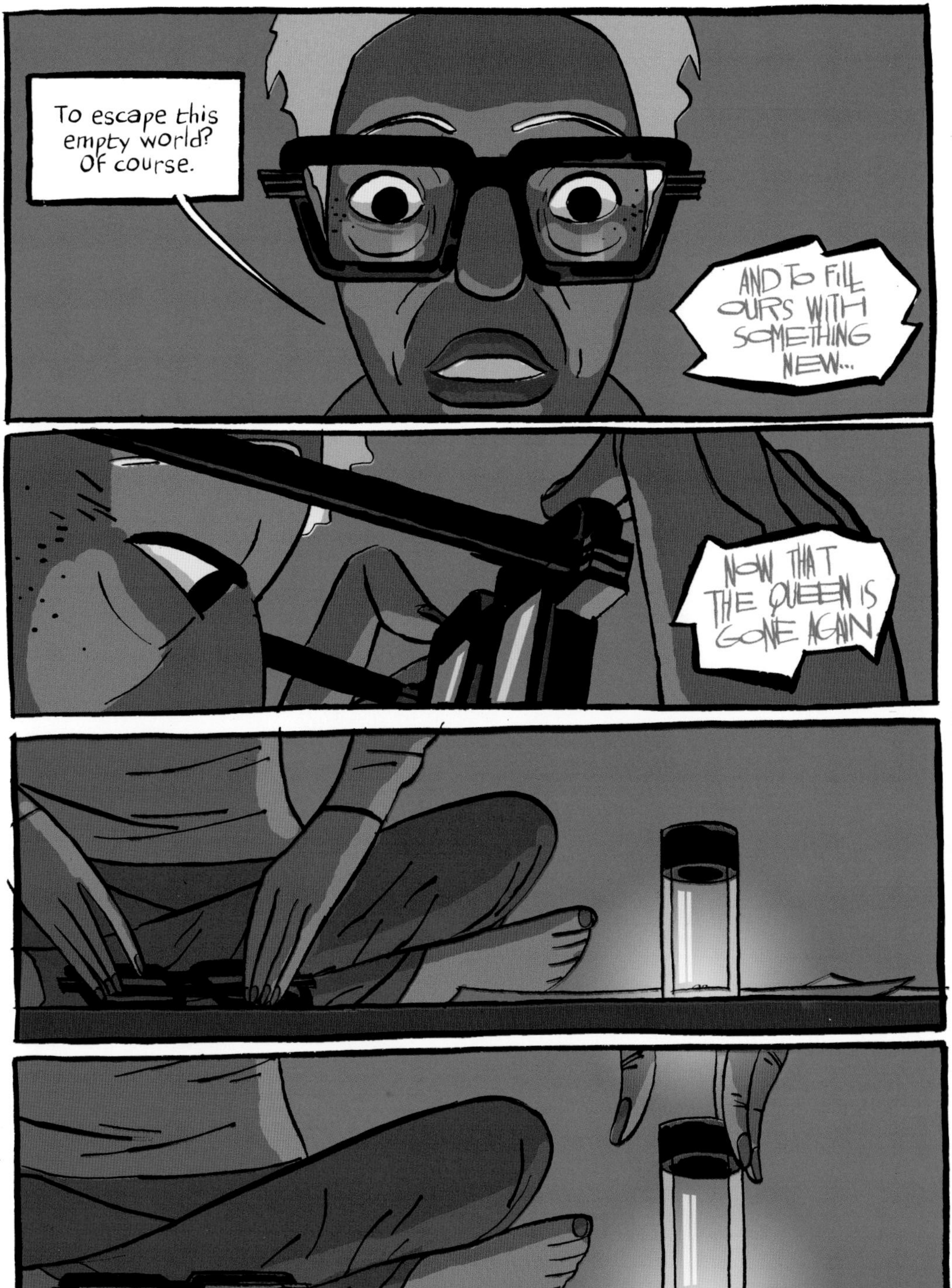
To escape this empty world? Of course.
AND TO FILL OURS WITH SOMETHING NEW...
NOW THAT THE QUEEN IS GONE AGAIN.

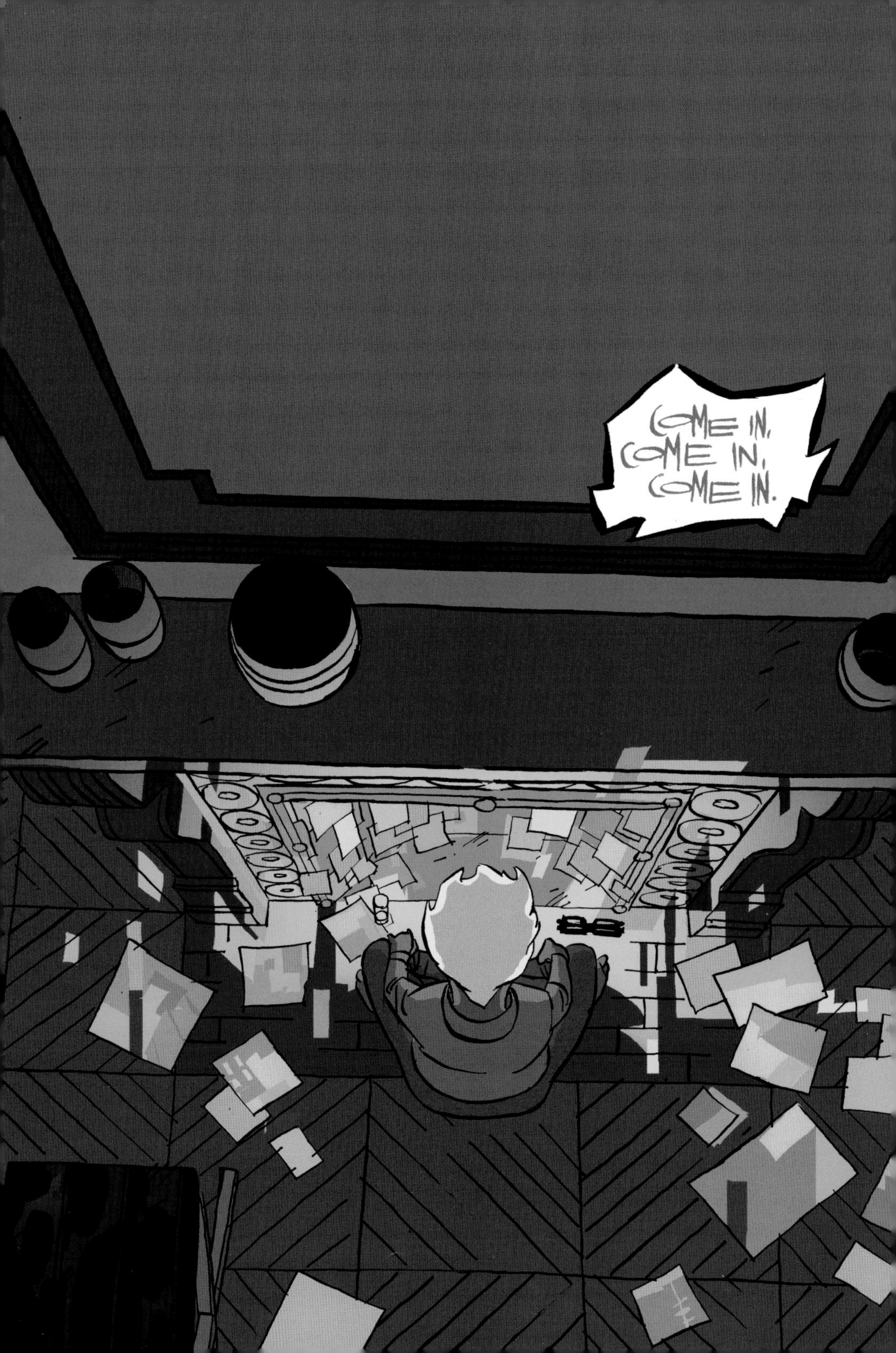
COME IN,
COME IN,
COME IN.

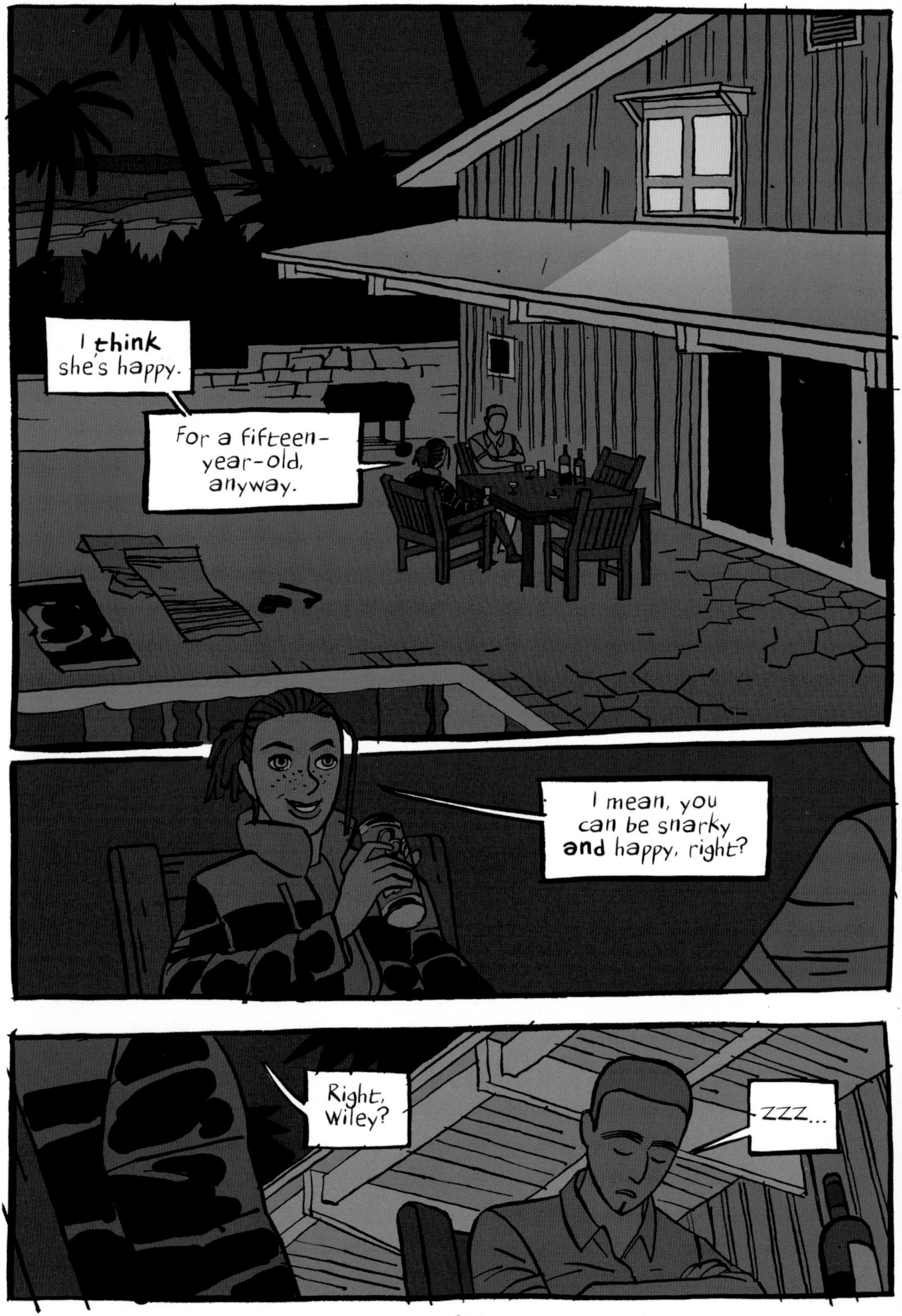
I **think** she's happy.
For a fifteen-year-old, anyway.
I mean, you can be snarky **and** happy, right?
Right, Wiley?
ZZZ...

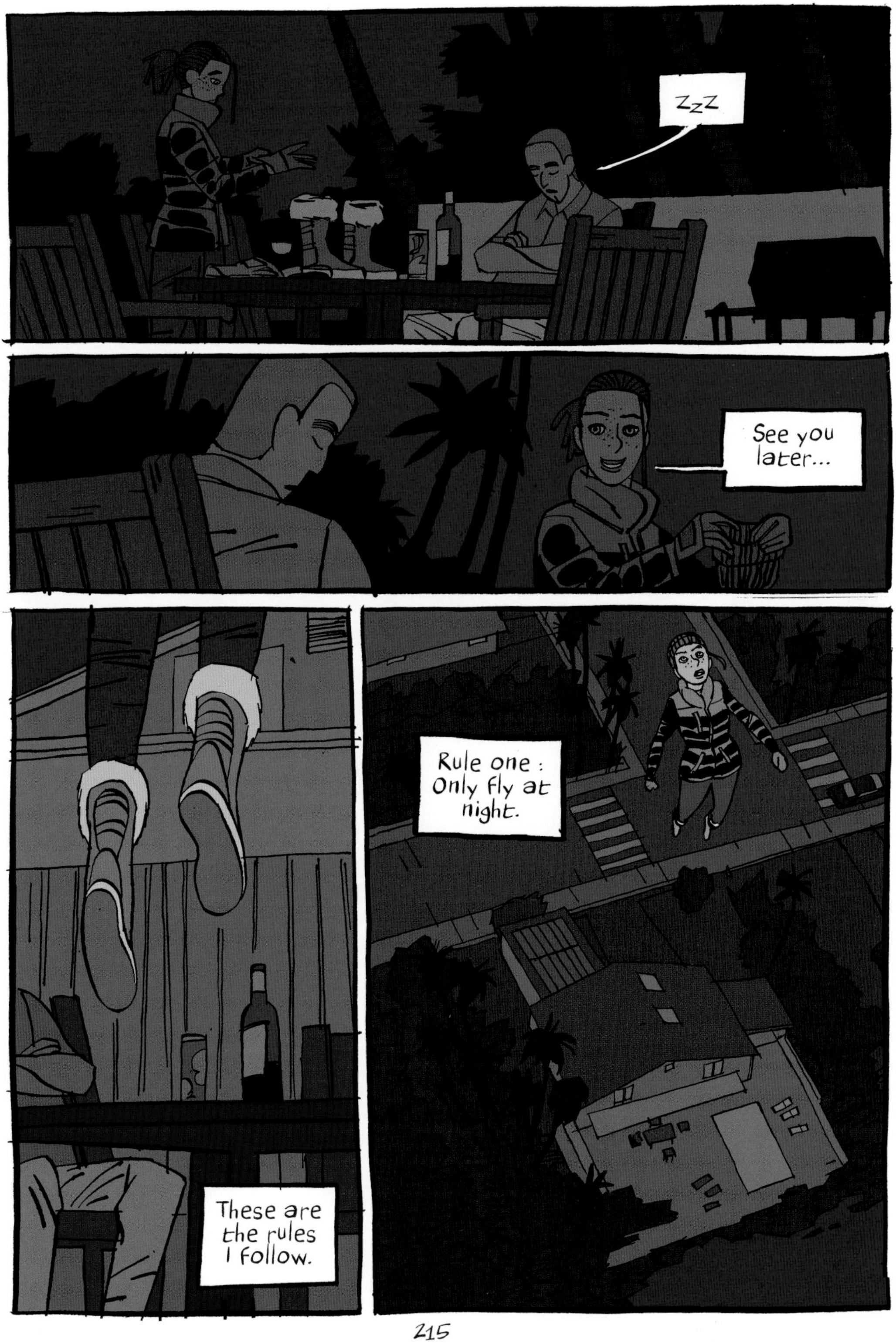
ZzZ
See you later...
These are the rules I follow.
Rule one : Only fly at night.

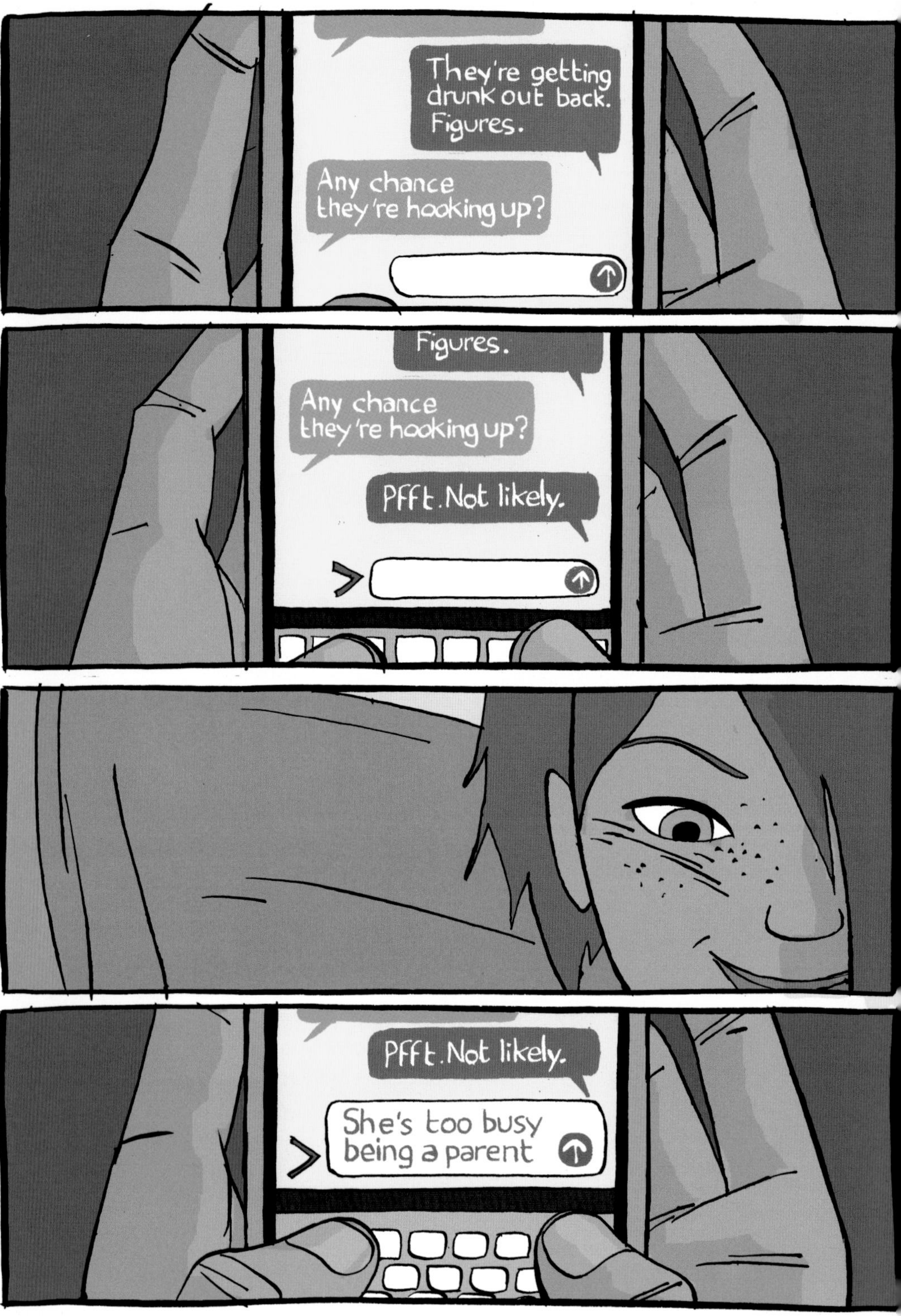
They're getting drunk out back. Figures.
Any chance they're hooking up?
Figures.
Any chance they're hooking up?
Pfft. Not likely.
Pfft. Not likely.
She's too busy being a parent

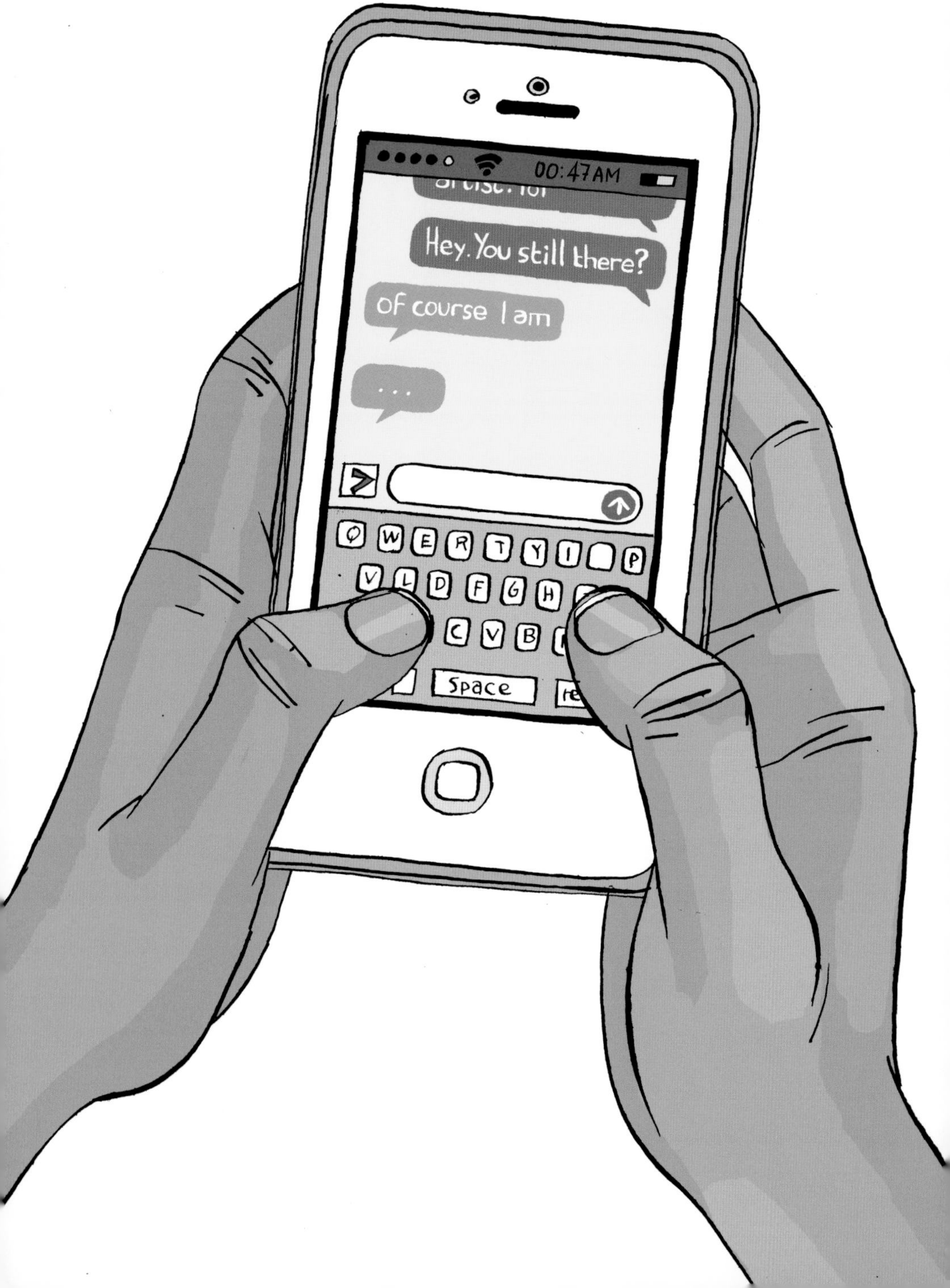
00:47AM
Hey. You still there?
of course I am
...
Space

For always and always kid.

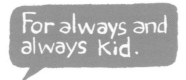

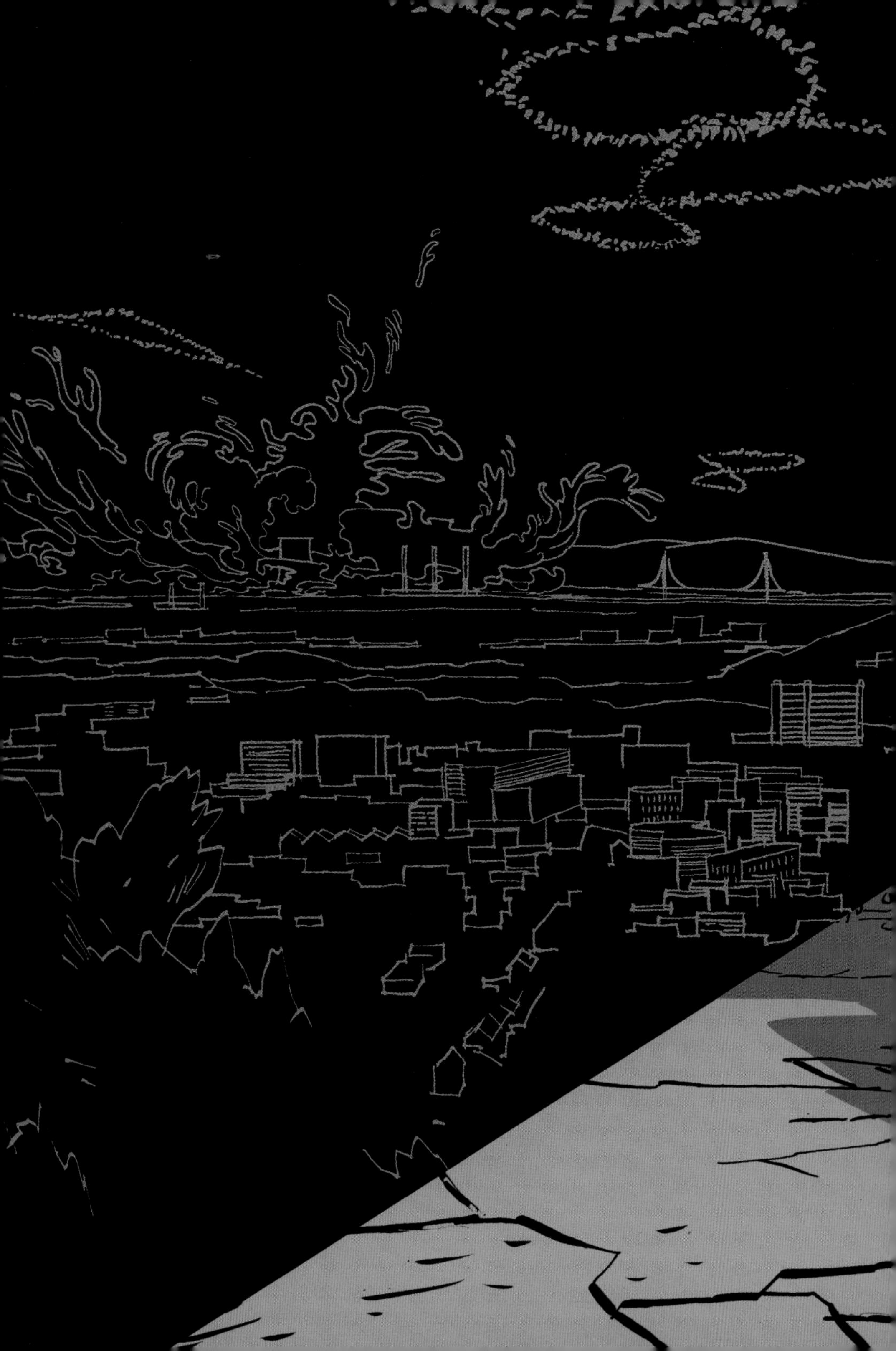

SPILL ZONE

RESEARCH and DEVELOPMENT

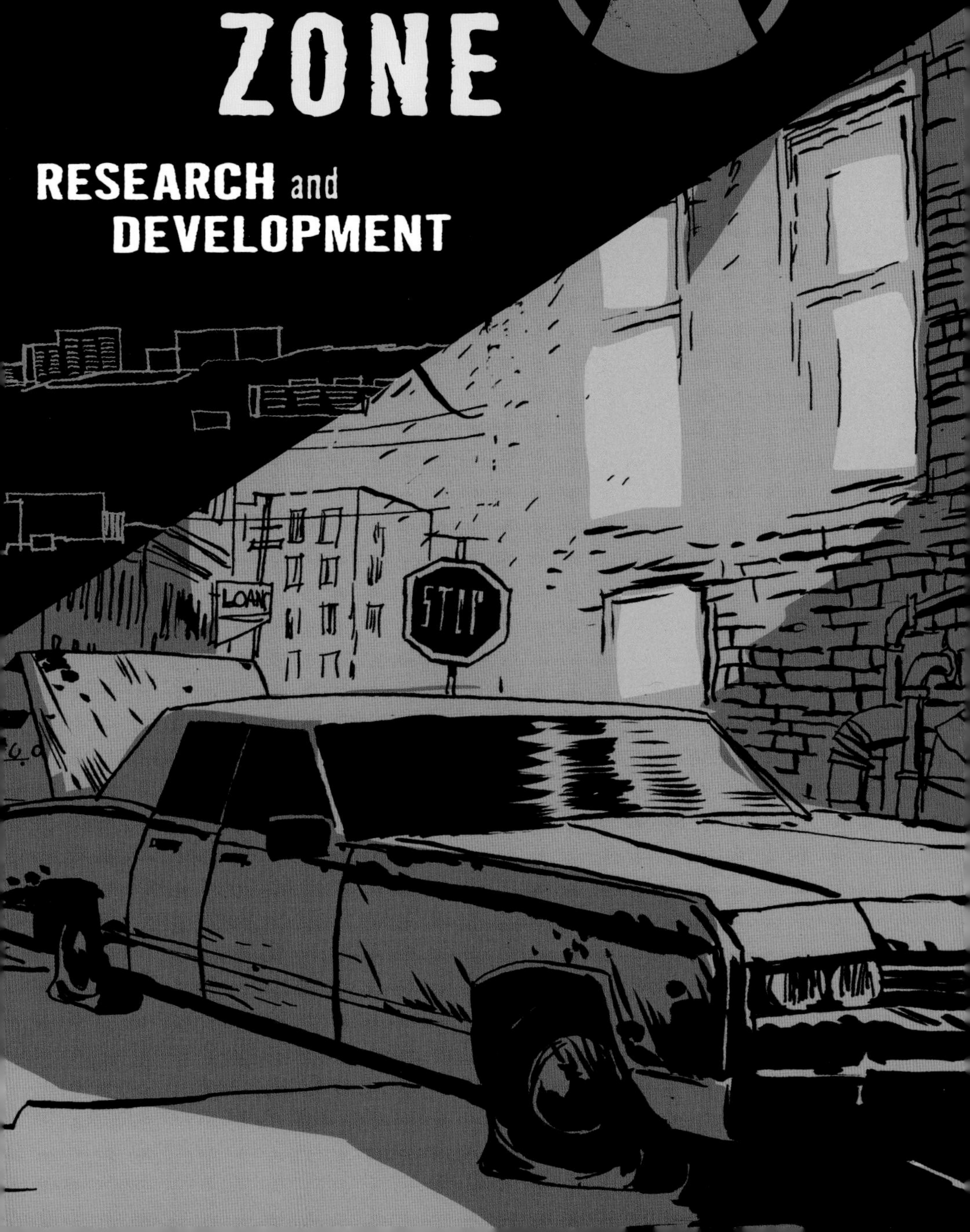

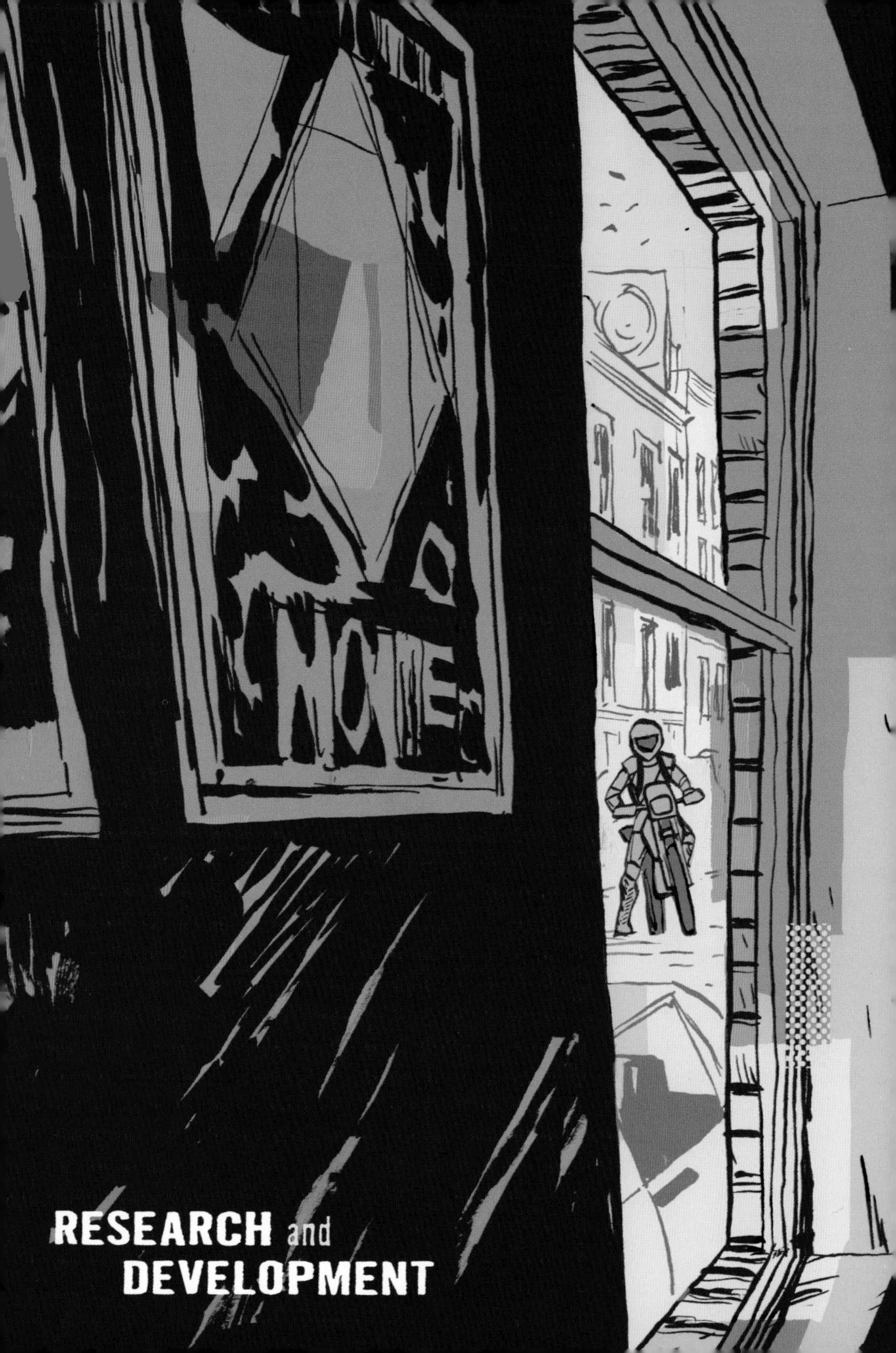

RESEARCH and DEVELOPMENT

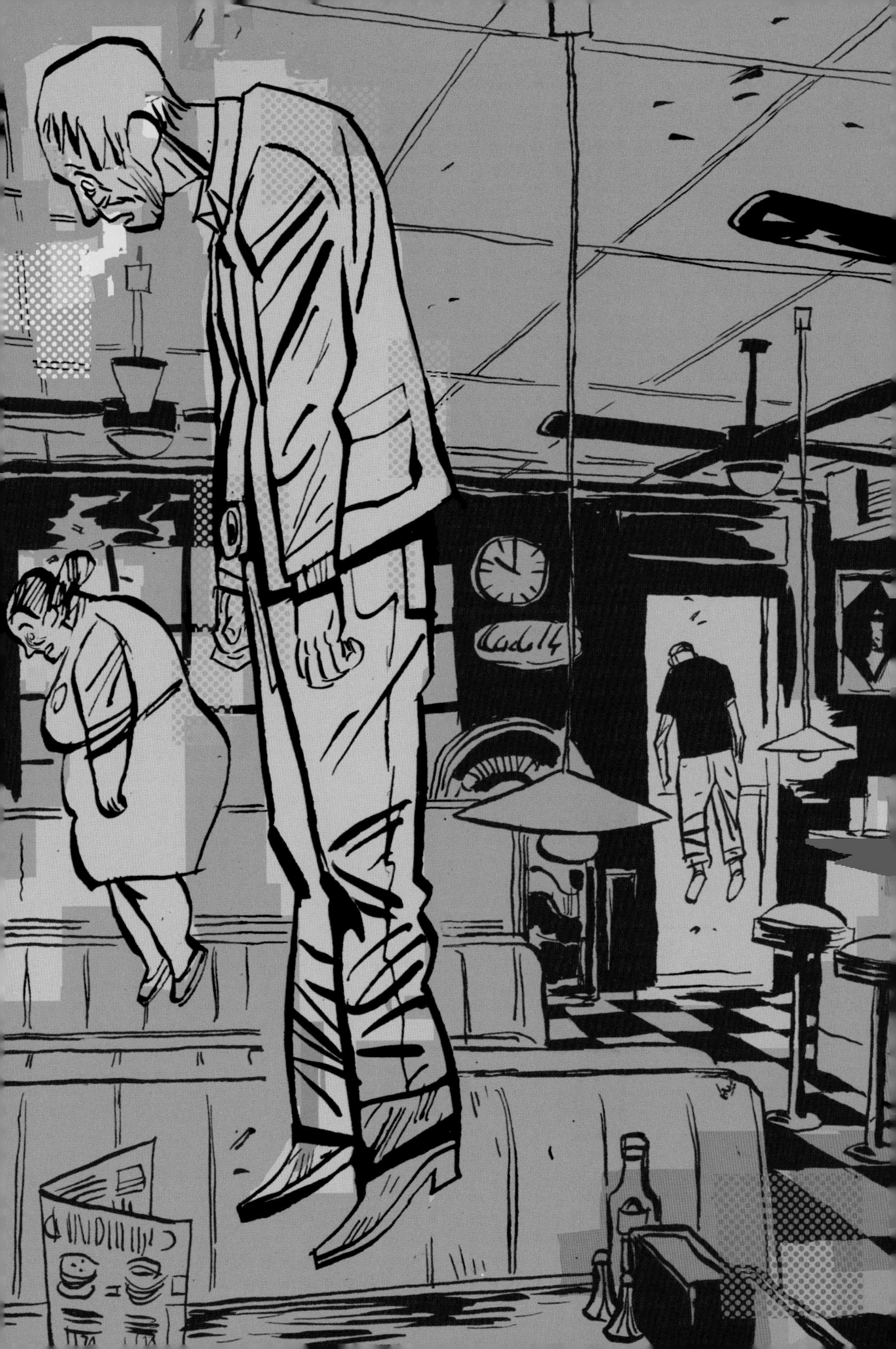

RESEARCH and DEVELOPMENT

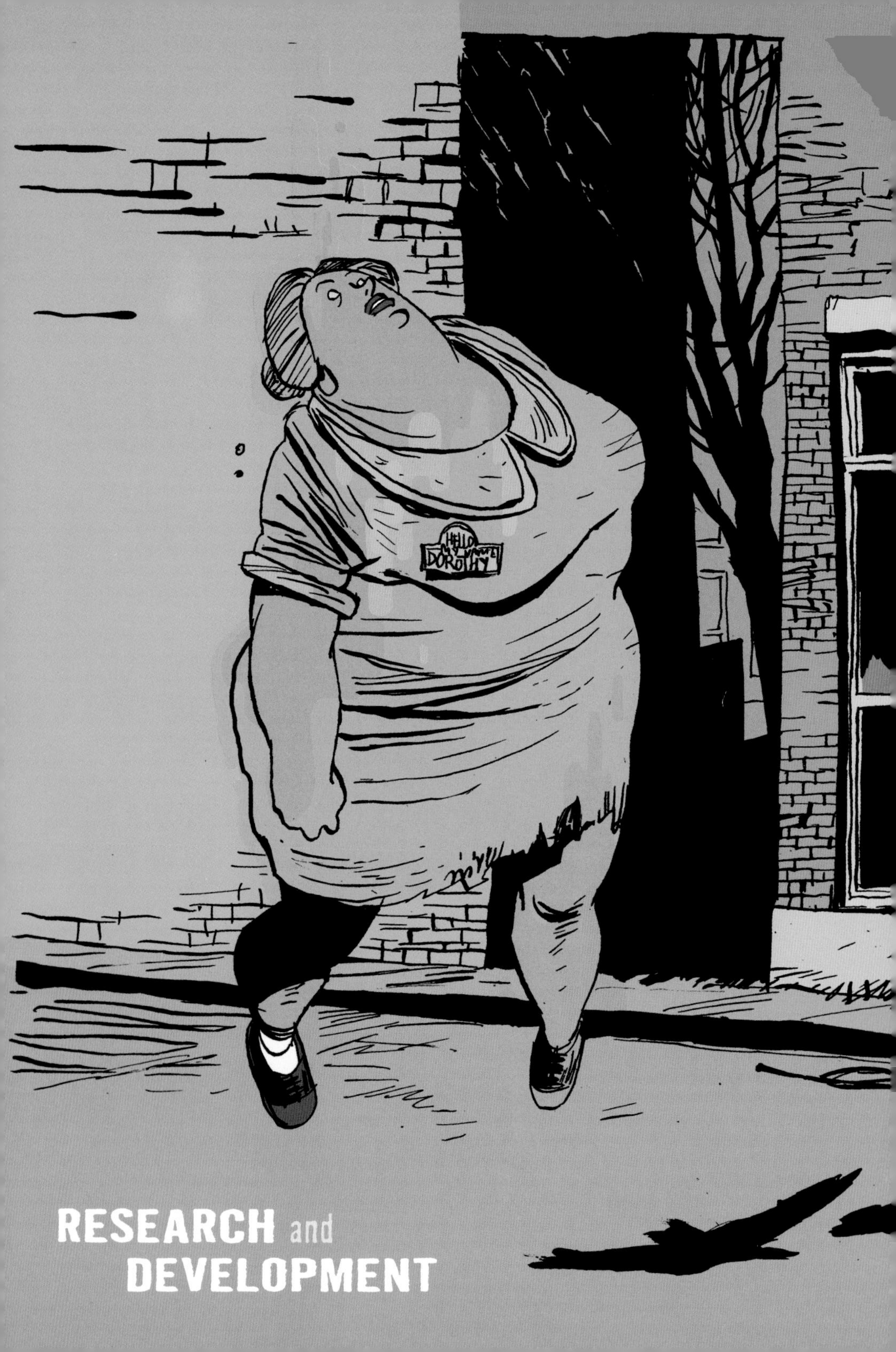
HELLO MY NAME
DOROTHY

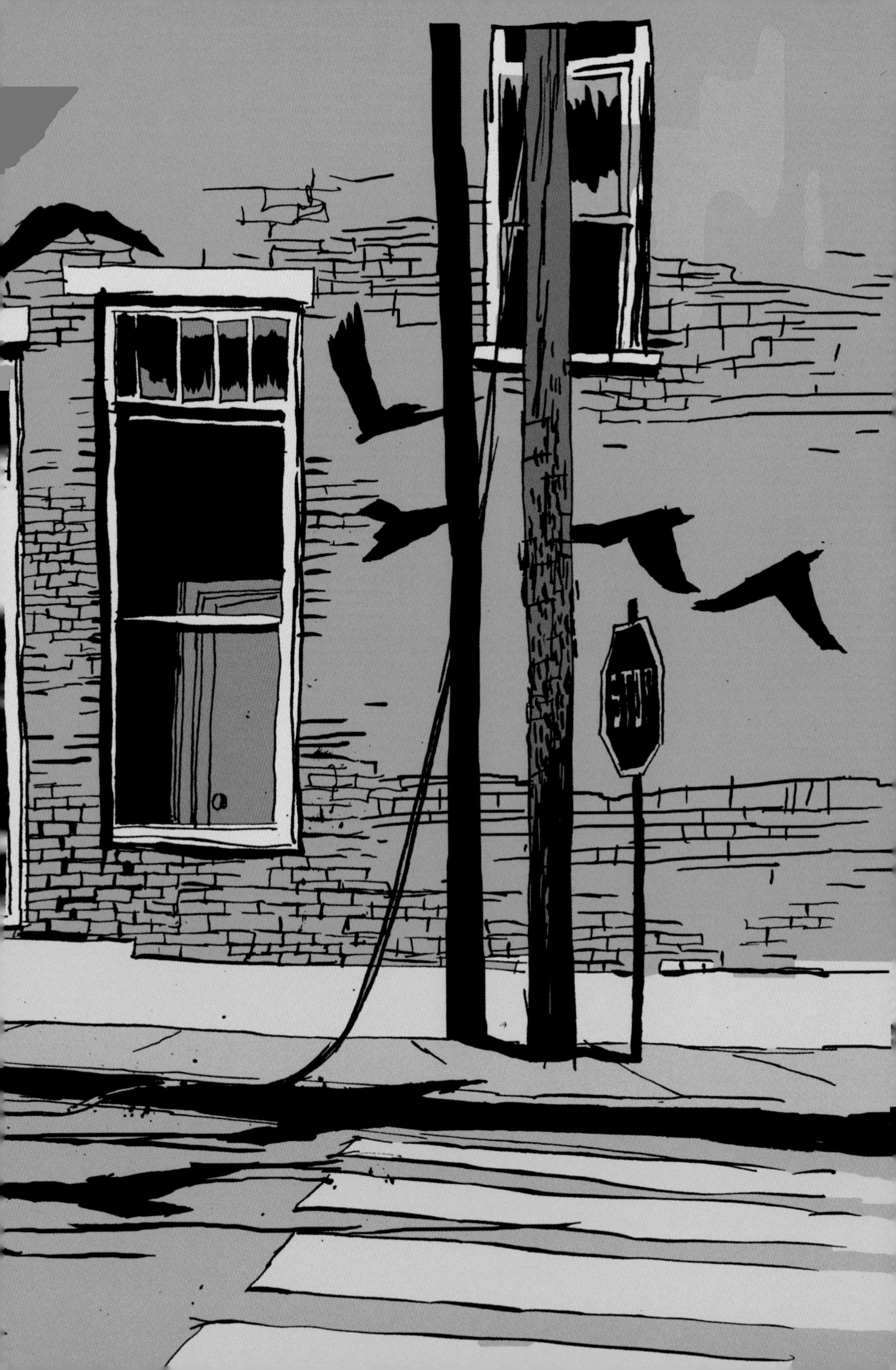

RESEARCH and DEVELOPMENT

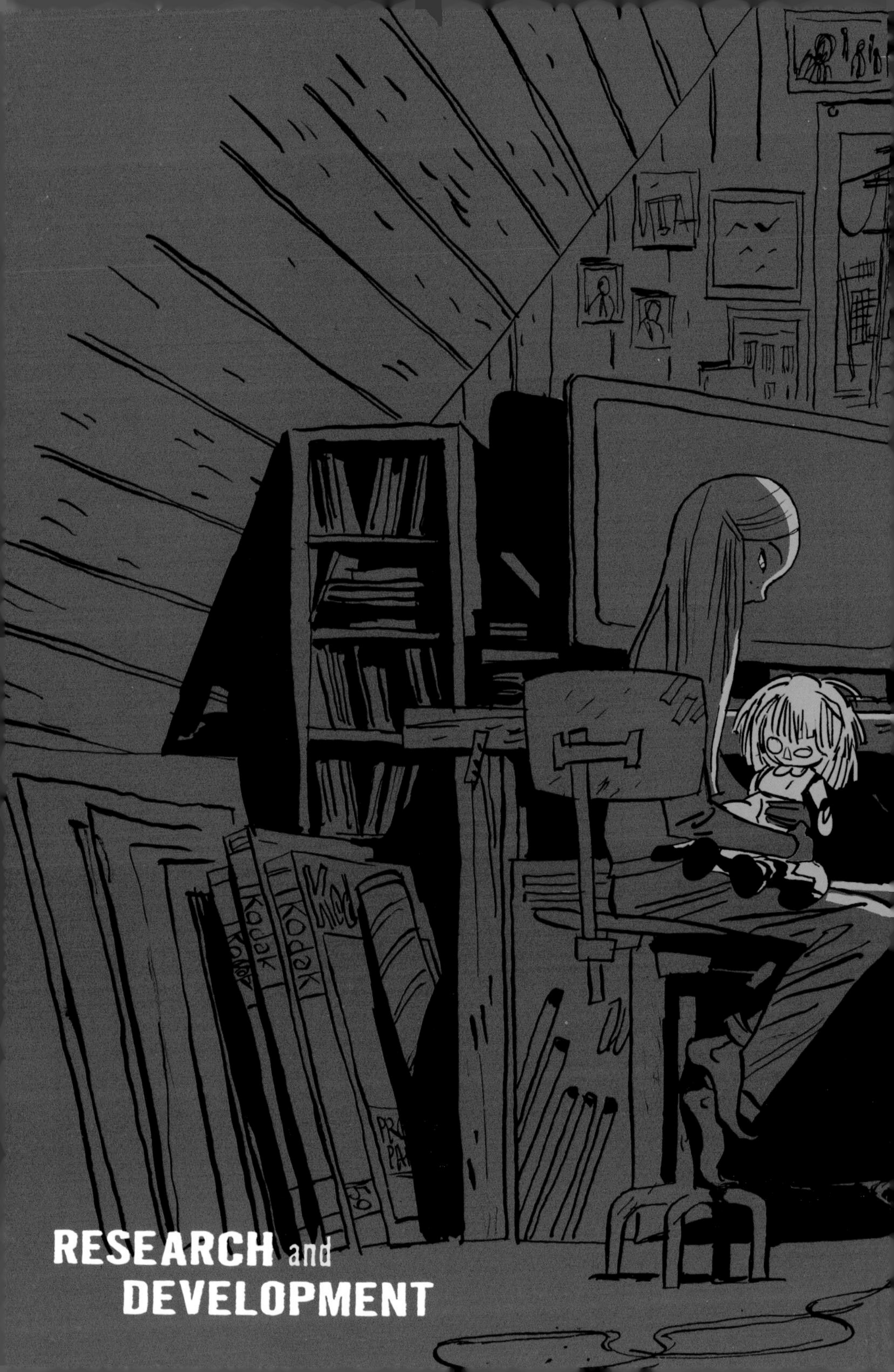
Kodak
Kodak

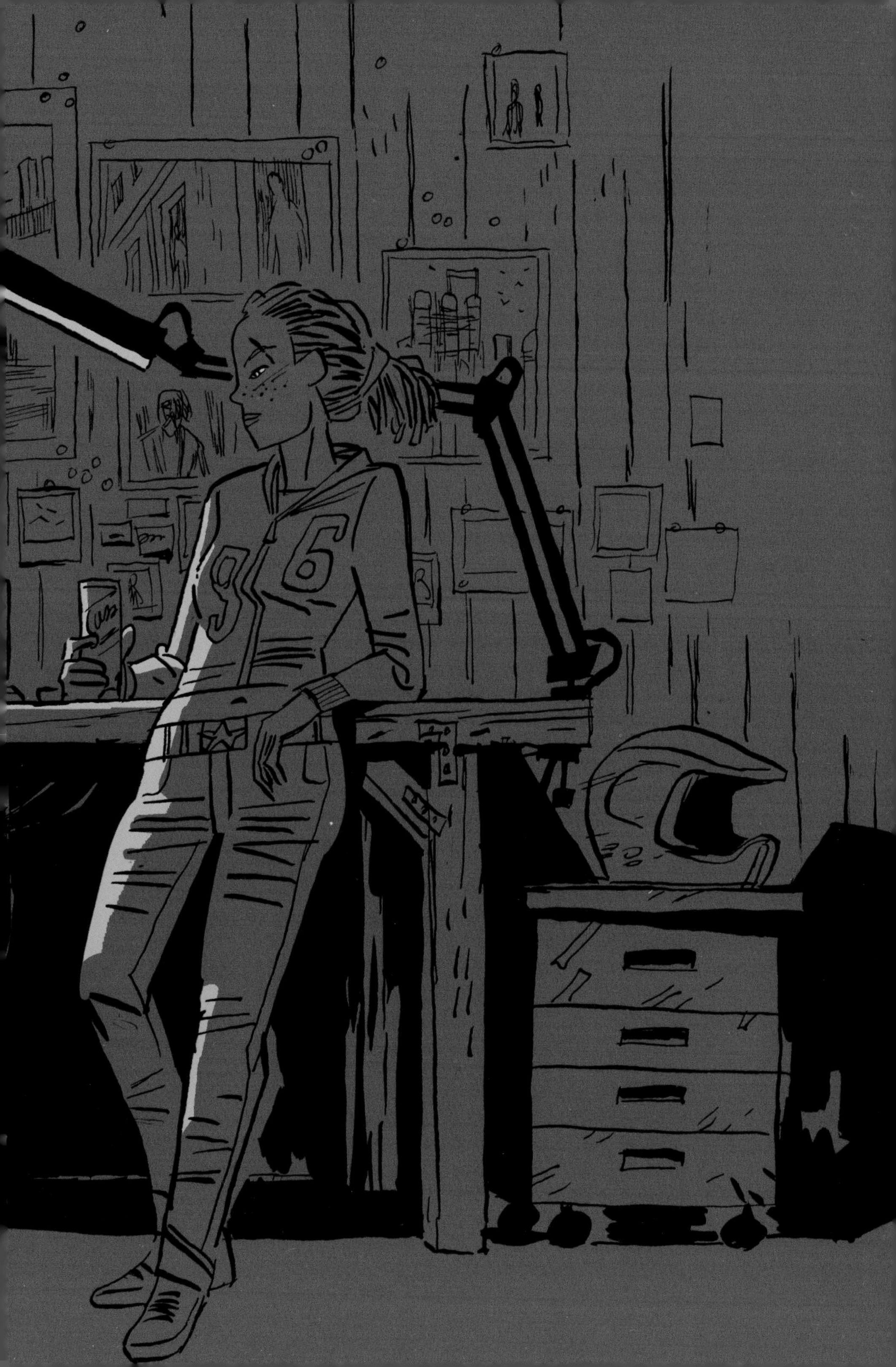

First Second
New York

Copyright © 2018 Scott Westerfeld

Published by First Second
First Second is an imprint of Roaring Brook Press,
a division of Holtzbrinck Publishing Holdings Limited Partnership
175 Fifth Avenue, New York, NY 10010

Library of Congress Control Number: 2017946157

ISBN: 978-1-62672-150-0

Our books may be purchased in bulk for promotional, educational,
or business use. Please contact your local bookseller or the Macmillan
Corporate and Premium Sales Department at (800) 221-7945 ext. 5442
or by e-mail at MacmillanSpecialMarkets@macmillan.com.

First edition 2018
Book design by Rob Steen
Printed in China by RR Donnelley Asia Printing Solutions Ltd.,
Dongguan City, Guangdong Province

1 3 5 7 9 10 8 6 4 2

Penciled and inked on regular copy paper
with a Speedball pen nib number 103 and a Pentel
brush pen. Colored digitally in Photoshop.